Resounding...
DIANE MOT...
and her delectab...
New York Times bestsell...
CRUNCH TIME

"Diane Mott Davidson's culinary mysteries
can be hazardous to your waistline."

People

"[An] undisputed master."

Philadelphia Inquirer

"Food and mystery are always the focus of Diane
Mott Davidson's excellent and very popular Goldy
Schulz mysteries, and her latest, *Crunch Time*, is no
exception. (The recipes alone are worth buying
this book for, but the story is great as well!)"

Wichita Falls Times Record News

"Davidson is one of the few authors who have been
able to seamlessly stir in culinary scenes without
losing the focus of the mystery. . . . [She] has made
the culinary mystery more than just a passing phase."

Fort Lauderdale Sun-Sentinel

"*Crunch Time* is full of surprises."

Houston Chronicle

By Diane Mott Davidson

Crunch Time
Fatally Flaky
Sweet Revenge
Dark Tort
Double Shot
Chopping Spree
Sticks & Scones
Tough Cookie
Prime Cut
The Grilling Season
The Main Corpse
Killer Pancake
The Last Suppers
The Cereal Murders
Dying for Chocolate
Catering to Nobody

DIANE MOTT DAVIDSON

CRUNCH TIME

AVON

An Imprint of HarperCollins*Publishers*

AVON BOOKS
An Imprint of HarperCollins*Publishers*
10 East 53rd Street
New York, New York 10022-5299

Copyright © 2011 by Diane Mott Davidson
ISBN 978-0-06-134816-7
www.avonbooks.com

First Avon Books mass market printing: February 2012
First William Morrow hardcover printing: April 2011

Avon Trademark Reg. U.S. Pat. Off. and in Other Countries, Marca Registrada, Hecho en U.S.A.
HarperCollins® is a registered trademark of HarperCollins Publishers.

Printed in the U.S.A.

10 9 8 7 6 5 4 3 2 1

To Ryan, Nick, and Josh

With many hugs, besos, and thanks
for lighting up our lives

When my love swears that she is made of truth,
I do believe her though I know she lies . . .
Therefore I lie with her, and she with me,
And in our faults by lies we flattered be.

—William Shakespeare, Sonnet 138

Chapter 1

When I heard that Ernest McLeod had been killed, I should have packed up my knives and left. Well, not *literally* left, because I was in my own kitchen, poised to slice a third pile of juicy heirloom tomatoes for a buffet Yolanda Garcia and I were catering the next day.

Then again, I could have left well enough alone. I also could have kept my mouth shut. But I've always had a hard time with that.

Yolanda, a fellow chef and caterer, never asked me for anything. I volunteered. Maybe she was a mind reader, or psychic. Perhaps she thought if she told me some of the things that were going on with her, her great-aunt Ferdinanda, and Ernest McLeod—who'd been housing the two women when he was killed—I would say what I did, which was *You and your great-aunt need to stay with us*.

Back before Ernest McLeod was forced to retire, he had been a very good cop. My husband, Tom, a sheriff's department investigator, had worked with Ernest and admired him.

While Tom was questioning Yolanda, she had repeatedly avoided his gaze. To Tom, this was a clue that more was going on than Yolanda was letting on. And as I already knew, he didn't trust her.

When Tom listened to Yolanda's tale, he pointed out that in Ernest's work as a private investigator, he'd had *clients*. His cases, as related by Yolanda, included helping an animal activist get a puppy mill closed; searching for something for someone, which sounded suspiciously murky; and looking at the circumstances surrounding what could become a very messy, expensive divorce. Not a single one of these investigations sounded particularly dangerous, but you could never be sure.

None of this was apparent on Sunday, the thirteenth of September. That afternoon, Yolanda and I were busy slicing, dicing, and sautéing. I hadn't gotten to the tomatoes yet. In fact, I wasn't even thinking about them. Instead, I was wishing we could be outside, perhaps picnicking, fishing in Cottonwood Creek, or hiking in the nearby wildlife preserve. Usually, Colorado's early fall weather is glorious—with the occasional blizzard, of course.

All summer, townsfolk had complained about our extraordinary rainfall. And then we'd had a reprieve. A warm Indian summer had unfurled over Aspen Meadow. Our mountain town is forty miles west of Denver, at eight thousand feet above sea level. Now, in mid-September, yellow cottonwoods lined the creeks. Higher up, golden aspen leaves shook like coins strung from bright branches, in stark contrast to the dusty blue spruce and deep greens of lodgepole and ponderosa pines. All the mountain gardens, including ours, were studded with sprays of purple Russian sage, bunches of amethyst viola, and brilliant daisies. The sweet air was still, as if it were waiting for the first blast of winter.

Alas, instead of enjoying the outdoor life, Yolanda and I were putting together a lunch for the following day. We didn't talk much as we bustled around my home kitchen, which the county health inspector had once again certified I could use for my business, *Goldilocks' Catering, Where Everything Is Just Right!* Yolanda was a hard worker, and I was happy to have her at my side. She inadvertently bumped into me when she was re-trieving a bunch of fresh basil from the walk-in, a type of refrigerator every restaurant or serious caterer needs. She gave me a tentative smile, which I returned.

At thirty-five, Yolanda, a Cuban-American, was a knockout. She had unruly masses of curly russet hair, a stunning face, large chocolate eyes, and a figure most women wouldn't get without a trainer. At André's, the now-defunct restaurant where we'd labored together years ago, at parties since then, and at the spa where Yolanda had worked until recently, I'd seen men give her looks of adoration. I always found this amusing, if somewhat deflating for yours truly, who was short and pudgy, with unremarkable brown eyes and unfashion-ably curly blond hair.

After several hours, we became so involved with our tasks that we didn't notice the weather turning blustery.

Despite the freeze we'd had the previous night, only a few clouds had salted the sky that morning. Now, without warning, gray masses obscured the sun.

I looked out the window and caught my own reflection. If I'd slimmed down a bit in the past few weeks, it was not from dieting, but from worry. Yes, indeed: worry, unease, apprehension—I had lots of those.

I forced myself to put the anxiety aside as I checked the thermometer. The external temperature had dropped twenty degrees in less than an hour, from seventy degrees to fifty. The fir and aspen that had drooped in the motionless air now slapped the sides of our two-story brown-shingled house off Aspen Meadow's Main Street. In the west, an ominous charcoal nimbus bloomed over the Continental Divide. Judging by the dark haze obscuring the highest peaks, it had already begun snowing above twelve thousand feet.

Hoping for a breath of coolness, I'd left some windows open when we started working. To me, the breeze was welcome, as the kitchen had become hot. The sudden scent of fall whisking through the house was as sweet as the cherries farmers sold off the backs of their trucks this time of year. When the wind became sharper, as it did before a storm, I actually laughed. Sudden blasts of cold air shrieked through the window jambs. I should have paid more attention to Yolanda, who jumped every time a chilly blast made the house moan. But my friend quickly smoothed her face each time she was startled. I wondered briefly what was bothering her, then dismissed the thought.

As if to calm her nerves, Yolanda ducked back into the walk-in. While I continued to knead the soft dough that would become loaves of Cuban bread, she brought out the last of the marinating pork shoulders, which she was about to roast.

Our plan for the next morning, Monday, was to slice the bread and the pork for the sandwiches that would be the centerpiece of our buffet. They weren't strictly "Cuban sandwiches," for which we would have needed several panini presses, mountains of cheese and ham, numerous jars of pickles, and a whole staff of cooks. But they would work for our guests. We were also serving prepared buffalo chicken wings and potato salad that my supplier had brought up from Denver the day before, plus sliced fruit, and Caprese salads served over tossed greens. For dessert we were bringing cookies and fudge—lots and lots of both, because our clients were teenagers.

The Christian Brothers High School had hired us to take the food down to Denver for lunch the next day. Although classes had started, scheduling glitches had prevented the school from administering the annual physicals required of students who played on, or planned to try out for, winter sports. These included basketball, ice hockey, and—most important from our family's perspective—fencing.

On Monday, the teachers had an in-service, and a full staff of medical personnel had agreed to come for six hours. My son, Arch, who had turned sixteen the previous April and now possessed growth-spurt long arms and legs, had been on the varsity fencing team the previous year. I wanted to be supportive, but when you're the mother of an adolescent boy, it's hard to be helpful without your child acting as if you're driving him nuts. So, to be encouraging without being obnoxious—I hoped—I'd happily contracted to do a buffet lunch for the would-be athletes. The lunch would be held out on the track if the weather was good, or in the gym if it was not.

I still couldn't believe Arch was now in his junior year. His fencing coach had already confided that he'd probably make varsity again. I'd told Arch that I was proud of his accomplishments, but he needed to keep all pointed weapons away from the house.

A moment before the sudden change in weather, Yolanda and I had been joking. How many rich people does it take to screw up a catered event? One, but she has to be plastered. Then a door slammed upstairs. Yolanda screamed as if she'd been hit.

"It's all right," I said, puzzled. "The wind's picked up. I'll go shut the windows." Before leaving the kitchen, I put my hand on her arm. "Are you all right?"

Avoiding my eyes, she shivered and nodded.

When I returned to the kitchen, Yolanda was removing one of the roasts from its marinade. When she saw me, she turned her head. I walked around in front of her. Tears had sprouted from the corners of her eyes.

"Yolanda, what is it?"

She closed her mouth and shook her head. At that point, I didn't know what was going on. I thought, *It's only a storm coming, right?* I mean, Yolanda had lived in Denver most of her life. A couple of years ago, when she became the head chef at the Gold Gulch Spa, she'd moved up to Aspen Meadow. So by now she should have been used to the mountain climate. Shouldn't she?

I frowned when Yolanda sniffed. I wondered if her eyes were watering from ingredients in the marinade.

Not likely. Was she mourning her recent job loss? Three weeks earlier, Gold Gulch Spa had been closed by the sheriff's department. The owner, as it turned out, had been doctoring the guests' food with illegal drugs. The guy had figured, people will love your food if you put cocaine into it. They'll have energy, lose weight, and keep coming back, right? You bet they will, until your long-term clients go home and writhe through drug withdrawal. Then you get caught. As Arch would say, duh.

When the spa closed, Yolanda had called me, begging for a job. She said no place in Aspen Meadow would hire her, despite her impressive résumé. I'd hesitated, because three weeks earlier, financial anxiety had begun to claim me, too.

Unfortunately, the closing of Gold Gulch Spa had coincided with the national economy undergoing one of its periodic convulsions. Months earlier, housing prices had tanked; then the stock market collapsed. Recently, large-scale layoffs had put all kinds of people out of work. The two restaurants on Main Street went out of business. Unemployed secretaries, engineers, and lawyers began traipsing into the Grizzly Saloon, our town watering hole, asking for anything, jobs as dishwashers and busboys included. The Griz said they had all the help they needed. So the newly unemployed stayed to drink, demanding the cheapest booze available. They peppered one another with questions: Know anybody who's hiring? Heard of any temp openings?

Oddly, the kitchen manager at Aspen Meadow Country Club had told Yolanda he couldn't have her working in his kitchen because he'd heard she had hepatitis C. Stunned, she protested that she was perfectly healthy. He hung up on her. Later, I called the guy myself, said who I was, and defended Yolanda. He said, "I don't care whether she's healthy or not. I can't hire anybody, period."

It's not as if I didn't know things were bad. Financial meltdowns make wealthy clients cancel bookings, either because they've lost their jobs, are afraid of losing their jobs, or think flaunting their money makes them appear insensitive. I'd made it through the summer relatively unscathed, as people still wanted me to cater their wedding receptions. But in the previous three weeks, I'd had so many parties called off, my brain was spinning like a cotton candy machine. I'd given up trying to sleep. I'd lost ten pounds, and not because I wanted to.

Tom, on the other hand, had suffered no decline in his work. Our local paper, the *Mountain Journal,* gave dire weekly reports on how crime was escalating. People were breaking into houses, dealing drugs, shooting at hikers in the wildlife preserve, and perpetrating every kind of financial fraud. In the previous month, Tom had heard all excuses imaginable for thieving, drunk driving, assault, you name it. And everyone, including yours truly, blamed their problems on the economy.

Still, I insisted to Tom after Yolanda called asking for a job, she was in worse shape than I was. I couldn't just let my old friend be thrown out of work when her greataunt Ferdinanda—whom Yolanda simply called her aunt—depended on her. Ferdinanda was seventy and confined to a wheelchair after an accident. Yolanda had COBRA benefits and Ferdinanda was on Medicare. But they had no income. I couldn't just ignore my friend's needs, could I?

Tom had cocked one of his cider-colored eyebrows at me, the same way he had since before we were married. He shifted his mountain-man build and gave me the benefit of his kind sea-green eyes. Usually when I want to do something he doesn't approve of, he exhales, thinks for a few minutes, then patiently tells me how completely and totally wrong I am. But when I talked about Yolanda, Tom said nothing, which unnerved me. So I ramped up my argument, pointing out that Yolanda and I had been friends since Arch was in grade school. Furthermore, Yolanda had helped me land my very first job cooking professionally, doing prep under the tutelage of Chef André, my deceased mentor. When Tom still remained silent, I demanded that he say something.

Tom said, "I don't trust the people she hangs out with."

"Who does she hang out with?"

"Never mind."

"Tom! That's not fair. Does she associate with known criminals?"

Tom shrugged. Sometimes he could be infuriating. "Miss G.," he said, "you don't have a whole lot of actual *work* to offer Yolanda."

"Don't change the subject. Who does she hang out with?"

"Forget it. If she hasn't told you, then I shouldn't."

"Well, I need her. Or I *will* need her, so I should hire her now. And if she doesn't mix with folks you like, then that's her business."

Tom sighed. "Goldy, just do what you want. You know you're going to anyway."

I'd called Yolanda and said she was hired. Tom had not brought up the subject again.

So here we were, on Yolanda's first day of working with me. On the phone, she'd seemed grateful. Now she was crying. Had she come to regret her decision? That, as Arch would say, was cold.

"Do you want to tell me what's bothering you?" I asked, my tone gentle. "Is it this storm moving in? I closed all the windows."

"You've been so nice to me. I just—" Her voice caught. She whacked the pork onto the counter and raced to the first-floor bathroom.

Oh-kay, I thought as I moved back to my bread. The bathroom fan couldn't quite muffle the sound of Yolanda weeping. I didn't want to intrude. All right, in all honesty, maybe I was a *tad* nosy about what was going on with her. But I would wait until she wanted to talk.

I finished the kneading, tucked the dough into a buttered bowl, and placed it over a pan of hot water in one of our turned-off ovens. I washed my hands, dried them, and leaned against the marble counter Tom had installed when he'd had to take over the remodeling of our kitchen from an incompetent contractor. I loved my new kitchen. Never mind that Tom had cursed to heaven when he'd put in the cabinets, and never mind that over the past few years, the catering business had encountered a few bumps. We'd gotten through it all, and I was determined that this would continue to be true.

I felt my face set in a scowl. Yolanda's sobs seemed to get louder. Was she worried about the national economy? I wanted to tell her that I was *positive* things would pick up soon. They always did, as I'd been reminding myself for the past three weeks. If a caterer ended up shorthanded and missed the wave of bookings that would occur once things turned around, that caterer wouldn't be doing all those profitable parties during the hectic Halloween-to-Christmas season. When everyone started whooping it up again, I did *not* want to be without help.

That was one of the reasons I'd offered Yolanda the job. Julian Teller, my longtime assistant, had returned to the vegetarian bistro in Boulder that employed him. The bistro owner always took August off, but once students returned to the University of Colorado, the owner demanded Julian's time. With him gone, I would need another professional at my side. *Eventually* I would need that professional. I didn't allow myself to wonder *if* or *when* clients would resume their celebratory ways, at least not during the day. Night, though, when I anxiously stared at the dark ceiling, was a different matter.

I took another glance out the window over the deep double stainless sink, also installed by Tom. Now the thermometer had dipped to forty-five. I sighed. Soon the doors to our local grocery stores would be flanked with spills of pumpkins. People would be calling, wanting to sign up *Goldilocks' Catering* for their holiday bashes. . . .

In the bathroom, Yolanda was blowing her nose. Whether there was a resurgence in bookings or not, I was beginning to have doubts about hiring her. Julian, at twenty-three, was even-keeled and mature. Yolanda, twelve years older than Julian, and whom I thought I knew well, was falling apart her first day on the job.

Could this be about the people that Yolanda hung out with, the people to whom Tom had referred? Who were these people, and why wouldn't Tom tell me more about them? I had no idea, but I resolved to interrogate my husband at the earliest opportunity.

Eventually Yolanda returned to the kitchen, her eyes puffy and her cheeks cinnamon red. She was wearing black capri pants under a plain white chef's jacket, and as usual, she looked like a model, not a cook. She seemed oblivious to how gorgeous she was. She hadn't cared about anyone in any deep sense until she'd met Kris. But hadn't she told me at the spa that she'd just broken up with Kris?

Ah.

The wailing, the pork slamming, and the dash to the bathroom might be because of the breakup with Kris Nielsen. Actually, as soon as this possibility occurred to me, I was sure of it. Tom would say I was jumping to a conclusion without evidence. Even though it was Sunday, Tom had been called into work. So without him there to inject logic, I could be as irrational as I wanted.

"Is this because of Kris?" I asked, still calm, as Yolanda picked up the first roast and placed it on a rack.

"That bastard!" Yolanda shrieked, and I jumped. When she whacked the pan back on the counter, the pork sprang off its moorings and bounced twice on the counter before heading for the floor. Yolanda quickly bent sideways with her arms outstretched. She snagged the meat a nanosecond before it landed, like an outfielder diving for a fly ball. Who says Cubans don't have God-given baseball skills?

Turning her back to me, Yolanda rinsed off the meat and returned it to the rack. Without elaborating on the bastard status of Kris Nielsen, she cleaned the counter, then washed her hands and placed the other roasts on the pan. Then she washed her hands again—caterers and chefs have the cleanest, driest hands imaginable—and preheated the oven I wasn't using for the bread. Quickly, as if to avoid my eyes, she strode back to the walk-in and opened the door.

"Breaking up really is awful," I called sympathetically in the direction of the cool interior. Yolanda did not reply. Was she thinking of making another dish for the kids the next day? We didn't have extra ingredients. In fact, the only things I could think of that were new in the walk-in were racks of lamb chops that I was preparing for a church fund-raising dinner, and a ham, which Tom had bought because he wanted it for our family. We were already serving the CBHS kids pork and chicken, so we didn't need more meat.

I returned to my own chore. With the bread rising, I needed to get going on the Caprese salad. At the sink designated for produce, I rinsed fresh organic tomatoes, which we would marinate in a basil-oil vinaigrette and serve the following day with chopped fresh basil and *ciliegine*—small, smooth, fresh mozzarella the size of cotton balls. I pondered Yolanda's situation as I moved my first pile of the succulent crimson fruit to one side. All right, breaking up is awful. But not always. I actually thought Yolanda had *happily* dumped Kris, and not vice versa. If he had ditched her, then I could understand the tears.

So maybe it was something else.

When I heard Yolanda emerging from the walk-in, I began slicing the tomatoes. I said comfortingly, and I hoped not too nosily, "You're right, he's a bastard." But she said nothing. When I looked over, she was opening the preheated oven. Her forehead wrinkled as she concentrated on sliding the roasting pan holding the pork inside.

I went back to work. I was aware of who Kris Nielsen was. Tall, muscular, and prematurely white-haired, he was a fixture around town. My best friend, Marla Korman, who was also the other ex-wife of our deceased ex-husband, unaffectionately known as the Jerk, had provided me with Kris's background. Marla thrived on gossip; the juicier the news, the faster she drank it in. She said Kris Nielsen was in his midthirties, had become stratospherically rich when he sold his Silicon Valley computer start-up, and had moved to Aspen Meadow, where he'd bought a "huge" house. If Marla, who was no slouch in the Wealth Department, said Kris's place was big, it was probably the size of an aircraft carrier. I hadn't been inside the house, because Kris had never hired me to cater for him. And he'd had no reason to. Until recently, he'd had a girlfriend who was one of the all-time great chefs. I set a second hillock of tomato slices aside and turned. Yolanda had gone back into the walk-in.

I said, "So . . . Kris is out of your life now, right?"

"I wish he was, that son of a bitch." Again Yolanda's tone was fierce. When she slammed the door to the walk-in, a thump made me think the ham had catapulted off its shelf. Yolanda, unheeding, strode to the produce sink with bunches of basil in each hand. "I wish Kris was *dead*."

I set my knife aside and entered the walk-in. The ham, still mercifully in its wrappings, lay on the floor. I set it back where it belonged, reentered the kitchen, and silently made us each an iced latte. *I wish Kris was dead?* This was more than idle kitchen banter.

"Time for a break," I announced as I placed the lattes on our kitchen table. I pulled out the sugar bowl and placed it carefully beside Yolanda's glass. The one time Yolanda's aunt Ferdinanda had made me a Cuban coffee, she'd put so much sugar into it that I'd gagged. Yolanda always spooned four sugars into her own caffeinated drink. The first time I'd seen her do this, I'd closed my eyes.

"So," I began after a sip, "why are you so upset all of a sudden?"

"The wind scared me," she said sullenly, "and I'm tired of being scared." She ladled sugar into her coffee. Not for the first time, I wondered how Yolanda could stay so thin while indulging in so much sweet stuff.

"Well," I said, "Kris is out of your life now, isn't he? I mean, is he . . . doing something to frighten you? Or, I don't know, are you trying to get some of your belongings from his house, and he won't let you in? Something like that?"

"Ha!" Her eyes blazed. Once again, I recoiled. "Having me in the same place with him is what he *wants,* Goldy. I told him he could take his house and shove it up his ass."

"All right, then. No house."

Yolanda did not smile. When I'd asked Marla for details about Kris's place, she'd told me he'd purchased a ten-thousand-square-foot stucco, red-roofed mansion on five acres, smack at the highest point of the ritzy local development known as Flicker Ridge. So not only was Yolanda talking about an anatomical impossibility, it was an anatomically impossible feat of gargantuan proportions.

I tried again. "So you don't want to get into his house. But he's doing something to upset you, and you want him dead. Why?"

Yolanda lifted her chin defiantly and brushed a mass of curls off her forehead. She was wearing large gold hoop earrings. When she opened her mouth to speak, her citrus scent wafted toward me. She stopped, inhaled, then started talking. "We broke up. Do you remember? I told you about it." When I nodded, she went on. "We were living together." She actually blushed, bless her heart. She was Roman Catholic, and I wondered if she'd confessed this sexual tidbit to a priest. If she had, and if she'd continued to live with Kris, could the priest absolve her? Hmm. Then Yolanda spoke so fiercely that I jumped. "Aunt Ferdinanda was with us. No matter where I live, I have to take care of her! And that takes a lot of time and money. You know that."

"I do," I said, remembering how faithful Yolanda had been that summer at pushing Ferdinanda's wheelchair everywhere. Ferdinanda, a steely-haired veteran—or so she claimed—of Castro's army, had become disillusioned with communism and, in the sixties, come over on a boat to Miami. Earlier this summer, Ferdinanda had been shopping in Denver when she'd been struck by a hit-and-run driver. With her leg broken in four places, she'd been forced to learn how to use a wheelchair during the long healing process. While Yolanda had been rolling Ferdinanda around, the older woman had protested that she was strong, could take care of herself, and just wanted to be left alone. I said, "So, what's the problem? Or what *was* the problem?"

Yolanda shook her head. "Whenever Kris and I weren't physically together, with me in the same room beside him, he was on my case. When I was working at the spa? You know we didn't get good cell phone reception out there. So Kris would call the switchboard, when the food staff and I were in the kitchen, prepping, cooking, serving, or washing the dishes. 'What are you doing?' he'd want to know, once I'd walked over to the office and answered the phone. 'When will you be back?' he'd say. Then, the very next day, he'd phone the spa real early, when we were making breakfast. So back I'd go to the office. 'How's it going?' he'd say. 'When will you be home?' It didn't matter what I said, how busy I told him we were. He'd phone all through the day. He always wanted to know where I was going, who I'd be with, when I'd be back. I never asked *him* where *he* was going or what he was doing. That was strictly a no-no."

I sighed as old memories intruded. I knew the story; it was familiar, as in like-the-Jerk familiar. He would always want to know what I was up to, every minute of the day. But if I asked him why he was home so late? I'd get punched in the face.

I resolutely put these thoughts out of my head and reminded myself for the millionth time that the Jerk was dead, thank God. Hmm, that wasn't a very nice thought. Maybe I was the one who needed to go to confession, although in general, Episcopalians aren't big on confession. Sinning, yes. Spilling our guts in hopes of absolution? Forget it.

Yolanda took a sip of coffee, added more sugar, and pushed her curly hair away from her face. She never wore a hairnet, as required by the county. She insisted that in all her years of food service, no one had complained. I hoped she was right.

She went on. "When Kris would ask me all these questions? I'd tell him, 'I'm in the car, taking Ferdinanda to the doctor,' or 'I'm on my way to the grocery store,' or 'I'm working, Kris, what do you think I'm doing?' And he'd always tell me I should quit, so that he could take care of me. But I never would. I don't care how much money he had or what he promised."

I sipped my coffee and nodded sympathetically. When I'd worked briefly at the spa, the staff had told me how, before Yolanda and Kris broke up, someone from the office always had to summon Yolanda to the switchboard. Yolanda would want to know who was calling, and when they told her, she'd just shake her head. When I'd heard this, I'd thought Kris was calling because he *cared* about Yolanda, or at the very least because he was worried about her. That lasted until Marla enlightened me. She'd found out from one of her sources that Kris was seeing other women while Yolanda was at work.

Seeing other women could explain why Kris had always insisted on knowing where Yolanda was, what she was doing, and when she'd be back. But I kept that thought to myself, because I didn't want to hurt Yolanda.

"So, you broke up," I said, adding a bit of cream to my coffee. "What, is he taking it hard?"

"Hard? Is he taking it *hard*?" Yolanda gave me a look that said, *You must be pretty naïve.* "Yeah. You could say that. He's taking it hard." She glanced out our back windows, at the clouds gathering over the mountains. "At first, right after we broke up, he called our rental house and hung up, called and hung up, called and hung up. His number was blocked, but I knew it was him. Then, maybe twelve times a night, he drove that damned Maserati of his past our place. You remember our little A-frame in Aspen Hills?" When I nodded, she went on. "Luckily, I was able to get back into it after Kris and I broke up, when Ferdinanda and I moved out of his house. But then, with him calling and driving by, I was really creeped out!"

"Of course you were."

"Weird stuff started happening. Twice, at night, Ferdinanda and I thought we saw someone looking in our windows. I talked to the owner, who also acted as the rental agent. She said nobody had asked who was in the house, and she had no idea who would be looking in the windows."

"Did you call the police?"

"After the second time, I did. A cop came out to talk to me, and that was it." Again she brushed the curls off her forehead. As I looked closer, I could see bags under her eyes and new wrinkles between her brows. When she felt me staring at her, she looked away. "I couldn't afford to move, because Donna Lamar—that's the owner/agent—said she didn't have anything cheaper. Sales are down and rents are up, according to Donna."

I groaned. After years of double-digit gains, the real estate market in Aspen Meadow had gotten very bad, very fast. My godfather, Jack, who'd sadly passed away the previous month, had owned the house across the street from us. The real estate agent had told us it could take up to two years for the house to sell—and that it would probably be at a loss. Jack had torn out the cabinets and closets with the idea of fixing it all up, but he hadn't had the chance to finish what he started. If Yolanda's rental wasn't working out, I couldn't imagine her being able to afford paying the unused part of a lease, making a deposit on another place, then picking up stakes, moving Ferdinanda, herself, and all their stuff yet again.

"So, are you still in the rental?"

Yolanda shook her head. "Besides working with you, I, uh, have another job."

I didn't follow. I hadn't asked if she had another *job;* I'd asked if she was still in the *rental.* This was a crucial miss on my part, but at the time, I glossed over it. Yolanda rushed on. "Ernest McLeod, do you know him?"

"Oh, of course. We adore Ernest," I said, hoping I didn't sound too enthusiastic, because I wasn't sure how much Ernest had divulged of his history to Yolanda. Despite excellent, long-term work for the sheriff's department, a bad divorce and a slide into alcoholism had led Ernest to rehab and forced retirement. He'd told Tom and me at the last department picnic that being a private investigator "isn't nearly as sexy as it sounds," which had made us laugh. To Yolanda, I said, "What are you, ah, doing for Ernest?"

Yolanda licked her lips, and her tone changed. *What's going on here?* I wondered. "I, you know, oh, for a while I was just doing his dinners for him," she said

without looking at me. "He hired me because he . . . wasn't eating right, and, you know. Oh, I might as well tell you, he didn't say I couldn't. Ernest is in AA. He said his sponsor—or maybe it was his doctor? Anyway, this person said she was worried about how Ernest wasn't eating right, so she told him he should pay someone to cook for him." Okay, so Ernest *had* told Yolanda his story, or at least the part about being an alcoholic. Yolanda went on. "So when the strange things started happening in the rental, and it was clear the cops weren't going to do anything, I asked Ernest if I could do his cleaning for him, too . . . in exchange for Ferdinanda and me moving in with him. It wasn't, like, a sexual thing—"

"I didn't think it would be," I said hastily, although, why not go that way, if it worked for you? Maybe because Yolanda was so pretty, folks assumed that she got *stuff* in exchange for sexual favors. Still, she probably wouldn't entertain the thought, at least not right off the bat. There was that Catholic thing.

Yolanda continued. "Ernest said yes. When I told him our story, I think he felt sorry for us. Well, anyway. Then once we moved in, I remembered he was a neat freak and that of course he wouldn't need me to be his housekeeper. So I felt guilty all over again and offered to do laundry or whatever he needed. He said just doing dinners every night would be fine, plus running errands now and then. He said he needed to work with his hands. He liked to clean, he liked to putter around his garden in the summer, and in winter, tend plants in his greenhouse. He said those activities kept him sane and sober."

I said, "It's been a while since I've seen him, but yes, Ernest is great." *And yes, he's a neat freak,* I added mentally. "He used to be partners with John Bertram, who's still on the force. John bought the land below Ernest's property, then built a place for himself and his wife." I thought, but did not say, *And John Bertram is no neat freak, trust me.* "The two of them, Ernest and John, worked for Tom." When Yolanda said nothing, I prompted her. "So . . . you moved in with Ernest? When? It must have been recent, since you just broke up with Kris."

She stirred her coffee, which she had stopped drinking. "Couple of weeks ago. Ferdinanda adores him. So do I, actually. It's been a long time since I had a man who was a real friend, you know, not trying to get something from me. And Ernest, well, he has that big house that he ended up getting in the divorce, so it's good for him, too, I suppose."

"You suppose? Don't you know?"

Yolanda swallowed some coffee. "Ernest's house is scary, too."

"Why?" I asked, my voice low, although no one was around except for our dog and cat, and I had no idea where they were.

"His clients." She looked around the kitchen, as if someone who had hired Ernest were about to jump out of the pantry. "He doesn't tell me much about them, but they frighten me."

"Why?"

Yolanda shivered. "Well, somebody's going through a bad divorce, and Ernest needs to get proof about something with that. We have no-fault divorce in this state.

Why do you need proof of anything? Then, you know, maybe I'm just paranoid, but it seems to me that unfamiliar cars are always driving past his house and slowing down."

"You think this is someone from the divorce case?"

"I don't know. Ernest also has an animal-activist lady who wants him to look into a puppy mill. Why didn't she just call the cops? You know, Furman County Animal Control? Or the SPCA?"

"Because *those* people need proof," I said, as I picked up my knife and started slicing tomatoes again. "They need evidence if they're going to move in and close somebody down. And anyway, don't worry. Ernest can take care of himself. Did he tell you he was investigating anything that would put him in danger? Or put you and Ferdinanda in danger?"

Yolanda shuddered. "He says he's looking for something for someone."

"Looking for something for someone? Looking for what, and for whom?"

She said, "I'm not sure, Goldy." Something about her tone of voice made me stop slicing and turn around. No one was there. When I faced her again, her big brown eyes were round. "Ernest didn't come home last night."

I asked, "Is that unusual?"

"Yes," Yolanda whispered. "He said he'd be back in the afternoon. I was fixing him seafood enchiladas for supper, and he said he couldn't wait. And then he didn't show up. I couldn't reach him on his cell. With his cases and his clients and my worry about Kris, I had a bad feeling. So did Ferdinanda. You know, she believes in Santería."

"I thought she was a communist."

"No! She's a Catholic." Yolanda continued softly. "It's not something you can explain. It's not like that."

I had to lean toward her to hear what she was saying. I was saying, "Not like what?" when Jake, our blood-hound, started howling.

Yolanda tensed, then hugged herself. "Does your dog always go off like that?"

Before I could answer, Tom and John Bertram, a for-tyish, well-built cop with a head of close-cropped fair hair, came around the back of the house. Tom's gaze penetrated the row of windows he'd put up along the rear wall of the kitchen. John Bertram, Ernest McLeod's ex-partner, saw only me. When he waved, I waved back with my free hand. Then his gaze snagged on Yolanda, and his arm fell. Yolanda got up, walked over to the sink, and stared into it.

I pointed the knife at the ceiling and gave Tom a what's-up gesture. He ignored me. He kept his eyes on Yolanda as he came through the back door.

"Tom!" I said. "John! It's so good you're here early, because we've made a lot of food, and you can taste-test—"

"Miss G., I'm working," Tom said.

"It's Sunday. Can't you just stay for a little while?"

Tom said flatly, "Ernest McLeod is dead. Yolanda, you need to come with us."

Chapter 2

I dropped my knife. Ernest McLeod was *dead*?

"Wait," I said.

Yolanda did not wait. She bolted for the bathroom again, where she turned on the fan.

Tom slumped into one of the kitchen chairs. I raised my eyebrows at him, but he just shook his head.

John Bertram rubbed his temples. After a moment, he crossed his thick arms. He started to say something, then ducked his chin and choked up. I picked up the knife, tossed it into the sink, and handed John a tissue.

"I'm sorry," I said.

John shook his head once, wiped his face, and stuffed the tissue into his pocket.

"Tom?" I said. "How did Ernest die?"

"He was shot."

I said, "Are you arresting Yolanda? Let me just say, she loved Ernest. She was telling me—"

"Goldy," Tom asked, his voice gentle, "would you please stay out of this?"

"No," I said. "And if you aren't arresting her, you can-*not* make her go with you."

We were all quiet for a few minutes, except for Yolanda, who again was sobbing. I washed the knife and my hands and looked at the tomatoes. But I couldn't concentrate.

Our bloodhound scrabbled at the back door. Desperate to have something to do, I covered the food we'd been working on, except for the bread, pork, and tomatoes, which were still rising, roasting, and awaiting slicing. I put the wrapped dishes into the walk-in, then let Jake in. He snuffled wildly around John and Tom, then cocked his ears when he heard Yolanda crying. In sympathy, the dog again started to howl.

"Jake, be quiet!" I hollered.

Jake shushed, but raced to the bathroom door and started scratching on it. Tom and John waited.

I didn't know what to do. Finally I washed my hands, picked up the knife, and began slicing the tomatoes again. "Is somebody going to tell me what is going on?" I asked, impatient.

Tom nodded at John. John said, "Near as we can tell, Ernest was killed less than a quarter-mile from his house. Our guys are combing the scene, which isn't far from my, from our"—he choked up again, then composed himself—"property line. Ernest must have been . . . I don't know, walking into town, hiking. . . . Our house is about a third of a mile from his, just above the back entrance to Aspen Hills." John crossed his arms again. "That section of Aspen Hills is pretty deserted, because most folks don't know about that way in, and if they do find it, they usually give up, because the road winds a bit."

I thought of Yolanda saying strange cars had been driving by and slowing down. Had she gotten a license plate?

John swallowed. "Ernest has, had, fifteen acres. I bought a couple of lots below his, so I could build our house and a big garage to work on my cars and trucks. There's a whole field of boulders just above the garage, below the forest service road. I didn't want somebody coming in and blasting, then putting in a house. . . ." He paused and, without embarrassment, tugged the tissue from his pocket and wiped tears from his eyes. "I can't believe he's gone."

"How has Yolanda seemed this morning?" Tom asked me.

"Her ex-boyfriend is driving her nuts. Plus, she was scared of Ernest's clients. She's a wreck."

"A wreck, huh?" Tom said. "You think it's because of the clients or because of the ex-boyfriend?"

"I don't know. She's just nervous. As I told you before, she doesn't have any money and she has to take care of her great-aunt. Anyone would be a catastrophe."

"I suppose," he replied. His green eyes regarded me thoughtfully. "I do think she has money, though. We found seventeen thousand dollars, cash, under a mattress in the guest room at Ernest's house."

"Seventeen thou— Wait. You searched a guest room when it was obvious someone was staying there?" I asked. "Did you have a warrant?"

"Miss G.," said Tom, "don't start. And don't mention

it to Yolanda, please. We know it's inadmissible, if it comes to that. I'm just telling you, she has money. We were looking for a weapon. And anyway—" Before Tom could elaborate on one of his favorite topics, which was that people should never keep valuables in the freezer, the back of their closet, or under their mattress, because those were the first places someone looking for weapons or valuables would search, Yolanda returned to the kitchen. She clenched a handful of tissues.

"Yolanda," Tom said, his voice kind, "please come with us down to the department, just to answer a few—"

"I can't," she said firmly, lifting her chin. "Aunt Ferdinanda is at the church, and I told the monsignor I'd pick her up at five. I have to . . . I want to . . . I mean, if Ernest is dead, then his friends need to be called, and then I . . ." Words failed her. After a moment, she said, "I should finish with Goldy, then get Ferdinanda, then go back—" Her mouth hung open and she blinked. *Then go back where?* She straightened with newfound resolve. "I have to go back to Ernest's to take care of his puppies."

"His *what*?" I said. Yolanda hadn't mentioned any puppies.

Tom gave me a be-quiet look. "Yeah, we saw all those dogs." He didn't elaborate, but seemed to be considering Yolanda. "Okay, look. We won't make you go down to the department. But we need to ask you some questions." He pulled a recorder out of his pocket. "And I need to tell you, anything you say can and will be used against you . . ." By the time he'd finished the whole Miranda speech, I thought I was the one who was going to run to the bathroom.

"I have nothing to hide," said Yolanda, lifting her chin.

Tom tapped the recorder. "I need your permission to use this."

Yolanda looked miserable again. She used a tissue to wipe her face.

I pressed my lips together and said, "Yolanda, please remember what Tom said. You don't have to tell them anything. You can ask for a lawyer. These things are important."

Tom said, "Goldy? Do you mind?"

Yolanda shook her head. "Sure, go ahead with the recorder." She made a point of glancing at the clock, which read five to four. "I just have to, you know, get Aunt Ferdinanda. *On time,*" she added.

Tom started the recorder and spoke into it, the usual drill of who was there, where we were, and the date. Then he pulled out his own notebook, as he distrusted technology. "We found nine beagle pups at Ernest McLeod's house. Where did he get them, Yolanda?"

Yolanda rubbed her forehead. "I don't know. The dogs were part of a case he was working on. A woman wanted a puppy mill closed."

"And how long had Ernest had these dogs?" Tom asked.

Yolanda said, "I, uh, how long? Let me think." She paused to compose herself. "He got them, let's see, to-day's Sunday . . . he brought them home late Friday night. He said they were important to the case," she repeated, her voice becoming distant. "Saturday morning, before he left for the dentist, he showed me how to feed them, give them water, and clean up the room where he'd put them. He said it was important, if he was ever away, and couldn't . . ." Her voice trailed off.

Tom said, "And you have no idea where he got them, or why he picked up nine of them?"

"I don't believe this," I interjected, which brought another fierce look from Tom. I thought, *Who needs nine puppies for an investigation? And picks them up at night? And why get nine, instead of, say, one?*

"I told you," Yolanda said, her voice bleak, "it had something to do with one of his *cases*. He was helping a lady who thought there was a puppy mill in Aspen Meadow."

There was quiet for such a long time in the kitchen, I thought Tom and John were waiting for Yolanda to say something more. But she didn't, and I knew better than to open my mouth again. Instead, I convinced Jake to go back outside. The meat thermometer beeped, so I brought the pork out to rest, then washed my hands and set the risen Cuban bread in the oven. I finished slicing the last of the heirloom tomatoes. Their juice filled the gutters of the cutting board.

"Yolanda," Tom said at length, "do you own a gun?"

I looked up in time to see Yolanda blushing deeply. "No," she said. "Of course not."

"Why of course not?" Tom pressed. "When you were living in your rental, you made a sheriff's department report that someone was looking in your windows."

In the silence that followed, I urged Yolanda, "Tell him about Kris."

Yolanda's voice was flat. "Kris Nielsen is my ex-boyfriend. He has a house in Flicker Ridge. Ferdinanda and I were living with him until a few weeks ago." She exhaled. "He knows how to shoot. He told me so."

Tom said, "He keeps a gun?"

Yolanda said, "Yes."

"You've seen it?"

Yolanda nodded in despair. "He insisted on showing it to me. I think he wanted to scare me. It worked."

"Do you know what type of gun it was?" Tom pressed her again. "The make? The caliber? Where he keeps it?"

"Tom," she said, "I don't know any of those things. I'm not even sure that it was his gun."

"This Kris, he's dangerous?"

"I'd say so. He was a very possessive boyfriend. Since we broke up, he's been driving me nuts. Calling and hanging up, driving his Maserati past the house where we used to live. Two times, my aunt and I glimpsed someone peeking in our windows—"

"Did you get a look at this person?"

She shook her head. "No. But we thought it was either Kris or someone Kris had hired. He has tons of money and can afford to hire people to do . . . whatever. I filed a report a couple of weeks ago, before we moved in with Ernest. The department should have it."

"And did Kris drive his Maserati past Ernest's house?"

"Not that we saw. But the past few weeks? There *were* strange cars driving past Ernest's house."

"Can you describe the cars?"

"One was silver, like a luxury car. It came past once, real slowly. But I didn't get any license plates."

Tom waited for her to say more. When she didn't, he asked John, "Could you go into the other room and have one of our guys visit Kris Nielsen?" John disappeared into the living room while Tom turned his attention back to Yolanda. "Could you take us through your movements, starting with Friday night?"

So she did. Ernest had gone out around half past eight, when Yolanda and Ferdinanda were watching a rerun of a *telenovela* on Ernest's basement television. Tom asked her which episode was on and what had happened. She gave him a wry look, thought for a moment, then told him. Tom wrote in his notebook. When the program was over, Yolanda rolled Ferdinanda into the guest bathroom and helped her get ready for bed.

John Bertram returned to the kitchen and flicked a glance at Tom. Tom asked Yolanda, "Do you know where Ernest had been that day?"

"Uh," Yolanda said, again discombobulated. "Friday? He was off doing investigating. I don't know if that had to do with the puppies or not. He came home, said he'd gotten some good pictures, and then I gave him dinner." She seemed unsure whether to go on. Maybe she thought someone was going to ask what food she'd made for Ernest.

"On Friday night, you gave him dinner?" Tom said, prompting her.

"That was my *job,* Tom," Yolanda explained testily, her eyes lit with defiance.

Tom shrugged. He did not mention the seventeen thousand bucks under the mattress. Nor did he bring up the people Yolanda hung out with, those folks he didn't like. Instead, he stood and walked into the hallway with John. Yolanda avoided my gaze.

When Tom returned, he smoothly picked up his earlier line of questioning. "So, Ernest said he got some good pictures?"

"Yes." Yolanda wrinkled her forehead. "He always kept his digital camera with him, in his backpack."

"His backpack?"

"Yeah, he kept his cell in there, too." Yolanda took a deep breath. "I never saw him go out without his red backpack."

"He didn't have a backpack with him. Just his wallet. Why would he carry a backpack?"

Yolanda said patiently, "He was trying to get more exercise. Whenever he would go out for a walk, he would sling it over his shoulders." Yolanda made an impatient movement with her hands. "I don't know, maybe he left the camera in his home office." When she stopped talking, there was another one of those long silences that were making me so uncomfortable.

I felt myself beginning to fidget, so I offered everyone coffee, even though it was twenty after four. There weren't any takers.

"Drink, then?" I asked. "As in wine or—"

"Goldy, please," Tom said. Then he asked Yolanda, "What did you make Ernest for dinner Friday night?"

"Grilled swordfish." Yolanda brushed her hair back from her face. "You can check the trash if you want. I also made him guacamole and put it on tomatoes. He liked that kind of thing, Tex-Mex, even though he didn't eat very much." Her brow wrinkled. "After dinner, he said he had to go out, but that he'd be back that night, hopefully with some dogs."

"Were you surprised by his mention of the dogs?" asked Tom.

"Nothing about Ernest surprised me," said Yolanda. A smile lit her face for a moment, then faded. "I did think he was kidding about the dogs. And then around midnight, he rolled up in his truck with a bunch of beagle puppies in cardboard boxes. I heard them yapping. In fact, they woke me up. Ferdinanda, too."

"Where exactly did you sleep in the house?" Tom asked, although I was sure he already knew the answer. He wanted to get it on the tape. He was up to something, I didn't know what, but I didn't like it, and my protective instinct toward Yolanda again flared up. I gave Tom a black look, which he ignored.

"We were in the basement guest room, I told you. We had to use that because of Ferdinanda's wheelchair. In addition to a little living room with the TV, there's a small kitchen. Why?"

Tom said, "You want to tell me about the seventeen thousand in cash under your mattress in that guest room?"

Yolanda's cheeks reddened again. She said, "No, I don't."

"Did you steal it from Ernest?" Tom asked mildly.

"No!" Yolanda cried. "I would never do that."

"But you didn't want to put it in the bank. Why?" Yolanda closed her eyes and shrugged. Tom went on. "I'm guessing it's because anything over ten thousand in cash gets reported to the federal government, since it might come from a drug deal."

Yolanda's eyes flared. "I don't do drugs, and I don't do drug *deals*."

"But you have seventeen thousand in cash," Tom said. "Was it severance from the spa? Something like that?"

"The spa doesn't have any money. I don't know why

you looked under my mattress. That's invasion of privacy."

"We were looking for the gun that killed Ernest. And you won't tell us where the money came from."

Yolanda stared out the window over the sink. A stiff breeze was churning the pine boughs. In our backyard, scarlet leaves of wild grass flattened themselves against flailing wands of gold, white, and pink yarrow. A gust of wind made the locks in the doors clatter.

"Why don't you go on with your chronology," Tom said finally.

"I will if you'll stop interrupting me," Yolanda shot back. When nobody threatened to jump into her narrative, she said, "I helped Ernest get the little dogs settled. He'd stopped to buy them chow on the way home, and together we brought in the bags from his truck. We gave the pups water, and—"

"When you went out to get the bags," Tom interrupted, which made Yolanda roll her eyes, "did you have the feeling somebody was watching you? Did you see anything, any movement outside?"

Yolanda exploded. "When I'm outside, I *always* feel as if someone is watching me! I figure it's either Kris or someone he's hired to spy on me." She paused, then went on. "Ernest knew this. That's why whenever he came in, he opened his garage with the remote, drove inside, and then closed the door with the remote. He knew I was scared. He knew that wherever I went, I was being followed—"

"Hold up," John Bertram said, actually showing Yolanda a palm. "Did Ernest actually *see* someone following you? Did he get a description, a license plate, or anything like that?"

"I don't know," Yolanda said, her voice despondent. "Goldy, may I take you up on that coffee? Do you have decaf espresso?"

"Sure." Once more, I offered some to Tom and John, who shook their heads. I fixed Yolanda and myself decaf iced lattes.

"So," Tom said, prompting her, "Saturday morning."

"Saturday morning." Yolanda exhaled and stirred sugar into her coffee. "We got up around seven, or at least, Ferdinanda and I did. She's an early riser, because she worked in a French restaurant in Havana before Castro took over. Back then, it was her job to make breakfast and start on lunch. Anyway, the habit stuck, and I like to help her get ready for the day. The night before, Ferdinanda had made a bread pudding mixture and put it in our refrigerator. We always wanted Ernest to have breakfast, even if I was only hired to make dinners. So I got Ferdinanda through the bathroom routine and getting dressed. I rolled her into the basement kitchen, preheated the oven—how much detail do you want here?"

Tom said, "No detail is too small. Especially if Ernest was acting odd, or you saw something outside the windows, or Ernest said anything that caught your attention."

Yolanda said, "I put the casserole dish into the oven and set the table. Ernest came downstairs, said it smelled great and that he'd be back in a little bit, after he took care of the puppies. He returned to the kitchen around, oh, eight? He washed his hands and had some of the pudding, which Ferdinanda announced needed more vanilla, cinnamon, and sugar. But Ernest said it was delicious. He wondered if the dentist would get after him for having it right before his appointment." She shook her head. "At that point he went off to brush his teeth. His dental appointment had been changed to ten o'clock—"

"Changed?" Tom said sharply. "When?"

"I don't know," Yolanda said, taken aback. "He just said it had been changed. The dentist had somebody who could only come in on the day Ernest was scheduled. So Ernest's appointment was changed from two weeks from now to yesterday, Saturday morning."

Tom and John exchanged a look. Tom poised his pen over his notebook. "Do you know who his dentist was?"

"Yeah, I do," said Yolanda. "I mean, I do now. Drew Parker."

Tom nodded to John, who got up and went into the living room to use his cell.

"Go on," said Tom.

"When Ernest didn't come home in the early afternoon, the way he said he was going to, I called his cell. There wasn't any answer. I left a voice mail asking him to call me."

Tom asked, "When was this?"

"About two? Ernest always called me back. Always. After half an hour, I tried his cell again. There was no answer."

John Bertram returned to the kitchen. To Tom, he said, "They're searching for Parker."

Yolanda looked feverishly at John. "When I couldn't

reach Ernest, I phoned your house! Didn't you get the message?"

John shook his head. "My wife and I don't answer our land line on the weekends. If the department wants me, they call on my cell that's dedicated to that purpose."

Yolanda closed her eyes. "I couldn't reach Ernest and I couldn't reach you. I just, I don't know, I panicked. I thought maybe he'd been in an accident, maybe he'd been the victim of a hit-and-run, like Ferdinanda—"

My business line rang. Everyone looked at me, so I checked the caller ID. It was the Breckenridges, the hosts for the church fund-raising dinner Yolanda and I were doing Tuesday evening. Saint Luke's, like every other charitable enterprise in Aspen Meadow, was hurting. Pledges were off, and the plate offering, according to our rector, Father Pete, was way down. Sean Breckenridge, the Saint Luke's senior warden, had had the bright idea to put on a dinner for the well-heeled. Tickets had been sold to twelve parishioners, who'd ponied up a thousand clams apiece. Father Pete thought he'd died and gone to heaven.

I picked up the phone and went into the other room. "Goldilocks' Catering—"

"It's Sean Breckenridge," our prospective host interrupted me. If he was going to cancel the dinner, for which I'd already bought the food, I would wring his neck, no matter what Father Pete thought of that particular crime.

"What's wrong?" I asked. "We're still on for Tuesday night, yes?"

"Yes," he said, but sounded tentative. Sean, fortyish, thin, with babyface good looks and dark hair, a lanky frame, and long fingers, did not work outside the home, although he'd been trained as an accountant. "Well," he said, "we have a problem."

"Problem, Sean?" I could just imagine his thin lips twisting as he spoke, his eyes crinkling at the corners, as if everything you said was amusing.

"I hear you have that Cuban woman working for you. The one with hepatitis C."

My skin broke out in gooseflesh. "First of all," I said testily, "Yolanda is an American citizen. She was born in this country, just as I assume *you* were. And she does *not* have hep C. Who told you that?"

"I heard it at the country club."

"Ah. From whom?"

Sean cleared his throat and said nothing.

I yelled, "Who did you hear it from, Sean?"

He paused, taken aback. "I'd, uh, I'd rather not say."

"I see. Well, Yolanda's fine."

"Will she be helping you on Tuesday night?"

"Yes, she will, unless you and Rorry want to come out into the kitchen and do the work yourselves." According to Marla, Rorry Breckenridge was the sole heir of the Boudreaux Molasses fortune, but—wait for it, Marla had said—Rorry had never so much as baked a spice cookie. I very much doubted she'd be willing to stand in for hardworking Yolanda. And Sean? Forget it.

"I just want everyone to be comfortable," he said. "I don't want anyone to worry about getting sick."

"The guests will be fine. Do you want me to make an announcement at the beginning of the dinner as to Yolanda's health?"

"No, no." He hesitated. "We had a call from someone who wants to come and bring a date. It's not too late to add another couple, is it?"

"Oh, Sean, for God's sake."

"Is it all right or not? This couple is willing to pay double the thousand dollars a plate. The church could use an extra four thou, Goldy. Besides, Rorry's table holds sixteen, so everyone would fit."

"Who is this extra couple?"

"Why does that matter?" Sean asked.

I wanted to say, *Because if it's Kris Nielsen and another woman, you can cater your own damn party.* As the silence between us lengthened, it became clear Sean was not in a sharing mood. "Oh, all right," I said finally, wondering feverishly about the number of racks of lamb chops I had on hand. "But no more. Fourteen people, and that's *it.*"

I thought he was going to sign off, but he said only, "Is your husband home?"

I was immediately wary. "Tom? Yes, why?"

"Does he . . . did he . . . know Ernest McLeod?"

"Let me give him the phone," I said noncommittally. But Sean hung up.

Well, now, *that* was interesting. I'd just found out about Ernest McLeod, and even if the news had been on TV, why would Sean call our house instead of the sheriff's department? And most curious of all, why would Sean Breckenridge be interested in Ernest McLeod?

I stared at the phone.

Had Ernest been investigating Sean, and Sean had somehow gotten wind of it? Or had Sean Breckenridge been one of Ernest's clients?

I returned to the kitchen, where the interview had apparently reached another stalemate. I wrote a quick note to Tom that Sean Breckenridge was curious about Ernest. He glanced at the note, nodded once, and mouthed, "Thank you."

"I *did* call the sheriff's department," Yolanda said at length, her tone miserable.

Tom said mildly, "When?"

"I told you."

"Tell us again."

"When Ernest didn't come home Saturday afternoon, which was when he said he was going to, and there was no answer on his cell, and no answer at the Bertrams', I got worried. He had told me how much he was looking forward to the seafood enchiladas that I was making that night. And then he didn't even give me a ring to say he'd be late? That just wasn't like him. So that's when I found out the name of his dentist—"

"Why?" Tom said sharply. "Why would you do that?"

Yolanda's face crumpled into a look of helplessness. "God, Tom! Because he was late! Because I couldn't reach him! Because Ferdinanda said he hadn't looked well when he went out! Because I have a crazy ex-boyfriend, and Ernest had told me about these cases, and I thought . . . oh, I don't know what I thought. And anyway, Ferdinanda was right, he did look weak when he left—"

"Weak?" Tom interrupted.

"I'm not a doctor." Yolanda rubbed her eyes. "But I was making his dinners, and even though he said he loved the food, I told you, he didn't eat very much. Then yesterday morning, he said, 'I'm going to walk to my appointment, get some exercise.' But he didn't come back. We were scared he'd been hit by a car or something. So I went through his Rolodex. Drew Parker has an office just above Main Street, in that new office complex. You know the one? That whole new building above Aspen Meadow Dry Cleaners, Frank's Fix-It Shop, and Donna Lamar's old office?"

"I know it," Tom said tersely.

"Frank's Fix-It Shop," muttered John. "The only thing Frank has fixed in the last twenty years is a joint he rolled himself."

"I know!" said Yolanda. "Saturday afternoon, late? I went to Drew Parker's office, looking for Ernest. There was nobody there. There was nobody at the dry cleaner, and Donna's office is for lease. So I went into Frank's Fix-It with a picture of Ernest, asking if anyone had seen him. Frank was so stoned, he just shook his head. He never said a word. And the place stank of weed. Why don't you people bust him?"

John Bertram said, "Well, we—"

"Who called Ernest to change the dental appointment, do you know?" Tom interrupted sharply, with a cautionary glance at John. *Let's not get distracted here.*

"I told you, by the time I got over there, nobody was *at* the dentist's office." Yolanda's tone was bitter. "Parker's the only dentist with an office right in town. So Ernest couldn't have been going to another dentist. Not on foot. When Ferdinanda and I couldn't find him, we went back to Ernest's place. I phoned the emergency clinic that's just outside of town. No one had been brought in. I called Southwest Hospital. Nothing."

Tom pressed his lips together. He was watching her, as was John. Anxiety for my friend gripped my heart.

Tom said, "Go back to before you made those calls. What made you go out looking for him, if you were afraid of your ex?"

Yolanda said, "Ferdinanda was driving me crazy, saying, 'We gotta go look for him.' I didn't want to go out." Her dark eyes implored Tom. "I was afraid. So I tried to be logical. I thought, *Maybe he's found out something about a case and he's pursuing it. Maybe he's lost his cell.* And Ferdinanda was saying, 'Maybe he's been hit by the same bastard who hit me. Maybe he's slipped on all the gravel between this house and town. Maybe he's unconscious in a ditch. We gotta go out in the van and look!' "

"You called Ernest. You went to the dentist's office and Frank's Fix-It. You came back and called the clinic, then the hospital. You didn't think to call anyone else?" Tom asked.

"I told you both, I called *John* here, whom I hadn't even met." Yolanda turned toward John. "Ernest said he trusted you like a brother. And before you ask, Tom"— she directed her attention back to my husband—"I found the Bertrams' home number in Ernest's Rolodex, too."

"Go on," said Tom. "You called John. When did you drive out to look for Ernest?"

Yolanda shook her head, dismayed. "Around four? I loaded Ferdinanda into my van and off we went. I drove slowly. I told you, there was nobody at the dentist's office and the guy at Frank's Fix-It was wrecked. We came home and I tried to call the Bertrams again." She gulped. "When Ernest still wasn't home at midnight, I called the sheriff's department. Since Ernest used to be a cop? They sent out a car, and the policeman took a report. Wait, I have his card." Yolanda rooted through her purse, then pulled out a sheriff's department card, which she handed to Tom. "The guy wrote down what I told him, and said maybe Ernest was working on a case. I told him Ernest would have informed us if he wasn't coming back for dinner. And he would have taken his truck."

Tom nodded. Presumably, he knew all of this already. He was testing Yolanda, asking the same details over and over, to see if she'd stick to her story.

John Bertram seemed pensive. "Did Ernest say anything to you before he left?"

"Nothing special," said Yolanda. "I was doing the dishes. Ferdinanda was out on the patio on the lower level. That's where she likes to sit, when the weather's nice." Yolanda gestured impatiently. "It was so she could smoke her cigars. Ernest would"—she pressed her lips together, then composed herself—"he would usually say a few words to her before he left. You can ask her."

"We will," Tom promised. He waited a beat. "Now, could you tell me if you knew whether Ernest had any enemies?"

"He had his cases, but he didn't talk much about them."

"Do you know if one of the people he was investigating had it in for him?" Tom asked.

Yolanda looked away. Not for the first time, I thought she was hiding something, or not telling the truth. Or something.

"Yolanda?" Tom said. "What was he working on?"

"Well, it would be in his files," said Yolanda. "They're in his study."

Tom raised his eyebrows. "How do you know where his files are?"

"Because he called me in there once," Yolanda replied, her tone steely, "and asked me to bring him a sandwich."

"Did you ever open the file drawers, say, when Ernest wasn't home?" Tom asked, his voice deadpan.

"Oh, Tom, will you stop?" Yolanda cried. "When Ernest worked at his desk, he sometimes had one of the drawers of his file cabinet open. It was a handmade wooden cabinet, really pretty, not one of those ugly metal ones. I asked him if he made the cabinet. He said that he had. He could build anything."

"Did you open the file drawers when Ernest wasn't home?" Tom repeated.

Yolanda crossed her arms. "I don't remember."

There was a silence. Tom gave John Bertram a small nod.

"So," said John, "do you know what he was working on?"

Yolanda looked very tired. "I know a bit. Someone was running a puppy mill, I told you. A woman named Hermie needed Ernest's help with proving neglect or some such thing. She's an older woman."

"Older?"

"Midforties, or maybe fifty, I'd say, but she looks sixty. She came over once, and I noticed she's missing a couple of fingers," Yolanda added. "I didn't ask her what had happened to her hand. She did tell Ferdinanda and me that her son thinks she's crazy, with her closing-down-of-puppy-mills crusade. She said her son didn't want to hear her stories anymore. He said she cares more about dogs than she does about him."

"You don't know her last name?" Tom asked.

"No."

"Um," I began, but Tom held up his hand. I knew someone named Hermie. Hermie Mikulski was a tall, buxom, gray-haired woman. This Hermie did have a son, and he went to the Christian Brothers High School. But I was pretty sure she had all her fingers, because she ruled the Saint Luke's Altar Guild with two tightly clenched iron fists.

To Yolanda, Tom said, "Anything else?"

"Ernest was working on a divorce case. I think there was a lot of money involved."

"The people getting the divorce?" Tom asked.

"I don't know," Yolanda said dully. "There was another thing. Ernest was looking for something for someone. I don't know the details."

"You have no idea what he was looking for?"

"No. And I don't know who the client was." She glanced at the clock, which read ten to five. "I need to be leaving soon, to go get Ferdinanda."

"Where is she again?" asked John Bertram.

"The Roman Catholic church. Our Lady of the Mountains. She's at the monsignor's house. She didn't want to stay at Ernest's place today, because he hadn't come home, and she, well, she said . . ."

"She said what?" Tom asked sharply.

Yolanda rubbed her forehead. "She said Ernest looked very bad to her yesterday morning."

"You already said that." Tom prompted her. "Are you talking about health or something else?"

"Ferdinanda says these things sometimes. She believes in Santería." I wondered how Tom was going to explain Cuban voodoo to his captain. Well, the captain could listen to the tape.

Tom asked, "Was there anything *you* saw that would make you think Ernest looked particularly bad?"

"His house frightened me," Yolanda said.

"Yolanda!" Tom's voice made me jump. "What scared you about Ernest's house? Were you worried he'd discover the money under your mattress?"

Yolanda pressed her clutch of tissues to her eyes. When Tom tried to ask her another question, she just shook her head.

I said to Tom, "May I see you in the living room for a moment, please?"

Tom turned off the recorder. "Let's take a break."

Once Tom and I were standing in the living room, I asked, "What in God's name do you think you're doing to my friend?"

"Since she won't go down to the sheriff's department, I'm interrogating her here."

"Yeah, well, they've discovered that torture doesn't work, you know."

Tom did not smile. "You stick to catering, and I'll stick to interrogation techniques that I have used for years, and that do in fact yield results."

"Why are you being so mean?"

"Mean? When I'm mean, Miss G., you'll know. At the moment, I want Yolanda to tell us about Humberto Captain. His father, Roberto Captain, brought Ferdinanda, her brother, and the brother's wife over on a boat from Cuba. The brother and his wife were Yolanda's grandparents."

"The Captains?"

"Roberto Captain was a good guy. His son, Humberto? Not so much."

I groaned. "This is one of the people Yolanda hangs out with, that you don't like?"

"This is *the* person," Tom said. "Listen, I don't for one second believe that Yolanda asked Ernest if she and her aunt could stay at his house just so they could clean and cook for him. I think the real reason she asked Ernest if they could bunk in with him was so that she could be paid by Humberto Captain to spy."

"To spy on Ernest? Why? And what kind of guy has *Captain* for a last name?"

"Roberto's original last name was something Spanish, but he legally changed it to Captain, because that's what everyone called him, since he was the skipper of a boat that made frequent trips bringing exiles over from Cuba. Roberto, El Capitán, became Roberto Captain. Roberto's dead now, but he ferried folks like Ferdinanda's family to Miami, after they became disillusioned with Castro." Tom tilted his head. "You don't remember Humberto Captain's picture in the *Mountain Journal*?"

"Remind me."

"The paper did one of those quizzes, 'Can you tell whose view this is?' The first ten people who guessed right got five bucks. The next week, the paper would run a picture of the owner, sometimes with other people, in front of the view. One of those was the view from Humberto's big living room. Then the next week, the picture was of Humberto, with his arm around a young woman, in front of the view."

"Wait. What does Humberto look like?"

"Like a guy who stepped out of a casting call for *Miami Vice*. He's in his fifties and is shaped like a Brazil nut, narrow at the ends and wide in the middle. He has orangey skin that looks as if he takes daily naps in a tanning bed. Is this sounding familiar?"

"Yes. I've seen him at parties I've done." Humberto Captain's shock of combed-back salt-and-pepper hair went well with the beige, yellow, and light blue tropical suits he wore—despite all the snow and mud we lived with in Aspen Meadow. The newspaper picture of him had made me shudder, and maybe that was why I'd blocked the memory. Humberto's pale suit seemed to match the light window casement. His tanned skin looked bizarre. His pearly whites were more brilliant than the chandelier he'd been standing under. I asked, "What does this guy have to do with Yolanda?"

"Everything, I'm sorry to say. Humberto is a thief, and Ernest was working on the case. You're going to have to let me tell you more about it later."

"But you think Yolanda is working for Humberto?"

"Yes." Tom ticked off the points on his fingers. "Ferdinanda is beholden to the Captain family for bringing her to this country. And Yolanda has covered for Humberto in the past. He had a big dinner for his cronies, including someone we were looking for, a smuggler. She catered it, but she would not say Word One about who was there, even when we showed her a photo array. We got the guy eventually. But Yolanda was singularly un-helpful."

"Why would she act that way?"

Tom cocked his head at me and raised his eyebrows, his gesture when he thought I was being naïve. "She keeps saying how scared she is? I think she's afraid of Humberto, Goldy." He ticked off another point. "She won't tell us where she got that cash under her mattress. Oh, and did she tell you why she had to leave her rental?"

"She was afraid of her ex-boyfriend."

"Yeah, right. The rental house burned to the ground."

"*What?*"

Tom shook his head. "Yeah, funny how she didn't mention that, huh? The fire was set, as in arson, okay? Accelerant was all over the place. Luckily, Ferdinanda and Yolanda were at the doctor. And near the house? We found a green and yellow Unifrutco oil can, the kind the United Fruit Company used to store fuel for their vehi-cles. It's also the kind of can Fidel and Raul Castro, and their people, filled with oil and dumped on the sugar-cane fields of their American oppressors, before burning the cane to the ground."

I stared at him. "You really can't believe Yolanda burned down the house she was living in, can you? I mean, if Ferdinanda came over in a little boat from Cuba, why would she make sure to bring an oil can with her? And keep it all these years? That doesn't make sense."

"No, Goldy," Tom said patiently. "We don't think Ferdinanda in her wheelchair burned down a rental when she was at the doctor. But we do think *Humberto* burned the place down."

"Why would he do that?"

Tom glanced at the kitchen door. "Our theory is that Yolanda wouldn't play ball and go spy on Ernest, whom she was making dinners for. Ernest, for his part, was working on a missing-assets case I'll tell you about later. That's what he was looking for, that Yolanda is being so vague about. As a private investigator, not a sheriff's department employee, Ernest wouldn't have had to bother with intrusive things like search warrants. Yolanda was already involved with Ernest in the dinner-making enterprise, so Humberto Captain must have figured, why not get her to do more? Why not have her ask Ernest if she could live there with Ferdinanda? And why not tempt her with cash in the bargain?"

"But then—"

Tom held up his hand. "We think Humberto found out Ernest was onto him. Humberto may have had Yolanda lift the file, destroy evidence, who knows what. Then, we think, Humberto killed Ernest."

"That's just beyond—"

"Beyond what?" Tom asked. "Let me tell you, Miss G. You shouldn't believe everything you hear from Yolanda Garcia."

Chapter 3

Tom walked out of the living room.

"Tom!" I called after him in a harsh whisper. "Why didn't you ask her about Humberto Captain?"

"I'm trying to, if I ever can get back to the kitchen." He paused. "Tell me about this Breckenridge character."

"He wanted to know if you were here, then he wanted to know about Ernest McLeod. Has it been on the news?"

"Yeah, 'fraid so."

"Look, what if Yolanda stayed here with us? And brought Ferdinanda? It isn't really safe for her to be at Ernest's place now, do you think? I mean, you don't know exactly how this was set up and you don't have a motive. So . . ."

Tom put his hands in his pockets. He said, "You want Humberto to come gunning for us, here?"

"Of course not. I just want Yolanda and Ferdinanda to be in a place that's safe for them, that's all. The rental's gone, Ernest's house will be off-limits for a while, and they certainly can't afford to stay in a Denver motel."

"With all the cash we found? They can afford the Ritz."

"Tom. I doubt she'll want to cater with me tomorrow. Arrangements will have to be made for Ernest. His AA group will have to be called. Someone will have to phone a church and plan a memorial service. All I'm saying is, we have more alarms on our house than a bank does. I want Yolanda and Ferdinanda to be safe. Please?"

He considered, then said finally, "Let me talk to my captain." He turned and pushed through the front door. Outside, the wind whipped the ornamental grasses Tom had put in. Another gust bent the Boulder Raspberry bushes, their white roselike blooms long gone. At the side of the house, wind-tossed pine branches slammed the shingles. Tom, who never seemed to be bothered by weather, pulled out his cell, punched in numbers, and began to walk up and down the porch as he spoke.

As Tom continued to pace, I watched him carefully, trying to figure out how the conversation was going. Tom looked into the living room. When he saw me glaring at him, he turned away. The kitchen was quiet, so I turned my attention back to Tom, who was stabbing the air with his free hand as he talked. Eventually he came inside and gave me a thumbs-up.

Only ten minutes had gone by, but it was now five o'clock. In the kitchen, Yolanda looked wrung out. Her normally glowing skin appeared ashen, papery, with a darkness under her eyes like bruises. She seemed fragile, very unlike the commanding presence she'd been in the Gold Gulch Spa kitchen.

Yolanda announced, "I *really* need to go get Ferdinanda. She worries about me."

"Just a couple more questions, Yolanda," said Tom. To John Bertram, he said, "Could you call the Catholic church and tell the priest we'll be picking up Yolanda's aunt presently?"

"You have to call his private line." Yolanda again rummaged in her purse, an intricately knotted beige bag, until she located another card, which she handed to John. "Please," she implored Tom, "don't make me stay here and talk to you. Ferdinanda may seem tough, but she's . . . not. She's easily disoriented. She claims she doesn't hear well, either, and I know her body has weakened since she's been in the wheelchair. I don't want you to scare her, the way—" She clamped her mouth shut. *The way you've scared me* hung in the air. She said suddenly, "You don't suppose Ferdinanda has heard from someplace else that Ernest's been killed, do you? Has it been on the news, I mean? She loves television and the radio. . . ."

"If she's visiting with the priest, she won't be watching TV or listening to the radio. Will she?" asked Tom.

"They might be watching television," said Yolanda. "He and she do that sometimes, when she's worn him out."

"I'm sorry, but the newspeople do know," said Tom, his tone a bit kinder. "Ernest's only kin is his ex-wife, who lives with her husband in Denver. The news outlets wanted information, and once we notified her, they got it."

"Oh, God," Yolanda whispered.

Tom turned the recorder back on. "You don't know of . . . anything that had been going on between Ernest and his ex-wife, Faye?"

"What do you mean, 'anything that had been going on'?" Yolanda asked. Her shoulders slumped.

"I mean, anything that would make her a suspect in his death," Tom said, his tone matter-of-fact. He brought his face a fraction closer to Yolanda's, which made her shrink back. "Did they talk? Did they argue? Like that. Anything you can tell us would be helpful."

"I don't think they had much contact, if any. He told me that Faye had an affair with some doctor in Wyoming, a while ago. The doctor wouldn't leave his wife. But then the doctor's wife died of cancer, the doctor moved to Denver, and the doctor and Faye got married. Aside from Ernest telling us he insisted on getting the house in the divorce, that's all he ever, you know, shared."

I knew the story of Ernest and Faye, the story of the house. But still Tom jotted a few words in his notebook.

"What?" asked Yolanda, her tone accusing. She eyed Tom's notebook. "Don't you believe me?"

"Should we *not* believe you?" Tom shot back.

"Tom!" I interjected. "You know what she's saying is—" But again I was stopped dead by Tom's look.

Yolanda muttered to herself in Spanish, something I didn't catch. I'd only occasionally heard her speak Spanish. Back when Yolanda and I were working at André's, she'd told me that she'd studied it in the Denver public schools, because she was tired of Ferdinanda talking to her fellow Cuban-Americans in a language she didn't understand. Now, I supposed, it came in handy, when you wanted to curse at someone without them knowing what you were saying. One of the few French words I remembered was *merde,* and just about everyone knew what that meant.

"Yolanda?" Tom prompted her. "Are you telling us the truth?"

"Of course I am." Yolanda looked at me for verification, and I risked Tom's wrath by nodding. "But you know what, Tom?" Yolanda said, turning her gaze to the window over the kitchen sink. "You can believe what you want. Can we go get Ferdinanda now?"

"Just tell me what you know about Humberto Captain."

Yolanda threw up her hands and narrowed her eyes, first at Tom, then at John. "You guys are always asking me about Humberto! Why?"

"Some months back? You catered a meal for him and his cronies, down in Lakewood," Tom replied evenly. "And you couldn't identify even *one* person who was there."

Yolanda protested. "That wasn't 'some months back.' It was over a year ago! And I was concentrating on the food, not the faces. Give me a *break.*"

"Did Humberto give you the cash under your mattress at Ernest's house?" John Bertram took over the questioning so smoothly, I wondered if Tom had signaled him in some way. "Seventeen thousand bucks? That's a lot of money for an out-of-work chef to have saved up and hidden."

"Oh," said Yolanda drily. "I see. You want to talk

about my money again. Did you do my laundry, too? Did you feed the dogs and clean up their poops?"

"You want to go get Ferdinanda," said Tom. "Tell us if Humberto gave you all that money under your mattress."

Yolanda clenched her teeth. "*Yes.*"

"Why?" asked John.

"Why did he give me the money?" Yolanda asked. "Or why did I put it under the mattress?"

There was a long silence. Finally Tom said, "Both."

Yolanda's fingers tapped out a drumbeat on the table as she looked out the back windows. "Humberto is a friend. His father brought Ferdinanda and my grandparents over on the boat from Cuba. So Humberto gave us the money because he knew we were having *problems*. I didn't have a job. We didn't have a place to live. He came around when we were packing up what we could salvage from the rental—"

"After it mysteriously burned down," Tom supplied.

"Yes, Tom. We didn't have insurance for our stuff. Our landlady, Donna Lamar? *She* had insurance. So why don't you ask her if she torched the place?"

I said, "Wait. Since when is Donna Lamar a *landlady*? You said before that she was an owner/agent. I thought she was just a, you know, rental agent and property manager." I pictured Donna Lamar, her dark blond hair pulled back in a messy ponytail, her gray sweatshirt frayed, her jeans unfashionably faded. She was a member of our church, but we went to different services, so I rarely saw her there. Invariably, though, I ran into her at the local hardware store as she absentmindedly pushed a cart loaded with cheap cans of paint.

Yolanda said, "Surprise, surprise, Goldy. Donna owns most of those little houses she rents out. Over the years, whenever somebody had a problem getting rid of a small place? Say the owners were going through a bad divorce, or the house was real remote, or it needed major repairs, and the owners had just been transferred? After the house sat on the market for a year, but before a short sale or foreclosure, Donna would creep in and offer half the asking price. If the owner or the bank refused her offer, she'd move on, buying houses after foreclosure or at auction. She wouldn't fix and flip, because nobody wanted that house in the first place, right? She'd fix and rent. On the low end of the market, renters aren't demanding. If Donna does have a difficult tenant, she just doesn't renew their lease. If you're renting at the low end? If you're desperate and you're just one step removed from sleeping in your car? Donna's your woman."

"How do you know all this?" I asked.

Yolanda shook her head. "I got to know Donna real well when I was renting from her."

"But she always looks so—"

"Poor and downtrodden? That's part of her shtick. Or it was. Lately, she's cleaned up her act. Maybe she's putting that insurance money to good use."

"How did Humberto know you were having problems?" Tom asked, giving me a dark, *stop interrupting this interrogation* glare.

Yolanda cocked her head at Tom. "You ever tried to keep something secret in this town?"

"Goldy didn't know your house burned down," said

Tom. "Goldy wasn't aware of Donna Lamar's circumstances."

Yolanda gave me a puzzled look. "Well, I haven't got a clue as to how you didn't hear the news about our rental, and about Donna." I stared at my friend. Somehow, her answer seemed . . . calculated. Was I picking up on Tom's distrust of Yolanda? That afternoon, my friend had told me all kinds of details about her relationship with Kris. And yet she had not told me that her rental house had burned down, or that her landlady was a jackal. Why not?

Before I could ask her some questions, Tom intervened. "So Humberto, your family's friend, somehow knew you were having problems, and he came around and offered to help you."

"*Yes*."

"He just showed up out of the blue."

Yolanda shook her head. "He heard it someplace, I don't know where. Maybe the news. You don't believe that he heard it through the town grapevine, then ask him how he knew. You want to hear the story or not?"

"I wouldn't believe a single word that came out of Humberto Captain's mouth," Tom replied.

Yolanda placed her hands palm down on our kitchen table. "Yes, Humberto showed up, out of the blue, as you said. He asked if we needed money. I said we did. He gave me that seventeen thousand. He wanted to know if we had a place to stay. I said I could ask someone I was working for if we could stay with him. At Ernest's, I put the money under the mattress because I couldn't think where else to put it."

I stood up and looked for something to do. This whole conversation was making me uncomfortable. First I was on Yolanda's side, then I was on Tom's, then back again. I'd be useless on a jury.

"But you didn't go stay somewhere Humberto supplied," Tom was saying now. "You asked Ernest McLeod if you could stay with him—"

"*Yes.*" Yolanda's eyes flashed. "So *what*?"

Tom leaned across the kitchen table. "You went to stay with Ernest McLeod, after your rental mysteriously burned down—"

"Would you quit saying the rental mysteriously burned down? I've only talked to sheriff's department investigators sixteen times about that stupid house, which was a firetrap, by the way. And no, I still don't know how somebody would go about getting a Unifrutco oil can these days, and using it to spread accelerant—"

"—and you had no place to go," Tom said, continuing as if she hadn't spoken, "despite the fact that you had a rich boyfriend with a big house who would have loved to have you back, with no conditions. But then Humberto Captain showed up while your rental house was still smoking. He appeared unannounced, wanting to give you money. And, let's see. I'll bet he was wearing one of his beige tropical suits. Makes him look like a Miami gangster."

"Gee whiz," said Yolanda, "I've heard of cops doing racial profiling before, but I'd never actually experienced it. And they're called duck suits."

"I was joking," said Tom, but he realized he'd made a mistake. "Sorry."

"Yeah," Yolanda muttered. "I'll *bet* you're sorry."

Tom went on. "And Humberto said, 'Here, Yolanda, take seventeen thousand bucks, and by the way, I don't actually have a place for you to stay, but I have an idea. To earn this money, could you and Ferdinanda go live with Ernest McLeod, because he's *investigating* me, even though he's not a cop anymore?'"

Yolanda said, "Ernest was investigating Humberto?" Once again, I detected a note of . . . what? Dishonesty?

Tom said flatly, "Don't try to convince me you didn't know that Ernest was looking into Humberto's affairs."

Yolanda closed her eyes. She said, "Okay, I knew."

John Bertram was summoned by his cell, and I found myself blinking rapidly. I was surprised by what Yolanda had admitted, but I still felt sorry for her. When my business had been closed after someone tried to poison a guest at an event I was catering, I'd been subjected to Tom's questioning. In fact, that was how we'd met. But I hadn't enjoyed the interrogation one bit.

Tom pressed her. "Did you know anything about the investigation?"

Yolanda took a deep breath. "Something about gold and gems."

"Yeah," said Tom, "something. Do you know if Ernest found anything?"

"I do not," said Yolanda, staring straight at Tom.

John Bertram returned and took a seat. "I just got off the phone with our guys who went to see Kris Nielsen. After the rental house burned down, why didn't you go stay with Kris? Just temporarily? He told our officers he offered to have you and Ferdinanda—"

"The *hell* with you!" Yolanda cried, jumping to her feet. "I told you, that man was *stalking* me—"

"He denies stalking you," John said simply.

"He's lying," said Yolanda.

"Was Ernest working for *you*?" asked Tom. "Trying to prove a case against Kris Nielsen?"

"I don't know." She glared at Tom. "But let me ask you something. When your guy went to see Kris, did the officer treat Kris the same way you're treating me? I'll bet he didn't, because Kris is rich. And white." While these words hung in the air like an indictment, Yolanda pointed first at Tom, then at John. "Kris Nielsen is my *ex*-boyfriend, and his house is the last place I would go. Ever." She reached into her bag and pulled out a faded gray nylon windbreaker, the kind that had been fashionable about twenty years ago. The jacket made a slithery sound as she put her arms into the too-large sleeves. I wondered if she'd bought it at Aspen Meadow's second-hand store, Julian Teller's favorite clothes shop. "I've had enough," Yolanda announced. "I need to go get my aunt, and then I need to drive back to Ernest's place and take care of the dogs. And *then* I'm going to start calling Ernest's friends."

"Actually, Yolanda," I interjected, "I'd feel better, well, actually, you and your great-aunt need to stay with us. With someone gunning for Ernest, and with Kris acting . . . you know, the way he is, I'd feel more comfortable all the way around if you were here."

Yolanda looked at Tom. "I told Ernest I'd take care of his puppies."

John Bertram piped up. "I can take care of the dogs

tonight. Feed them, take them out before we go to bed. But my wife's allergic, so I can't have them in our house. They'll be all right at Ernest's place after you get your stuff."

Yolanda had not stopped staring at Tom. "Are you sure *you* want us here? I can go back and forth to take care of the dogs."

Tom's tone turned gentle. "Yes, I already checked with the department. It's fine, really. You know how Goldy worries."

"You want to spy on me," Yolanda said to Tom.

"We want you to be safe," Tom replied.

Yolanda pushed through the kitchen door and moved down the hall. "I'll think about it," she called over her shoulder. "Now I'm on my way to the church."

"I told you, we're coming to talk to Ferdinanda," Tom replied.

Yolanda pushed the kitchen door open and again pointed at Tom. "When you talk to Ferdinanda? If you treat her the way you treated me, she'll spit in your face."

"I thought you said we'd frighten her," said Tom. "I thought you said she was vulnerable and weak."

"If you frighten her, it doesn't matter how vulnerable and weak she is, she'll hit you. I am *not kidding*."

Tom shook his head mildly. "We'll be nice."

I thought, *Uh-huh.*

I went out to the driveway with them, because I wanted to make sure Yolanda was okay. Tom and John, meanwhile, tried to settle on who was going with whom and what vehicle they were going to take. Out back, Jake began to howl, as if he wanted to get his two cents in. The wind had picked up even more strength, and whenever one of us tried to say something, the words were whipped from our mouths. Finally, Tom huddled in next to Yolanda and spoke to her. She rolled her eyes, dug in her purse, and came out with a ring of keys. Then Tom walked over to me and came close to my ear.

"Drive Yolanda's van, would you please, Goldy?"

"Sure. Can you lock the house?"

Tom walked back up the steps and made sure our front door was secure and the alarm was set. When he returned, he dropped the key ring into my hand. "We'll drive her to the church. We want her to be with us, in case she decides to share any more information. Then you can drive Ferdinanda and Yolanda over to Ernest's place, so they can take care of the puppies and pick up their stuff before they come back here."

"What if they don't want to stay with us?"

"Then I'll come get you at Ernest's."

"Will department investigators still be at Ernest's house?"

Tom glanced at his watch. "They should be."

"Whatever," I said as I marched to Yolanda's vehicle.

It was an ancient van that had been retrofitted with a small elevator for a wheelchair. Even with that, the vehicle couldn't have cost more than a few thousand dollars. Formerly turquoise and white, it was now mostly rusted. I gingerly opened the door. Inside, it was immaculate, although the carpet was worn and the windshield cracked. I cranked the key in the ignition, shifted into

Drive, took my foot off the brake, and turned the steering wheel. When nothing happened, I gently stepped on the accelerator. After an initial hesitation, the behemoth growled and jerked away from our curb. It listed to starboard and the engine made a horrible grinding noise.

As I moved down our street behind Tom, John, and Yolanda, the hair on the back of my neck prickled. Was I being followed or watched? Or was I being paranoid? Maybe our discussion in the driveway, or Jake's howls, had brought unseen neighbors to their windows. I checked the van's pitted rearview mirror but saw only tiny stalks of silvery snow-in-summer. Tom had told me it was a favorite perennial in Aspen Meadow because it spread rapidly and withstood the summertime hail that crushed more delicate flowers. Tom had helped Trudy, our next-door neighbor, plant a dozen of them along the fence in her front yard, and with this summer's record rainfall, the invasive plant had taken over.

I refocused my attention and checked the street. No one was behind Yolanda's van. The sidewalks were empty. The FOR SALE sign in Jack's front yard rippled in the wind. *Oh, Jack,* I thought, *I miss you.* My heart twisted in my chest.

The wind kicked up waves of dust as our vehicles lumbered down Main Street and up toward Aspen Meadow Lake. The water itself formed dark wavelets that mirrored the charcoal sky. My watch said it was only quarter after five, but it seemed like much later.

Our Lady of the Mountains loomed on the hill just above the lake. Despite the cold wind, Ferdinanda and the monsignor were out in the parking lot. The priest, short, slender, and already half-bald, was shivering in his clericals. Ferdinanda, stout, square faced, and frizzy haired, sat tall in her wheelchair. She wore only a shapeless brown dress that looked as if it had been prison-issue from the former Soviet Union.

I wondered why they were outside. But that was clear soon enough, as Ferdinanda was smoking a cigar. She waved it jauntily when she saw the van, but when she realized it was accompanied by a police car, her chin dropped. She stared through the cracked windshield, as if she were trying to make out Yolanda.

I threw the vehicle into Park and jumped out to re-assure her, but that only made matters worse.

"Where's Yolanda?" she demanded of me, pointing the cigar in a menacing manner. "Why is she not here?"

I said, "She's over in that other—" And then I waved at the police car.

Ferdinanda began to wail. "What's he done to her now?" she cried.

"Who's that?" asked Tom as he eased his way out of the prowler. "What has who done to her?"

"Where is Yolanda?" she demanded.

"*Estoy aquí,*" called Yolanda as she rushed to her aunt. *I'm here.* Yolanda fell to her knees in front of the wheelchair and hugged Ferdinanda's knees. I could make out enough of their Spanish to understand that Yolanda was telling her great-aunt that Ernest was dead, that he had been murdered, and that the police were here to question her.

Ferdinanda's mouth turned downward. She dropped

the smoking cigar on the asphalt and leaned forward to embrace Yolanda. The priest worriedly crushed the cigar with his toe, then asked Tom and John if there was anything he could do to help.

"Yeah, go back inside, Father, if you would," said Tom. "We're just going to talk to Ferdinanda for a few minutes."

"Oh no you're not," said Ferdinanda. "Put me into the van, Yolanda. I want to go home, take care of the dogs." Ferdinanda began to roll herself toward the van.

John Bertram abruptly stepped in front of the wheelchair, as if to stop her. "Tom, do you want me to—"

John Bertram did not see Ferdinanda reach beside her hip and pull out a telescoping baton. As Yolanda and Tom both cried, "No!" Ferdinanda pressed a button to extend the baton and whacked a startled John Bertram across the knees.

John hollered, "Christ!" and fell to the pavement.

"You just assaulted a police officer!" Tom yelled at Ferdinanda. The monsignor knelt quickly beside John and spoke softly to him. John, for his part, cussed and held his knees. Was the monsignor used to police officers being hit by the disabled in the church parking lot? Probably not. But the priest seemed okay. John Bertram did not.

"Ferdinanda!" shouted Tom as he hustled to John's side. "What were you thinking?"

"That man tried to block the way of a handicapped person!" Ferdinanda hollered right back. "I'll call my lawyer! I'll sue the sheriff's department!"

Yolanda stood protectively next to Ferdinanda. At the

same time, she tilted her head and gave Tom a raised-eyebrow I-told-you-so look.

Tom ignored them both, knelt next to John, and asked the priest to step aside. Then my husband expertly felt around John's knees, told him nothing was broken, that he was probably just bruised.

John said something unintelligible.

Tom talked in low tones to John, who must have agreed to something. Tom asked the monsignor for help. Eventually, John put one arm around Tom's shoulders, one around the priest's, and the three of them moved haltingly to the squad car. They eased John into the front seat. Tom thanked the priest, who waved to Ferdinanda and Yolanda and hustled back to the rectory. He was probably saying a prayer of gratitude that he was getting away from this particular mess.

With John still inside, Tom got out, slammed the driver-side door, and walked over to us. But instead of losing his temper, he kept his tone even.

"John says he's okay, just in pain," Tom said to Yolanda. "I couldn't feel anything broken, but I want him to be checked out, just in case. Let's get your aunt into the van. We can talk for a few minutes, before I take John to the hospital."

The old van had chilled quickly. Once Ferdinanda had gone up the motorized lifting device and was strapped in the back, Tom sat in the passenger seat. I saw him take in how decrepit the vehicle was, with its split seats, torn dashboard, cracked and pitted wind-shield, and worn carpet. Yolanda got behind the wheel and turned on the engine so it could warm us up. I took the lone seat in back, beside Ferdinanda.

Tom turned to face us. "I need to ask you a couple of questions about Ernest, Ferdinanda. Please."

"I'm not saying anything without a lawyer here," Ferdinanda said defiantly.

"You're not a suspect," Tom replied. "Will you talk to me?"

Ferdinanda patted her frizz of hair. After a moment, she said, "I suppose."

"What time did Ernest leave the house on Saturday?"

"What?" she replied, and then I remembered that Yolanda had said she was hard of hearing.

Tom raised his voice a notch. "When did Ernest leave his house Saturday morning?"

"About half past eight," said Ferdinanda. "He said he was going to walk, try to get some exercise. He'd told us it helped alcoholics if they get high from walking or running, instead of from booze."

"Is that what he said that morning?"

Ferdinanda turned the sides of her mouth down, considering. "No. That was what he usually said. He didn't say it that morning."

"What did he say that morning?"

"I was out on his patio, smoking a cigar. Yolanda was doing the dishes. Ernest? He said, 'That thing will kill you, Ferdinanda, you ought to stop.'" She paused for a moment. "I don't hear so good anymore. I think that was what he said."

"Did he say anything else?" asked Tom. "Anything about being worried? Anything about someone wanting to hurt him?"

Ferdinanda rubbed the sides of her mouth with her tobacco-stained thumb and forefinger. "A woodpecker was at his feeder. I think Ernest said, 'I'm going now. If anything happens to me, ask the bird.'"

"'Ask the bird'?" said Tom. "That's what he said?"

"I think so. I told you, I don't hear so good anymore. I laughed. He laughed. Then he walked away. He didn't come home last night. Didn't Yolanda tell you? She called all over. We were worried sick. We drove over to the dentist's office, but the dentist wasn't there. Ernest wasn't either. Yolanda, she called the clinic, the hospital—"

"When he was saying something about asking the birds, did he say he was going anywhere else besides the dentist?"

Ferdinanda lifted her chin. "No. Ernest promised us he was coming home right after his appointment. He wanted Yolanda's seafood enchiladas."

"Was Ernest carrying anything?" Tom asked. "When he left? His cell phone, something like that?"

Ferdinanda's wizened face looked blank. "He just had on his backpack, the way he always did."

"One last thing," said Tom. "When you asked, 'What's he done to her now?' what did you mean? Who were you talking about?"

"That Kris Nielsen," Ferdinanda replied. Here she took out a handkerchief from an unseen pocket of the brown dress and spit into it. She wadded up the kerchief and stowed it in another invisible pocket. "Yolanda got sick. Sexually transmitted disease."

Yolanda protested, saying, "Oh, Tía, no—"

Ferdinanda held up her hand to shush her niece. "Yolanda's doctor asked who was she having sex with.

She said only Kris. The doctor said Kris made her sick. So Yolanda asked Kris if he was sleeping with other women, someone with a disease. Do you think he cared about her, about how she was sick? No. He picked up a broom. I knew what he was going to do, so I rolled myself in front of him. That bastard pulled off my *eleke* and then pushed me aside."

"*Eleke*?" Tom asked, bewildered.

"A beaded necklace," Ferdinanda explained. "It is sacred. But listen. That bastard Kris took that broomstick and hit my dear Yolanda two times. *Crack,* on one arm. Then *crack,* on the other."

My mouth dropped open as I glanced at Yolanda. Her left hand covered her eyes in shame.

Ferdinanda concluded by saying, "That's when we decided, we have to move out."

"You didn't tell me," I whispered to Yolanda.

"I couldn't tell you, Goldy," said Yolanda, still not looking at us. "I was ashamed." She did glance up at me then. "He hit me so hard I thought my bones were broken. They swelled up, then turned black and blue. My long sleeves covered up the bruises."

"Yeah," said Ferdinanda. "Tell her about the VD, too."

Inside the dark van, I could just make out Yolanda's face turning scarlet. She said, "Crabs. I've been treated. I got it from him, but I'm all right now. It was nothing that would affect food handling. I told Ernest, in case he didn't want me fixing his dinners. He knew all about STDs and their treatment, and he told me not to worry about it."

"Did you file a police report, Yolanda?" asked Tom gently. "Over the fact that Kris hit you?"

"No," she replied in a low voice. "Later, when we were in the rental and things started happening, I called the police. But back then? When he hit me? I just wanted to get out of there."

Chapter 4

I interrupted. "Tom, let me get them back to their place."

"Just remind me," said Tom, his tone still gentle, "was Ernest investigating Kris? Trying to prove he'd been harassing you?"

Yolanda looked down and sighed.

Ferdinanda shook a gnarled index finger at Tom. "Not yet. But Ernest, he promised he would help as soon as he finished up some other things."

"Some other things?" said Tom.

Yolanda intervened. "He *was* going to help me. But he had to finish up the divorce case, the puppy mill, investigating Humberto and the missing assets. After that, he was going to go after Kris. Ferdinanda is right. He promised." Another sob escaped her lips.

Ferdinanda dug in her pocket for the tissue. She muttered, "Humberto," and spat into the tissue.

Tom pressed her again. "Did Kris by any chance *know* that Ernest was going to investigate him?"

Yolanda looked out the van windshield. "I'm not sure. But Ernest did say he was going to, you know, open a file on Kris."

"When did he say this to you?" Tom asked.

"I don't remember."

Tom's fingers tapped the dashboard. "He was going to open a computer file? A paper file?"

"I told you, he had a nice handmade cabinet, with hanging files in it." Yolanda's tone had turned sour again. "I didn't check to see if he had a file on Kris."

"Tom, please," I said again. "It's getting late. The puppies need to be fed. Can we go?"

"Just one more thing. Does either one of you know how to shoot?"

"Tom!" I cried. "You said they weren't suspects."

Yolanda sighed. "It's all right, Goldy. No, I told you before, Tom. I do not know how to shoot a gun, and I don't want to learn."

Ferdinanda frowned in defiance. "*I* know how to shoot. *I* was a *francotiradora,* how do you say, *sniper,* in Raul's army. Somebody comes after me or Yolanda? I will shoot them."

"And that's all either one of them is going to say without a lawyer," I interjected.

Tom turned in his seat to eye me directly. "Listen to me. I want you to *ask permission* of the investigators at Ernest's house before you go in and touch anything. Understand?"

"All *right*," I said.

"Yolanda," said Tom, "do you have a remote to get into Ernest's garage?"

"Uh," she said, "yes."

"Good," said Tom. "Still, when you all see the police car, I want you to honk or something before you go in. Understand? Yolanda, I know you and your aunt may want to stay there, but I just don't want the investigation messed up."

"Okay," said Yolanda.

I asked, "Could you call me when you know what's going on with John? Because if Yolanda and Ferdinanda decide to stay with us, and John can't let the dogs out tonight, I'll need to find somebody else to do it."

"Yup," said Tom as he heaved himself down from the van. "Thanks for your help, ladies."

"Tell your friend I'm sorry I hurt him," said Ferdinanda.

When Tom said, "He knows," I wanted to hug him.

A clap of thunder startled us as we drove toward Aspen Hills. Yolanda had asked if we could trade places, so she could be in back with Ferdinanda. Once they were sitting next to each other, they began to speak in Spanish. I would have tried to follow what they were saying, but they began to speak so fast that there was no way I could make it out.

Which they no doubt knew.

I couldn't help but wonder, *Did Yolanda take Humberto's money to spy on Ernest? And did she actually spy on him and tell Humberto what Ernest was doing? What is the story on those missing assets?*

The sky began to spit large drops. I glanced at my watch. The storm had been brewing all afternoon, and now, at ten to six, it was hitting us. The television meteorologists were always warning that this time of year in Colorado could yield "unsettled" weather patterns. For a caterer, this means "unsettling," because if you had an outdoor event scheduled, you could, at the last moment, be hustling a lot of chairs and tables inside. Thank goodness for CBHS's alternate plan to use the gym the next day. Thank goodness we didn't have anything we needed to cook outside. Thank goodness Arch had his own transportation that night and wasn't depending on me. Thank goodness . . .

I recognized my own thought pattern. I was trying to calm myself, trying to get distracted, before something potentially *unsettling* was due to take place. As Yolanda's tires ground up the hill into the back entrance of Aspen Hills, I swallowed hard. Up, up, up we went. The engine gnashed its innards as I turned the steering wheel hard for first one, then another switchback.

On our right, John Bertram's house, then his garage, came into view. A hundred yards beyond that, crime-scene ribbons wrapped around rocks and posts fluttered in the wet breeze.

As John Bertram had told us, Ernest McLeod's house was a third of a mile farther up. When I saw it, my heart plummeted. So much for just worrying about weather, cooking, transportation, and other insignificant issues.

"Hey, you two," I said to Ferdinanda and Yolanda. "Everything all right?" They'd both begun sniffling, so *no*.

I peered ahead into the gloom. I could not see any police cars. If Ernest had had one garage remote and

Yolanda had had the other, how had they gotten in? Well, presumably John Bertram had a spare key to his friend's house and had given it to the sheriff's department. And even if John hadn't, the police had their ways. They'd already gotten in once and found the seventeen thousand under the mattress.

But if Tom wanted me to honk at the police car, then to get permission to go inside, how was I supposed to do that if I couldn't see anybody there?

Yolanda and Ferdinanda were still crying. I pulled over onto the graveled shoulder, then reached into my bag and handed tissues back to Yolanda, who kept one and gave the other to her aunt. Ferdinanda wiped her eyes and then tucked the tissue into another unseen compartment of her wheelchair. I wondered where she kept the baton, and how often she used it.

We were just above the highest location of the crime-scene tape stretching around a boulder. The rain pelted down; the yellow ribbons blew sideways. I strained to see up to Ernest's house. There was no police car. Could the investigators have been dropped off by another team? There were no lights. Was it possible they were done already?

Tom had said they would be there. I honked three times. There was no reponse.

I punched in first Tom's cell, then his office number, but was directed to voice mail both times. I left messages saying I couldn't see a department car at Ernest's house, and that I'd honked, to no avail. If I couldn't see the investigators or reach them, should we go in?

Could the team have left already? That didn't seem

likely. County investigators usually stay on a fresh murder for hours in pursuit of clues. I didn't know which investigators were assigned to Ernest's place. I wasn't sure I wanted to risk Tom's wrath by going into the house without the permission I'd promised him I would get.

I called Tom's cell four more times during the next ten minutes. I tried Sergeant Boyd, his most trusted subordinate, and got voice mail there, too.

On my last try to Tom, I said that even if Yolanda and Ferdinanda decided to stay with us, they would need toiletries, clothes, and so on. I knew he wouldn't want us to come back to Ernest's house when it was completely dark and the team had left, would he? I supposed we could go to the grocery store for essentials, I said, and run the washing machine for Yolanda's clothes for tomorrow. . . .

I reluctantly hung up. Ferdinanda and Yolanda had started up their Spanish conversation again. Shame or no shame, I wanted to ask Yolanda why she hadn't felt the confidence to call me when Kris hit her. She knew my history. Had she been too proud to ask for help? I wondered.

While waiting for Tom to call back, I contemplated Ernest's dark house, which was barely visible now through the relentless downpour.

The weathered-gray-clapboard-sided house had originally been a one-story summer vacation home for a public school teacher. The teacher, who'd had the old-fashioned name Portia, had lived and worked in Denver from the end of the Second World War, when the house had been new, until the early seventies. Never married, Portia had lived year-round in the house after her retirement. Like many Aspen Meadow residences of that era, the place had been small—only two bedrooms and one bath. But its glory had been the fifteen gorgeous, sloping acres that commanded a spectacular vista of national forest.

I stared at my cell phone, willing Tom, Sergeant Boyd, or someone from the department to call me. Nothing. I shook my head and stared back at the house.

Over the years, Portia had told Ernest, she'd had multiple offers from builders riding various booms. He told us this story as he waved his hand, the way she had, as if Portia had been a princess who'd dismissed suitors who weren't up to snuff. These builders, Portia had angrily told Ernest, were trying to take advantage of unincorporated Furman County's lax building restrictions. They wanted to put sixty structures on one-quarter-acre parcels. How could anyone enjoy the view with all the houses cheek by jowl? No, no, Portia told Ernest. She put her house up for sale several times, to take advantage of rising prices. But she stood firm in one area: Whoever purchased it had to sign a legal notice that he or she would never tear down the original house nor subdivide her land. Buyers weren't interested in a small, outdated, ramshackle place with only two bedrooms and a single bath. Builders were scared to death to sign away their desire to develop.

And then along came Ernest McLeod, a cop who was unmarried at the time. Ernest charmed Portia and asked if he could have her permission to buy her house and

add on to it. No matter what, he promised, he would
never subdivide her land. And for the addition, he would
use the same siding, let it weather, and keep Portia's
style of architecture, which even an amateur art critic
would sneeringly call *nondescript.* Ernest also insisted
he would do all the work himself and, as if to prove it,
showed Portia pictures of the addition he'd done to his
place in Denver. He'd also told her he'd just been accepted into the Furman County Sheriff's Department.
He wanted to live in Aspen Meadow, because the people
were so nice. And, he said, he would be using the land
only to host picnics for his fellow law enforcement officers.

Portia, a lifelong Republican who was a great believer
in law and order, had gladly sold Ernest her house. Shov-
eling the long driveway might have kept her in shape for
the first decade of her retirement years, but the winters
had begun to grind on her. She wanted to move to Arizona. The deal was made, and they were both happy.

Portia had sent Ernest postcards from Tucson, which
he'd shown us. In reply, he'd sent her pictures of her old
house, with whatever project he was undertaking high-
lighted in "before" and "after" snapshots. Ernest had
begun by adding a garage and a cantilevered second
story that featured a second, new kitchen, a new living/
dining room, and two more bedrooms, plus two more
baths. He'd then moved on to building a deck in the
middle of the second-story façade, with a greenhouse on
one side and a glassed-in winter porch complete with
wood-burning fireplace on the other. He'd carved a sign
that said PORTIA'S PERCH and hung it outside the winter

porch, then another one that read PORTIA'S PARCEL, which he'd staked next to a boulder. Portia had written back to Ernest that they were her favorite photographs; she showed them to everyone in her retirement home.

Even after Ernest married Faye, who divorced him three years into their union for the Wyoming doctor, he'd sent snapshots to Portia, until his last letter was returned, stamped "Addressee Deceased." He'd told us about her passing with tears in his eyes, and shortly after that, his casual drinking had turned heavy, then addictive, and he'd been forced into early retirement. Still, he'd told us at one of the department picnics he still hosted at his house, he'd found spiritual renewal through AA and a "new way to fight the bad guys," as he put it, in his job as a private investigator.

Tom and I had often admired the view from Ernest's deck. Every house in Aspen Meadow had a slightly different view. It was that same puzzle posed by the *Mountain Journal,* which Tom had reminded me of: "Whose view is this?" For a whopping five bucks, you could drive around and try to figure it out.

Portia, for her part, had hated the newspapers and had called the cops when the *Mountain Journal* had shown up, uninvited, to take a photograph of her view. Ernest said Portia called the media "a bunch of pinkos." Remembering, I smiled as I recalled Tom putting his arm around me as he pointed out the spectacular vista of national forest, with its steep nearby mountains. Around Ernest's house, the land was peppered with quartz and granite boulders, towering lodgepole and ponderosa pines, stands of aspen, and the occasional perfect,

Christmas tree–shaped blue spruce. After some December poachers had come in with chain saws, which they'd used to cut down over two dozen of the spruce, Ernest had put up signs every twelve feet that read ABSOLUTELY NO TREE CUTTING, although he'd told us we could come get a tree anytime we wanted. We demurred, saying Portia wouldn't have wanted it.

I sighed and stared at the house, which, with all the additions, had a hodgepodge look to it. The place already showed indications of neglect, although Ernest had been gone—I couldn't bring myself to think *dead*—for only two days. It was hard to make things out through the wind, the rain, and the gathering gloom. The PORTIA'S PERCH sign hung at an angle. The long deck had the painful look of abandonment. When Ernest hadn't returned Saturday night, Yolanda clearly hadn't known to bring in the pots of annuals. These massive displays—petunias, geraniums, nicotiana, and a dozen other florals—had died from the frost we'd had the previous night. Every spring, Ernest had grown the flowers from seed in his greenhouse, before placing them outside on the deck. Now they looked scraggly and forlorn, as did the whole house, come to think of it. I felt a rush of sorrow.

After fifteen minutes, I still hadn't heard back from Tom. No one appeared. Yolanda and Ferdinanda seemed to have exhausted their conversation. Ferdinanda's voice sounded like stones scraping together when she said she needed to go to the bathroom.

I called John Bertram's house, since it was just down the road. There was no answer, and the place was dark. I started the van, moved it to the end of Ernest's driveway, and honked again. There was no response.

Finally, I told Yolanda and her aunt that I would call out to whatever law enforcement people were in the house, if there were any, to get their permission to come in.

Pulling on my jacket, I took the remote that Yolanda handed me and jumped from the warmth of the van. I was immediately stung with freezing rain and another clap of thunder, but I trotted up the driveway to the garage door anyway. When I opened it, only Ernest's pickup was inside.

"Hello?" I called.

I raced to the door leading into the house, tentatively calling, "Tom Schulz sent me!" and "Hello!" The only response was a chorus of yips. Nine puppies? Only nine? The place sounded like a kennel at feeding time.

"Is anybody here?" I yelled when I pushed through the door.

No one answered. The house did have a slightly peculiar smell, but I couldn't place it. Not rotting food, not puppy mess, but something else . . . what? My mother had always claimed I had overdeveloped olfactory receptors and that I could sniff scents that she couldn't. This was common among foodies, I later discovered, and so it was only natural, I told my mother much later, that I should go into catering. Then it had been her turn to sniff, but that was another story.

I pressed switches on a nearby panel, which brought illumination to the shadowy interior. Then I raced back to the van.

"Let's go," I said as I shook drops out of my wet hair. I eased the van into the space next to Ernest's pickup truck, and Yolanda brought Ferdinanda into the basement.

"We've decided to stay with you," said Yolanda. "Will it be all right for us to make calls from your house? We still need to phone Ernest's friends and make arrangements."

"Absolutely," I said. "But we'd better go as quickly as possible," I warned them. "I was supposed to get permission for us to be in here."

"Five minutes," Yolanda replied. "We don't have much stuff."

"Do you have suitcases?" I asked, but my words were drowned out by the barking of the puppies. "Should I go do something with them?" I called to Yolanda, who was rolling her aunt into the bathroom.

"No, I can do it," said Yolanda. "Ernest told me what to do. It'll just take me a few minutes to—"

"I can figure out what the dogs need," I called back. "You've got enough to worry about already."

"Thanks, Goldy." Her beautiful face was filled with gratitude. "You do too much for me."

"Where are the dogs?"

She pointed at a door. Before I could go through it, though, my glance snagged on a section of the small living room where Yolanda and Ferdinanda watched television. The hearth of the tiny moss-rock fireplace was covered with a cloth topped with various statues: the Virgin Mary, a metal chalice with a rooster on top, and a mask of some kind, with cowrie shells for eyes and a mouth. It was some kind of . . . well, what? Altar?

The dogs' crying pulled my attention away, and I pushed through the door Yolanda had indicated. It opened into a small, linoleum-floored storage room, which also served as the laundry room. I flipped on the lights and was immediately greeted with a barking storm and a horde of beagles.

"Wait, wait!" I cried as I tried to get my bearings in a world of stink. Whatever order Ernest had imposed on this room, where he had placed a row of metal cabinets, all labeled alphabetically, *Auto* to *Yard,* was gone. The floor was strewn with stained wet newspapers. The beagles raced about, clambering over my feet, clawing my legs, and falling every which way. They were probably the cutest animals I'd ever seen, a tumble of brown, black, and white fur and lovable baby hound faces. Still, I resisted the urge to get down on the floor and play with them. The stench of dog urine and feces was so strong that my eyes watered. I looked around wildly. Ernest had hung a mop, a broom, and other cleaning items next to the washer and dryer. Above the machines was a shelf that blessedly contained a neat pile of newspapers and a spray bottle of disinfectant. On the floor was a trash can lined with a plastic bag. Hooray.

I gathered up all the soiled papers, shoved them into the garbage, and sprayed the entire floor with disinfectant. This was no easy task, as the puppies kept yipping madly, whining, licking my ankles, digging their tiny teeth into my calves, and rolling onto their backs to have their tummies rubbed. When they decided to go off and play with their pals, their paws slid every which way on whatever part of the floor I'd just mopped. I pushed the sponge-on-a-stick as best I could to get the whole floor, then sprayed again and mopped again. When I got on my hands and knees to lay down clean newspaper, the puppies decided I was the Eiger and began to climb. They also licked my face, my hands, and my arms before they went back to whining.

"Did you feed them?" Yolanda asked from the doorway.

"I haven't even rinsed out the mop."

"I'll do the mop," she said, grabbing it. "You feed them."

"Okay. Where's the puppy chow?"

Yolanda looked around and frowned. "We put the bags of food right there." She peered at the shelf, as if willing the chow to appear. "Oh, wait, I finished the first bag he bought this morning. Damn. Do you see more in here?"

I looked around the storage room. "Nope. Would it be in one of these cabinets?"

"I don't know," she said, her voice frantic. "I'll do the mop and take this stinky bag out to the trash bin in the garage, and then I'll give them fresh water." From the distance, Ferdinanda called to Yolanda. Yolanda inhaled and closed her eyes. "Goldy, could you go look for more puppy chow? Maybe John Bertram's wife has already been in here and she moved it. She's a slob without the first clue about how to keep a house." Like her husband, I thought, who was a slob who couldn't find a police file if his life depended on it. Yolanda went on. "I wouldn't doubt that she moved it, 'cause in addition to being messy, she's also absentminded. Oh, yeah, and allergic to dogs. Still, I know Ernest bought several bags of puppy chow. In the kitchen, maybe? I'll check the garage. Ernest is—was—a neat freak, so we should be able to find it somewhere, no problem. Thanks, Goldy," she said as she rushed off, clutching the mop handle, to tend to Ferdinanda.

John Bertram! I wished I had his cell number. But then I remembered that he was down at Southwest Hospital. He was having his baton-bashed knees examined and treated. Maybe that was where Tom was, too, which could explain why he wasn't getting my calls. I was willing to bet that SallyAnn Bertram was also at the hospital. Whenever a cop is hurt badly enough to be taken to the emergency room, the spouse drops everything to go check on his or her loved one. Staying at home, imagining how bad things could be, did not help.

I phoned the Bertrams' home number and waited until I was connected to voice mail. I left a message for SallyAnn, asking that she please get in touch with me. Guiltily, I added that I hoped John was all right.

I climbed up the stairs, then poked around from room to room, ostensibly looking for puppy chow, but also to figure out if the cops had finished their investigation. Ernest had made one bedroom his own. It was a masculine blend of brown and white, with a white rug and chocolate-colored Roman shades. The cops had pulled the mattress and linens off and emptied the drawers. I wondered what they'd found.

Ernest had turned the other bedroom into a study. It was only slightly more tidy. The wooden file cabinet was open, and a single file lay on Ernest's desk between the computer and telephone. A bag filled with papers was on the floor. Had the sheriff's department's guys been interrupted? It certainly looked that way.

That slightly odd smell I'd noticed when I first came in was a bit stronger upstairs. It wasn't like spoiled food, it wasn't like men's cologne or soap, and it wasn't from one of those plug-in air fresheners. It was like . . . clover. Or maybe alfalfa. I was extremely curious, but I was on a mission for puppy chow.

En route to the kitchen, I passed the large room that Ernest had made into a living and dining space. A white leather sectional sofa stood atop Navajo rugs, all new since Faye had moved out. The dining table and chairs were a contemporary mahogany style, and I wondered if Ernest had made them or bought them locally.

When I moved into the kitchen, I wondered how anyone could keep a cooking space so sparkling clean. But Ernest had. He'd put up old-fashioned pine-paneled cabinets that he'd reclaimed from a log cabin that was being torn down. Ernest had been big on recycling materials before it was fashionable. I smiled when I saw a framed poster for a local production of the Oscar Wilde play *The Importance of Being Earnest* in the kitchen, where he'd refinished the cabinets and put down a hickory floor. The effect was dazzling.

I moved from one highly organized cabinet to another: No puppy chow. I sighed in frustration. The last thing we needed was more delays before getting back to our house. Even if Yolanda and Ferdinanda were able to get every last bottle of shampoo and deodorant they needed, I still foresaw a trip to the store on the way home, and I hadn't given a thought to dinner. I tried to think what we had in the refrigerator, in case Arch arrived first. . . .

The phone startled me. I looked around and saw it on the wall. On the third ring, I figured Yolanda was still dealing with Ferdinanda, so I glanced at the caller ID. It read *Captain, Humberto.* Was he calling Yolanda, on Ernest's home number? And should I pick up the phone, or not? Well, what harm could come if I did answer it? I picked up the receiver and pressed Talk.

"This is Goldy Schulz."

Click.

I slammed the phone down and made a mental note to tell Tom about the call. Yet even as I went back to hunting for puppy chow, I felt guilty. I didn't want to believe that Yolanda was working for Humberto.

I checked both bathrooms for puppy chow. Nothing. The winter porch was next, but it was cold and empty except for the bent-twig furniture Ernest had put in there.

"Doggone it," I muttered, and headed off to the greenhouse, the only room left that I hadn't searched.

Because of the black clouds, rain, and fog, darkness seemed to be falling quickly, even if it was technically still summer. I turned on the lights by the greenhouse door before entering. The alfalfa-type smell was stronger in here. But the switches I'd flipped also contained an exhaust fan. I coughed and looked around. Ernest had been growing string beans, peppers, and tomatoes. The reclaimed glass Ernest had used for the walls made the darkness outside seem huge, despite the overhead lights. At the far end of the greenhouse were some big, bushy green plants and—victory!—a bag of puppy chow.

Only, would somebody please tell me what dog food

was doing in the greenhouse, next to big bushes? Wait a minute. As Tom was always saying, "I may have been born at night, but I wasn't born *last* night."

These weren't ordinary bushes . . . they were marijuana plants. Hello!

I counted them: six. I knew that under Colorado law, you could grow six plants legally if you were the provider for a card-carrying medical marijuana user. But . . . Ernest was a recovering addict. Was it really such a good idea for him to be growing a plant with narcotic properties? And why had he left the puppy chow up *there*? So the dog food would absorb some of the marijuana's properties and the puppies would sleep through the night?

And why, oh why, had the cops missed this?

Or had they?

Okay, I'd graduated from the University of Colorado, one of the top party schools in the nation, and I hadn't been born last night, either. I knew enough about weed to know that it was the bud, and not the leaves themselves, that provided a quality high. Harvested leaves only produced what was known to folks in the know as *schwag,* and everyone from stoners to stockbrokers knew that schwag was junk.

Ernest's marijuana plants each boasted large buds, so they were ready for harvest. Without thinking, I walked over to Ernest's shelf of tools, picked up a pruner, and snipped off a large bud.

It was then that my vision caught a movement outside: what looked like a small rock, only not on the ground, because it was moving. For the first time since I'd entered the house, fear scurried down my spine.

I squinted. What with the rain and fog, it was hard to make things out. I watched for a moment, and saw the moving rock was a person, a tall, heavyset person who was carrying something in one of his hands. Was he a cop? I doubted it. The guy was moving in too stealthy a manner. Was he a looter?

I swallowed my fear and tried to think. *Kill the lights,* my inner voice said. *Try to get a better look at him, without his seeing you. And call the cops.* I shoved the marijuana bud deep into my jacket pocket, reached for the switch, and turned off the greenhouse lights. I rooted around in my pocket for my cell while keeping my gaze fixed outside.

The man seemed to be wearing a dark jacket. My dousing of the lights had not bothered him—just the opposite, in fact. My mouth dropped open in disbelief as the intruder used his free hand to pick up a large rock. He reached back and heaved it at the greenhouse.

I ducked as the rock exploded through the glass. *Damn it! Where is my cell phone?* Rummaging for it, desperate to call 911, I saw the intruder bring a small object out of an unseen pocket. He fumbled with the thing, whatever it was. Then a light flared in the near-darkness. The man was bald.

This guy had a lighter? What was he going to do, have a cigarette while he waited for us to come out? Or maybe Ernest was his medical marijuana provider, and he was going to smoke his last joint before getting some new buds?

He was going to do neither. He lit the thing he was holding in his other hand. It flared hugely. It was a cloth, hanging out of a glass bottle. *Oh my God, the man is holding a live Molotov cocktail.* He reached back and flung the flaming bottle toward the hole he'd already smashed through the greenhouse glass.

"Yolanda!" I screamed as I raced out of the greenhouse. I dug my hand into my pocket and finally grasped my cell. "Get out! Get Ferdinanda out! Right now!"

The Molotov cocktail crashed through the hole in the glass. There was a sudden whoosh that actually propelled me headfirst down the stairs to the basement. The cocktail had reached its target. *Damn,* I thought as I rolled and got awkwardly to my feet. *Damn, damn, damn.*

My cell phone had skittered across the floor. I grabbed it and pressed 911. "I need a fire truck up here right away!" I hollered at the operator. "Ernest McLeod's house, I don't know the address. Sorry." Then I hung up and stuffed the phone in my pocket. I knew enough about emergency services to know that the operator could figure it out. I barreled toward the garage as Yolanda raced in from it. We barely avoided colliding.

"Goldy!" Her face was filled with alarm. "What is it? Why were you up here yelling? What's going on—"

"Somebody's trying to burn the house down!" I grabbed her and turned her around by the shoulders. "You need to get Ferdinanda out right now! And, and, and we need to take the puppies out, too!"

"I'll put Ferdinanda into the van," she called over her shoulder, "and open the garage door. Where is this person? Where is the, the fire?"

"In the greenhouse! When you get Ferdinanda into

the van, wait for me to bring the puppies. Then back the van well out into the street and keep the windows closed. Be *sure* you lock the doors!"

"Where will you be while I'm getting Ferdinanda—"

"Just do it!"

Yolanda raced off to her duties. I rushed into the puppy room, where the dogs were barking crazily. Either they already smelled smoke, or they had picked up on our sudden anxiety, or both.

I glanced out the window in the storage room but could not see the bald man. Then I looked wildly around the room. What was I going to put the puppies in? What had Ernest used?

I didn't know, and couldn't find out on short notice. I yanked open the storage closet marked *Yard* and dumped out a cardboard box of spades, gardening gloves, and fertilizer. Fertilizer! What if Ernest had kept fertilizer, which was highly combustible, up in the greenhouse? Rain or no rain, this place would go up like a tinderbox.

Upstairs, there was another *crash, tinkle,* and *whoosh.* The bald arsonist had sent in another Molotov cocktail.

"You son of a bitch!" I screamed. The puppies were crowding around me, whining and yipping. "Okay, dogs, I didn't mean you." I put five beagles in the first box, then hustled it out the garage door. Smoke was already filling the house, and the smoke alarm was beeping so loudly I couldn't think.

I ran into the garage, trying not to jostle the puppies too much. Yolanda was in the driver's seat of the van. Ferdinanda was in back, next to several plastic bags of stuff, which I assumed contained as many of their belongings as they'd been able to pack. I wondered fleetingly where the seventeen thousand bucks was.

"Can you help me?" I asked Yolanda. She immediately unlocked the rear door, slid it open, and took the box of dogs. Ferdinanda gripped the sides of her wheelchair.

"If *only* I had my old rifle," she said fiercely.

I moved bags around, trying to figure out where we were going to put the other box of dogs. The old woman's wrinkled hand tapped my arm.

I said, "Ferdinanda—"

"With my scope, I could see Batista's people—"

"Ferdinanda," I cried cheerfully, "not to worry. Tom has a gun at our house! Now, I need to go back—"

"That *bastard,* Kris," she said, her tone still stubborn.

Yolanda begged, "Please let me help you, Goldy."

"Guard Ferdinanda," I ordered tersely. "Close the van windows and call nine-one-one. I've already phoned them once, but I didn't have the address here."

I sprinted back into the house. Smoke stung my eyes. It did not smell like marijuana, I noted bitterly. *I should have put a wet rag over my nose and mouth,* I thought, too late. It was hard to think with the fire alarm continuing its high shrill.

In the storage room, I pulled open the door marked *Trains* and dumped out another cardboard box, this one filled with tracks for an HO set.

"Sorry for the accommodations," I muttered as I chased the last four puppies, who'd decided that they didn't like me after all. I finally corralled them all into the box. I dashed to the van, placed this second puppy box on the floor of the passenger side, and jumped in.

"Hit the gas!" I yelled to Yolanda. As she backed out of the garage, I stared into the night to see if I could see the bald man. The fire, which was now raging, lit only the long grass, trees, and rocks on Ernest's property. "Hurry!" I called to Yolanda.

Alas. We had barely turned out of Ernest's driveway when the strobe lights of not one but *two* police cars lit the street in front of us.

"What the hell?" I asked. "Where were they, in the neighborhood?"

The police cars blocked the roadway, so Yolanda pulled over. I looked behind us. Ernest's house was completely ablaze.

A barrel-shaped uniformed cop approached us, shining a blinding flashlight at us. When he was some distance away, he called, "What are you doing at this house?"

"Getting my belongings," Yolanda cried.

"It's okay," I said as relief washed through me. "We know this guy. Remember Sergeant Boyd? He's great."

"Getting your belongings?" Boyd shone the light into the van. When he saw me, he said, "Goldy? What the hell are you doing here?" He directed the flashlight at Yolanda. "Yolanda? Is that you?"

"Yes." But her voice wavered, as if she weren't quite sure who she was.

"Please listen," I begged Boyd. "Yolanda and her aunt are Ernest McLeod's friends. They were living here."

Boyd exhaled. "Anybody in the house now?"

"No, thank God. But a bald man threw two Molotov cocktails at Ernest's greenhouse! He may still be around here."

"Armed?"

"I don't know."

"Description?"

I did the best I could, but the enveloping mist and darkness, plus my surprise at the bald man's actions, made it hard to recall details beyond "sort of hefty, maybe tall."

Boyd nodded anyway and spoke into his radio to officers fanning into the field around Ernest's house. Then he put his hand on Yolanda's shoulder. Romantic sparks had flown between these two when Boyd had come out to the spa to help me the previous month. Now he said gently, "Are you okay?"

"No," she said, staring straight ahead.

"Hang in there."

I said, "Do you know if the fire trucks are on their way?"

"Hold on." Boyd again spoke into his radio, and received a reply that the fire engines would arrive in less than ten minutes. Boyd clipped the flashlight onto his belt and rubbed his scalp. His once-black hair was turning to gray at the sides, but he still wore it in an unfashionable crew cut.

"Where *were* you guys?" I asked. "Why weren't investigators inside the house? I called and called, but nobody answered."

Boyd ignored my question and looked back at Ferdinanda. "Yolanda, would you introduce me to your aunt?"

I smiled. Apparently, courting rituals took precedence over the deliberate setting of a house on fire and the destruction of evidence. But when Yolanda patiently went through introductions, she seemed to calm down.

Finally, Boyd said, "The team in the house got a call that shots had been fired five miles away. It's the next neighborhood over, and they were the closest cops. They couldn't find anything, but then they got another call. More shots fired. So they called us, and a couple more of us raced up here. We kept looking in that neighborhood and in this one, but we didn't find anything."

The puppies whimpered at me, and I patted them.

"Did you take anything else?"

"No," I said guiltily, keeping my eyes on the puppies. It felt, of course, as if that big bud of marijuana was burning a hole in my jacket pocket. But I didn't want to tell Boyd about it in front of Yolanda and Ferdinanda. I needed to tell Tom about it first, I decided.

Boyd rubbed his forehead. "Do you know where Tom is now?"

I said, "He's supposed to be at Southwest Hospital."

"Why there?"

"He's, uh, with John Bertram," I said, trying to avoid giving the reason.

"What happened?" asked Boyd, his voice on edge.

"I hit him with my baton!" called Ferdinanda from the back. I heard the unmistakable sound of Ferdinanda snapping her weapon open. She thrust it through the window at Boyd, who jumped back. "You be nice to Yolanda, or I'll hit you, too!"

I put my head in my hands. It was going to be a long night.

Chapter 5

We missed the fire engines arriving, although we could hear their approach behind the screeching of Ernest's alarms. As smoke and ash billowed from Ernest's house, Boyd stepped away from Yolanda's van long enough to call the sheriff's department.

A few of the dogs were still whining. The rest had slumped against each other and fallen asleep. One of the ones who were awake climbed the cardboard directly in front of me. This puppy was crying and looking so pathetically unhappy that I brought him up in my lap. He, or maybe it was a she—I wasn't going to check in the poor light—liked having his back rubbed, I discovered. Within a couple of minutes, he'd stretched lengthwise on my thighs, his nose over my knees, his little legs splayed out so that his paws just touched my stomach. Like his pals, he succumbed to slumber.

Boyd pocketed his cell and came back to the van. "Goldy, we're going to your house," he announced. His expression was unreadable.

I sighed. I didn't know whether going back to our place was a good thing or a bad thing, but I couldn't bear to watch Ernest's hand-built house being consumed by fire. To make matters worse, the smoke was making Ferdinanda cough.

I asked Yolanda to head back toward our place, and she pulled to the left, off the shoulder. *Ferdinanda smokes cigars,* I reminded myself as she coughed relentlessly. The old van's engine ground in protest as Yolanda hung a U. Ferdinanda was gagging; I thought she was going to be ill. It was the cigars, I told myself. Still, I was too tired to talk about the perils of smoking. Like the puppy in my lap, I was too exhausted to think.

As Yolanda piloted the van down the street away from Ernest's house, Ferdinanda stopped coughing. Oddly, hunger made my stomach cramp. Ferdinanda and Yolanda had missed dinner, too, but too much had been going on to think about eating. My mind jumped to my usual worry: Where was Arch? He had his own car, a used VW, but I vaguely remembered that he wasn't driving it at the moment. No matter what, he had not checked in, and that was anxiety-producing.

I so wanted to talk to Tom. I debated dislodging the beagle and reaching for my cell but reasoned that we'd be home momentarily and I could find out exactly where he was.

We hadn't gone a hundred yards in the direction of town when Boyd flashed us with his strobe lights. Yolanda shook her head and pulled over to the dirt shoulder on our right.

When Yolanda rolled down her window, thick smoke billowed in.

"Okay," said Boyd, who was barely visible, "the fire trucks are asking us not to go down this way. They need access to the hydrants, and they're blocking off all traffic into the neighborhood. We need to take the service road."

"*What* service road?" Yolanda asked.

"Follow me."

So we did. Boyd expertly pulled in front of Yolanda's van and gunned his vehicle downhill. Just before the crime-scene tape, he signaled to turn left onto the shoulder where we'd initially stopped, when we were trying to see if there was a police car up at Ernest's. The gravel area passed through two spruce trees and materialized into a road, if you used the term loosely. The narrow lane was pitted and deeply grooved, but Boyd expertly swung his prowler from one side to the other. I prayed there were no cliffs nearby.

While I clung to the puppy in my lap, Yolanda worked hard to follow Boyd. Despite my efforts, the puppy awakened anyway and started shivering. I used my feet to stabilize the cardboard box on the floor, from which much canine whimpering issued. Ferdinanda's wheelchair was locked in place, and she assured us she was leaning over and was holding on to the box of dogs on the backseat.

My eyes stung from the smoke. Still, I could see Yolanda's headlights pick out a tiny U.S. Forest Service sign in front of a boulder on our right. The Forest Service had built many such roads into the mountains, for fighting flames in remote regions. The summer before the one we were technically still in had seen numerous wildfires, which had been followed by flooding. The word in town was that it would take another year or more to get some of these roads rebuilt. From a forest-fire perspective, the fact that June, July, and August had seen record amounts of rain had been a blessing.

Boyd veered right, left, then right again. There were no streetlights, of course, but Boyd knew the way, and Yolanda managed to keep up. Thanks to the rain, the police vehicle wasn't kicking up much dust, but it occasionally spit a shower of dirt onto the old van's windshield. Yolanda cursed but kept going. After a few minutes, we made a hairpin left turn, then headed steeply downward. Boyd made a sharp right turn onto a paved road, right near a gas station that was barely visible in the gauzy light.

I peered outside. We'd landed on Lower Cottonwood Creek Road, below town. I looked up; a sudden breeze had sent the smoke back up the hill behind Ernest's place, and I could just make out an exterior light on a building that had to be John Bertram's large garage. I wondered how John was. Okay, I hoped.

We passed Saint Luke's, and within a moment we were back on Main Street. The wind had stopped, and downtown was dark, foggy, and quiet. The only exception was the Grizzly Saloon, where light spilled from the double doors. A batch of cowboys and bikers were hanging out under the porch roof. Heads turned as the prowler passed.

Despite the cold and fog, Tom was waiting on the porch. Carefully, I moved the puppy from my lap and put him back in the box, so he could snuggle with his compatriots.

"Miss G.," said Tom as he helped me out of the van. He looked down. "Did you get all the dogs out?"

"Yes."

"Miss Goldy?" Tom asked, putting one of his big hands on my forearm. I was shivering. "Did you see who set the fire?"

"Yes. A bald guy. I described him to Boyd."

"Let's all get inside," Tom said, "and we can talk."

Despite Ferdinanda's protests, Tom worked to bring her onto the lowering mechanism of the van, then rolled her up our driveway. Thank God, it stopped raining. Nevertheless, it seemed as if the temperature was still dropping.

Boyd offered to bring the battered suitcases and bags of stuff that Yolanda had managed to pack up before all hell broke loose. I hauled out the box of puppies from the passenger-side floor while Yolanda pulled on her big shoulder bag and, before I could protest, lugged the other box of puppies from the back. What a troop we made: two caterers, two cops, nine puppies, and a great-aunt in a wheelchair.

Boyd put down his load and raced forward to aid Tom in lifting Ferdinanda and her wheelchair to the front door. I realized that we would need a ramp if they ended up staying more than a single night. At this point, I didn't care that there was one more thing still to be done. I was grateful we'd all gotten out alive.

"Hey, Tom!" Ferdinanda called. "You got any hand weights? Five pounds, ten?"

"Not here," Tom said patiently as he wheeled Ferdinanda into the house. "But Goldy's pantry shelves are undoubtedly groaning with cans that would work for you. Why? Are you going to start working out?"

"Start?" exclaimed Ferdinanda. "*Start?* What are you talking about? I already lift. Gotta stay in shape. Gotta be ready."

I didn't say *Ready for what?* because I knew what she was worried about: our own house burning down.

"Couple times now, I haven't been ready," Ferdinanda muttered, once she was situated in the living room. Yolanda, walking by with her box of puppies, gave her aunt a warning look. Ferdinanda clamped her mouth shut.

As Yolanda and I carried the boxes of puppies through the house, Scout the cat streaked by, heading fast in the opposite direction. Our bloodhound had been asleep in the pet containment area, but the sudden arrival of nine fellow canines brought him fully to life. Yolanda and I put all the dogs into the backyard, where they gamboled to and fro merrily. They were undoubtedly covering themselves with mud, but if it made them happy, then I didn't care.

Tom greeted us in the kitchen. "Yolanda," he said noncommittally, "could you go out into the living room and answer Sergeant Boyd's questions?"

Yolanda shot me a questioning glance but then complied. I inhaled deeply. The luscious scent of roasting ham made my head spin. Bless Tom's heart; he'd made dinner.

As soon as Yolanda closed the kitchen door, Tom enclosed me in a hug. "I was so worried about you, Miss G." He put his face close to my ear. "You scared me half to death, I swear."

"I didn't *do* anything."

"Yeah, you always say that." He inhaled. "You smell like smoke. Why don't you go upstairs, have a shower, then come back down? Boyd won't harass your friends."

"Actually, he's been great." I pulled him close to me. "Where's Arch?"

"He called and said he was staying with Todd. You remember he doesn't have his car? You wanted to get snow tires for it?"

I rubbed my forehead. Of course. But snow tires were about the last thing on my current agenda.

Tom went on. "The Druckmans will bring him down for the physical tomorrow. You ready to eat? I roasted that ham, and made a macaroni and cheese from scratch. I found some applesauce, too. We're talking comfort food here. I also chopped fresh basil to put in your Caprese salad. Sound good?"

"It sounds *phenomenal*." Then I felt guilty. "We can celebrate Ernest's life when we eat." I was still clinging to him. "Uh, Tom? I do have something to tell you."

"More?" Tom held on to me. "Is this a good something or a bad something? I mean, since Ernest's house is being incinerated even as we speak. We were *not* able to retrieve any of his files, by the way. Two bogus calls of shots fired yanked our guys away before they could go through Ernest's study."

"I heard." I cleared my throat. "Ernest McLeod was growing marijuana in his greenhouse. Six plants. And that's the exact place where our arsonist tossed his Molotov cocktail."

Tom shifted away from me. *"What?"* His handsome face went from concerned to incredulous. "Pot? Ernest was growing weed? Our guys didn't get as far as the greenhouse, but . . . and I thought Ernest had given up—" I shook my head and pulled the somewhat smashed bud from my jacket pocket.

"Here you go," I said. "I managed to snag this before the arsonist threw in the first Molotov cocktail."

"You just managed to snag it, huh?" Tom retrieved a new brown paper bag from a drawer. "Drop it in," he told me. Once I complied, he gave me a quizzical stare. "Does either Yolanda or Ferdinanda know about this?"

"I'm not sure. Honestly, Tom, before that guy showed up and started throwing things, all we talked about was the puppies. When I was looking for their chow, I found the bag next to the plants in Ernest's greenhouse."

Tom carefully folded the top of the bag down, then put it on the counter. "Know what?" He pulled his notebook out of his pocket. "I'm going to come up and question you while you shower."

The bathroom mirror confirmed that I looked as bad as I felt. My face was gray, wet, and smeared with dirt. Ash had settled into the wrinkles under my eyes, and my hair looked as if a large family had dumped the contents of their grill on top of my head. My clothes, which had become soaked in the rain, had absorbed so much dust they were unrecognizable as the jacket, shirt, and jeans I'd put on that morning.

Tom said he would turn the shower water on. I hunted for clean underwear, pants, and a turtleneck, then returned to the bathroom and peeled off every item of clothing I'd been wearing.

"I like what I'm seeing," said Tom, who'd pulled a small chair in next to the hamper.

"I look like crap."

"Far from it, Miss G."

I stepped into the steaming shower and shivered in the luxurious stream of heat. Tom scooted the chair over to the tub.

"Begin with when you got there," he said.

"I tried to call you. Oops, no washcloth." I blinked in the stream of water as Tom's large hand pushed the shower curtain aside and offered me a clean cloth and new bar of soap. "Thanks." I scrubbed up quickly. "The investigators weren't there, and I wasn't sure whether we had permission to be in the house when they weren't there."

"I remember telling you that. I also got your messages after I left the hospital. Sorry about that."

"So we went up, finally." I told him about Ferdinanda and Yolanda gathering up their belongings while I concentrated on the puppies. But their chow was missing, I added, so I went around the house looking for it. Clearly, the investigators had been there, because some files were opened in Ernest's study. I looked all over for the chow and finally found a new bag next to the marijuana plants in the greenhouse.

"That seems odd," Tom observed. "Ernest was a careful, conscientious investigator. Why would he leave puppy chow next to marijuana? Do you think he forgot it there? That's just not like him."

"I don't know." I drenched my hair, shampooed it, and rinsed. "You're right about the conscientious bit, though. Except for the places where your team had been, the house was neater than a magazine spread on compulsive organization."

"You 'bout ready?"

"Just need a couple of towels."

His hand appeared again with two plush cotton towels. I wrapped them around my head and torso and stepped out. "Thanks. Are you going to keep asking me questions while I get dressed?"

"I'd rather be doing something else," he said warmly, "but unfortunately there's this damn job I'm obligated to. So you found the chow and the weed, and pulled off a bud."

"Right." I dried quickly and pulled my clothes on. "Oh, sorry, forgot to tell you. The phone rang while I was looking for the dog food. It came up on the caller ID as Humberto Captain. I answered, but whoever it was hung up." Tom wrote, and I continued. "Anyway, when I was in the greenhouse, I saw a flash of movement from outside. It was a man holding something. I killed the lights in the greenhouse to get a better look. First he threw a rock through one of the windows. Then he lit the rag, or whatever it was, going into a bottle of accelerant. I saw him more clearly then."

"Describe this man."

Again, I did my best with that while rubbing my hair dry. No, I didn't get a good enough look at his face to go through a police photo array. What could I say about him? He was tallish, bald, and white. I stopped talking for a moment, then asked, "If the arsonist was the source of your false reports, and he was destroying evidence, say, why would he wait half an hour before torching the place?"

Tom looked at the floor. "Maybe he was watching Ernest's house. Waiting for you all to come back. I don't like that one bit."

"Neither do I. But at least Yolanda, Ferdinanda, and I, plus all the puppies, got out of the house before it went up in flames." As I told Tom this, a rocklike tightness formed in my chest. "I don't know what we're going to do with the dogs. I have no idea why Ernest would have been growing pot. And what about that crazy bald guy? Tell me. Do you think he was trying to destroy evidence? Or was he trying to kill us?"

"Come here." Tom stowed his notebook, stood up, and gently tugged me toward him. "I don't know the answers to your questions. But clearly, Ernest pulled somebody's chain. It's already making Yolanda crazy, as you've seen. I need you to keep a steady head, all right?"

"Yeah. Sure."

"Let's go see how Boyd's doing."

When I walked into the living room, Boyd stood up, which I appreciated. Tom and I sat down. I did feel sorry for Yolanda and Ferdinanda, who looked as ragged and ash covered as I had fifteen minutes before.

"Tell him, Goldy," Yolanda said. "Tell him you came down the stairs when you knew someone was trying to burn down the house. Didn't you—"

"I'm sorry," said Boyd, stirring uncomfortably in his wingback chair. "I have to ask you these questions."

Tom held up an index finger, meant for me. *Don't get involved in this.*

Boyd began again. "So where were you exactly when you heard glass breaking? Downstairs, you said? Where downstairs?"

"I don't know," said Yolanda. "I don't remember. I just heard Goldy screaming about a fire. Then she fell down the stairs, I think because she was in a hurry, or maybe the big explosion made her lose her balance—"

"Did you smell anything unusual?" Boyd asked.

"Like what?" demanded Ferdinanda, turning to Boyd. She tapped one of the metal arms of her wheelchair. "Burning *pasteles*?"

Yolanda gave her aunt another warning glare. "If you mean like gasoline, no, I didn't."

"And where were you when Goldy screamed at you?" asked Boyd.

"*Dios mío*," said Ferdinanda, slapping her forehead. "I'm *hongry*."

"Look," pleaded Boyd, "I'm doing the best I can here."

Ferdinanda shook a bent forefinger at Boyd. She leaned forward and waggled her head at him. Her steely, determined face made him draw back. "We answered your questions, the same ones you've been asking since we got inside. I'm tired and I'm going to eat this wheelchair if you don't leave us alone. The place where we were staying burned down. That's all."

"Boyd," interjected Tom. "Want to stay for dinner?"

"I would love to," he said. "But I promised SallyAnn I'd go see Bertram." Tom's invitation, though, signaled that Boyd didn't have to ask Yolanda and Ferdinanda any more questions.

"Goldy." Boyd handed me a pad of paper he'd produced from an inner jacket pocket. "Humor me here. Could you write down everything you saw, and exactly what happened, and when, while you were at Ernest McLeod's house?"

"Tom's already asked me questions," I said.

"Sorry," said Boyd. "I need it for the record."

"Okay, but I want to get Yolanda and Ferdinanda settled first. Just five minutes?"

"No," Tom interrupted, and I flinched. Tom said, "Yolanda? Ferdinanda? Did you know Ernest was growing marijuana in his greenhouse?"

"What?" Yolanda sat up straight, a stunned look on her face. "Are you kidding me?"

"No," said Tom. "I'm not."

"I never went up to his greenhouse," said Ferdinanda. "This wheelchair can't climb steps."

"So neither of you had *any idea* Ernest was growing marijuana?" When they shook their heads, Tom said, "Did you ever smell marijuana smoke?"

Yolanda shook her head in puzzlement. Ferdinanda said, "Yeah. I smelled it a couple of times."

Tom narrowed his eyes. "Did you ask Ernest about it?"

"No," Ferdinanda said emphatically. "It was none of our business. And before you ask, no, I didn't tell Yolanda, either."

"Ferdinanda!" exclaimed Yolanda. "I tell you everything."

When the old woman shrugged, it looked as if her whole body was rising out of the wheelchair. "I am older than you. I don't have to tell anybody anything. Now, I'm not going to say any more until Goldy shows us where the bathroom is, so we can clean up."

There was a brief silence in the living room until Tom said, "Fine. Thanks for giving us your statements. If you think of anything else, please let us know. Actually," he said, "why don't I show you the way to the first-floor bathroom while Goldy writes out her statement? Sergeant Boyd needs to wait for it before he goes down to the hospital to see John Bertram." He said this last part without inflection, but Ferdinanda did drop some of her steely façade at this. She knew she was responsible for poor John's injury.

I started writing out a statement while Tom showed Ferdinanda and Yolanda the dining room, where they would be sleeping, and the little bathroom off the kitchen. Once they were bustling around in there, Tom poked his head back in the living room and said he was going to make some calls, to see if he could palm some of the puppies off on people we knew.

Without warning, Yolanda appeared beside him. "Palm them off forever?" she whispered.

"Yolanda," said Tom gently, "you find a new place to live, you can take a couple back. How's that?"

Yolanda, whose lovely face was creased with fatigue and fragments of cinders, nodded but did not move. I finished writing on Boyd's pad—this time, I added the whole bit about finding the marijuana plants—and then handed it back to him. Boyd scanned it and said if he had any more questions, he would call me.

"Thank you," I said weakly.

"You need me to go out and buy anything for you?" Boyd's dark eyes moved from Yolanda to me.

"Puppy chow," I said meekly. "That's what we need."

"No problem. One of the grocery stores is open late."

I said, "Thanks."

Boyd muttered something about it being no problem again, rubbed his scalp once more, and said he would be back in twenty minutes.

Yolanda and Ferdinanda were still in the bathroom. I wondered if they had been able to pack any clean clothes into the stuff they'd brought or if they needed me to launder things for them. Well, I supposed they would tell me. Ferdinanda was not someone who kept her needs and opinions to herself.

"Success!" said Tom when I came out to the kitchen. "I called Father Pete first, because he'd be upset if we didn't. He's coming over tomorrow afternoon and taking three dogs. Marla's taking three, and she's going to call her cleaning lady, Penny Woolworth, who will probably be over tomorrow morning, early, before she starts work. According to Marla, Penny's been saying she wants a dog, since Penny's husband, Zeke, is now in prison for stealing cars. Knowing Marla, she probably has more information on Zeke and Penny than I ever did. Oh, and Marla's coming for dinner, too. I thought the least I could do was invite her to stay. I told her our meal could be a memorial to Ernest, whom she knew, apparently."

I said, "Goodness. I'll set us up, then hunt for a bottle of wine to go with the ham."

"No need for the latter. Marla's bringing us, and I quote, 'a couple of bottles of the good stuff.' She said, and I quote, 'If Ernie had still been drinking, that's what he would have wanted me to do.'"

"'Ernie'? 'The good stuff'?"

Tom shrugged. Since Marla's idea of good wine began at a hundred bucks a bottle, I just shook my head and started setting the table. Boyd returned almost soundlessly, a bag of puppy chow in hand. He and Tom worked on settling the little dogs in our pet containment area with food and water. With Yolanda and Ferdinanda still in their bathroom getting cleaned up and changed, Tom and Boyd trundled off to set up cots in the dining room and make them up with clean sheets. They made a path through the furniture to the bathroom, wide enough for the wheelchair. Tom hung a clothesline across the opening between the living room and the dining room and slung a sheet over it, for privacy. Yolanda and Ferdinanda were set, for now at least.

I showed Boyd out, thanking him profusely as we walked down the hall. He merely nodded.

Fifteen minutes later, the doorbell rang and Marla swept in. She was clothed in full autumn regalia: orange and brown leopard-print St. John's jacket, russet pants, pumpkin-colored silk scarf, and tobacco-hued Italian leather loafers. She'd had her hair colored so that it appeared bronzed. It was pulled back from her face with clusters of citrine-crusted barrettes that matched dangling citrine earrings. Her face was merry, and she held up a canvas bag that clinked with wine bottles. The effect was dazzling.

"I'm so sorry to hear about Ernie," she said.

"We all are."

"He was killed?"

"Yes," I said quietly.

She leaned forward. "Can you talk about it?" she whispered.

"Not yet. Sorry. Tom may be able to tell you more." When I hugged her, there was the sound of glass clinking. "Careful of the wine, Goldy," she said. "I brought a bottle of Dom, plus two of Bordeaux. You shake the Dom, and it'll explode all over the place." I let go of her and offered to take her jacket. "Not yet," she said, "I need to stay warm. The temperature's dropping fast. Plus, you wouldn't believe the mess I had to come through on the way over here. I about froze to death in the Mercedes while waiting for a fireman to wave me through. They've got half the roads going into Aspen Hills blocked off with water trucks, apparently. It looks as if some asshole started another forest fire, which you wouldn't think would burn when it's raining, but—" She stopped talking when she saw my face. "Oops. Are *you* the asshole who started the forest fire?"

Before I could answer, Yolanda emerged from the kitchen. "Marla!" she cried. "I am so glad to see you, you have no idea."

Marla gave me a questioning glance. I said, "Yolanda and her great-aunt, Ferdinanda, are staying with us for a few days. They were staying with Ernest McLeod, and it was his house that burned down . . . while we were inside. We got out, thank God."

Marla shook her head and quirked her eyebrows at Yolanda. "You were living with Ernie? The last time I talked to you, out at the spa, you were living with Kris Nielsen."

Yolanda's face darkened. "We'll bring you up to date over dinner. Come meet my aunt Ferdinanda."

"You call her your aunt, and not your great-aunt?" asked Marla. No detail was too small to be caught by Marla's antennae.

"I call her my aunt," said Yolanda. "It makes things easier."

We moved into the kitchen. Tom relieved Marla of her sack of bottles, then shook his head when he took the first one out. Tom knew his wine values, and Marla's generosity, even if it did come from inherited money, always amazed him. I put out five crystal glasses while he put a towel over the stopper in the Dom and began the gentle job of twisting it out. Before he could finish, his cell beeped urgently.

Tom put down the bottle and towel and went into the living room to take the call. I twisted the stopper in the Dom until it popped out in my hand, followed by a small gush of bubbly. So someone had done some expensive shaking. I carefully placed the bottle in a champagne bucket, then stuck crushed ice around the edges.

Yolanda and I scooped the food into serving dishes while Marla gave Ferdinanda her usual third degree: When had she come to this country, why were she and Yolanda together, how did she end up in a wheelchair? As usual, it went over the borderline between showing interest and being nosy, but Ferdinanda was happy to be the center of attention.

Tom returned. His eyes were hooded, and he gave no indication of what the call was about. He poured the champagne and handed each of us a glass.

"To Ernest," he said. We lifted our stems and drank.

Chapter 6

After we'd prayed, Tom busied himself slicing the ham. I passed around the applesauce, the Caprese salad, and—yum—the homemade macaroni and cheese. A crust of cheddar had browned over the creamy lake of pasta, and I took a bite that was both crunchy and soft. When my eyes widened in amazement, Tom smiled. The ham, which Tom had glazed with brown sugar and Dijon mustard, was meltingly tender, and the chunky cinnamon applesauce set it off perfectly. The meal was a wonderful way to remember Ernest.

Marla stopped eating momentarily, took a sip of wine, and turned her attention to Yolanda. "So, when did you and Kris break up?"

"That *pendejo*," interjected Ferdinanda. "Don't mention Kris to me. Don't mention him at this table."

Taken aback, Marla cleared her throat and touched one of her jeweled barrettes.

I said, "Ernest invited Yolanda and Ferdinanda to stay at his place." I omitted the part about the rental burning down, knowing that would bring another torrent of questions. "Yolanda was fixing his dinners—"

When Marla waved her fingers to interrupt me, all her gems glittered in the kitchen light. "After the Jerk and I got divorced? And Ernie and Faye did the same thing? Ernie and I used to drink together at the Grizzly. Then he got sober and I had a heart attack, and that was the end of that." She reflected a moment. "I hadn't seen him in a while . . . and now you say—" She stopped talking, shocked into silence.

Tom mildly asked Marla, whom everyone in Aspen Meadow would agree was the most reliable source of town gossip, if she had any idea whether Ernest had any enemies.

Marla twisted her mouth to one side. "Well, let's see." Then her eyes twinkled. "I heard from a source at the church that he was investigating Brie Quarles."

"The junior warden?" I asked, incredulous. Brie Quarles, a short, slender lawyer, had a head of wavy blond hair, light blue eyes, and porcelain skin. She was thirty but looked twenty, *and* she had separated from her husband . . . but then I'd heard they were getting back together. They did not have children. So, Brie was being investigated? "Why would Ernest be interested in her?" I asked.

"Don't know," Marla said matter-of-factly. "And no, I don't know who the client is. Maybe Father Pete. I'm sure he doesn't want his vestry doing things that could get the church bad press."

Ferdinanda had blanched. At the possibility of wrongdoing in the church? Sad to say, Episcopalians didn't have the market cornered on *that* one. Tom, meanwhile, had furtively taken out his notebook and written down a few words that I was sure included *Brie Quarles*.

"So anyway," I said, groping for any topic beyond the ecclesiastical, "Yolanda and Ferdinanda will be staying with us for a little while. Tom? Will you and Boyd put in a ramp for Ferdinanda?" I asked brightly, nestling a second juicy piece of ham beside a heap of applesauce.

"Tomorrow morning," Tom replied, not at all fooled by my digression. "That was Boyd on the phone. He'll be here at seven."

"But," said Marla, also one not to be put off by conversational diversion, "you don't think Brie had anything to do with—"

"We don't know yet," Tom said. "We're open to all theories. Who was your source on that piece of information?"

It was rare to see Marla blush, but this was one of those times. To hide it, she again turned to Yolanda. "Do *you* know if Ernest had any enemies?"

"We've already questioned Yolanda," Tom said firmly. "Who's your source of information?"

Marla closed her eyes and sighed. "My cleaning lady, Penny Woolworth. If you talk to her, she'll never tell me anything again."

Tom made another mark in his notebook. He said quietly, "We won't mention you."

Marla scowled at him, then smiled at Yolanda. "So, when did you move out of Kris's?"

"A few weeks ago," said Yolanda before Ferdinanda could offer another opinion of Kris Nielsen.

"That *bitch*," said Marla.

"What bitch?" I said. "Who are you talking about?"

"Penny Woolworth, my cleaning lady! I share her with Kris Nielsen and a couple of other people," Marla said. "*She's* the bitch. I pay her extra to keep me up-to-date on the romantic affairs of all her clients."

"A cleaning lady sharing dirt," I observed drily.

"I remember Penny," Yolanda said weakly, looking into her wineglass. "She used to clean Kris's house once a week. She was nice. It was too bad about her husband going to prison."

Marla went on. "Yes, well, our little mountain town doesn't keep secrets all that well. This not-keeping-secrets is something Kris should have known, or at least have figured out. Penny Woolworth, as you know, is a young woman who's fallen on hard times, since some-body"—here she looked at Tom—"got her husband sent to prison for car theft."

"Zeke Woolworth," Tom said matter-of-factly, "stole not just one or two ultra-expensive cars, but more than thirty, which he eventually sold to chop shops. Unfortunately, before he sold the cars, Zeke would speed all over the place. Sometimes he even crashed into something, usually a pylon, or a street sign, or sometimes a lane divider. He got caught not just once, but eight times. He served short stints, but when he stole a Ferrari and sped up the interstate to Aspen Meadow at more than a hundred miles an hour, he was, yes, finally sent away for two years. He's getting out soon, but in the interim we've all been a lot safer."

"Maybe so," said Marla. "But with no income, Pen-ny's had to work for me and four other people."

"Marla," I interjected, "it's really not right for you to pump Penny for information on her clients—"

Marla waved this away. "How do you think I found out Ernest was investigating Brie? She cleans Brie's next-door neighbor's house, and Brie told the neighbor she thought someone was following her. The guy was driving a red pickup truck. I got the neighbor to ask Brie the license plate of the truck, which Brie told her, and Penny got it from the neighbor, who told me. *I* recognized the license plate as the one Ernie had on his old pickup. You see, Goldy," she said triumphantly, "you're not the only one in town who can figure things out."

Tom shook his head. "Did you tell Brie or her neighbor it was Ernest who was doing the following?"

Marla frowned at Tom. "What do you think I am, nuts? No, I wanted to call Ernie first, but then I forgot."

Tom wrote in his notebook. Marla turned her scowl to the notebook, then raised her eyebrows at me.

She went on. "Anyway, Penny did tell me that Kris Nielsen's huge house in Flicker Ridge cost over a mil. But he can afford it," Marla said. She took a sip of wine. "Penny says that she had to work there late one night, because it had snowed in the morning, and she couldn't get through until the late afternoon. By the time she left, Kris had had more than a few drinks. While Penny was waiting to be paid, she asked him if he knew about expanding a business, because she had more clients than she could handle, and she wanted to hire some more people. She figured he would know the answer, because supposedly he was a successful businessman. He said he wasn't a businessman, and did she want a drink. She said yes, drank with him, and he ended up telling her that he'd inherited all his money from his dead mother."

"*What?*" exclaimed Yolanda. "He told me he'd started a company in Silicon Valley and sold it, and that was how he made his money."

"What was the name of the company?" Tom asked mildly.

"I don't know," said Yolanda, dumbfounded. "I didn't ask."

"Hmm," said Tom, in a way that showed he would look it up.

"Well," said Marla, "I guess sharing the 'I inherited all my money' tidbit with his cleaning lady made her recoil in horror. She said, 'You don't have to work?' And he shut up about it. The next time she cleaned, she pressed him again on the business thing. He said he'd turned over all his hiring to the human resources people at his company."

I said, "For crying out loud."

Marla beamed. "Penny thinks that Kris should be serving time for being lazy. Penny says it's not fair that poor dear can't-keep-from-boosting-cars Zeke is in prison."

"I agree that Kris should be serving time," said Ferdinanda. She squinted at Marla. "Does this woman have any real dirt on Kris?"

Marla regarded Yolanda somberly. "Did you know he was, ah, being unfaithful to you?"

Yolanda's voice was weak. "Yes, I did know that. I mean, I figured it out." She knew that if she mentioned the venereal disease to Marla, it would be in next week's *Mountain Journal*.

"And you know how he did it?" asked Ferdinanda emphatically. "While Yolanda was working at the spa, Kris hired a nurse to take me out for a drive. Every day I had to go out with that woman so he could have some 'free time.' Free time to do what? I always asked that nurse. He's not going to a *job*. But she never told me."

"Do you remember the name of the nurse?" asked Tom, as mildly as before.

"Just her first name," Ferdinanda replied. "Patty. I called her Pattypan, because she squashed any chance I had to take a nap."

"Ferdinanda?" I said. "You didn't protest? You just made a joke out of it?"

Ferdinanda pulled herself up tall. "I tried to protest, but I didn't have a weapon. That's why I had Yolanda buy me the baton, when we moved out of Kris's."

Nobody spoke for a moment. Marla finally said, "Penny doesn't know anything about this nurse, at least not that she told me. *She* claims Kris drives her nuts because he's in the house a lot, not out working, and because he loves to go shopping for stuff he doesn't need, stuff that she then has to dust. But she neglected to tell me that you had moved out, Yolanda, which I am sorry about—"

"Don't feel sorry for me," Yolanda said, her tone bitter. "I'm fine." As if to prove it, she took another swig of wine. "Can we change the subject?"

"I'm still mad at Penny," Marla said stubbornly. "She should have told me that Yolanda had moved out, and then I wouldn't have had to ask about it. Oh well," she said. She looked around the kitchen. "Tom? Could you open that second bottle of wine? We should be talking about Ernest, not about problems with cleaning ladies."

Tom opened the wine and filled the glasses again. When he sat down, he said, "Unlike many cops, Ernest was a neat freak. His desk was always the cleanest one I've ever seen in the sheriff's department."

And so we talked about Ernest. Ferdinanda said he was without prejudice and welcomed them into his home. Marla became weepy, and Tom diplomatically moved the open wine bottle off to a cupboard. Yolanda said Ernest cared about his clients. "He cared about everybody," she added. "Even us," she whispered.

It seemed as if the conversation was going to veer into something maudlin requiring more boxes of tissues than I knew I had on hand.

Marla and Ferdinanda began to talk about other topics, thank God. The two women seemed to have a natural affinity and found that they agreed on a variety of issues, from immigration reform (they were for it) to using margarine (they were against it). Neither Kris Nielsen's nor Ernest McLeod's name came up again.

Concentrating on food kept us from talking about all that had happened. Yolanda gradually seemed to relax. Tom winked at me several times as we ate and talked, and I found the stress melting out of my own body as well.

Speaking of men who love to shop, Tom had gone browsing in some specialty food stores the previous day, before all hell had broken loose with the murder of Ernest McLeod. He'd picked up a box of my favorite toffee, which was made with butter, cream, chocolate, and almonds. He chopped it, placed it on a plate, and passed it around. Marla restrained herself and had only one piece—there was that heart attack, after all—but Ferdinanda and Yolanda each had three pieces, plus coffee into which, as usual, they measured so many teaspoons of sugar, I couldn't watch.

"If you want me to get those dogs bedded down at my place for the night," Marla said at last, "I need to get cracking. Penny comes tomorrow afternoon, and I'll find out why she held out on me regarding—" But when Marla saw Yolanda's stricken face, she broke off. People may love to gossip, but when they discover how much being the subject of gossip hurts others, they often don't love it so much anymore. "Sorry," Marla mumbled.

"I'm doing the dishes," Yolanda announced as she got up.

Tom protested. "You're a guest. Besides, I'm the only one who knows where everything goes."

"You cooked," said Yolanda. "As soon as I get Ferdinanda settled in the tub, I'm cleaning up. Please just give Marla her three puppies." Her voice cracked when she said, "Cleaning will help me." Tom backed off.

Reluctantly, Tom and I gathered up a promising-looking trio of the little beagles. Outside, the weather had become even colder. When we picked up the puppies, they were covered with mud.

I felt horribly guilty. "We should have brought them in earlier."

"They'll be all right," said Tom. "They've been out here having fun. Let's just commandeer the kitchen sink and rinse them off in warm water. Can you get some thick bath towels that you don't mind having stained?"

"You bet," I said as I carried one of the squirming

puppies into the house. While Yolanda pushed all the plates to one side of the counter, I put the first puppy into one half of the double kitchen sink, then turned the warm water on in the other sink.

"Good Lord," said Marla, peering down at the grimy animal. "Please tell me you're going to get those animals clean before they plop down in my Mercedes that I just had detailed."

"Of course," I called as I nabbed baby shampoo from the pantry and handed it to Tom. Then I headed to the linen closet.

When I returned, Tom was using a warm spray of water to rinse the shampoo off the puppies. He handed me the first beagle, and I rubbed it down with the old, plush towel.

"Very odd," said Tom as he handed me the second puppy.

"What is?" Marla and I asked in unison.

"Every single one of these puppies is a female," said Tom.

"So?" I asked as I dried off the third puppy. Marla was already hugging her first charge to her shoulder.

"Well, it looks as if they've been spayed already," said Tom as he towel-dried his puppy. "I want to take a picture of this little pup and have my guys canvass the town's veterinarians. I want to know who did these surgeries and why. It might explain why Ernest took them."

Once Tom had taken photos, we got the puppies into a box and the box onto the floor of Marla's expensive German car. By that time, she appeared to be having second thoughts. But she soldiered on. Like Yolanda, she wanted to do whatever it took to honor the memory of Ernest McLeod.

After shampooing the rest of the puppies, plus Jake, we bedded down all the dogs on clean newspaper in the pet-containment area. Tom showered and we finally fell into bed an hour later. I was so exhausted that I couldn't even contemplate the prospect of catering the next day. But I dutifully set the alarm and snuggled in next to Tom.

"Thanks for a fabulous dinner," I said.

"Miss G., when I think about that fire, and our guys being pulled off that house, and you in there, unprotected, I just . . . it's not like you're a regular vic, for God's sake. You're my wife."

"We were fine. But we do still need to find out why someone wanted to hurt Ernest, and then why that person would try to destroy his house, and maybe us in the process. I wonder if it's the same guy who was peeping in Yolanda's windows at the rental. And could this guy have burned down that house, too? Really, we need to figure out if this is all the same person."

"Who's 'we,' woman?" said Tom. "The *department* needs to find out. Not you. Please don't meddle in this."

"I'm not meddling. I'm trying to help Yolanda, who is, remember, my longtime friend. Boyd likes her, don't you think?"

Tom kissed my ear. "I don't know and I don't care. Your friend, who's now been at the center of two arson investigations, was not particularly helpful, in case you didn't notice."

"She was downstairs in Ernest's house, trying to help Ferdinanda—"

"There are caps you can wear that make you look bald," Tom said.

"I know, Tom. But this person was husky."

"There are big coats."

I was about to disagree with him, but his cell rang. He rose quickly and punched the Talk button. "Schulz."

He listened for a while, then said, "Is that a fact." It was not a question. Then, "Okay, thanks, buddy, I'll see you in the morning."

"Now what?" I asked.

Tom pulled me in playfully. "I thought you weren't going to meddle."

"Okay, don't tell me."

"That was Boyd again. Nobody in town saw Ernest. So they're now pretty sure Ernest was on his way to the dental appointment when he was shot. It looks as if he was trying to get away from somebody on foot. There were shell casings nearby, from a thirty-eight." Tom sighed. "But that being-on-the-way-to-the-dentist part? Seems Drew Parker, the dentist, left for Hawaii on Friday for a two-week vacation. So of course he didn't have *any* appointments on Saturday. He gave us permission by phone to break into his office. We couldn't find evidence that a receptionist or dental hygienist was working there in his absence, and Parker thinks he's the only one with the right key, besides the building manager, who used to be with the department and is a good guy."

"So who—"

"Ernest McLeod *had* been put down in the computer schedule to have a crown put on in a couple of weeks, right after Parker returned. That was probably the appointment that someone changed. We just don't know who that person is. Parker says he recently fired his secretary, because she was snorting cocaine when she wasn't getting patients into their chairs. The dental hygienist is a woman who always goes to Arizona at this time of year to see her widowed mother. Parker gave us the hygienist's name and contact information."

"If he fired his secretary, who's he using as a receptionist, typist, cashier, and so on?"

Tom sighed. "He said he's been using a temp service when he needs it, but he couldn't remember what it was called. He did recall the name of the last temporary receptionist, which was Zelda. Apparently, she misfiled everything and charged patients either too much or too little, depending on her mood."

I said, "Did she have her own key?"

"He can't remember whether she did or not. Time change to Hawaii, you know. Plus, our guy thinks Parker had had too many mai tais."

"So, is he hard on secretaries, or is he hard to work for?"

"Don't know. But *somebody* used the phone in Parker's office to change Ernest's appointment. There's no record of the appointment in the computer, but we dumped the numbers from Ernest's home, and there was a call from Parker's office on Thursday." Tom lapsed into thought. Finally he said, "There's more. The department got a call from Ernest McLeod's lawyer, Jason

Allred. He saw the news about Ernest on television."
Tom took a deep breath. "Ernest McLeod went to him
last week."

"Because?"

"Ernest changed his will. We originally thought all
the files in Ernest's house were destroyed. But it turns
out our guys did get a single box of files. In it was the
file with his will, which our guys read. When Allred
called us, he said yes, the document we have is indeed
Ernest McLeod's last will and testament." Tom paused.
"Ernest left ten thousand dollars to the Sheriff's Department Widows and Orphans Fund. He left the rest of his
money, plus his house, to Yolanda."

"He did *what*?"

Tom went on. "So now we don't know for sure if
Yolanda knew about the weed, and we don't know if she
was aware she was inheriting Ernest's house. Yolanda
broke up with Kris while you were working at the spa.
That's what, three, four weeks ago? She moved back
into her rental and it burned down after a week. So she
and Ferdinanda had been staying with Ernest for less
than two weeks. And yet he'd changed his will to give
her almost everything. It's very strange."

"Yes," I agreed. After a moment, I said, "What was
that she was saying about the gold and gems? Do you
know about that?"

"Yup. You ever heard of the Norman Juarez family?"

"The Norman Juarez family? No. Do they live up
here?"

"Norm owns a bar and restaurant near the department. He and his wife have a house next door. When

Ernest and John were partners, one of the most challenging cases they worked concerned this family."

"The Juarez family," I repeated, for clarification.

"Right. Norm, who originally had a Hispanic name and changed it, claims that *before* the Juarez family left Cuba, they gave a box of gold, gems, and a valuable necklace to Roberto Captain, who promised to keep them safe until the family could leave Cuba and come to America."

"Where did they get gold and gems in Cuba?" I asked. "It's not like they're natural resources on the island."

"Miss G.," Tom said patiently, "I don't know. Last time I looked, what they have in Cuba is nickel that they mine, cane that they cut to make sugar, and tobacco they grow for cigars. Anyway, according to Norman, five years or so after giving Roberto the box with the goods, the Juarez family tried to cross the gulf with someone else piloting the boat. The vessel was torn apart in a storm. There was only one survivor, a teenage boy who knew that if something happened to his loved ones, he was supposed to get in touch with Roberto Captain."

"And did he?"

"The son, Norman Juarez, made it to Miami by clinging to a piece of wreckage and kicking as hard as he could. But he couldn't get in touch with Roberto Captain, because El Capitán had died of a heart attack the year before. Cancer took his widow soon after, and their child, Humberto Captain, who was about twenty at the time, was nowhere to be found."

"Oh, Lord."

"Norman got a job as a dishwasher, then a server, and

eventually, a restaurant manager. He kept looking for anybody who could tell him where Humberto Captain was, because he, Norman, wanted his family's necklace and the other stuff."

"These were the gold and gems Yolanda mentioned?"

"Apparently. What we do know is that Norman Juarez finally tracked down Humberto Captain in Aspen Meadow, which is not that big a town. Still, it took Norman thirty, count 'em, *thirty* years to find Humberto, who might have thought he was smart to move far away from Miami, but he's a risk-taker, a crazy-ass big spender, and a guy who thinks he's never going to get caught—at anything. Anyway, no matter how arrogant Humberto is, it's not because of his intelligence, because he wasn't smart enough to change his name. With the advent of Google, Norman was able to find Humberto Captain, no sweat. Norman moved out here with his wife. He found Humberto and confronted him about his family's assets. According to Norman, Humberto said he didn't know what Norman was talking about."

"But if Humberto has money he can't prove he earned—"

Tom sighed. "Financial crimes are hard to prove, Miss G. Humberto has a little export-import business on the Internet, which is all he needs to cover his tracks. Norman Juarez came to us, asking for help. Ernest and his then partner, John Bertram, worked on the case when they had time, but they didn't get anywhere. Couldn't get a search warrant, couldn't get Humberto to cooperate, the usual. Then Ernest retired. Case closed, or so we thought. But then, this morning? After we found Ernest, and before anything was on the news? Norman Juarez called us and asked if we'd heard from Ernest McLeod."

"So," I said, "Norman had hired Ernest, and that's why he was investigating Humberto."

"You jumped to that one, Miss G. Norman was indeed one of Ernest's clients. When Ernest became a private investigator, *he* called Norman to see if he was interested in a non-cop looking for his stuff. Norman hired him."

I inhaled. I almost didn't want to hear what Tom would say.

Tom went on. "This morning Norman was anxious, because he couldn't reach Ernest. Norman said that Ernest had called him, all excited, Friday morning, as in two and a half days ago. Ernest said he had retrieved some of the Juarez family goods. But then Norman didn't hear back from him. According to the coroner's preliminary guess, Ernest was shot sometime on Saturday. I wish the canvass had turned up something, but up to this point, nothing."

"And the gold and gems?"

"So far, we can't figure out what was going on in Ernest's search for the assets. But here's the significant part. We suspect Yolanda was spying on Ernest in exchange for cash from Humberto Captain. She already admitted she got the money from Humberto, and she told us that she knew Ernest was investigating Humberto regarding assets. But there's a lot she hasn't told us, such as whether she knew Ernest had left her the house."

"She's been through hell," I said gently, and then brushed my hand over his chest. "Her ex hit her with a broom and gave her a sexually transmitted disease. She's traumatized."

"Uh-huh. And Ernest leaving her the house?"

"Tom, of *course* she didn't know about that. She would have told me." But suddenly, then, or maybe not so suddenly—perhaps this had been building throughout the day—a seed of doubt planted itself in my brain. Did *I* believe Yolanda?

Understandably, she had not told me about contracting a venereal disease from Kris. But less comprehensibly, she had not told me that he'd hit her, with a broomstick, no less. I felt suddenly cold and pulled up the bedcovers. Had I heard something outside, or was it just the unfamiliar sounds of Yolanda and Ferdinanda being in the house?

"Miss G.? You going to sleep? I think I hear someone moving around in the kitchen. Yolanda, do you suppose?"

"I don't know."

Tom eased out of our bed and pulled on his robe. "I'm going to go see what's going on."

While he was gone, I tried to regain my thought process. Okay, Yolanda had not told me about her rental burning down. Yesterday, the day before, and the day before that, when we'd been talking about the high school catering, she hadn't mentioned that she had moved in with Ernest or that he had undertaken problematic investigations, especially Humberto Captain versus Norm Juarez's claim to stolen gold and gems.

And of course, she hadn't said anything about dope, beagles, or inheriting a house.

When Tom returned, he said, "It was just Ferdinanda."

"She's probably like me. When she's trying to figure something out, she cooks. Listen, Tom. Maybe Yolanda *didn't* know she was inheriting Ernest's house. That happens, doesn't it?"

"Yeah, it does. But think of this another way. Maybe Yolanda went through Ernest's files and found, then read, the new will. And maybe she was helping somebody. Humberto, say. Humberto wanted her to discover what Ernest had on him. Maybe Humberto or somebody else had promised Yolanda a big payout if she could come up with information. Maybe this person had said he'd chip in to build Yolanda a new house on that site that Ernest had promised good old Portia he would never develop. Plus, we don't know how much Ernest had insured the place for, but with all the adding-on he did, you're probably looking at three, four hundred thou. And the property, with unobstructed mountain views, but close to town, is worth at least ten times that. Maybe the prospect of a big payday is why she's been crying. Tears of guilt. Or maybe they're tears of joy, over her big inheritance."

I said quietly, "At the moment, Tom, she's *sad*. Plus, I have to say that in *all* the time I've known Yolanda, she has never been anything but honest and upright."

"I know she's your friend, but I have to treat her just the way I would treat anyone else in a murder case. I can't just take her word for everything. But I understand if you do, with that big heart of yours."

I said softly, "You have a big heart, too. And I miss you."

He put his arms around my waist and pulled me toward him. Then he made love to me so tenderly, so lovingly, that afterward—around midnight, I suppose, when the house was finally quiet—unexpected tears of gratitude slid down my own cheeks.

Chapter 7

Monday morning, I awakened well before the alarm went off. Tom was still asleep, and I didn't want to disturb him. But a thought had niggled my brain to full consciousness. I glanced at the clock: It was half past four. Problem was, I wasn't quite sure of the nature of the question, if that was even what it was. I looked outside and frowned. A hard frost had iced the trees. Thick fog enveloped the streetlight near our bedroom window. I closed my eyes. What was that idea that was just out of reach? The more I tried to grab for it, the more it eluded me.

I eased out of bed and tried to relax my way into whatever the bothersome notion had been.

Before Arch became a teenager, and thus too cool for such pursuits, I used to take him fishing in the Aspen Meadow Wildlife Preserve. My job was to hold the net and collect the squirming trout, so I could take my son's picture, with him proudly holding his catch aloft. All this would have to be done quickly, because Arch always threw back his haul. Now, it seemed, I was thrusting wildly with the net, but whatever I was trying to snag remained maddeningly out of reach.

There was only one thing to do in this kind of situation, I thought as I put on jeans, a sweatshirt, and walking shoes. *Cook.* I'd been told that working with your hands to prepare food engages your left brain. So, the reasoning went, your right brain was free to wander around and capture intuitions. It had happened to me enough that I trusted the process.

I crept down to the kitchen. I didn't expect the household to start moving for at least a couple of hours. I looked forward to savoring the quiet, the time to think and—

Someone was crashing around in our pantry. I simultaneously pulled the pantry door open and screamed bloody murder.

"Dios mío!" cried Ferdinanda, her hand clutched to her heart. "What are you yelling about?" Instead of answering her, I stared at the pantry shelves, which were all jumbled. She had cleared off one whole area and now had a dozen cans in her lap.

Tom, wearing his undies, appeared at the door to the pantry. He was holding his .45 in both hands. When he saw us, he lowered it and said, "Uh, ladies?"

Yolanda, her face full of fear, stood shivering in the doorway to the dining room. "What happened? Did someone try to break in?"

"It's okay," I said. "I apologize, everybody. Please go back to bed. I heard someone and hollered. It was just . . . Ferdinanda." Yolanda disappeared back into the dining

room. Tom, his gun lowered, shuffled across to the desk
and pulled out the remote control to the garage, which
was where he stored the .45, in a hidden compartment.
But he had not gone outside to get it. He just happened to
have it upstairs? I knew better than to ask him about his
weapon while others were around. Tom, for his part,
shook his head, put the remote back down, and left the
kitchen. A moment later, I heard him clomping upstairs.

"Goldy," Ferdinanda scolded, "what are you doing up
so early? Weren't you tired from last night?"

"Ferdinanda, what were you *looking* for? Why are
you up at this hour?"

She wheeled herself out of the pantry. "Guava marmalade. And I'm awake now because I always am. During Batista's time? I worked in a café in the mornings. I
had to show up at four o'clock and make the bread. I've
got our breakfast almost ready. I just needed some good
jam to go with it."

"Is this what you were doing last night?" I asked. The
kitchen was empty, clean, and cleared of cooking utensils, except for a mixing bowl and a beater turned upside
down to dry on the counter.

"Yes. When Tom came down to see what the noise
was." Ferdinanda rolled herself to the kitchen table,
where she deposited the cans. Then she took off for the
walk-in. She said over her shoulder, "I'm glad you're
here, you can help me."

My shoulders slumped. I was so looking forward to
having this time to myself. "What do you—"

I was interrupted by Tom, who'd pulled on sweats and
now reappeared in the kitchen with his gun. He picked

up the garage remote and disappeared, then came back a moment later. "Goldy? How long has this remote been dead?"

"Uh," I said, trying to remember something, anything, about our supply of batteries. While Ferdinanda continued to crash around in the walk-in, I searched my brain. I had no idea where the batteries were or even if we had any. "Why did you even have the forty-five in the house, anyway?"

"Target practice yesterday," said Tom. After a fruitless rummage through the desk drawer, Tom whispered, "All right, didn't you just change the code for the panel?" Our detached garage was a remnant of the time when our brown shingle house had been built, in the twenties. There were two entries to it: the main one facing the street, and another on the side, a regular door which we kept locked with a key. The main door could be opened by either a remote—one that worked— or a numbered panel on the side.

"The panel code is Arch's birthday," I replied.

"Yeah, yeah," said Tom. "Tax day." He tossed the dead remote back into the desk and shuffled off. A moment later, the garage door rumbled open.

"Here we go!" cried Ferdinanda, triumphant. She emerged from the walk-in with a plastic-covered glass pan in her lap. "This is a bread pudding that sits overnight. I'll make a rum sauce later. That's as good as marmalade."

"This is all very sweet of you," I forced myself to say as I peered around her into the walk-in's dark interior. Make a rum sauce out of what?

"Just leave the pudding on the table for a while," Ferdinanda said as she piled large cans of beans and broth back in her lap. Outside, the garage door thundered closed. I certainly hoped we hadn't awakened any of the neighbors with all the screaming and clanking. Ferdinanda gave me an expectant look. "Can you push me into the dining room? I need to do my exercises."

"Sure," I said. Tom reentered the house, reset the house alarm, and walked upstairs. I felt a shudder of guilt for getting him up so early.

"Goldy?" asked Ferdinanda.

"Right." I pushed the wheelchair through the swinging door to the dining room, which Ferdinanda could have easily opened herself, and clearly already had when she came out there. As Ferdinanda placed most of the cans on her cot, I looked around our guests' temporary bedroom. Years ago, when I'd done the minimal amount of decorating required for a house, I'd only put up sheer curtains over the long mullioned windows. But the sun was not up yet, thank goodness, and the room remained dark. Yolanda, inert on her cot, had pulled the sheet up over her ears.

With a sigh, though, I realized that I had also awakened the puppies. This was becoming the opposite of a quiet morning of relaxation.

I crept back to the pet-containment area. Scout the cat was nowhere to be seen. Jake was asleep with four of the puppies leaning up against him. I picked up the two whining puppies and carefully snuggled one against each shoulder. Then I rocked them until they went back to sleep. With as much care as I would have used handling newborns, I placed them next to Jake's warm back. He did not open his eyes, but his tail thumped twice in acknowledgment.

Finally I retreated to the kitchen, where I washed my hands and put on a clean apron. I hadn't remembered whatever it was that had awakened me, and with all the commotion and no caffeine, I sure couldn't bring up the thought to net it.

What kind of cooking would aid my thought process? And could I work in the kitchen so quietly that Tom, Yolanda, and all the dogs would be able to sleep?

I fired up the espresso machine, ground freshly roasted beans in my new burr grinder, and cast my mind over things we'd eaten lately that we'd enjoyed. There was the toffee Tom had bought. I decided to make another cookie for the high school buffet: a conglomeration of sweet, tangy, and crunchy ingredients that I would call Crunch Time Cookies. In the walk-in, I nabbed unsalted butter and a couple of eggs. I thought the cookie should not be *too* sweet, so I picked up some cream cheese to add tang. I gathered oats and other dry ingredients, plus our favorite Mexican vanilla, from where Ferdinanda had moved them in the pantry. I looked around at the mess in there. When was I going to get this all cleaned up?

While the cookies are baking, my mind supplied. *And after you have some coffee.*

I made myself a quadruple-shot cappuccino, then sipped it as I measured brown and regular sugar and sifted together flour and leavening agents. I was making toffee cookies, so I thought I could use semisweet chocolate chips as well as toffee bits. Pecans have always been my favorite nut, so I thought, *To heck with almonds and tradition, I'm going to add the crunch of toasted pecans.*

The nuts tapped against the side of the sauté pan as I heated them oh-so-quietly and took tiny mouthfuls of my luscious coffee. *Think,* I ordered myself.

Tom had said that someone had set Ernest up, by. arranging, or, to be more precise, rescheduling, a dental appointment that he wasn't due to have for two weeks. The dentist, in Hawaii, didn't know anything about it. But he wouldn't have been the one to attend to the calendar; his *secretary* would have. But Drew Parker, DDS, didn't have a full-time secretary anymore, and he claimed Zelda, his temporary secretary, was a ditz. Had anyone else done his office work? Dr. Parker himself said he used a service, the name of which he could not remember. And it was *that* aspect—the service—that had awoken me that morning, full of curiosity concerning an idea that was just out of reach of my mental net.

After ten minutes of stirring the pecans, I turned them out onto paper towels to cool. I softened the butter and cream cheese a bit in the microwave, then emptied them into the mixer bowl and let the beaters rip. Next I combined the sugars and slowly added them to the mixing bowl, continuing to beat until the mixture was ultra-creamy and very soft. Next came the eggs, then the vanilla. While that mixture melded, I sifted the dry ingredients; combined the oats, chocolate chips, and toffee bits in a bowl; and roughly chopped the pecans.

Okay . . . I'd repeatedly heard about people like Dr.

Parker, who'd let secretaries and other assistants go. Sometimes they said all the business could afford was a temp. My cynical view was that usually the business was trying to rid itself of the cost of providing benefits to a full-time employee. But never mind that; *what had I been thinking?*

The sheriff's department, going into Parker's office that day, ought to be able to locate the name of the temp service he used in his Rolodex or in his files. *The temp service. What temp service?*

I stared down at the chopped pecans. They smelled so good, I couldn't resist popping a still-warm nut into my mouth. It was crunchy and sweet.

Finally, something about a temp service swam toward me. I could see a face; I could recall a vaguely unpleasant personality.

I stopped the mixer and stirred in the flour and leavening agents, plus the pecans, chocolate chips, and toffee bits. I figured the cream cheese would ripen the flavor of the batter if I let the batter chill for a while. It would have been better if I could have let it sit overnight, but I didn't have overnight. I covered the bowl with plastic wrap and put it in the walk-in.

Then it was time for a little CPR on the old memory bank. I pulled out the phone book and searched through the yellow pages until I came to "Secretarial Services." Some in Denver, Lakewood, and Littleton had advertised there, but . . . there was only one in Aspen Meadow. It was called Do It! and their slogan was "Secretaries Do It Behind the Desk." Right. I looked closely at the proprietor's name. Finally, I snagged the thought that had awakened me at half past four.

The owner of Do It! was Charlene Newgate. And I knew her. For crying out loud, of *course* I knew her. I fixed myself another cappuccino and sat down at the kitchen table.

I'd met Charlene, who I thought must now be in her fifties, when I was doing outreach work at St. Luke's. At that time, our parish had had the only food pantry in the mountain area. Back in the dark old days before the government had more resources to track down deadbeat dads, Charlene's husband abandoned her and her daughter. Habitat for Humanity built Charlene and her daughter a house, but Charlene also had a series of live-in boyfriends. They, too, packed up and shipped out. All this left Charlene with only the barest welfare income. She came into the church from time to time for tuna, peanut butter, canned ravioli, and breakfast cereal. Unfortunately, Saint Luke's hadn't offered free counseling sessions to people coming for food, or I would have suggested them to Charlene.

As a teen, Charlene's daughter got pregnant. She gave birth to a son, but shortly thereafter went to prison for dealing drugs. One time when Charlene had come in and asked if we had SpaghettiOs, she'd shared with me that she was determined to raise her grandson, little Otto, by herself. Otto, who loved SpaghettiOs, was a year younger than Arch. In elementary school, Otto had been even more uncoordinated than Arch, and my heart had bled for them both.

When the Jerk had finally popped for tuition money for Arch to go to Elk Park Preparatory School—a disaster of monumental proportions—Charlene had complained bitterly to me that she was unable to afford such opportunities for Otto. I'd wanted to say, *You want your son to be ostracized for not having money, not belonging to a country club, not being athletic, and not going to Europe for the summer? Be my guest.* But I'd said nothing. After one year of hell, I'd quietly taken Arch out of Elk Park Prep and put him into the Christian Brothers High School, which cost half as much as Elk Park Prep and had none of the aggravation. Charlene somehow found out where Arch was and told me that she wished she were rich—!—so that she could send Otto to a Catholic school like the one where Arch was.

I finished my coffee and cleaned up the mess of eggshells, butter wrappers, beaters, and measuring cups. Then I thought, *Oh, why not make a batch of those cookies right now?* They would probably be better if I baked them later, but I wanted to see what I'd invented. Delayed gratification had never been my thing, and anyway, the cookies had oats in them, so they were sort of breakfasty. I preheated the oven, slapped a silicone pad on a cookie sheet, and tried to remember more about Charlene Newgate. I needed to figure this out, doggone it, because I was willing to bet several pounds of unsalted butter that either she had been the secretary for Drew Parker or she'd sent one of her temps to work there.

Charlene got the idea for her business while visiting the church, when she'd seen other single mothers lining up for food for their families. If the mothers' children were in school, Charlene figured, why not see if the ladies could be plugged into gaps in the business world in Aspen Meadow? She'd started Do It! and found work for office assistants, bookkeepers, and office managers, and after that, personal organizers, house cleaners, pet sitters, nurses, and paralegals.

I took the bowl of batter from the walk-in and carefully scooped out twelve balls of dough, which I gently flattened before putting into the oven. I set the timer, booted the kitchen computer, and popped online. Bingo. Charlene Newgate and Do It! had a website and a phone number. Best of all, her e-mail address was also included.

After some thought, I sent an e-mail to Charlene, making up some BS about catering a party for a doctor and wondering if her secretarial service would be willing to address and stamp invitations. It was the best I could do on short notice.

I finished cleaning up after myself and realized I needed another coffee. I steamed some whipping cream, poured it into a china cup, and pulled two double shots of espresso on top. While I drank it, I cleaned up the pantry. The sheet of cookies came out, and after letting them set up for a couple of minutes, I moved them over to a cooling rack.

A moment later, the computer made that little *bink!* noise that indicates you have mail. I was sure it was an ad for Viagra—I get a lot of those, and trust me, that's the last thing Tom needs—but I was curious. It was twenty after five in the morning, Mountain Time. Who would send me an e-mail at that hour?

Charlene Newgate, that's who. She wrote, *I'll be at the physicals today at Christian Brothers High School. Otto is a student there and trying out for sports. I knew you were catering the lunch, because Otto brought home a notice about it. How's noon?* She concluded by giving me her cell phone number, in case that time didn't work.

Before I could think about it, I wrote, *Sounds great. See you in the gym.* After I'd sent the message, I wondered if Tom would approve. Still. Why wouldn't he? What was Charlene going to do in a crowded gymnasium, throw a file cabinet at my head? She ran a secretarial service, and if she had hired out a temp for Drew Parker, the cops were going to discover it anyway. The worst she could do, I thought, was refuse to talk to me, once she discovered the doctor's-party bit was a sham.

I picked up one of the cookies, bit into it, and entered heaven. The crunch of toasted pecans combined with the soft chocolate and chewy texture of baked toffee bits made me swoon. And of course, it went so well with the coffee. I made a latte for Tom, put a couple of cookies on a plate for him, and zipped back up the stairs.

It was just before six, and Tom was making his usual shaving noises in the bathroom. There was water running somewhere else, too, I realized, but I couldn't figure out whether someone downstairs was having a shower or Yolanda was in the basement, doing a load of laundry. Clearly, having a couple of extra females in the house would take some getting used to.

I placed my load on a night table, sat on the floor, and closed my eyes. Very slowly, I began my yoga routine. My muscles were tight, either from getting up early to bake and think or from all the stress they'd undergone escaping from the inferno at Ernest's place. My backside was sore, too, no doubt from the tumble I'd taken down the steps to his basement.

I breathed, stretched, and endeavored to relax. Unfortunately, now another question came squirming to the front of my mind. *Why* set up Ernest by moving a dentist appointment?

Maybe the killer had not even known Ernest would walk into town. Maybe he or she had thought to follow Ernest at a safe distance, then shoot him by his dentist's empty office.

But then why burn down his house the following day? If you wanted to kill Ernest, why not just set the house on fire and be done with it?

I stopped midstretch. Of course, Ernest had had excellent fire alarms, and Yolanda, Ferdinanda, and I had made it out, along with nine puppies.

Nothing made sense. And before I could ponder the situation any more, the doorbell rang. I was about to stop my routine and go answer it when there were voices: Boyd was out on our front porch talking to Yolanda. They started laughing, and then she invited him inside.

A moment later, there was mad yipping from the puppies, accompanied by Jake howling his head off. Scout the cat streaked into our room and slid under the bed.

Let's see: I had company to entertain, a crazed cat, six extra dogs plus the one we already had . . . and I hadn't even gotten through the Salute to the Sun.

Tom appeared at the bathroom door and eyed the plate with the cookies beside his coffee cup. "You've been busy." He leaned down and kissed my head. "Did I just hear Boyd arrive?"

"You did. I think Yolanda's showing him the puppies. Please taste a cookie and have some coffee."

Tom chewed thoughtfully, then smiled and pronounced it excellent. He drank the coffee in just a couple of gulps—working in the sheriff's office makes you impervious to the heat of drinks—and glanced outside. "Boyd said he would bring wood for the ramp, which was awful nice of him. He said he was bringing a ham, too—"

"Another *ham*? Why?"

When Tom grinned, the skin on each side of his sea-green eyes crinkled. "Aw, don't get after him. He's had a thing for Yolanda ever since he came out to the spa to keep an eye on you. When I talked to him last night? He said he was going to pick up something for breakfast. I thought he meant cinnamon rolls. But then he said he was bringing a ham. Maybe he wants to come back for dinner. We could have a hamboree."

"Not funny. Please don't invite him. Yolanda and I have enough on our plate today already."

"Listen to the caterer: enough on her plate. Know the definition of *eternity*?"

"Tom? Please."

He said, "A ham and two people."

"We're not two people, though, are we?"

"Do your yoga, Food Woman, see if it improves your mood."

"Well, I do have some news in the food department. Guess who's making breakfast?"

"Ferdinanda."

I smiled up at him. "Correct. Remember how Yolanda said her aunt was an early riser? That she used to work in a café before Castro's revolution? Well, the noises we heard last night were Ferdinanda making a breakfast dish that has to sit overnight in the refrigerator. She'll probably love serving it with the ham."

"She survived being screamed at while she was in the pantry?"

"She made a mess of the place, moving things from one shelf to another. Looking for guava preserves, she said. She had her lap full of cans, too. They were for her workout."

Tom shook his head. "Glad I didn't scare her with the gun. How long does she have to stay in the wheelchair?"

"Probably until Thanksgiving, Yolanda told me."

Tom eyed the empty plate and coffee cup. "Want me to bring you a latte?"

"I've had one too many espresso drinks already this morning. Better make it decaf. And thanks."

I moved through an abbreviated yoga routine while Tom steamed more milk and pulled the shots. I could hear him talking to Ferdinanda, who must have finished her strength exercises. I wondered if I should tell Tom about the fact that I'd set up a time to talk to Charlene. Maybe he could give me some tips on subtle interrogation. Plus, our talk about Ferdinanda reminded me of something else I wanted to know.

"Here you go," he said. He placed my steaming mug on one of the needlepoint coasters he'd ordered with the Adirondack chairs for our front porch. "And get this: Ferdinanda has preheated the oven and poured the juice."

"Thanks a million." I got up on the bed and took a sip. The creamy beverage shot across my taste buds.

"And it is yummy, too." Scout the cat cautiously pawed his way out from his hiding place, then leapt up on the bed and snuggled next to me. I patted his back and said, "It's a shame about Ferdinanda's accident. A broken leg can heal, but it sounds as if hers is going to take forever." I shook my head. "Did the Denver cops investigate the hit-and-run?"

Tom groaned. "Yup. No reliable eyewitnesses, no license plate, just a few mentions of a big black SUV." He looked out the window that had a view of our street. "The Denver guys' question to me was, 'Do you know that old woman would not tell us why she was down here in the first place?' There was a small ethnic grocery store nearby, and the proprietor said he recognized her. He said she doesn't like to say what she's doing or why. After the accident? She told the grocery store proprietor, this country has freedom of speech, and freedom of no speech, and that was what she was doing."

The stairs creaked, and I jumped. "Who's that?"

Tom gave a half grin. "Just Boyd. I recognize his step." He started to leave.

"Wait. Tom, I looked something up on my kitchen computer this morning." I rushed forward before he could object. "I was thinking about Ernest's appointment being changed, and Dr. Parker saying he couldn't remember the name of the secretarial service he hired. Well, there's only one secretarial service in town, and it's run by a woman I know from Saint Luke's, or at least from when she used to come to the food pantry. Her name is Charlene Newgate. I've already sent her an e-mail, and we're going to see each other at the physicals today. Her grandson is a student at CBHS. He must be new because I haven't seen him at any school functions—"

"Miss G., what are you saying to me? You want to know if she worked for Dr. Parker? You want to question this woman about Ernest's appointment? And wait, you want to wear a wire, too?"

I sipped the coffee and tried to think. "No, I just want to know if it's okay with you. That I talk to her, I mean."

Tom shook his head and sighed. "Be very careful. And be nice—"

"I'm always nice."

Tom chuckled. "Right. If she worked for Parker, we're going to figure that out anyway. But don't press her, got it? I want to hear what she has to say, and in particular, how she acts with you."

Boyd knocked softly on our door. When Tom answered, Boyd said he needed to get into the garage to get the toolbox. Tom gave him the code, said he'd be right there, and came over to give me a kiss.

"See you, Miss G."

"Thanks, Tom. You know I'm only trying to help Yolanda." I sipped the coffee again. In a moment, banging began to echo up the stairs. "And one more thing—"

Tom slumped. "Only one more?"

"Is there a laptop up here? I don't want to use your computer in the basement, and I don't want to use the one in the kitchen. I want to use one up here."

He quirked an eyebrow at me. "There's that new desktop in Arch's room." When I didn't mention why I needed it, Tom said, "Oh, man, Miss G., don't I know you." It was not a question. "You want to start a file, make a list of what's happened, that kind of thing, right?" I pressed my lips together and looked out the window. Tom went on. "And you want to be up here to do it, not in the kitchen, because despite what you say about loving good old honest Yolanda, you want to keep what you're putting down to yourself."

I shot him a glance. "Yeah, okay, I'm just being, well, circumspect. Do you know how to password-protect a file? I don't want to mess up Arch's stuff."

"Wouldn't he just love you for that. Come on, I'll show you."

While Tom booted Arch's Mac, I looked around my son's room. His memorabilia crowded the shelves above his desk. There were pictures of Arch with Julian on a fishing trip, Arch smiling broadly with the Christian Brothers fencing team, another of him brandishing his new épée. Another photo showed him in front of a cake on his sixteenth birthday, flanked by his best friend, Todd Druckman, and his newfound half brother, Gus Vikarios. We called the trio the Three Musketeers. Most amazingly, to me, anyway, were the fencing trophies between the photos. DENVER AREA FENCING CHAMPION-SHIP, THIRD PLACE. BOULDER FENCERS, THREE-TIME KING OF THE HILL. WESTERN REGIONAL RUNNER-UP, UNDER-EIGHTEEN ÉPÉE TOURNAMENT.

This was, all of it, a sea change from Arch's life up to a few years ago. In elementary and middle school, he'd been steeped in misery—not unlike little Otto Newgate, who had taken his grandmother's last name. Otto was even younger and smaller than Arch. For his part, Arch had been unathletic, bullied constantly, addicted to role-playing games, and torn apart by my divorce from the Jerk. But in a gradual change, he'd turned away from Dungeons and Dragons, secretiveness, and despair, and made friends besides Todd. At CBHS, he'd ventured into fencing. He'd focused and concentrated at school and, best of all, started to gain confidence, even joy. And then my heart twisted in my chest, because I realized at what point this change had begun to occur: It was when the man in front of me, now busily tapping on Arch's keyboard, had come into our lives, and stayed.

"Thank you, Tom," I said, putting my hand on his shoulder.

"Yeah, yeah, it's just a file. Here you go, Miss G." He stood and held out the desk chair for me. "Your password is *Havana*. Now, if you'll excuse me, I'm going to go see if any of Ferdinanda's breakfast dish is ready. Don't be long, 'cause Boyd and I do have to do some work today, as in down at the sheriff's department."

"Wait. I have a quick question regarding Yolanda's problem with Kris. If he was threatening her, and she could document it, couldn't he be charged with menacing?"

Tom nodded. "She made a report, remember? But in order to sustain a charge of menacing, Miss G., we need *documentation* and *evidence*. Same with harassment. We have to have something to go on, and she didn't even make a sheriff's department report when he hit her with the broom."

"And the investigation at Ernest's house? When will

you know about accelerant, what's been destroyed, canvass of the neighborhood, ballistics on the gun that shot him, that kind of thing?"

"Today or tomorrow."

"And you'll tell me?"

Tom crossed his arms and smiled. "If you can keep it to yourself."

"Thanks. I'll be down in a few."

Once Tom had quietly closed the door, I stared at the screen.

1. *Ferdinanda:* Mid-June, victim of hit-and-run. Was she a target? If so, why? What was she doing in Denver that she won't divulge? Or is she just naturally difficult? Hates Kris. Loved Ernest. Ask her about Humberto.

2. *Yolanda:* Beginning of July, moves in with Kris. Mid-August: VD diagnosis. He hits her with broom; she moves out. While in rental, strange things happen; she thinks Kris is stalking her but has no proof. Twice, she and Ferdinanda see shadowy form at window; makes police report. Lost job at end of August, won't give specifics about why Humberto gave her 17K in cash, found at Ernest's house. (Did the cash burn up? Find out.) Won't talk about Humberto; acts evasive. August 26: Rental mysteriously burns down. Unifrutco oil can nearby. Next day, she moves in with Ernest McLeod. She claims she is afraid of some of his clients: Hermie who's

missing fingers but loves puppies; some divorce
clients; Juarez, who's missing gold and gems.
Ernest decides to leave her the house. Why?
After Ernest is shot, his house is burned by
arsonist. Why?

3. *Humberto Captain:* Being investigated by
Ernest for theft of gold and gems from family of
Norm Juarez. According to Tom, HC is slimy
and uncooperative. Can a little export-import
store provide him with the extravagant lifestyle
he is rumored to have?

4. *Kris Nielsen:* Wealthy. Tells everyone he started
a company and selling it made him rich. But he
drunkenly confessed to Penny Woolworth, the
cleaning lady, that he had inherited wealth.
Penny tried to find out more about running a
business, but Kris clammed up. Tom is trying to
find out name of company Kris sold. Worse than
all this: Yolanda says he is obsessed with her. He
was unfaithful to her, gave her VD, hit her. Is he
involved in the murder of Ernest? In the fire at
Ernest's house? If so, how? And why?

5. *Brie Quarles:* Being investigated by Ernest.
Why? Is she the one with the messy divorce?

6. *Hermie:* Trying to close puppy mill. Are the
beagle puppies from that mill? Is this why Ernest
was killed, because he had discovered it?

7. *Ernest McLeod:* Investigating Humberto.
Surveilling someone with messy divorce.
Following Brie Quarles. Investigating puppy mill
for Hermie. Why was Ernest growing marijuana
in his greenhouse? Why did Ernest change his
will? Why was Ernest killed?

I stared at that last question and thought if I could
figure that out, I'd know who had shot Ernest while he
was walking to his non–dentist appointment. I glanced
around Arch's desk, as if looking for clues there. All I
saw was the bright orange flyer he'd designed for the
athletes' lunch today: *Yes, There Is Free Lunch! (But
You Have to Have a Physical First).* And then there was
a cartoon of a doctor listening to the chest of an athlete,
who in turn looked longingly at a steaming plate of food
that was just out of reach. *Oh, Arch,* I thought as I
picked up the flyer and stuffed it into my pocket. *You
must have gotten your sense of humor from Tom.* I
saved and closed the computer file, then raced downstairs for breakfast.

Yolanda looked as if her night's sleep had not rested
her at all. But she didn't complain; she merely hugged
me when I came into the kitchen. Ferdinanda rolled
around the kitchen with purpose, giving Yolanda stac-
cato orders for setting the table and making coffee. I
wished she would not ride Yolanda so hard, but that issue was not, as we used to say when I was growing up,
any of my beeswax. Ferdinanda commanded that I make
a rum sauce, the directions for which she had written out
and placed next to the stove. Rum, rum . . . did we have
rum?

"I found your bottle of rum in the dining room cabinet," Ferdinanda told me, as if reading my mind. "It's there on the counter." And so it was. I sighed and began working on the sauce.

Tom and Boyd traipsed in and washed up. When Ferdinanda's golden, puffed bread pudding emerged from the other oven, I was impressed. While Boyd removed the ham from the oven, Ferdinanda instructed me to pour the hot rum sauce over the bread pudding, which I did. And then we all dug in.

Ferdinanda's dish consisted of raisin bread soaked in a spiced cream-and-egg concoction that became a rich custard when baked. The result was moist, fluffy, and luscious, especially when dripping with the hot syrup. Ferdinanda beamed when I complimented her. Boyd proudly cut each of us thick slices of the ham he had brought. We all insisted the combination of salty meat with a slightly sweet dish was perfect.

While Ferdinanda and I did the dishes, Tom and Boyd finished work on the ramp. Yolanda took care of the puppies, and I was thankful Boyd had bought more chow the previous night. With Yolanda and Ferdinanda staying there, I thought we might need more food, besides ham, that is. Once the dishes were out of the way, I nabbed an index card to start a new grocery list. Ferdinanda asked me shyly if I could pick up some guava marmalade.

"Sure. Where do you get it?"

When she described the location of an ethnic grocery in Denver, I wondered if it was the one she'd been going to when an SUV had mowed her down. Could someone have been following Ferdinanda? Why would someone do that? And was I becoming as paranoid as our two houseguests?

Yolanda came in from tending the puppies, said they were all fine, and washed her hands. Then she asked if it was all right for her to make Boyd and herself another coffee.

"Yolanda," I replied, "you know that old *mi casa es su casa* saying? Just take whatever you want."

"In that case," interjected Ferdinanda as she shrugged into an old jacket of Tom's, "I'm going to have a cigar. You know what the Mexicans say? *Después de un taco, un buen tabaco.* Except we didn't have tacos for breakfast, we had my bread pudding. Better put on your coat, Goldy! It's freezin' out there." With this, she rolled down the hall toward the front door, not into the dining room, her makeshift bedroom. Did she already have her cigars with her? I didn't remember her bringing anything in from the van. Where did she *put* stuff? I suspected that if we turned Ferdinanda's empty wheelchair upside down, we would shake out an umbrella, a set of false teeth, and a baby pachyderm.

A short while later, I zipped up my winter coat and accompanied Yolanda out to the front porch. I held the door open while she walked through with a tray of coffees—I'd made another decaf for myself—and the ubiquitous sugar bowl. When we arrived, Tom grinned. Boyd, with his dark crew cut, muscular body, and kind face, positively lit up. Ferdinanda, clearly happy with whatever was going on between her niece and the police officer, blew cigar smoke toward the neighbors.

As Ferdinanda had warned, the air temperature had plummeted since the previous evening. A thick gray blanket of cloud lay low over the mountains. In years past, we'd had snow in mid-September, so perhaps our short-lived Indian summer was indeed over for good.

I sat down with my latte—grateful it was unsweetened in addition to being decaffeinated—and admired the progress the men were making on the ramp. Then, quite unexpectedly, I had one of those frissons you get when you know you're being watched, or judged, or threatened.

I put my coffee down and walked out to the center of our street. Almost from habit, I checked Jack's empty house. The FOR SALE sign was still there, if slightly askew. The place looked deserted. Our bloodhound wasn't howling; Tom and Boyd continued to work.

I shivered and did a one-eighty, right in the middle of the street. Nothing.

I pulled the sleeve up my right wrist; my skin was covered with gooseflesh. I swallowed. I'd seen a TV nature show where the narrator had been giving a discourse on the African savanna and how gazelles were "warned" by birdcalls when predators were nearby. The question being discussed in the program was, how had gazelles learned bird language? But I hadn't heard a birdcall, because most of our birds had flown south at the end of August. What, then?

I tried to look nonchalant as I again glanced up and down the street. Except for our little crew, no one was around. There was the usual rumble of traffic from Main Street. From about two blocks away, an approaching school bus chugged along. But then I heard something else: a metallic growling, grinding noise, like a set of gigantic axes being sharpened. Once, twice. *Vroom, vroom.*

"¡Ai!" cried Ferdinanda from the porch. "It's Kris."

Yolanda, frozen in place, dropped her coffee cup onto the cement floor of the porch, where it broke. Tom and Boyd were immediately on guard. Boyd went so far as to pull his firearm out of its holster.

"Take the women inside!" Tom called to me.

I sprinted back and did as commanded. We watched through the living room windows while Tom and Boyd split up and walked to opposite ends of the street. The detritus of the ramp-making lay higgledy-piggledy across our front yard. I glanced at my watch: half past seven. Yolanda and I had to leave at eight for the Christian Brothers High School, to be there by nine so we could start setting up. But I wasn't as worried about that as I was about Yolanda, who was trembling.

"It was his car," Yolanda said under her breath. "Kris's."

I said, "You could tell by that grinding noise?"

Ferdinanda and Yolanda said in unison, "Yes."

"He drives a Maserati," Yolanda said, "because it's expensive and he wants to show off. Problem is, he has trouble with the Formula One gears, and when he's stopped, like he's set the car in Park? He hits the accelerator so the exhaust makes that *vroom-vroom* sound." I thought of Zeke Woolworth, in prison for grand theft auto. I bet he would know how to make Kris's car hum.

"He's around here somewhere," Ferdinanda said, her voice flat. "He followed us to this house."

I wanted to disagree with her, to say we'd left Ernest's house by a back service road not known to many people, least of all to Kris. She was being paranoid. Still, I'd had that frisson. What had my nerves sensed?

Well, well. It was not Kris in his Maserati who came driving up our street a minute later, as Boyd and Tom returned, holstering their weapons. Instead, a long black Mercedes pulled to our curb and disgorged a tall, heavy, Hispanic male. Despite the weather, he wore a beige suit. He was very wide in the middle but narrowed as you glanced at his feet or head. His curly black hair was threaded with gray. His tanning-bed face and hands were the color of papaya flesh.

I recognized him from newspaper photographs: Humberto Captain.

Chapter 8

Hello, officers!" Humberto called loudly, with a papal-style wave. Ferdinanda, Yolanda, and I were still standing in front of the windows. The two women exchanged an unreadable glance. Tom and Boyd stopped Humberto on the sidewalk, where the three of them spoke in such low tones that we couldn't make them out.

"What do you all want to do?" I asked.

"See if they argue," Ferdinanda replied without moving her gaze from the window.

They didn't exactly quarrel, but the conversation did not seem to be going well. Humberto gesticulated adamantly at the house, until finally Tom accompanied him to the porch, where he admonished Humberto in a raised voice to stay put. When Tom came inside, he was shaking his head.

"He wants to know how the girls are," Tom said. "That's his term, not mine. And he means Yolanda and Ferdinanda, not you, Goldy."

"Did you ask him why he called Ernest's house last

night, right before the arsonist hit?" I asked with more heat than I intended. "Did you ask him if he was the arsonist?"

Tom inhaled patiently. "Goldy, I am building a *ramp*. Last night, our guys did question Captain. He says his cell phone was stolen last week. He also says he was at home when the Molotov cocktail was being thrown at the greenhouse." Tom lifted his chin at Ferdinanda and Yolanda. "You want to talk to him?"

"He is our . . . family friend," Ferdinanda said. I wondered why she did not sound enthusiastic about the relationship.

Yolanda closed her eyes. "Let's get this over with."

Well, that was not the way I would want my friends to talk about me when I dropped in, but never mind. To Tom, I said, "How'd he find out Ferdinanda and Yolanda were here?"

Tom lifted his hands in despair. "How d'you think? He called Marla very early this morning, saying he had stuff for Yolanda and Ferdinanda. Woke her up, he says. I can just imagine how popular he is with Marla right now. Let's go out there and see how quickly we can finish this."

Once we were all on the porch, Humberto focused his attention on Yolanda and Ferdinanda. He opened his hands in a lavish gesture. "My dear friends and countrywomen," he began.

"Hey, Julius Caesar," said Yolanda, her tone cool. "I was born outside of Miami."

Humberto continued as if she hadn't spoken. "I am here to offer help." He walked back to the black car, reached inside, and brought out a bag. He carried it to the porch and handed it to Tom.

Tom checked the contents and said, "This is nice. Cheese, crackers, and rum. Thank you."

Humberto nodded. But then he eyed the half-empty coffee cups that sat on the wooden table between the Adirondack chairs. He pulled his mouth into a moue of distaste when he saw the shards of another cup on the porch floor. He turned to me and lifted his graying eyebrows expectantly. Well, if he thought I was going to offer him caffeine or explanations, he was mistaken. "I heard . . ." Here he faltered and cleared his throat. "I heard that the, the home where you were staying burned down last night. Ferdinanda and Yolanda, you may come and stay at my house. It is much bigger and more comfortable"—here he did his regal wave again, indicating our humble abode—"than this, I assure you."

"We're happy here," said Yolanda, lifting her chin. "I'm working with Goldy, so this is convenient for us. But thanks for your offer. We'll remember you want to *help*." She put a peculiar emphasis on that word, which once again made me wonder exactly what was going on with Yolanda.

"I am happy to help you, Yolanda. Our families have always been friendly with each other. Our Cuban community needs to stick together, especially in times of tragedy." When no one said anything, Humberto said, "Yolanda, if you would not like to stay at my house, allow me at least to invite you, Ferdinanda, and your kind hosts to my house on Black Bear Mountain for dinner. Shall we say, Wednesday night?"

Before Yolanda could answer, Tom said, "Fine," his tone flat. "We'll be there."

Humberto drew himself up. He looked confused by Tom's unenthusiastic acceptance of the dinner invitation. "You will remember my house, perhaps? The police were less than cooperative when I experienced a break-in not so long ago."

Boyd lifted his eyebrows. "Would that be the break-in where your cell phone was stolen?" he asked, crossing his arms.

"No," said Humberto, "my cell phone was taken . . . from my jacket. I told the police this. I . . . was having mojitos with a very attractive woman, and I left her for a moment . . . during that moment, the phone was taken."

Ferdinanda shook a gnarled finger at Humberto. "You gotta lay off those mojitos, amigo." It was her first comment since we'd all come out there. "But thank you for wanting to help your Cuban *friends*."

Even I was surprised to hear Ferdinanda's sarcasm, and once again, I could not figure out exactly what the dynamic was between these three.

Boyd said, "So you had *another* theft, Mr. Captain?"

Humberto was defiant. "I did. But your department was unhelpful."

Tom said, "Mr. Captain, if you won't tell us the details of your security system, and you won't tell us what was taken from your house, how can we help you? How can we not feel that coming all the way up to your place and taking a report is a complete waste of time?"

Humberto straightened his shoulders, but you could

see by the way his arms hung helplessly at his sides that he felt he'd failed to get whatever he wanted by coming here. He made a last stab. "So, did you find out . . . anything of interest in Ernest's house? I mean, was there anything inside to, to tell you who burned it down?"

These were the wrong questions. Tom walked to Humberto, who shied back as if he were about to be hit. But Tom only gently took his arm. "Read the newspaper, Mr. Captain. That's where to get the latest news. See you Wednesday."

Humberto allowed Tom to escort him to his car, but then turned and stood steadfast for a moment, despite the bum's rush from Tom. "Six o'clock! And, ladies! Would you like to bring a special dish on Wednesday night?"

This reminded me of a wedding invitation I'd received once, back in the bad old days when I was a doctor's wife. It was from someone I barely knew, but this person had scrawled across the heavyweight bond, *Bring salmon salad for twelve.* Guess what didn't happen?

"What would you like, Humberto?" asked Yolanda, solicitous. "Dessert? An appetizer?"

"An appetizer would be lovely," he replied, smoothing back his long salt-and-pepper hair.

"I'll fix my famous spinach quiche," Ferdinanda hollered as he got into his car. "It's part Italian and part French. I used to make it for the rich people who came into the café in Havana. Now that you're a rich person, it will be perfect!"

Humberto pretended he did not hear. His long black car pulled away smoothly from the curb, and he was

gone. I knew export-import businesses could be profitable, but I did wonder if they could enable you to afford
a house on Black Bear Mountain or a top-of-the-line
Mercedes.

Yolanda and I made serious inroads on the packing
up that is an essential part of any catering undertaking. I
asked her once if she knew what Humberto did for
money, but she said only what I already knew about his
business. I wanted to ask her about Tom's insinuation
that Humberto had had a hand in a big jewelry theft, but
since Tom hadn't brought it up again, I didn't feel I had
permission to jump in.

We worked feverishly against the clock. But leaving
on time was not to be, alas. I figured I must have uncon-
sciously put out a karmic sign to the universe that day,
one that said, "Open house today! Please drop in to ask
for anything you want before eight in the morning."

When Yolanda and I were packing the last box for the
school's buffet lunch, the doorbell rang again. Jake and
the six remaining beagle puppies started howling. I
wondered where I'd put our headache medication.

Yolanda gave me another one of her fearful looks.

"Don't worry," I said. "If it was someone untrust-
worthy, Tom and Boyd would have stopped him or her."
But I raced down the hall anyway.

I looked through the peephole at a fortyish woman.
At first I couldn't place her, but then I remembered: This
small, mousy-looking lady with brown eyes like tiny
buttons and a cap of short, straight, dyed brown hair was
Penny Woolworth, Marla's and Kris Nielsen's cleaning
lady. Last night, Marla had told Tom that she'd ask if

Penny would take three of the puppies. I couldn't open the door fast enough.

"Hey, Penny, come into the kitchen. I'm catering today, and—"

"What's Ferdinanda doing out on your front porch?" she asked. "Why are your husband and that other man building a ramp? Is it for her?"

Well, great. Was Yolanda in danger? If Ferdinanda spent most of every day on the front porch, smoking cigars and monitoring the goings-on in the neighborhood, then it really wouldn't be long before the whole town knew they were at our place. Humberto Captain, obviously in a hurry to find out where Yolanda and Ferdinanda had taken up residence, had gone right to the source: Marla, early in the morning and without caffeine. I made a mental note to call my best friend and tell her not to give the news to anyone else.

I tried to think of what to say as I hung up Penny's coat. Penny did, after all, work for Kris Nielsen. Was there any way to prevent her from finding out exactly why Ferdinanda was outside? Was Yolanda still in the kitchen? That would not be such a big deal. Still, between the kitchen and the dining room, there was only a swing door. I gestured for Penny to precede me back down the hall. Unfortunately, as she walked into the kitchen, she quick-stepped over to the dining room door and swung it open. When she saw Yolanda making up the cots, Penny turned and faced me, her mouth formed into an O of surprise.

"Penny!" I exclaimed. "What the hell? Do I come into your house and nose around?"

She blushed scarlet. "I was just trying to—"

"Yeah, I know what you were just trying to do." I forced myself to soften my tone as I pointed to the far end of the kitchen. "Meet me over there." When we were by the back door, I said, "Please *don't* tell Kris they're staying here."

"He says he loves Yolanda more than life itself," Penny whispered. She crossed her small arms over her chest. "He's not a bad person, really, I mean, not really, *really* bad, he just has a hard time being faithful—"

"Penny?" I said, interrupting. "You want to keep your job with Marla, don't you?"

She gave me an angry frown. "All right! I won't tell Kris she's here. You don't have to threaten me. And anyway, Zeke and I have been talking about getting some dogs just forever."

My heart warmed toward her. "You're helping us by taking the dogs."

She hugged her sides in anticipation. "Won't Zeke be surprised when he hears I've adopted *three* beagles?"

I merely smiled and said, "Yolanda and I are about to leave for our catering assignment. Would you like to take a latte with you?"

I ground more coffee beans while Yolanda packed up the dogs, along with a can of Jake's food and some old towels I'd given her to line the cardboard box. She began weeping when she handed the container to Penny.

Penny, misreading the situation, said, "Kris will take you back, Yolanda." She heaved up the box, sending it slightly askew. The puppies slid sideways in the box and began whining. "No worries. I've got them. Look, Yolanda, Kris really misses—"

"I don't care about Kris! I'm just sad to lose the dogs,

Penny," Yolanda said, dashing the tears from her eyes. "They belonged to a friend."

"Oh?" Penny was immediately curious. "Who?"

I set the wand to steam Penny's milk on High. This was a neat trick to drown out conversation, because it sounded as if the space shuttle was taking off in the kitchen. Yolanda gave me a grateful glance while I pulled the shots. I quickly poured Penny's latte into a paper cup, and was glad when Tom and Boyd tromped into the kitchen to say the ramp was done and they were leaving.

"Let's us go, too!" I cried merrily as I used my non-latte-holding hand to grab Penny's arm, the way that Tom had taken Humberto Captain's. I stopped Penny in front of the hall closet, where she put down the box. I helped her into her coat. She gave a curious glance back at the kitchen before again picking up her box of dogs. "Yolanda," I said over my shoulder, "could you open the front door so Penny can walk to her car without having to put down the box again? I don't want to spill her coffee." Yolanda did so, and soon Penny and I were outside, where the chill seemed to be deepening by the minute.

"Goldy, just tell me," Penny said as she scrambled along beside me down our walk, "who had these dogs before you? I mean, why do you have so many? What's the big secret?"

"There's no secret." I noticed she had no purse. "Where are your keys?"

"Coat pocket."

I rummaged around in Penny's pocket and pulled out a tangle of keys. After opening her Jeep door, I placed the latte in the cup holder, took the box of puppies from her, and laid them on the passenger-side floor. In back were all manner of brooms, mops, and vacuum cleaners. Once again, I felt immensely sorry for her. It wasn't her fault her husband was a criminal; she'd been forced by his car kleptomania into a brutal schedule of house-cleaning.

"All right, Penny," I said. "They belonged to a friend who used to be a cop. He adopted them . . . and then he . . . died suddenly."

"*That* sucks." This seemed to satisfy her, as she got behind the wheel. "Well, I gotta go if I'm going to get these puppies home and then be at my first job."

"Wait. Penny? I need to ask you something. What day do you work for Kris Nielsen?"

She tucked in her tiny chin. "Why?"

"I just want to know who will be taking care of the dogs that day."

"Thursday," she replied. "Look, Goldy. I work every day. The dogs will be fine in our fenced backyard over in Spruce. If it snows, I'll put them in the basement. You don't believe me, you can come over on Thursday and check on them. Kris usually does his shopping that day, so I can get finished in just a few hours."

This answered my second question, which was if Kris was there when Penny cleaned.

"Thanks!" I said, then waved and walked back to the house. I was catering that day, the next, and Thursday night. But on Thursday during the *day,* I had absolutely no intention of checking on the dogs.

Chapter 9

In the Rockies, a storm is often preceded by strong winds, followed by a period of icy calm. Then the gale starts up again and the storm hits. Maybe that was what it was like when you were in the eye of a hurricane—minus the ice. As we passed Aspen Meadow Lake, the entire tinfoil sky, the pines, the aspens on the banks, were reflected in its silver surface. Frost had coated each pine needle and blade of wild grass. The effect was magical.

That morning, unfortunately, I was not able to appreciate the beauty of nature. If I thought Yolanda would not fret on the way to Denver, I was mistaken. Her frequent checks of the rearview mirror were punctuated by worries about Ferdinanda.

"She'll catch cold if she stays outside all day. What if she can't remember the security code to get back in?"

Then, "She smokes too much."

And finally, "What if the person who burned down Ernest's house finds out where we are and comes over and attacks her?"

"Yolanda," I said as we drove down the ramp to the interstate, "*please*. Your aunt strikes me as someone who can take care of herself." I wanted to ask whether she knew Ernest had made her such a huge beneficiary of his will. Another issue continued to niggle the back of my brain: What was the nature of Yolanda and Ernest's relationship, exactly? She'd said they were just friends, but did you leave a "friend" your house and property? Or did you leave it to a lover because you were afraid you were going to die soon?

Either that was the possible title of a morbid country song or I needed more coffee.

Anyway, Tom would kill me if I broached these subjects. So . . . I tried to stay nonchalant as I asked, "Do you want to talk about Ernest?"

"I am afraid. I'm afraid of his clients. I'm afraid of Kris. I'm afraid of whoever burned down our rental, of whoever burned down Ernest's house. I never used to be afraid, and now I live in fear."

I took a deep breath and tried to remember how I used to deal with Arch when he had unreasonable panic attacks during the divorce from the Jerk. I'd get him to catalog the fears, and then I'd try to defuse each one.

"What are you most afraid of? It doesn't have to be sensible."

"Kris. He hurt me."

"He hurt you," I repeated, and glanced over at Yolanda. Her spill of russet curls glinted in the cold light. She stopped talking and stared at her lap. This immediately made me paranoid, and so I felt it was now my duty to check the rearview mirror for . . . well, for what, exactly? I'd seen one Maserati in my entire life-time, and I'd thought it was a sports car made by Chrysler.

"Yes," she said, and her voice caught. "I keep think-ing about what he did to me and how I failed to pro-tect myself, protect Ferdinanda—"

"You know what? Enough already," I said as I sig-naled to exit the interstate.

"Enough of what? Where are you going?" Yolanda said. She looked around wildly. "Why are you taking this exit?"

"I'm just removing the threat." *Or trying to,* I added mentally.

I headed back west, took the exit for Aspen Meadow, then zipped through the entrance to Flicker Ridge. Yolanda shook her head as I raced to the top.

"You are making a mistake, Goldy," she warned, and in that moment, she sounded like Tom. Oh, well. I was going to do what I'd always wished I'd done with the Jerk: confront him, damn it.

I said, "That remains to be seen."

My van had more pickup than Yolanda's, so we were at the entrance to Kris Nielsen's mansion in less than two minutes. The place was all one level, and consisted of vast expanses of yellow stucco and numerous win-dows. The house was topped with a long red tile roof. It was enormous and looked less like a residence than the corporate headquarters for Taco Bell.

"Goldy," Yolanda said sharply, "*please* listen to me. This is a *very bad idea.*"

"You don't even know what my idea is," I said mildly,

although I wasn't quite sure what it was myself. How would I parry a thrust from a broom handle? I narrowed my eyes at the road. In my post-Jerk days, I'd taken self-defense lessons. If I needed that training, hopefully it would come back.

At the side of the road, I pulled behind a large cedar tree to conceal my van. Then I got out and jogged down the long driveway.

Well, well. Why was I *not* surprised to see Penny Woolworth's Jeep parked at the side of the house? If she'd left the dogs out in that cold car, I'd throw her carefully made latte in her face.

I stepped quickly around to the battered Jeep and checked the interior. No puppies. Was Penny leaving them there? Was it possible Kris Nielsen had thousands of square feet of white carpet? I certainly hoped so. I walked back to the front of the house, where I checked the porch for security cameras. There were none. I rang the bell, then stepped off to the side, out of the line of sight of the peephole.

"Who is it?" Penny's voice called meekly through the heavy wood a moment later.

"*Mountain Journal*!" I shouted, making my voice husky. "Need to see Mr. Nielsen!"

There was a pause. "Uh, about what?" Penny's tentative voice called back.

"Harboring stolen puppies! Open this door or I'm calling the cops! Like now, lady!"

She opened the door a crack. "The puppies aren't his, they're—"

I slammed the door open and stepped into a stuccoed

foyer. In my head, I could hear Tom's voice saying, *No, no, no.* But I pressed forward anyway. I stopped at the edge of the foyer beside the living room, which was filled with chrome and leather contemporary furniture. Beyond it was a dining room, its glass dining room table surrounded by uncomfortable-looking modern chairs. Overhead, a complicated tubular crystal chandelier glimmered. I whirled and glared at Penny Woolworth. "You work for him on *Thursdays,* huh? Today's Monday. Where is he?"

"I can't—"

"Listen to me, Penny, you tell me where he is, or I will call Tom and have Zeke held—"

"What's going on here?" asked Kris Nielsen from the dining room. Tall, with his shock of prematurely white hair swept back, Kris looked first at me, then at Penny, with genuine puzzlement. He wore a T-shirt, basketball shorts, and running shoes. The shirt made his arm and chest muscles pop out. I swallowed and realized what a really terrible idea it *had* been to come here. Kris walked toward me, holding out his hand. "We met once before, didn't we? You're Goldy?" His blue eyes were kind, merry even. "Is there a problem?" He looked back at Penny for some kind of explanation.

"I got the puppies from her," said Penny, looking down at an asymmetrically designed area rug.

"And?" asked Kris, still confused. I didn't shake his extended hand, so he dropped it to his side. When neither Penny nor I followed up on his question, he said, "Goldy, would you like to stay for a cup of coffee?"

"No, thanks," I said stiffly. "I have to be somewhere." I felt my courage evaporating, so I squared my shoulders and pointed at Kris. "Leave Yolanda and her aunt Ferdinanda alone. Leave *me* alone. She may have been afraid of pressing charges against you or of swearing out a restraining order against you, but *I am not.* Do you understand?"

"What?" he said in disbelief. He swayed back on his heels, as if I'd slapped him.

I turned my body and my pointing finger on Penny. "Whatever he's paying you for your efforts, it is *not worth it.*"

"I, I, I . . . ," said Penny helplessly. "Goldy, wait, you don't understand."

But since she offered no explanation of what I didn't understand, and since Kris was still struck dumb, it was time for me to boogie. In the distance—the garage, probably—I could hear the puppies whining. I raced back to the van.

"How'd it go?" Yolanda asked, staring straight ahead.

"About as well as you'd expect." I started the van and pulled away from the curb. When we reached the exit of Flicker Ridge, I picked up my cell and hit the speed dial for Tom. If Tom couldn't do anything else, he could at least come up here and get Ernest's beagles back . . . or something.

Unfortunately, Tom picked up on the first ring. "Miss G.? I just got off the phone with Kris Nielsen. What were you thinking?"

Nonplussed, I steered the van toward the interstate. This particular turn of events was not what I was expecting. I stared hard out the windshield and said, "I wasn't exactly thinking."

"*That* much is clear." He was quiet for so long, it made me uncomfortable. Yolanda, staring out her window, was no help. Finally Tom sighed. "He was very upset. Says he has no idea why you barged into his house. He says he invited you to have a cup of coffee, and you threatened him. Did you threaten him? You didn't take a weapon into his house, did you? A knife, say? Tell me you didn't."

"Tom, I didn't even take a wooden spoon in there."

"Well, that much is good, I suppose. I did some shucking and jiving with him, said we had strong anti-stalking laws in this state, that I'd heard his Maserati myself this morning—"

"You heard it?" I said, incredulous. "You never told me that! How did you know it was a, ah—" I glanced over at Yolanda. I didn't want her to know what I was talking about. "How did you know what it was?"

"Oh, Miss G. If I didn't know my cars by now, I would not be worthy of the title *Police Officer*." He paused. "Neither Boyd nor I actually saw Kris this morning, and he insists he was working out on his exercise machines. At home. Maybe it was somebody else's Mas, who knows. But people in our neighborhood can barely afford to put clothes on their kids' backs. They don't have the dough for that kind of vehicle."

"Exactly!" I said. "That's why I—"

"Miss G. I have to go. I'm in the middle of a homicide investigation, remember? I promised Kris Nielsen that you would *not* attempt to contact him in *any way* in the future, all right?"

"Oh-*kay*."

"Those anti-stalking statutes apply to you, too, Miss G. Do you understand?"

"Tom, please stop." We signed off, not happily.

"What did Tom say?" Yolanda asked.

"Nothing, really. He just wants me to leave Kris alone."

Yolanda snorted. "That's rich."

Outside, the mantle of gray cloud had grown much darker. The wind started up again, this time with such force that it violently swept leaves, pine needles, and bits of trash across the highway. The thermometer in my van indicated the external temperature was thirty-one. When we reached the Ooh-Ah Bridge, with its spectacular view of the Continental Divide—which was behind us—the first snowflakes began to fall.

I cursed silently. These were tiny flakes, the kind that signal a true storm, not a flurry. Worse, the snowflakes didn't drift slowly downward, they sped sideways with such ferocity and thickness that a sudden, dense white curtain made visibility difficult. First the view of the plains, usually so clear when you're heading east, disappeared. Then I couldn't make out the road a hundred yards in front of us. Eventually, I couldn't see the road ten yards ahead. I got into the middle lane and slowed the van way down.

Yolanda transferred her worry to the weather. "Think they'll still have these physicals? It looks pretty bad. Maybe you should call and see if the school is going to cancel."

"Something involving sports at a Catholic high school?" I replied, straining to see out the windshield.

"Those kids and parents would turn out if we had flash floods, a tornado, and ten inches of basketball-size hail."

And they did. By the time we got to Denver and turned onto the street that led to the Christian Brothers High School, the snow was mixed with rain. We passed the crowded parking lot and pulled up near the kitchen entrance. We were late, but it was only half past nine. We needed to be done setting up in two hours. The buffet lunch wasn't due to start until noon, but hungry teenage athletes would be ready to eat at half past eleven, if not earlier.

Plus, I had to make sure I connected with Charlene Newgate at noon. I hoped I'd be able to find her in the gym.

Alas, the kitchen doors were locked. Yolanda guarded the van—in case someone came along and told us we had to move—while I went inside to hunt for the athletic director, Tony Ramos. Tony was supposed to have unlocked the kitchen doors, and I didn't have his cell phone number.

A deafening amount of noise echoed off the tiled walls of the hallways. I checked Tony Ramos's office: empty. I shot down the hallway and pushed my way into the gym, where the din was even louder than in the halls. Parents, students, doctors, nurses, and volunteers packed the space in a free-for-all atmosphere that was like a postgame celebration. The walls were hung with banners announcing championships the school had won in various sports. Someone with a bullhorn was trying unsuccessfully to impose order on the chaos. Parents called to one another in recognition, teachers made out name tags, and there was an excited buzz among the kids: Would the developing storm mean school might be canceled the next day?

While I was looking for Tony Ramos, I bumped into Sean Breckenridge. This was not a metaphorical bumping but a quite literal one, as my attention was focused on searching for Tony. Sean had been holding an over-size camera up to his eye, and neither of us saw the other until I'd whacked his lens and ended up on the gym floor. My elbow immediately screamed with pain, but I pressed my lips together.

"Oh, gosh," he proclaimed. "I'm sorry!"

"It's my fault," I said after he'd helped me up. "Are you all right? Did I mess up your camera? I'm sorry." As I said this, I pushed up my sleeve, which had torn. Blood spurted from my elbow.

Sean looked away quickly. "Did I, did I do that?"

"No, I did," I said, pulling my sleeve down to my wrist. "Sean?"

He looked back at me cautiously. When he saw my sleeve was back in place, he used the long fingers of his free hand to brush his thinning dark hair over to one side. He glanced at his camera, which seemed to have weathered my impact. "Yes?"

"Are you all right?"

Embarrassment flooded Sean's thin face. He cleared his throat. "Fine, thank you."

He clearly wasn't, but since the last time we'd talked he hung up on me, I said quickly, "Have you seen Tony Ramos? The athletic director?"

"Yes," Sean said slowly "I just took a picture of him with the basketball team. I'll show you where he was."

I followed Sean's tall, bowlegged body. The camera seemed to weigh him down, so that he listed like a leaking ship. At one point, he seemed to remember something and reached into his pocket. He pulled out a tissue and wiped his face.

"Are you sure you're all right?" I asked.

"I'm fine," he said, then hoisted his camera again and resumed his slow, tilted walk across the gym floor.

Wait a minute. Camera?

"Sean, what are you doing here?" I rushed up to his side. I mean, he was the senior warden of our Episcopal church in Aspen Meadow, and his only child was five. Marla had said the kid was precocious, but I doubted he was in high school already. "Are you the official school photographer?"

Sean shook his head as we threaded our way around clumps of students and parents. When we passed the entrance to the locker rooms, the odor of sweat almost knocked me flat. Sean said something unintelligible, and I hustled up to his side.

"I didn't hear you," I said.

"I'm the *volunteer* school photographer. They needed somebody, so here I am." After a moment, he said bitterly, "There's Tony."

He pointed at Tony Ramos, a short, muscular fellow with close-clipped gray hair straight as a bristle brush. Tony Ramos had been the subject of media coverage this summer, when a national sporting goods company had bought a contraption he'd invented for the CBHS girls' fast-pitch softball team. Tony had christened it the Pitch Bitch, but when the sporting-goods company had bought the thing for an estimated eight figures, they'd vowed to change it to something more "acceptable to young women." Tony, not the most garrulous of people in ordinary circumstances, had said, "No comment." When asked if he would retire from CBHS, he said merely, "No." Now he was listening to a very pretty woman whom I could see only in profile. She was making comments, bending in toward Tony, and then laughing flirtatiously. When she turned and put her hand on Tony's arm, I cringed. I recognized her: Brie Quarles.

"Tony?" I said. Sean Breckenridge slithered away. "Sorry to bother you, but we need to—"

"The kitchen door!" he said, slapping his forehead. "I'm so sorry, Goldy. Brie," he said, turning to her, "I'd love to hear more. Some other time, okay?"

"All righty!" said Brie as she caught sight of me in my workplace kitchen duds. Her smile faded and she turned away. Even though we were both parishioners at St. Luke's, and we both ostensibly subscribed to the idea that being Christian meant, at the very least, being *nice* to each other, I clearly wasn't important enough to merit a bit of conversation.

"Hello, Brie," I called after her. She stopped and turned around, giving me as blasé a look as possible. Despite the weather, she wore a pink polo shirt, khaki shorts, and flashy metallic flats. I certainly hoped she had a good winter coat somewhere in the gym. I said merrily, "I'm catering the church fund-raising dinner at the Breckenridges' place tomorrow night. You're going to be a guest?"

"What is this," she asked, "twenty questions?" And with that, she whirled on one of her flats and flounced away to talk to someone more important.

Well, I thought as I accompanied Tony Ramos to the kitchen entrance, *that was interesting.* A truism I'd heard expressed on the radio suddenly came to mind: that the Church of England—in America, the Episcopal Church—is the last bastion standing in the way of the spread of Christianity. I wasn't quite that cynical, because I did love Saint Luke's, and the parish did a great deal of good in the community. In any event, I would have to grill Marla on the possibility that the reason the *married* Brie Quarles had been under surveillance was that she was fooling around with the *married* athletic director of Christian Brothers High School.

Tony, feeling remorseful about not being where he was supposed to be when we arrived, helped us schlep in all the boxes. The man was strong, I'd give him that. He then commandeered four athletes to move the two long tables we'd be using to serve food in the gym. In fact, Tony and his soldiers helped so much, our work took half the time I'd allotted.

And lo and behold, who should walk into the kitchen but Arch! I hadn't seen my own sixteen-year-old son for two days. As usual, I noticed how he was becoming tall and gangly. Also as usual, his disheveled, toast-colored hair looked as if it hadn't seen a comb lately. The gray circles under his brown eyes indicated he'd stayed up too late with his pals. But he looked happy.

"Hey, Mom." A shy smile flickered across his face. "How're you doing?"

"Fine, thanks." I tilted my head at Yolanda, who was arranging the pork on large platters. "Yolanda and her great-aunt, Ferdinanda, are staying with us for a few days. They're on cots in the dining room."

Arch lit up as Yolanda walked over. "Cool! Is this the aunt who smokes cigars?"

Yolanda grinned at him. "Yup. But you're not allowed to have any."

"I'm in training," Arch joked. "No smoking, no booze."

"Arch!" I cried.

"Gotcha, Mom." He surveyed the food. "Looks great. I need to ask you for something. One of the kids on our team? He's been diagnosed with leukemia and started his treatment. Could I bring him some lunch?"

"I'll do it," I said, and swiftly put together cutlery and a dish full of food.

"He'll never eat that much," Arch warned as he blinked at the loaded plate. "He's here because he missed being with the team. But he doesn't want the other kids to stare at him in the gym, so the team is gathered in one of the halls with him, and his mom's going to pick him up by a side door."

"Just lead the way."

Arch did. We entered a warren of hallways and eventually came to a tunnel of lockers with a clutch of boys at the end. A pile of sabers, épées, and foils indicated practice was over. The kids were seated around an emaciated, bald classmate whose skin was a terrible color. I got down on my knees, introduced myself, and handed him the plate. Arch had brought a bottle of water.

"Thanks," the boy said as he looked at me with eyes that looked huge. "I'm Peter."

"Well, enjoy," I replied.

Peter's forehead wrinkled. He said to his teammates, "So am I going to eat this while all of you are watching me?"

"Yeah," replied one of the kids, "and after that, we're going home to shave our heads, so we can look like you, too!"

They all laughed, then started talking, apparently to divert attention away from Peter so that he would not, indeed, be embarrassed. Several of the boys began to gather the equipment, while a couple got to their feet to open their lockers. Then there was a crash and a whoop of pain.

Everyone stopped moving and looked at Peter, who swallowed what was in his mouth. "It wasn't me, guys."

"It was me!" shouted one of the boys, whom I couldn't see. "What the hell, Boats," the kid, still invisible, shouted, "can't you look where you're opening your locker door?"

Boats, aka Alexander Boatfield III, closed his locker door, revealing a kid holding on to his nose, which was bleeding profusely. "Oh, Jesus," said Boats. "I'm sorry, Mikulski. I didn't see you there."

"That's obvious!" cried the offended Mikulski. I did not know this kid, whose last name was Mikulski. He must have been a new member of the team. What worried me more at the moment was that his hand could not contain the red flood from his nose. Blood dripped down his shirt and onto the floor.

"All right," I said authoritatively, "I want to take you to the nurse. Arch, give him a shirt. Mikulski, sorry I don't know your first name—"

"Brad!"

"Brad," I said calmly, "we need to see if your nose is broken. Let's go." I took Brad's free arm and signaled to Arch to lead the way back.

"This sucks!" Brad howled as I guided him down the hallway. "I'm going to look like shit for the school picture!"

"Cool it, Mikulski," Arch said in a low voice once we'd turned a corner. "Peter's a lot worse off than you, and you don't hear him crying."

"Jesus, Arch, I'm in pain here! Have a little compassion!"

Arch looked at me and rolled his eyes. The three of us tried to hustle along, but since Brad had his head tipped back, it was slow going. Just before the next hallway corner, I heard a clanking that I could not immediately identify. Then Sean Breckenridge, carrying all his photographic equipment, hove into view, and before Arch and I could pull Brad Mikulski back, Sean banged right into him.

"Jesus H. Christ!" hollered Mikulski. "Is this the blind leading the blind or what?"

"Omigod," murmured Sean Breckenridge, looking at me. "I'm sorry, I was in such a hurry that I didn't pay attention to where I was going. Goldy, have you seen—" In midquestion, Sean happened to look over at Brad

Mikulski, who had lowered his chin to see who'd plowed into him. Brad's blood was everywhere at this point—on his face, his shirt, Arch's shirt—and it was dripping onto the floor.

Sean Breckenridge's mouth dropped open and his cheeks paled. His eyes rolled upward as he keeled forward.

"Arch!" I shouted. "Catch him!"

Arch deftly stepped into Sean Breckenridge's trajectory, absorbed the weight of his fall, and lowered him to the floor.

"I swear, this is getting out of hand," said Brad Mikulski, staring down at an unconscious Sean Breckenridge. "We're going to have to open a ward on hallway B. Somebody needs to call a priest."

"Sit down on the floor, Brad," I ordered. "Arch, run and get us some help, would you, please? Ask them to bring compresses and ammonia salts."

Brad Mikulski sat on the floor, lifted his chin, and cut his glance sideways at Sean Breckenridge. "It's just a little blood, man. Why do you have to be such a wuss?"

Moments later, Arch reappeared with two nurses. One was fortyish and slender; the other, young, bulky, and blond, appeared to be an assistant. Both wore the blue PJ-type scrubs common these days among their profession. Unsure of the extent of the injuries, each was carrying a first-aid kit. The older one gave instructions to the younger, who held a small tube of ammonia salts under Sean's nose. He jerked awake, looking confused. The other nurse shook her head at Brad Mikulski, who, in turn, was watching the goings-on with Sean Breckenridge with interest.

The older nurse said wearily, "What have you done to yourself this time, Mikulski?"

While Brad Mikulski was in the middle of his protestations that he hadn't done anything, the problem was what had been done to him, the nurse interrupted him. She told me she and her colleague would handle the situation, and that Arch and I could go back to whatever it was we'd been doing before the collision.

"Do you know how to get to the gym from here?" Arch asked me.

When I said that I was sure I did not, my son began to lead me. As we walked along, I asked about Peter's condition.

"We don't know much," Arch said protectively. "Please don't ask me a bunch of questions I can't answer."

"Oh-*kay*." Was I *that* nosy? Well, probably yes.

Arch furrowed his brow, as if he were trying to remember something important. "Somebody said that— outside?—it's snowing to beat the band."

"It's coming down in Aspen Meadow," I said. "You won't be home too late, will you?"

"Gus's grandparents invited Todd and me over for dinner. They said they'd bring me home, too. Remember, my car's in our garage? You were afraid the radials weren't going to be good enough to get through the winter, and you wanted to get real snow tires for it."

"Right, we'll get to that. Speaking of which, I'm worried about the weather. The snow is coming down *really* hard, so please ask the Vikarioses to bring you home early. Like nine at the latest?"

"Sure." He deposited me at the door of the kitchen. "Thanks for being nice to Peter. And to Mikulski, too."

"Arch, of course I would be nice to—" But my son had taken off. As I watched his retreating back, I wished I'd asked who Peter's mother was. I simply couldn't imagine being in her shoes. The pain she must have been feeling . . . I wondered about Peter's prognosis. Arch was always accusing me of nosiness, so it sure didn't feel right to be digging around in this.

Then again, what about Brad Mikulski? Was his mother Hermie, the one who might have hired Ernest to look into the puppy mill, over her son's supposed objections? Brad didn't come to church, so I hadn't seen them together. Still, I shook my head at the fact that I'd been too preoccupied by Brad's blood and Sean Breckenridge's reaction to it to ask. I took a deep breath and focused on the work at hand, which was feeding a big crowd of athletes, parents, teachers, and medical personnel.

When I returned to the gym, Tony Ramos was speaking into the bullhorn, and the kids were organizing themselves according to his instructions. The physicals would continue through lunch, Tony announced. When Yolanda and I started to serve at quarter to twelve, two lines of more or less disciplined kids moved along both sides of the tables, piling their plates high with salads, buffalo wings, sandwiches, and cookies. The school provided the drinks: water, milk, and juices—no pop, thank goodness—so that was one less thing to deal with.

As I spooned a refill of Caprese salad into one of the buffet bowls, I saw something that gave me a start. It was a kid, a boy, not very tall, overweight, with tufts of light brown hair sticking out at all angles from his head.

He was holding himself somewhat apart, which made his lumpy stomach stand out even more. I'd never seen him at CBHS, and if he was from our church, I didn't recognize him. But I knew him, somehow. Arch had re-entered the gym with his team, so I caught his eye and motioned him over.

"Don't look now," I said surreptitiously as I deposited the last few tomato slices into the bowl, "but there's a heavy kid nearby, and he looks familiar. Is he from Aspen Meadow? Is he new to the school?"

Arch leaned over the salad bowl. "I don't need to look. It's Otto Newgate, and he was a year behind me at Aspen Meadow Elementary. I tried to talk to him, you know, welcome him to CBHS, but he said he didn't want to be here at all, that his grandmother insisted he come. And get this. His grandmother wants him to try out for the basketball team, so he's getting his physical. This school won the state *championship* last year. One member of the team is thinking of skipping college and going straight to the pros. Even CBHS's *junior* varsity beat other *senior* varsities. Otto has exactly no chance of making either basketball team."

"Oh, no."

Arch said, "I mean, I feel sorry for Otto. I do. But if he doesn't want to be here, then he should just tell his grandmother, no dice. Can I go now?"

"Yes, buddy. Thanks."

Charlene Newgate! It was ten minutes after noon, and I'd been so busy worrying about Arch's sick teammate, and dealing with the buffet, I'd almost forgotten I was due to meet her. And I certainly hadn't put much thought into what I was going to say when I saw her, beyond bluffing about invitations to a doctor's catered event. I knew I needed to ask questions that wouldn't scare her off or do anything else to upset Tom.

I asked Yolanda to take over, which she did. I scanned the gym bleachers for Charlene. Would I even recognize her? I wondered.

Finally I caught sight of her, up high, wearing a fur, yes, *fur* coat that she had wrapped tightly around her. It wasn't particularly cold in the gym, either. What with all the animal lovers in the Denver area, Charlene was running a risk wearing real fur anywhere outside her house. Still, the CBHS kids were not, I thought, the paint-throwing types. At least, I hoped they weren't.

To the best of my knowledge, Charlene hadn't come through the line, so I made her a sandwich and put large servings of Caprese and potato salads next to it. Then I double-timed it to the top bleacher.

"Charlene!" I greeted her, gasping from the exertion of climbing. "Sorry I didn't make it right at noon. Please have some lunch." I handed her the plate.

"I was beginning to wonder if you'd remembered, Goldy." She shrugged off the coat. Charlene looked older than someone in her fifties. No doubt, the stress of being both a single mother and a single grandmother had taken their toll. Like her grandson, she had thin, light brown hair that formed uneven tufts around her head. She was a bulky woman, but instead of the jeans and T-shirt I'd always seen her in, this day she was dressed stunningly, in charcoal wool slacks with a matching sweater. Her thick ankles were swathed in black leather boots.

"Charlene," I said, "you look like you've won the lottery."

She spooned a bite of salad into her mouth, taking care not to get any on her clothes. She chewed, nodded her approval, then said, "I have a new boyfriend." Her whole face seemed to twinkle as she smiled at me. "He's good to me."

"How nice." I meant it. "Is he here? Can I meet him?"

Distrust flared in her eyes. "No. He has lots of business projects. You wanted to talk to me about those invitations you need addressed?"

"Well, actually," I said, improvising, "it was a Halloween party, for a dentist? Drew Parker? He called just as we were leaving the house to come here. He's in Hawaii—it must have been the middle of the night there—anyway, his practice isn't doing so well, so he's not having me cater the party after all. In fact, he's not even going to have a party."

Charlene snorted and looked away. "All these years, I've been slaving away running a secretarial service. I've watched the doctors, dentists, lawyers, and businessmen I work for get richer and richer. Now I'm the one doing well, and I have no sympathy."

I ignored her very palpable resentment, sat down next to her, and pretended to focus on the kids in the gym. "It's so good your business is doing well. So, do you know Drew Parker? I mean, do you ever do work for him?"

She eyed me again, and I put on my most innocent-looking face. She trained her gaze on the gym floor. "I've already talked to the police, if that's what you're getting at—"

"Oh, no!" I lied. "The police? About what?"

Charlene looked away. "My service has worked for a lot of professionals in Aspen Meadow. Practically all of them, if you want to know the truth. I told the police, Drew Parker's name doesn't ring a bell."

"I understand. I have a *lot* of clients, too. By the time I've finished serving dessert? I can't remember half of their names." I paused. "My business is suffering, though. I'm glad yours is doing well."

She gave me a look that would have curdled cream. "You have enough money to send your son here," she rejoined. "Now Otto can have all the advantages that other kids have." She lifted her wobbly, stout chin. "He's going to do real well." She opened her light brown eyes wide at me, and I blinked. She leaned in toward me, and I got a whiff of her powdery scent. "Who says money can't buy happiness? Not me!"

Tony Ramos interrupted us with his bullhorn. He announced that the athletes had to finish their lunches and get their physicals, if they had not already done so, because the doctors and nurses needed to leave.

"Goldy Schulz!" A harsh female voice interrupted my visit with Charlene.

"Oh, Christ," said Charlene under her breath. She picked up her plate and handed it to me. "Keep me away from that crazy woman, will you?"

I said, "What crazy woman?"

"Go!" Charlene told me. "Get out of here!"

I held the plate carefully with both hands, turned around so as to face the gym, and scanned the bleachers.

"Goldy Schulz!" the abrasive voice called again. The

parents who sat all around, instead of paying attention to Tony Ramos, turned to look at me. Even some of the kids out on the gym floor stared upward.

At length I saw the woman calling me. My heart plummeted. Hermie Mikulski, her prematurely gray hair crimped in sharp curlicues all around her head, her tall, commanding body encased in a tube of pale gray wool, stood at the bottom of the steps, her hands on her hips.

"Coming!" I called weakly. I hadn't seen Hermie Mikulski since the annual meeting of our parish, the previous January. Whenever I'd greeted her at church, I'd received a cold nod in reply, which I figured was just her way. But now she was screaming at me? Why? Was she blaming me for her son's bloody nose?

When I reached the gym floor, I clutched Charlene's plate between me and Hermie, like a kind of shield. To forestall a verbal attack, I quickly said, "Is Brad your son? I'm sorry that he—"

Hermie tossed her head. "I'm not here about Brad." The area between her gray eyebrows furrowed. "Why were you talking to that woman?" When Hermie pointed up at Charlene, I noticed something that made my mouth fall open. Where two of Hermie's fingers on her left hand should have been, there were only stumps.

"Hermie?" I asked. "When did—" In my mind, I could hear Arch's voice saying, *Being nosy, Mom?* I had the presence of mind to say, "What woman would that be?"

"That welfare cheat, Charlene Newgate! Look at her up there, wearing a *fur coat*. I pity the animal who died for that woman. Oh," she trilled, squinting and nodding ominously in Charlene's direction, "Charlene's got herself a sugar daddy now. Never mind that he's a criminal."

"A criminal? Who is he?" I asked breathlessly.

When Hermie turned her angry, trembling chin at me, I felt something like wool at the back of my throat. Hermie said, "I heard on the news that Ernest McLeod was dead. I take it your husband is looking into it?"

"Well—"

Hermie drew herself and her massive bosom upward, and took a deep breath. "Ernest was working for *me.*"

I swallowed. Was I supposed to let on that I already knew this? I said, "Oh? Doing what?"

"How far along is your husband in the investigation?"

"I don't know," I said truthfully.

"Have him call me," Hermie said. With that command, she turned on her squat heels and marched away.

"You could always call him," I said to empty air.

I had wanted to ask Charlene Newgate more questions, and I now certainly wanted to ask Hermie Mikulski more questions, such as *What happened to your hand?* But it seemed both women had dismissed me. I dashed across the gym to help with the cleanup.

Yolanda was already hard at work, washing the metal serving dishes. We'd used paper plates and cups, as the school didn't want even the possibility of broken china or glass on their expertly sprung gym floor. The washing-up operation took less than an hour. A few stragglers were still in the gym, one doctor, three kids, and assorted parents. Sean Breckenridge had left. Brie Quarles was still there, and once again she was hanging on to

Tony Ramos. What in the hell was going on with them? I wondered. Maybe Brie wanted *her* son to make the basketball team. Well, Marla would know.

Otto Newgate and his grandmother were among the last to leave. Charlene had expertly wrapped a scarf around her head. She lifted that chin of hers and pulled her fur around her, Tallulah Bankhead bidding me a grand farewell. Otto held on to his wide stomach. He looked absolutely miserable.

Outside, the rain had completely turned to snow. An astonishing six inches had already accumulated on the school's football field. The pavement, which had been slightly warmer, only had about four inches of white stuff, but the snow was falling even harder than it had been when we came down from Aspen Meadow.

"We'd better hurry," Yolanda said as she heaved one of our boxes into the van. "I'm worried about Ferdinanda."

Ferdinanda! "Oh, dear," I said as I pushed in my last box. "I promised her I'd go to an ethnic grocery store and get her some guava marmalade, or preserves, I can't remember which. Do you know?"

Yolanda said, "I sure do. Want to let me drive?"

With a check from the school stuffed into my pocket, I relaxed, finally, in the passenger seat. Yolanda revved the van engine and got in line to exit the school parking lot. I was stunned by the amount of snow we were getting, but knew there was nothing we could do about it. It was while I was looking out the window that I saw something else that astonished me. Charlene and her grandson were getting into a car, hers, apparently, because she was easing herself into the driver's seat. The bumper sticker read, SECRETARIES DO IT BEHIND THE DESK.

It was a 7-series BMW. That was some boyfriend.

It took longer than either Yolanda or I would have imagined to get to the Capitol Hill area of Denver and the ethnic grocery store. Even though Denverites are used to driving in snow, the *first* snowfall of the season, whether it comes in September, October, or even November, invariably paralyzes the city. Plus, since it was technically still summer, I doubted most folks had given a thought to snow tires, which slowed them down even more. Still, we eventually arrived at the store, which was called merely Ethnic Foods. Their parking lot was almost full. This told me that people had convinced themselves that they absolutely had to have their picante sauce and caviar if they were going to be snowed in, whether it was for a day or a week.

"Was it near here that Ferdinanda was hit?" I asked nonchalantly.

"Yes. Why?"

"Just wondering."

Yolanda pointed me in the direction of the jams and said Ferdinanda liked guava marmalade. She said she needed sour pickles and would meet me at the front. I snagged a basket, found guava marmalade, and put it in my basket. Mission accomplished, I headed toward the row of cash registers, eager to get home before rush hour.

And we would have made it, maybe, if a huge crash, shattering, and tinkling of breaking glass, plus a lot of screaming, had not emerged from one aisle over.

"Get away from me!" Yolanda screamed. "Who sent you? Why did you bump into me? To scare me? Did Kris send you to hurt me?" There were more explosions and splinterings of glass. I rushed toward the ruckus.

"Stop it!" a male voice pleaded. Wait, that was a voice I knew, didn't I? "You're not acting logically," the man said, his voice raised. "Stop hitting me! I don't want to hurt you!"

"I'm calling the police!" Yolanda shrieked.

I raced toward the source of the racket. It was hard to see what was going on, because light reflected off a field of glass shards. The acrid scent of brine made me pull back. What looked like at least twenty broken jars of pickles and olives were strewn everywhere. Yolanda, stricken, was holding herself flat against the pickle shelves. And on the floor, disheveled, drenched in pickle juice and olive brine, his face red with mortification, was the man who loved to cook with genuine kalamata olives, our very large, very Greek, Saint Luke's parish priest, Father Pete.

"Yolanda, it's all right," I said soothingly. "This is our priest. Our rector. It's okay." I realized I was still gripping my basket, which I put on the floor.

"He pushed me. He bumped into me hard, on purpose," she said. She pressed her lips together, perhaps realizing that a priest would not intentionally hurt her.

"I'm sorry, I didn't mean to touch you," said Father Pete. "I was reading a label, and I thought I barely touched you. Okay, look, I'm sorry I bumped into you. I'm absentminded. Mea culpa."

"I don't believe you," said Yolanda, her voice still trembling.

"I can vouch for this man," I said to Yolanda as soothingly as possible. I turned to our poor rector, who was, indeed, absentminded, and renowned for trying to do two things at once, like backing up and reading a label. Usually, like this time, he failed at both undertakings. "Father Pete, are you all right?" I swallowed. "Can I help you get up?"

Father Pete grunted. "I'm fine. I can get up on my own." He brushed his dark, curly hair away from his face and groaned as he heaved himself to his feet. He then tried to step around the olives and pickles littering the aisle. A clerk appeared, a cell phone in one hand and a mop in the other. She looked from one person in our little trio to the other, waiting for direction.

"It's all right," I told her, trying to sound authoritative. "We had a little mix-up here. Sorry about the mess."

"If everyone would just leave the aisle," she said miserably, "I can clean up."

So we did, and Father Pete, who looked much worse than Yolanda, wanted to know if we were all right. Father Pete seemed particularly concerned about Yolanda, whom he tried to help away from the pickles, where she remained flattened. She bristled at his touch.

"I've known Father Pete myself for several years," I murmured to her. "He's a good man. Please come out of the aisle, so the grocery lady can clean up."

Yolanda moved away, finally, after picking up her brine-soaked purse and taking two jars of pickles, which she clutched in each hand like weapons. I nabbed my basket and headed toward the cash registers. Father Pete abandoned his cart.

While Yolanda paid for her merchandise, Father Pete whispered to me, "I promise, Goldy, I didn't hurt her."

"I know, Father Pete," I replied. "She's a little touchy these days." While Yolanda talked to the cashier, I lowered my voice even further, thinking I would try to explain the situation to Father Pete. "Do you happen to know Kris Nielsen?" I asked. *Oops,* I thought. I had not received Yolanda's permission to talk about her problems with Father Pete.

"Oh, Kris is wonderful." Father Pete's tone was suddenly warm, and he gave me the benefit of his benevolent brown eyes. "He's been *very* generous to the parish, and he's always trying to help those in need. Why?"

"He's a member?" I had never once seen Kris Nielsen at Saint Luke's. I looked up at Yolanda, who was watching me talk to Father Pete. I signaled that I'd be there in a moment, and she went back to talking to the cashier.

"He's not officially a member," Father Pete replied. "He travels a lot with his work, so he can't come on Sundays."

What work? I wondered. Kris didn't work. Maybe he wanted to sleep in on Sundays. I said, "And what do you mean, Kris is always trying to help those in need?"

"Oh, my! He outfitted our Sunday school rooms with all new furniture. He bought a lovely rug for the parish meeting room—"

"You said he helped those in *need*," I reminded him. "Like, people."

Father Pete straightened. "Yes, yes. A couple of months ago, he called because he was looking into convalescent facilities in Denver. I can tell you about this, without giving any names, since you ask. Anyway, Kris said he knew an elderly woman who belonged in a nursing home. He was willing to foot the entire bill. But this woman's great-niece, who was a dear friend of his, could not see the problem. So Kris said he needed me to step in. I asked him if the elderly woman was of sound mind. Kris said she was not. I asked if a doctor would sign off on the elderly woman's mental incompetence, and Kris said, 'Oh, well, she's very clever, she could fool anyone.' I told him I probably couldn't aid him, then, and he was saddened by that, because he clearly wanted to help his friend, the great-niece."

I said, "Clearly." *Yeah, right.* I wanted to tell him about the venereal disease, about the broomstick attack, about the possibility that Kris had been stalking Yolanda. But I knew that both Yolanda and Father Pete would not want me to. "Father Pete, I wonder if you could keep this whole incident in the grocery store between us? You, me, Yolanda, the pickles, and the olives?"

Father Pete's look of puzzlement was replaced by what I thought of as his smooth, pastoral expression. If I wanted him to keep something quiet, that was exactly what he would do. "Do you and Tom still want me to take in some rescue puppies?"

I rocked back on my heels. I'd forgotten that Father Pete was our last adoptive parent for Ernest's dogs. "Yes, please, oh, yes." I looked outside at the snow, now a raging blizzard. We'd be lucky to get home without incident. "Will tomorrow be all right?"

"Of course," said Father Pete, brightening. "I have a four-wheel-drive vehicle, if this snow becomes too much." He held his hand up to Yolanda, as if to bid her a fond farewell. Then he leaned into me, while he continued to smile at Yolanda. In his low voice again, he said, "I think your friend needs professional help."

Chapter 10

I tried to keep my teeth from chattering as we dashed to the van. Neither of us had worn a jacket that was thick enough. It was my fault; I should have packed us each a down parka and a pair of waterproof boots. I guess I really hadn't believed that a storm of this magnitude could happen in the middle of September. Clearly, I'd been in denial.

There was no denying this, though: Heaven was blowing snow down on us with unmitigated ferocity. I piloted the van to Eighth Avenue and headed west. Traffic was heavy. It was just past five, so we were in the full grip of rush hour. All around, taillights glowed like rubies in the mist.

Every now and then, the snow would sift downward in a straight, fast-falling curtain. Most of the time the wind buffeted the tiny flakes crazily, first from one side, then from the other. The drivers around us braked carefully, even allowed people in when they turned. In general, Coloradans try to help one another during storms, for which I was thankful.

I asked Yolanda if she was all right, and she said she was fine. She was shivering, though, so I insisted she snuggle under an old blanket kept stashed in the van's back. She nabbed it and wrapped it around herself.

The radio announced that a genuine winter storm was upon us. *Gee, d'ya think?* Denver was due to get high winds and up to a foot of snow by midnight. Up to eighteen inches was predicted for the mountains, including Aspen Meadow. People with four-wheel-drive vehicles were asked to bring doctors to local hospitals, in case they were needed. Some ski resorts, the announcer breathlessly concluded, were hoping to open in October. At least some people were happy.

The van inched westward. I gripped the steering wheel while trying to make out the shapes of the cars around us. I hoped, but did not really believe, that Gus's grandparents would cancel the dinner they'd planned for the boys. I tried Arch's cell but was connected to voice mail. I left him a message asking that he call when he was on his way home.

"Would it be all right if we phoned Ferdinanda?" Yolanda asked.

"Of course." I handed her the cell.

A moment later, Yolanda was talking to Ferdinanda, once again in Spanish. I understood "*¿Cuándo?*" and "*¿Marla?*" and "*Tres,*" and that was about it. Eventually, she promised we'd be home in about an hour, if we were lucky, two if we weren't. Or at least, that's what my limited command of the language made out.

"Ferdinanda's fine," Yolanda informed me. "So are the puppies. When it got cold this afternoon, she brought them inside and cuddled them in her lap. Oh, and three people came to your house."

"Three people? All together? Or one after another?"

"I got the impression they were all together. Judging from the way they were dressed, she thought they might be from a real estate agency. But she wasn't sure. Anyway, she didn't answer the doorbell, because she was afraid that if they were bad people—her words—they could overpower a person in a wheelchair and come inside and rob the place." I glanced over. Yolanda was rubbing her forehead. "I know, I know. She's paranoid."

I thought, *She's not the only one, O smasher of pickle jars,* but said only, "Somehow, I think Ferdinanda could handle three people. Was there something in there about Marla?"

"Yes, she called, and Ferdinanda answered that one. You're supposed to return the call ASAP. Ferdinanda says there might be other messages on your machine, but she's afraid to mess with voice mail. She's not exactly a technological whiz," Yolanda said apologetically.

"Don't worry about it." I asked her to hit the speed dial for Marla, and a moment later, I felt relieved to be connected with my best friend. But if I expected succor after my long day of running around, catering, and surviving an ethnic grocery donnybrook, I was mistaken.

She began with, "Where the *hell* have you been all day?"

"Down in Denver at Arch's school, then at an ethnic grocery store, why?"

"An ethnic grocery store? Buying what?"

"Guava marmalade and sour pickles, Marla. Now,

what's going on? If you have an emergency, why didn't you call my cell?"

"It's not really an *emergency*. Or group of emergencies, rather. I just kept thinking you'd be home. Well, first. I wanted to tell you I'd given Yolanda's location to Humberto Captain. I'm so sorry. He woke me up early this morning, and the phone discombobulated me. He insisted he had some things for Ferdinanda and Yolanda, and that he just couldn't wait. Was that okay?"

"The ship on that one has sailed, Marla. He did come over this morning. Early. But Tom was still there. And what he had was a care package." I eyed Yolanda, but she was looking out the window at the falling snow. "Please, *please* don't tell anyone else she's staying with us."

"All right, all right. Sorry," Marla mumbled.

"While we're on the subject of this person, ah, that you just mentioned—"

"Oops! You've got Yolanda right there next to you?"

"*Yes*. I need you to find out what he does for a living. Where he gets his money, to be more exact."

Marla said, "I thought he owned a little export-import business."

"Besides that, if anything."

"Ooh, juicy. I'll work on it. I thought he didn't do anything, really, besides just, you know, acting rich. Well, never mind, I'll dig into it."

"Thanks."

She went on. "Couple more things I need to talk to you about. Rorry Breckenridge called me. She only has your home phone number. I figured you'd be mad at me for telling Humberto where Yolanda was, so I didn't give Rorry your cell." Marla waited to be congratulated for this odd bit of illogic. When I said nothing, she rushed on. "Rorry's frantic. She's had to add four people to the dinner tomorrow night, you know, the one that raises money for the church? She wanted to make sure that was okay."

"Does this include the two extra people that Sean already told me about?"

"Don't know. She said it would be eighteen people total."

"Omigod." This did include the two Sean had added. So now we were up to eighteen people for the church's fund-raising dinner, and it was snowing like gang-busters, which would mean no way to get extra supplies. I groaned.

"You don't sound happy," Marla said.

"I'm not." I mentally reviewed what I was making for the dinner. Back when we'd thought it would be held on a warm September evening—ha!—and that the twelve guests—ha! ha!—would be eating outside—ha! ha! ha!— Rorry Breckenridge and I had agreed on an assortment of cheeses, crackers, and fruit for a first course; lamb chops with garlic, mint jelly, *salades composées,* and hot rosemary focaccia for the main course; and a flourless chocolate cake for dessert. I calculated what was in the walk-in. I could thaw some more lamb chops and stretch out the salad ingredients I already had on hand. But I'd have to make an extra cake and an extra loaf of bread. This was not my idea of fun.

"Goldy?" Marla said. "You there?"

"Yeah, sorry. I was thinking about how to readjust my menu."

"No need for that. Rorry told me that Sean insisted that one of the guests was willing to pay an extra thousand dollars if you'd make Navajo tacos."

"Navajo tacos?" I asked, incredulous. I said flatly, "Navajo tacos are not gourmet food. Besides, I don't have a recipe."

"Oh, so what if it's not something a French chef would serve? And call Julian for a recipe. Didn't he come from Bluff, Utah? Isn't that in the middle of Navajoland?"

"Yes, but Navajo tacos have meat in them, and Julian's a vegetarian—"

"Details, girlfriend."

"All right, all right! I'll figure out how to do it," I said, "since it's for the church."

"That's the stuff."

I said, "Do you know the names of the people she's adding, by any chance?"

"Well, the four she added *today* are Humberto Captain and a date, and Tony Ramos and his wife."

"*Who?*"

"Goldy, jeez, are you not getting a cell phone signal down there? You didn't think I'd have her tell me about four extra people, and that I would say I'd call you, until I knew who these folks were, did you?"

"Sorry to be grumpy. Is that it?"

"No." She took a deep breath. "I heard through the grapevine that Jack's house sold today."

"Jack's—" I couldn't breathe. I actually braked, even

though we'd entered Sixth Avenue westbound, which was an expressway with no red lights. Luckily, no one honked, and I accelerated cautiously. If Jack's house sold, then that would mean he was really gone. "Do you know who bought it?"

"Nope. My source said she thought it was a family with kids, but she wasn't sure. Something about wanting to get in before the school year really got under way. I think the parents were going over there today with the real estate agent."

Could this be the three people who showed up? But why would they come over to our house? I said, "I can't stand this."

"I know, I know. Jack was so great. But I thought you'd want to hear it from me."

"Anything else?"

"No, except we're getting a boatload of snow up here. Are you almost home?"

"I just got on Sixth Avenue. Listen, I need you to do a little more research for me. A few items, and they could be . . . fun for you."

"Make my night."

"Could you dip into the Brie Quarles story a bit? I'm wondering if the person she's fooling around with is Tony Ramos."

"Brie?" said Marla, disbelieving. "Brie Quarles? There's no *way* she'd go for an ordinary high school athletic coach. No way. She's a barely practicing attorney who thinks of herself as high society. I haven't had the heart to tell her there *is* no high society in Aspen Meadow. There's money and there's no money, with all the shades in between. But now Tony's made himself a load of dough, so maybe Brie's interested in him. Who knows? Brie equates money with status, poor girl. All right, I'll look into it. What else have you got?"

"Do you know anything about Charlene Newgate having a new boyfriend? One with a lot of money?"

"Charlene Newgate? Remind me."

"Oh," I said, without referring to the hard time I'd had bringing Charlene to mind myself. "She used to get money and food from the church, until she started a secretarial service?"

"Charlene Newgate, right. Just saw her at my lawyer's office a couple of weeks ago. That woman gives me the creeps. She wears resentment like a second skin. She has a *boyfriend*? What, is she in junior high?"

"She told me she had a new boyfriend," I said as the van crawled through the snow.

"I hate being the last to know something. I suppose Charlene would have had the chance to meet plenty of men, but still, *Charlene Newgate*? She's a bitch who's worked for every lawyer, doctor, and other well-moneyed professional in this town. I've never heard of *anyone* being interested in her. Whenever she sees me, she tells me that while *she* has to work, I am a wealthy, overfed layabout who's done nothing with her life. Which may be true," Marla admitted, "but I don't need Charlene Newgate to tell me."

"That's an extremely cruel and untrue thing to say about you."

"Thanks. But anyway, what guy could possibly want someone so negative for a girlfriend?"

"My question exactly."

Marla said, "This one will be fun. Anything else?"

I paused before asking, "Do you know any doctor in town who's prescribing medical marijuana? Or anyone who's using it?"

Marla laughed. "I know country club parents whose kids use *plain* marijuana, and the only thing that ails them is their need to get stoned."

I glanced at Yolanda, whose face above the blanket held an amused expression. "Can you make some discreet inquiries?"

"I can make inquiries, but I passed *discreet* when I was in my twenties, and I've never looked back. Anything else?"

"Ernest was looking into a divorce. And no, I don't know whose, and I don't know whether his client was the man, the woman, or someone else."

Marla said, "Uh, that's not much to go on. But I'll try."

"Thanks, girlfriend. See you tomorrow night at the Breckenridges'."

"Sounds good. I'll bring highbrow beer to go with your lowbrow tacos."

We signed off, and Yolanda said, "I know how to make Navajo tacos. But here's my question: If the food business doesn't work out, you're going to grow weed?"

"Why not?" When she gasped, I said, "Just kidding."

What I didn't mention to Yolanda was the thinking I'd done that afternoon, after I'd met Peter, the member of Arch's fencing team with leukemia.

Ernest McLeod had been getting thin, and he needed

Yolanda to prepare meals for him. Maybe it wasn't Ernest's *sponsor* who'd suggested he hire a cook; maybe it was his *doctor.* And if he'd been in pain? I'd have to ask Tom about how the laws worked, but it was possible Ernest had been growing marijuana for his own—legal—use.

And, most significantly of all, if Ernest had learned he was terminally ill with cancer, he might have decided to change his will.

I didn't mention any of these theories to Yolanda. There was no point.

Aspen Meadow looked like a wonderland, albeit the kind you might find in Siberia. The lights around the lake glowed in the fog. Snow fell steadily. In winter, we get huge amounts of the dry, powdery stuff that is much prized by skiers. But after the initial fall of tiny flakes, this storm had brought a foot of fat, wet flakes, the kind that blanket our town in the fall and spring.

My van, which had good snow tires but no chains, groaned when I turned off Main Street and tried to climb the hill to our house. I slid one way, then the other, and finally backed down to the nearly empty parking lot of our town's Chinese restaurant. We were half a block from our house, and I figured we could traipse uphill the rest of the way. I threw the van into Park and prepared to abandon ship.

"But your leftovers!" Yolanda protested.

"Not enough to amount to anything. Take the blanket, put it over your head."

We jumped out of my vehicle and moved up the hill

to where I judged the sidewalk to be. Since the snow was so deep, our progress was reduced to a shuffle. A drapery of white was still streaming down, and the streetlights were enclosed in gossamer. The neighborhood was hushed. Flakes stung my cheeks, eyes, and unprotected neck. My feet, which were still in caterer's walking shoes, became numb as I pushed through the drifts the wind had sculpted between the street and people's front fences.

When we finally arrived at our driveway, I noticed our garage door was open. I wondered idly if Tom was home, if he'd gotten out the snowblower and for some reason it hadn't worked, so he was working on it inside. Arch's Passat, with a veil of snow blown over the trunk, stood in the garage next to the lawn mower, hedge clippers, and gardening tools, none of which we would need for at least six months. I prayed the Vikarioses had excellent tires and chains and would get Arch home safely.

"There you are!" Ferdinanda cried when we came through the door. The wonderful aroma of a home-cooked meal filled the house. I hadn't realized I was hungry until that moment, and I almost fell to my knees in thanks. "I got some dinner going." She looked us over. "You two need hot showers right now, else you gonna catch your death of colds."

Yolanda gave me a worried look. "Is there enough hot water for the two of us?"

I said, "Sure. You go first."

Ferdinanda eyed me up and down. She wore a sheriff's department sweatshirt and pants. Whether they were gifts from Tom or Boyd, I knew not. "Goldy, you need to go put on dry clothes at least. Don't want you gettin' sick so you can't work."

"Yes, I do have to be able to work, doggone it. What's the delicious scent?"

"Sense?"

"What's the wonderful smell?" I asked, a bit louder. I'd forgotten Ferdinanda complaining to us about having trouble hearing.

Ferdinanda put on one of her sly looks. "Nothing around here but ham, bread, eggs, and cheese, plus a can of chiles and a jar of picante. So I threw them together and put it in your refrigerator. Yolanda said you'd be home between one and two hours, so I waited an hour, then put it in the oven. It took you an hour and a half to get back," she said, concluding triumphantly, "so it should be about done."

I moved to embrace her, but she drew away. "Oh, you Americans with your hugs! Just go, put on some warm clothes. And hurry up about it." But she was grinning.

"Is Tom here?" I asked. "Working with the snow-blower?"

"What is it Americans say? Nobody here but us chicken?"

"But . . . do you know why the garage door is open?"

"Nope."

"All right, let me go close it." I zipped myself into a hooded jacket and traipsed outside, where the snow was still coming down fast. At the side of the detached garage, I pressed four-one-five into the panel. The door obediently closed. I realized with a pang that I had forgotten to buy more batteries for the accursed remote.

Back inside, I asked Ferdinanda, "Have you heard from Arch?" The niggle of worry about my son was spreading.

"No. But I haven't been answering the phone since Marla. I was afraid Kris might call, and I didn't want to give us away."

I wasn't up to telling her that thanks to Penny Woolworth, *that* ship had sailed, too. Instead I took the puppies outside. They didn't want to stay long, and they seemed to have figured out that if they did their business, they could come in and be cleaned up and fed. I did both, then went to look for dry clothes.

While rummaging around, I remembered that I hadn't ratted on Penny to Marla, although I'd meant to. I thought I'd save that threat for when I really needed it. Still, I had to do *something* about Penny's treachery.

I nabbed my cell phone and called her house. She sounded tired when she answered. When I identified myself, she said, "Uh-oh."

I said, "When are you cleaning Kris's house this Thursday?"

"Early afternoon," she said meekly. "But he won't be there, so you can't—"

"I don't want to see him. I just want to look around."

She cursed, but agreed.

"Another payment for your betrayal of Yolanda," I said blithely, "will be your tidying whatever house we use for a get-together to commemorate Ernest's life. Don't worry, I'll pay you."

She cursed again, but said she'd do it. When I thanked her, she hung up on me.

I disrobed, scrubbed myself with a wet washcloth,

and shrugged into a turtleneck and sweatpants. Then I hopped back down the stairs.

Ferdinanda was rolling herself around the kitchen, snagging bananas, apples, and Italian plums to slice for a fruit salad. Without a cooking duty, I pressed the phone's playback.

The first two messages were from Rorry Brecken-ridge, who was very apologetic to be calling just after eight in the morning, but she desperately needed to talk to me about the dinner the next night. In the second message, she said she would try Marla. The third was from Trudy, our next-door neighbor, who'd also called this morning. Trudy said she'd just had a "strange" visit from a real estate agent and an older couple, who said they were buying Jack's house. They'd heard the famous caterer lived across the street, and they wanted to meet me. Now here, according to Trudy, was the strange part: She'd asked for their card so good old Goldy the caterer could call them, and they'd said no, they would just come back later. I shook my head.

Also on the voice mail was an afternoon call from Tom, saying he would be late, and that he'd given a sweat suit to Ferdinanda, and for me not to worry, as he had plenty. He also told me not to be anxious because of the snow. He could be home as late as ten, and that someone with four-wheel-drive would bring him.

There was nothing from Arch. I put in another call to his cell, which went unanswered.

"Ferdinanda?" I asked. "About the garage door. During the day, did you see anyone fooling around out there, trying to get in?"

"I told you. No." She was slicing bananas with one of

my ultrasharp Japanese stainless steel knives, and did not lift her eyes from her task. "Why?"

"Somebody got in there and left the big door facing the street open. Tom doesn't usually do that." I did not mention that actually, Tom *never* did that. That was why we'd had the flap about the remote with no batteries, and the code for the panel. There was a false wall at the far end of the garage, beside his power tools. In the wall, Tom's gun was in a compartment that acted like a medicine cabinet: The hinges were hidden, and you had to know just where to press on the uninsulated part of the wall to get it open.

There was also a side door that faced our backyard. We kept a key to that door under a nearby rock, in case we just wanted a rake or hoe in summer, or the snow shovel or blower in winter, and didn't have the remote, batteries, or memory of the numbers on the side panel for the big door.

"Probably Boyd left it open," Ferdinanda said, moving on to the plums. "He was in a hurry to get out of here."

This was equally unlikely, but the last person I wanted to argue with about anything was Ferdinanda. Instead I put another call in to Arch.

"Yeah, Mom, what is it?" he said with a note of impatience, as if we'd just been speaking ten minutes earlier and I'd called to remind him of something.

"Hon, I'm so worried about you! Where are you?"

"I'm at the Vikarioses', I told you." He lowered his voice. "Peter came, too. We're having pizza."

"Are you still coming home tonight?"

He groaned. "Yes. School hasn't been canceled yet, and I'm out of clean clothes. Gus's grandmother offered to wash what I have on, but I feel bad asking her to do that. And anyway, Peter lives on the other side of Cottonwood Creek, and he has to get his medication tonight. So I don't want him to feel as if he's the only one who has to go home." Someone called to Arch, and he about broke my eardrum when he yelled, "Yeah, I'll be right there!"

"Okay, go have fun with your pals. Please tell the Vikarioses our road hasn't been plowed. They might want just to leave you off on Main Street."

"Oh, great, and me with plain old shoes." Someone nearby spoke in the background. "Never mind," Arch said. "Gus just came into the living room to find me, and he's going to loan me a pair of snow boots. Gotta run, Mom."

And with that he was gone. I looked out our front window and checked the street. It was still snowing. I glanced over at Jack's dark house. An older couple, with young kids about to start school? Well, a lot of folks didn't start having children until later these days. I would have to ask Trudy more the next day.

Ferdinanda's ham and cheese casserole was delicious. I'd give her this: She could do wonders with egg-soaked bread. That morning she'd served us a bread pudding with rum sauce. The dinner featured layers of cheddar melting over ham and buttered sourdough, over which she'd poured a mixture of eggs, cream, and spices, and on top of which she'd sprinkled green chiles and picante. She'd garnished the dish with fresh chopped cilantro, which gave it a snazzy gourmet appearance. The fruit was a perfect complement, and it looked lovely on the plate. For the first time, I realized that it was probably Ferdinanda who'd given Yolanda her passion for food preparation.

I opened one of Marla's extra bottles of red wine to go with our dinner. Beer would have worked better with the Mexican food, but we didn't have any. Anyway, with all the snow outside, it was more of a red wine kind of night.

Neither Yolanda nor I mentioned the incident with Father Pete at the ethnic grocery store, which was probably just as well. Instead, Yolanda talked about how nice the kids were at Christian Brothers High School, and how much they'd appreciated the food. Ferdinanda beamed; she knew CBHS was a Catholic school.

It was then that I ventured to ask her about our trio of visitors. Ferdinanda's face darkened. "They had a bad aura," she said. "They were bad people."

"Is that your professional opinion?" I asked, pouring us all more wine.

Ferdinanda set her chin. "I know about these things."

I didn't ask her if she'd been able to read Raul and Fidel Castro's auras, too, and what they had told her. We were having a relaxing evening after a long day, and I wasn't going to wreck it. Arch was coming home soon, and Tom would be along.

Ferdinanda again insisted on doing the dishes. "I've been doing nothing all day—"

"No," I said, interrupting, "you haven't been doing anything except making a wonderful dinner and—"

"Whatever you say, Goldy," she said, interrupting me right back, wagging that crooked index finger of hers at me, "I am more stubborn than you and will last longer—"

"You've been up since half past four!"

"I had a nap!" she retorted as she piled plates in her lap and wheeled toward the sink. "Now go make phone calls or something! Yolanda, you look terrible. I know you didn't sleep well. I heard you thrashing around. Go to bed." Once I handed Ferdinand the throat of our faucet, which was placed at the end of an expandable hose, she was able to squirt water on dishes and then expertly pivot to put them in the dishwasher.

Yolanda yawned. "It's only eight o'clock."

Ferdinanda said, "So?" I had the distinct impression she won every one of these discussions.

While Ferdinanda banged about in the kitchen, I took the phone and my wineglass out to the living room. Was it too late in the evening to build a fire? I knew that after getting up early, cooking, catering, running hither and yon, and then slogging home in the snow, if I now sat down on the couch with a second glass of wine, it would be about ten minutes before I was fast asleep. So I fancied myself actually exercising as I moved around the living room, piling up logs and kindling, crumpling newspaper, and finally setting a match to my creation.

It was for Tom, I told myself, and Arch. The fire would welcome them home from the blizzard. I said this to myself as I settled on the couch in front of the blaze and took a sip of my wine. It couldn't have been more than ten minutes before I was in Slumberland.

I awoke to a horrific scream. It was not the shriek of a woman, either. I listened carefully and heard another prolonged "Aargh!" It was as if someone were being tortured, and nearby, too. It was a grown man's voice, and now he was yelling, "Stop it! Hey!" This was followed by yelling and . . . banging. Where were these noises coming from?

A loud thud crashed against the side of the house and rattled the windows.

Yolanda and Ferdinanda both were screeching. Groggy, I looked at the clock. It was twenty to ten. Arch wasn't home, and neither was Tom. Or at least I hadn't heard them. With Yolanda and Ferdinanda yelling, I raced into the dining room first. Blinking madly, I thought I should have picked up the phone en route.

"What is it?" I cried. It was still dark in there, so I turned on the light, a used chandelier I'd bought at a garage sale and Tom had rewired. "What's wrong?" I persisted. "Why are you screaming?"

They both pointed at the dining room window. This was my house, damn it. Undaunted, I walked across the room and looked outside.

The light spilling from the window illuminated Arch's face. He was wearing a woolen hat. My son stood facing me, knee-deep in snow, openmouthed. He blinked. In one of his hands he was holding Tom's long, sharp-pointed weeder. It was covered with blood, and the blood was dripping into the snow.

Chapter 11

"Come inside," I called. "Arch!" I motioned to him. "Quickly!"

When Arch turned, he clung to Tom's weeder, as if to protect himself. I raced outside, heedless of the snow, and embraced him, avoiding the weeder.

"Is that your blood?" I yelled. "Arch? Are you all right? Did someone hurt you?"

"I'm fine," he said weakly. "I want to go inside."

I put my arm around him. He was still clinging to the weeder as we plodded as fast as possible to the front. Yolanda pulled the door open as we traipsed in.

"Did you call the cops?" Arch asked me. He tossed the weeder on the floor, where it clattered against the wall. I tried not to look at the blood, but couldn't help myself.

"I did," said Yolanda as she closed the door. Barefoot and shivering, she hugged her sides. "They're sending a couple of cars and notifying your husband of a Peeping Tom or possible intruder."

To Arch, I said, "What happened?" Arch's teeth were chattering, and his hands were shaking. I said, "Wait. Come out to the kitchen and warm up."

He unzipped a borrowed white parka, which he dropped on the other side of the hall from the weeder. "I'm freezing." He paused in the hallway and hugged his sides. "I just stabbed somebody."

I said quickly, "Somebody was trying to break in?"

Arch's brown eyes were huge as he looked at me. "Yeah. At least, I think so."

"Oh my God, Arch," I said, embracing him again. He pulled away from me awkwardly. "I wish you wouldn't have—" I wished he wouldn't have what, exactly? Tried to protect us?

Arch pulled off the borrowed hat. He was bald.

"What the *hell*—"

"Oh, Mom, don't. We really did decide we were all going to shave our heads, in sympathy with Peter." He used his heels to push off the borrowed snow boots and clomped out to the kitchen.

Ferdinanda and Yolanda's mouths dropped open when they saw Arch's hairless head, but to their eternal credit, they said nothing.

Ferdinanda, who was busily making my son cocoa, said, "You are a good boy." She slapped down the whisk and, despite what she'd said about Americans and hugs, leaned out of her wheelchair and pulled Arch's waist toward the metal frame. "I know your mother is proud of you. We are all proud of you."

"You are a *very* good boy," echoed Yolanda.

As Ferdinanda continued to hold him, and without

Yolanda and Ferdinanda able to see him, Arch gave me a helpless look. I shrugged.

"Did you see who was outside?" Yolanda asked Arch, once we were all gathered around the kitchen table. "Was it someone trying to break in?"

"I think so," said Arch. "I was coming up our road, once the Vikarioses left me off on Main Street—"

He was prevented from continuing by the crashing sound of our front door opening.

"Goldy?" Tom called.

"That was quick," said Ferdinanda.

And then, before I could even get to the door, Tom was through it. "What happened?" he demanded. He was standing in the hall, shaking and staring at the bloody weeder. "I was on my way home when the call came through."

"We're just hearing about it from Arch," I replied. "In the kitchen. So far, all we know is that Arch stabbed the guy, with your weeder there." I pointed at the dripping garden tool. Tom shook his head, glanced at the weeder, then stormed down the hall. I followed. Boyd had come through the front door; he brought up the rear.

"Have somebody bag that thing for evidence," Tom ordered Boyd, who relayed the message to an officer behind him. "And have somebody else bring the dining chairs that are in the living room into the kitchen, would you please?"

"He was outside the dining room window," Arch was saying to Ferdinanda and Yolanda, "and then I—"

"Arch, are you all right?" Tom asked, taken aback by my son's bald-egg head.

"I'm fine. Well, sort of." He sipped cocoa. "You want me to start over?"

"Yes, please," said Tom. In that command-taking way Tom had, he motioned for Yolanda and me to sit at the table flanking Arch. My son must have seemed like a pretty cool customer for someone who'd just attacked a would-be intruder with a garden implement. Boyd brought in extra chairs and put them down carefully. Tom placed a recorder on the table and pulled out his notebook. Then he and Boyd sat, while Ferdinanda rolled her wheelchair over to be beside Yolanda.

"What happened to your hair?" Tom asked Arch.

"One of the guys on the fencing team has leukemia, and the chemo has made all his hair fall out. So the other team members and I shaved our scalps. You know, in sympathy."

Tom nodded. "Okay. Begin about an hour ago, and tell me what happened. Don't leave anything out."

"An hour ago," Arch said, "let's see." His hand trembled as he put the cup back on its saucer, and liquid spilled across the table. Maybe he wasn't quite as cool as I'd thought.

"I'll get it, you talk," said Ferdinanda, already on her way to the sink for a sponge.

Arch inhaled. "An hour ago is about when Gus's grandparents left off our sick friend, Peter, at his house on the other side of Cottonwood Creek. The Vikarioses couldn't get up our hill, so I told them I could walk. I was coming up our street, and I"—here he swallowed—"I saw someone peeking in our dining room window. So I cut through the neighbor's backyard, then slipped into our garage—"

"How'd you get in there?" asked Tom.

"Someone, the guy probably, had broken open the side door. The snow was making everything quiet. The guy was still looking into our dining room, so I tried to figure out what I could use against him. I don't know how to shoot, but I do know fencing. I figured I'd have the most luck with your weeder, Tom. So I took it off its hook and came up behind the guy. He was pushing the numbers on a cell phone, maybe to call someone, maybe to text. He didn't hear me, so I lunged at him, the way I'd learned in épée. Got him in the back. He *squealed.* He whirled around and tried to get the weeder away from me. But I did a parry and riposte and stabbed the front of his shoulder. He howled again and fell against the house wall. I was about to gouge him again when he gave up and started running toward Main Street. He was yelling his head off."

"Schulz," said a patrolman from the door. "We've got a blood trail from outside your house to Main Street, where we lose it. Looks like the perp had a car parked down there. No outside surveillance cameras on any stores, either. He might have dropped this, though." The patrolman held up a black watch cap.

"Yeah, yeah, he was wearing that!" Arch interjected as Ferdinanda expertly wiped up the spilled liquid, placed the cup back on the saucer, and patted Arch's arm.

"Thanks," said Tom. "Check for boot prints or anything he might have dropped, all right?" *Like a cell phone,* I thought, but dared not hope. To Arch, Tom said, "I need you to remember everything you can about this guy. How tall he was, hair color if you saw any hair, like his eyebrows, say. I need to know whether he was fat or thin, how old you think he might have been, what he was wearing. No detail is too small."

Arch drained the last of his cocoa. "He was taller than me, but not as tall as you. Maybe just under six feet? He was stocky, but I couldn't have said how old he was. Not a kid, though. A man. I don't remember his eyebrows, because I was concentrating on attacking him. He was dressed all in black. I'm like, 'Dude, you're trying to break into somebody's house in a blizzard! Why not wear white?'"

"Dressed in a black coat? Or a jacket? Black jeans?"

Arch closed his eyes as he tried to remember. "I don't know what kind of pants they were. He had on a bomber-type jacket, only it wasn't leather, or the weeder wouldn't have gone through." Worry suddenly creased Arch's face. "You don't think I really hurt him, do you, Tom? I mean, you don't think I *killed* him, do you?"

"If you'd killed him," Tom said matter-of-factly, "we'd have a body. You probably just grazed him." Tom stood, as did Boyd. Tom put his big hand on Arch's shoulder. "You did a good job."

"Thanks."

Tom said he was going outside to work with his colleagues.

"Wait," I said, then took Tom into the hall. "The main garage door was open when I got home."

Tom cocked his head. "Any idea who opened it? Or how?"

"Ferdinanda thought Boyd might have left it open. She's not sure. Anyway, I closed it. Sorry I didn't see the side door broken into."

"That piece-of-crap flimsy hollow door," Tom said, fuming. "I should have replaced that thing months ago—" Arch poked his head into the hallway. He wanted to get online with his pals to tell them what had happened. Was that okay? Tom asked him to hold off. "Anything else I need to know, Miss G.?"

"Trudy said there were three people sniffing around here today—"

Boyd appeared in the hallway. "Tom," he said, his tone ominous. "You'd better come look at this."

Tom shook his head and followed Boyd. Curious, I threw on a coat and trailed behind them to the side door to the garage, which was now blindingly illuminated with sheriff's department lights.

I shivered when I saw what they were all looking at. The medicine-type cabinet where Tom had installed the hidden compartment was open. His forty-five was gone.

The investigative team split up. Half worked the garage scene, the other half the area outside the dining room window. The snow continued to fall.

A buzzing began in my brain. *One more thing,* it said over and over. It would take hours, I knew, for Tom to fill out reports regarding our watch-cap fellow's attempted burglary—if that's what it was—and the actual one, of a firearm being stolen. Because if the guy had had a gun, why wouldn't he have used it on Arch? I shivered and felt suddenly nauseous.

Yolanda and Ferdinanda went to bed; whether they would sleep was anybody's guess. Tom insisted that we keep the security system armed at all times. I returned

to the kitchen, too nerve-racked to sleep. The Breckenridges' party loomed. I decided to mix extra bread
dough for the double batch of focaccia. It would taste
better if it rose overnight in the refrigerator, anyway. I
mixed yeast, spring water, flour, sea salt, and fresh rosemary, and placed the savory-smelling concoction into a
buttered plastic container, which I covered and put in
the walk-in.

The police were still outside, and Tom and Boyd with
them. I decided, *What the hell, I'll go ahead and make
the two flourless chocolate cakes*. Initially I was going
to make only one, but with the addition of six people,
Sean's two, plus Humberto and Tony and the women accompanying them, there was no way one would work for
everybody.

I preheated the oven, prepared the pans, then melted
unsalted butter and bittersweet chocolate in the top of
my double boiler. I sifted cocoa and sugar onto waxed
paper and set them aside. Unfortunately, that same ter-
rifying thought invaded my brain: *What if the man
who'd stolen Tom's gun had used it on Arch?* I felt dizzy
and began breaking eggs. *Why oh why had Arch felt he
had to attack someone?* I gritted my teeth and folded
the ingredients together, then poured them into the prepared pan and placed the pan in the oven.

As I sat at one of our kitchen chairs waiting for the
cakes, waiting for Tom, waiting for clarity, I felt so much
nausea and vertigo I had to put my head between my
knees. I probably had some medication to treat this condition somewhere. I also probably had batteries somewhere. But when you're nauseated and dizzy, the last

thing you can remember is where you put important stuff.

I would have to talk to Arch, who looked especially vulnerable with his shaved head. Then again, he knew what I'd gone through with the Jerk, and he worried when I got into scrapes with bad guys. Like Brad Mikulski, Arch worried about his mother. Now that he was older and knew fencing, it was no wonder he'd thought he could take on a would-be intruder. I shook my head.

When the puffed cakes emerged, they looked and smelled heavenly. I placed them on racks. I cleaned up after myself and finally felt tired enough to think sleep might be possible. I left a note for Tom. When he came in, could he please cover the cakes? Thanks.

As I was heading upstairs, Boyd walked quietly through our front door. He said if it was all right with me, he wanted to stay at our house until all this blew over. *Like a storm,* I thought. When I hesitated, Boyd said he'd already asked Tom, and he'd said it was fine, as long as it was okay with me.

"Yes, yes, of course," I said. Arch's room had two beds, I told him, and he was welcome to one of them, as long as Arch didn't mind. But Boyd replied that if we had a sleeping bag, he would prefer to bunk on the living room couch. It was a lumpy sofa, I warned him, but he said he'd slept on a lot worse when he was in the army. I found one of our sleeping bags and handed it to him.

In the bedroom, I closed our curtains, changed into pajamas, and lay on our bed to wait for Tom, and for the sleep that my body had promised. But my heart started thumping again, and my skin suffered wave after wave of gooseflesh.

The Breckenridges' dinner was scheduled for the next evening, and my jumpy mind said all those extra guests would be a challenge. But Yolanda would be there to help, and Ferdinanda had proved her mettle in the kitchen. Plus, we would have Boyd. He didn't enjoy cooking or serving. Still, when Tom had sent him to watch over me when I was doing an event, and Boyd had been involved in culinary duties, he'd been stoic. Now his only work would be to keep us safe.

Around midnight, Tom came into our room.

"Are you awake?" he whispered. When I told him I was, he said he'd covered the cakes and stored them. He was going to have a quick shower and then come to bed.

"Size-eight boot," he said without preamble when he slipped between the sheets ten minutes later. "Same as what we found in the mud over at Ernest's. Our guys are trying to get good photographs of the print. And we're sending the weeder to the lab to have the blood ana-lyzed, see if we get some kind of hit. The watch cap's going, too. It didn't look to us as if there were any hairs in it. But it's dark out, so maybe the techs will find something we couldn't see."

"But you're thinking it's our bald guy."

"That's my guess at this point."

"So," I said slowly, "you're giving up on the idea that Yolanda burned down Ernest's house? And her rental?"

"At this point, yes." Tom paused. "This guy. In a twenty-four-hour period, he burns down Ernest's house and maybe he steals my gun, although if he had it, it's a miracle he didn't use it on Arch. I don't get it. What's he up to?"

"I have no idea. Maybe he thinks we have clues to some of Ernest's cases? Maybe he's somebody who's been sent to scare Yolanda? They think she knows something?" When Tom said nothing, I said, "I have a few things to tell you. Charlene Newgate, the secretarial service lady? I've known her for a long time, and she's never had any money. But she's got lots of it now."

"You saw her at the CBHS event, the way you planned?"

"I did, and I was very circumspect—"

"You? Circumspect?" Tom interrupted, with a smile in his voice.

"Stop, okay? I asked if she'd ever worked for Drew Parker, and she clammed up."

"I know. Our guys found the number of the secretarial service in Parker's office, and she gave them the same silent treatment."

I continued. "Well, Charlene said she didn't even know who Parker was, but I think she was lying."

"My wife, the human polygraph."

I ignored this. "Charlene is not attractive, okay? But she said she had a new boyfriend, which Marla promised to look into. Charlene was wearing fancy clothes and was driving a Seven-Series BMW."

"Nice boyfriend. We'll try to take another run at her tomorrow."

"Something else. Remember the Hermie Yolanda mentioned, with the missing fingers? I know her. Her name is Hermie Mikulski, and I saw her today at CBHS.

She has a son there, named Brad. Hermie's missing two fingers on her left hand, Tom. That's new since the last time I saw her. She wants you to call her. And she isn't old, the way Yolanda said, she just has prematurely gray hair. I can't believe this is the same Hermie—"

"Let me talk to Boyd again." Tom put his clothes back on, picked up his cell, and disappeared.

Half an hour later, when I was beginning to wonder if I would ever get any sleep, Tom returned and again began to undress. "Hermie Mikulski's neighbors say she hasn't been living in her house for a while. She told them she and Brad would be staying in different motels for a while, until some problem she had is resolved. They know she lost two fingers, but they don't know how. We left a message on her home phone, we're trying to get a cell phone number for her, and we're trying to find out where she is. So far nothing."

"Doesn't the school have a number for her?"

"Not at this time of night." Tom slid between the sheets. "How are you doing?"

"Not so hot," I said honestly. "Listen, Tom. Marla said something else. Apparently, the house across the street from us sold. The buyers are an older couple with school-age children. Remember when I told you that three people were here this afternoon? The real estate agent who handled the sale of the house brought these people over *here* to talk to *me*. When Ferdinanda wouldn't open the door, they went to Trudy's."

"Trudy didn't see anything." He sounded discouraged. "We asked her—"

"She can't see our garage from her place," I interrupted. "Did she tell you any more about the three people?"

"Just a description. Older couple, both brown-haired, with a gray-haired woman who said she was a real estate agent. But she wasn't wearing a badge and wouldn't give Trudy a card. They were only interested in talking to you, but they wouldn't say why."

I let this sink in—again. "Can you find out who bought Jack's house?"

"I can try. Sometimes that kind of thing takes a few days, though, if the agent gives us a hard time or the sale hasn't closed. Anything else?"

"Well, I wanted to let you know an odd thing that happened." I waited for him to say what he usually did, which was that odd things were always happening to me. But he didn't, so I related the story of Yolanda going Chernobyl with Father Pete at the ethnic grocery. "He thought she was certifiable," I concluded. "Poor thing. She's been through too much."

"After the surprised way Kris Nielsen acted this morning when you confronted him?" Tom said. "Does this second incident make you even wonder if Yolanda might be exaggerating the stalking phenomenon? I mean, I know, he was unfaithful and gave her a sexually transmitted disease and hit her with a broomstick. And those things are awful. But—"

"If somebody did all that to me," I said, "I'd be scared to death."

"You're right. But . . . do you believe her?"

"Yes," I said, but I could hear the uncertainty in my voice. "You?"

"I never believe anyone, Miss G. But I can hold both possibilities in my head. Yolanda is exaggerating and stretching the truth. Yolanda is telling the truth and we're dealing with a dangerous guy."

I considered this. "There's something else I want to tell you. This Peter kid Arch mentioned? The one with leukemia?"

He pulled me close. "Yeah?"

"It made me think, Tom. Ernest was getting thin. He hired Yolanda to cook for him. He invited her to stay in his home, and in exchange all he wanted was meals. He was growing marijuana in his greenhouse. He changed his will all of a sudden, leaving the place to Yolanda—"

"You're on the right track, Miss G. Our preliminary autopsy indicates he had esophageal cancer."

Ice formed in my chest. "That poor man. Why do you suppose he kept on working, doing investigations?"

"Some people don't want others to know they're terminal, because they don't want pity. The investigations were probably what was keeping him alive. They were giving him a sense of purpose."

"And we don't know where his files are."

"Except for the one with his will, they burned, Miss G. Forgot to tell you. The fire guys said Yolanda's seventeen K is toast, too."

I sighed. "Still, I know that money's an issue. Why Humberto gave it to her, and what she's going to do now, besides work for me. But with the filing: Wouldn't Ernest have had a backup system of some sort?"

"Not necessarily. Ernest was old-school." Tom exhaled. "Speaking of which, his former partner, John

Bertram, isn't in very good shape. Not because of Ferdinanda whacking him, but because he didn't know Ernest was sick. He's having a hell of a dose of survivor's guilt, I can tell you. We're having a get-together at their house on Thursday night, you know, the way we do. We're going to share our recollections of Ernest—"

"I want to help," I interjected. "And I'm sure Yolanda and Ferdinanda will want to, too. Did John Bertram even know that two women were living in Ernest's house?"

"Nope. But remember, Yolanda and Ferdinanda hadn't been there that long." Tom exhaled. "You might as well know the rest. It looks like Ernest's body was moved. He was shot in the chest, near the fire road that goes behind John Bertram's garage. Then he was pulled out of sight of the main road, behind a boulder. As far as we can tell, Ernest wasn't armed."

"What was he doing back there?"

"We don't know. There's no path going from his house to where we found him. Our theory is that he heard or felt someone following him along the main road, so he ducked down the fire department's wide dirt trail, which most people don't even know about. Then when he thought he was safe, he started walking back toward the main road. Whoever was waiting for him jumped out and shot him with a thirty-eight."

"Shell casings?"

"They're working on a match now."

I said, "Were there defensive wounds? I mean, if Ernest struggled with our bald guy, and the bald guy wanted to know what Ernest was up to or what he had discovered, maybe the perp would have tortured him."

"No defensive wounds. His wallet and anything else he had on him are gone. But it wasn't a burglary, apparently, or somebody wouldn't have thought to come back to torch his house. We're thinking the motive was to shut him up. About what, we don't know yet."

"What about Humberto? Does he have an alibi?"

"More or less. His guards are vouching for him, but our guys who interviewed them say they had rum on their breath, and it's clear they spend most of their time down in the gatehouse that's outside the high fence surrounding Humberto's property. So that may not mean much. No matter what, there's not evidence for a warrant. Kris Nielsen claims he was having brunch in Denver. He paid cash and kept the receipt."

"Oh, that reminds me. Something else about Kris Nielsen. This summer, he called Father Pete and said he was trying to get an elderly woman involuntarily committed to an institution. The woman sounded like Ferdinanda, and it made me wonder more about Kris Nielsen."

Tom exhaled. "He has financial resources, no question. As does Humberto Captain. We just don't know what we're dealing with here. Plus, we don't yet know if Marla's story about Brie Quarles is true, but we're going to talk again to Brie. Our guys are still checking the scene and Ernest's house, or what's left of it. Maybe they'll find something."

"I hope so." A cramp had spread from my chest to the pit of my stomach. Ignoring it, I asked, "How about the pictures you took of the puppies? Did you get any information from one of our town veterinarians?"

Tom sighed. "This past summer? A hiker brought a

small beagle puppy that was bleeding into one of our local guys. The puppy was female but hadn't been spayed." Tom paused. "The puppy had some buckshot in its backside."

"What?"

"Don't worry, the little gal made a full recovery. The veterinarian offered to put it up for adoption, but the hiker said he wanted to adopt the thing, that it was karma. Or dogma, whichever you prefer."

"Who would shoot a puppy?" I asked.

"There are bad people out there, Miss G., in case I need to remind you. My question is, what was a puppy doing out on a remote hiking trail? If the hiker hadn't found her, she would have died, that's for sure. The vet said the hiker was a real animal lover, and that he went back to the same trail the next day, looking for more casualties. He didn't find any, but he did hear gunfire."

"Oh, for God's sake." My stomach clenched again.

"Miss G., relax," said Tom, reading my mind. "The vet is going to look through his files to see if he recorded who this hiker was and where he lives. We'll talk to him." Tom pulled me closer. "And for now? We're in our own house, the security system is set, and there are two cops under this roof."

"I think Boyd is developing an attachment to Yolanda," I whispered. "That's not going to screw up the investigation, is it?"

"It didn't hurt the investigation when I developed an attachment to you when there was an attempted poisoning at a party you catered, now, did it?"

* * *

The next morning, we were awakened by the sound of water trickling through our gutters. As quickly as it had come, the evidence of the blizzard was disappearing. I pulled back the curtains and looked outside. The sun shone through sprays of drops, spangling our bedroom wall with rainbows. Melting clumps of snow were already dropping from our street's pines and aspens, and a recognizable thump on our deck indicated the load of snow on our roof had thawed enough for the whole thing to slide off. Shining rivulets of water snaked down the middle of the street. I was pretty sure Arch would have school. Would Brad be there? Would Tom be able to find Hermie? I wondered.

I also wondered how the fencers' bald looks would go over.

I didn't dwell on these thoughts. Instead, more sinister worries surfaced, like memories of nightmares: *In the darkness, did the cops get a good enough photo of our would-be burglar's boot prints to match them absolutely to the ones at Ernest's house? Did that same guy break into our garage and steal Tom's gun? And how would the guy know where Tom kept the gun? Who were the three people who came to our door yesterday, and what did they want? And in a buyer's market, who would purchase the house Jack had gutted, when he'd intended to remodel it and it looked horrible? The house has only been for sale for a few weeks. So what gives with that?*

Am I being paranoid, or does someone want to keep an eye on us? If so, why?

The answers to none of these were forthcoming. I

allowed the thoughts to drain away as I moved through my yoga routine. The scent of ham drifted up the stairs.

When Tom finished shaving, he came out and sniffed. "Sure smells like someone's cooking a super breakfast again! When Ferdinanda gets out of her wheelchair, maybe we could move her and Yolanda into our basement." He winked. "Not that your breakfasts aren't fabulous, Miss G. It's just good to have a break now and then."

"From me?"

"*You* need a break from cooking. I thought I heard Arch moving around." His forehead furrowed. "Wonder if anyone woke up Boyd?"

But someone had. In the kitchen, the newly bald Arch sat next to Ferdinanda and across from Boyd and Yolanda. In front of my son was a plate of ham, eggs, and a slab of toasted Cuban bread spread with guava marmalade. He was forking in food while asking Ferdinanda questions.

"So you don't really inhale the cigar smoke?" he said around a mouthful.

"You inhale it a little," Ferdinanda replied. "You gotta get the taste."

Rather too loudly, I said, "*Hello?*"

"I'm just asking her, Mom." Arch shoveled in more food, then announced, "I checked online, and we do have classes today. There wasn't enough snow to close a school of fish. Speaking of pets, how cool are those three puppies, Mom? Why didn't you tell me about them?"

"We were being foster parents for a day. Father Pete's coming to get them this morning. Speaking of which, did anyone take care of them this morning? Food, water, and the rest?"

Arch said, "I did, Mom. And Sergeant Boyd came outside with me while we were in the backyard." My son turned his attention to Tom. "I can't drive my car, though, right? I mean, isn't the garage still a crime scene?"

"Yes, it is. Sorry, buddy. It'll probably just be for today. I can drive you down there, if you want."

"No, thanks," Arch replied. "I'll manage. Wait, I can call Gus. His grandparents felt really bad that they couldn't get their car up our hill, so I know they'll want to take me." He turned to Ferdinanda and Yolanda. "Thanks for breakfast. It was super." And then, bringing joy to my heart, he hugged first Yolanda, then Ferdinanda, who both grinned widely.

When the Vikarioses arrived, Tom walked Arch out to their van. Boyd rubbed the top of his unfashionable crew cut. For a moment, I wondered if he, too, wished he were bald. But Boyd said only, "You've got a good kid there, Goldy."

Yolanda said, "You've got a *great* kid."

"Hoh-kay," said Ferdinanda as she wheeled toward the stove. "Next shift. And I don't want anybody getting in my way!"

Since arguing with Ferdinanda never got me anywhere, I merely fixed hot lattes for everyone else. I usually didn't change from iced caffeinated drinks to hot ones until October, but since cold and snow had made an early appearance, I thought it was time. When Tom returned, he and Boyd told Yolanda, who again looked exhausted, to stay put while they cleared Arch's detritus and set the table for the five of us. While the ham and eggs cooked, I spooned a bit of guava marmalade onto my plate and tasted it. It was *sweet*. But it had a distinctive taste, and I thought I could use it in an American-style coffee cake. I wanted to experiment, because I had some thinking and phone-calling to do, and I did those best while working with food.

Ferdinanda's scrambled eggs were studded with chopped ham and sliced, caramelized onions. She'd added something else to them—whipping cream, I thought, or butter—that gave them an ineffable creaminess. She'd used the last of the Cuban bread to make a crunchy toast that she'd cooked in a frying pan—in some more butter. Every bite was heaven. I told her that the whole point of being the guest in someone's home was that the *host* took care of the guests, not vice versa. She said, "Yeah, yeah, yeah," and asked me for the marmalade.

"Now I'm going on the porch to have a cigar," she said as she pushed away from the table. "You don't want me to do the dishes, I won't."

"I'm coming with you," Boyd announced. He stood up.

"Nah, I don't need you!" she called over her shoulder. "I'm ready for anything, I told you! Do you think I survived with Raul and the army, up in the mountains, because I was a wimp?"

"I'm just keeping you company," said Boyd mildly as he opened the front door for her.

We called our thanks to her as she rolled outside.

"When does she see the doctor again about her leg?" asked Tom, sotto voce.

"Our calendar burned up in Ernest's house," Yolanda replied. She looked at the ceiling. "Along with the seventeen thousand in cash, the fireman says. We were in too much of a hurry, with the fire and the puppies, I just forgot about the money." She sighed. "I'm getting used to starting over. But anyway, I'm going to have to call the doctor and find out when Ferdinanda's appointment is. It might even be today. I've been so frazzled, I haven't kept track."

Once Tom had left, Boyd stayed outside with Ferdinanda. Every now and then as Yolanda and I did the dishes, we would peek out at them. With Ferdinanda smoking, Boyd shoveled our sidewalk, the steps to the porch, and the ramp. When he came around back to clean off the deck, he rolled Ferdinanda in front of him. She complained the whole way. We could hear her through the walls.

When Yolanda and I finished the dishes, she asked if she could use our phone so she could try to reach Ferdinanda's doctor. I replied that she could, and she didn't need to ask. If she could just use the house phone, I said, I could keep the business line clear, in case clients called.

When she retired to the dining room with the phone, I removed the extra lamb chops from the freezer for the Breckenridges' party. Then I checked that we had plenty of garlic and said a silent prayer of thanks that we did. So now I was going to think and cook.

I buttered and floured two pans and preheated the oven. Then I pulled out unsalted butter, sugar, flour, sour cream, leavening, vanilla extract, a lemon, an orange, and the guava marmalade. As I creamed the butter and sugar, I ran all the questions about the case through my head. Tom thought Ernest had been murdered to shut him up. With Ernest's house then burned to the ground, whatever evidence might have been in there was gone— more shutting up.

I sifted flour, salt, and leavenings, then zested a lemon and an orange and minced the result. What had Ernest found out that would make him have to be killed to shut him up? There were lots of possibilities but no certainties. If the motive was to keep something quiet, did the shooter question Ernest, to see if he knew something? Because if so, you'd expect signs of a struggle, and there weren't any. Maybe the shooter already knew what it was?

I stirred the vanilla, zests, and marmalade into the batter, then carefully folded in the dry ingredients. I divided the batter between the two pans and placed them in the oven.

Ernest McLeod had been a good man, in addition to being kind and generous. Somehow, I felt as if Yolanda was holding out on me, but I had no clue how to elicit information from her. She seemed like a deer perpetually caught in the headlights, and the stabbing of a Peeping Tom the night before was not going to make her any less nervous.

Yolanda returned to the kitchen and announced that as she feared, Ferdinanda's follow-up doctor's visit was that afternoon, just when we would have the big push for the Breckenridges' dinner. In catering terms, this meant right now, it was Crunch Time.

We began in earnest on the menu for that evening's dinner: Rorry was providing cheeses, crackers, and fruit for people to munch on while they drank wine, which was being provided by a parishioner. Thank goodness Marla was bringing beer to go with the Navajo tacos. We would have to do the fry bread for the tacos on the spot, Yolanda said, because that was how it tasted best. But we could sauté the ground beef and seasonings, plus chop the tomatoes and lettuce in advance. I thanked the Lord we had iceberg lettuce, and plenty of it, because I'd meant to use it to make lettuce cups for the Caprese salad but then decided not to at the last minute. The ingredients for the *salades composées,* along with the flourless chocolate cakes, were already in the walk-in.

Yolanda and I swiftly divided the prep duties. She would work on the ingredients for the composed salads. I pulled the focaccia dough out of the refrigerator and set it aside to rise. Next I minced the garlic in the blender.

With a sinking heart, I sautéed the ground beef with taco seasoning. Maybe it wasn't haute cuisine, but a client's eccentricities were not my problem, I always told myself. As the beef sizzled in the pan, I chopped a mountain of lettuce, another one of tomatoes, and a final one of scallions. Yolanda finished the salad ingredients and made a large bowl of guacamole. Finally, I grated so much cheddar I thought my knuckles were going to give out. Still, when we were done, Yolanda insisted we stand back and admire our work. It helped.

The doorbell rang, startling both of us. Boyd looked in from the deck, held up his hand for us to stay put, then rolled Ferdinanda into the kitchen.

"This is too much," she muttered, but opened her eyes in admiration when Boyd drew his gun and walked carefully down the hall.

He called to our visitor to identify himself.

Father Pete yelled back, "I'm Goldy's parish priest! Why don't you identify *yourself*?"

"Look here, Father," Boyd called through the door.

"And furthermore," Father Pete hollered, "I am not afraid of you! In fact, I'm calling the sheriff's department!"

"It's okay," I said to Boyd, who was looking through the peephole.

Boyd, still defiant, holstered his weapon and opened the front door. "I *am* the sheriff's department," he said to Father Pete, who was punching numbers into his cell phone. "We had an incident here last night."

Father Pete pocketed his phone and passed by Boyd. The priest gave the cop a decidedly frosty look. Father Pete, who had been a boxer in his younger, thinner days, had twice won the Golden Gloves. He might have been a match for Boyd at some point in his life, but not today, when he came striding down the hall, unafraid, but burdened by a large cardboard box.

Before he got to the kitchen, Father Pete asked me, "What kind of incident, Goldy?" But then he caught sight of Yolanda, who was holding the door to the kitchen open. Father Pete's mind made an unfortunate leap. "Mistaken identity again?"

Yolanda turned on her heel and shut the kitchen door in our faces.

"Let's go into the living room," I said to Father Pete. To Boyd, I said, "Could you bring us the remaining puppies, please?"

"Goldy," Father Pete whispered to me, "what is *going on*?" Then he glanced around the living room. Boyd had neatly stacked his pillow and sleeping bag at one end of the couch. The makeshift curtain between the living and dining rooms was pulled back, revealing the cots. In the kitchen, Yolanda and Ferdinanda were again speaking Spanish in fierce, low tones. Father Pete said, "Is that woman staying with you? Who else is at your house?"

I sighed. "That other cot in the dining room is for her great-aunt. Did you hear about Ernest McLeod's house burning down?" When Father Pete nodded, I said, "They were staying there, and now they're spending time with us. The sheriff's department deputy who greeted you at the front door is bunking on the couch. We had a—" Well, what had it been, exactly? "We had an attempted burglary last night. It's possible it was the same man who burned down Ernest's place."

"Goodness gracious." Father Pete sat in one of our wing chairs and put his box on the floor. "Is there any way I can help?"

I rubbed my temples and tried to think. In the kitchen, Boyd was talking to Yolanda. He clearly had the puppies, because their whining was louder. I asked Father Pete, "Do you know where Hermie Mikulski is staying?"

Father Pete lifted his wide chin. "I do, and she is fine.

I cannot, however, tell you where she is. I mean, I promised her."

I sighed. Maybe Boyd would be able to get it out of him. I said, "Well, do you remember Charlene Newgate?"

"With the secretarial service? Yes. She hasn't been around the church in a while. Of course, the food pantry is at Aspen Meadow Christian Outreach now . . . why? Does she need food?"

"No, I don't think so. But do you happen to know . . . if she has a rich new boyfriend?"

"That bald fellow? Is he her rich boyfriend? I saw them at the Grizzly one time, when I was trying to help an alcoholic parishioner—" He stopped talking when he saw my shock. "What is it? What's the matter?"

I almost couldn't get the words out. "Do you know the bald fellow? Do you know his name?"

At that moment, Boyd came into the living room carrying a puppy in each arm. Yolanda was right behind him, snuggling the last one to her chest. They wordlessly deposited them in Father Pete's box.

Yolanda said, "I'll go get a can of food."

"That's not necessary," Father Pete said. "I already have puppy chow." He squirmed a bit in his chair, as if he were having a change of heart but couldn't find the words to match. "Young lady—"

"My name is Yolanda," she said, brushing her tumble of russet curls away from her lovely face.

"Yolanda," Father Pete said warmly, "I am sorry you are having so many difficulties. If you need the church in any way, we are prepared to help you—"

"Thank you," Yolanda said stiffly. "I am fine now." She patted the puppies one last time, then left.

"Sergeant Boyd," I said breathlessly, "Father Pete knows where Hermie Mikulski is. He can't tell me, but he may tell you."

"I cannot tell either of you," said Father Pete.

I shook my head. "Father Pete has also seen a bald fellow who may be our perp. He was with Charlene Newgate." I didn't know if Tom had filled Boyd in on Charlene's background, and I didn't want to do it now.

Boyd looked at me skeptically, but he sat in the other wing chair. He pulled a notebook from his back pocket and nodded at Father Pete. "Tell me what you know, please."

Reluctantly, I left the living room. I wished I could hear what they were saying, but the crying of the beagles drowned them out.

Chapter 12

Back in the kitchen, I couldn't help it. I called Tom. He wasn't at his desk yet, so I announced into his voice mail that Father Pete knew where Hermie Mikulski was. Father Pete also had seen Charlene Newgate's new, rich boyfriend, who might be our bald perp. Emphasis on the *might,* I added.

I then tried Tom's cell, but he must have been in one of those folds in the mountains that prevented reception. I repeated my message anyway and hung up. In the living room, Boyd and Father Pete were still conversing in low tones.

"What is it?" Yolanda asked as I held myself next to the kitchen door.

Ferdinanda gave me a steely stare. "Why are you listening? Is the father hearing the cop's confession? If so, you are doing something very bad."

"No, no, no," I said impatiently, "Father Pete isn't performing any sacraments. He's talking to the policeman because he might *know* something about what's been happening to you two. But if I can't eavesdrop, I can't tell what the priest is telling the cop!"

Ferdinanda's gray eyebrows shot up. "Does the father know who burned down Ernest's house? Was it the same man who was here last night?"

"I don't know," I said truthfully. "Maybe."

At that moment, the front door opened. The puppies' whining decreased as Father Pete went through. That was it? Fewer than five minutes of questions?

Still in the living room, Boyd got on his cell. Ferdinanda announced she was going into the dining room to rest. Uh-huh. I wondered if she wanted to do some eavesdropping herself. Yolanda moved to the pet-containment area and poured food into Jake's bowl. Ordinarily, our bloodhound noisily gobbles up his food, but this morning, he wouldn't look at us. There was a resolute silence from his bed.

"What do you suppose is the matter with him?" Yolanda asked me as I tipped out kibble for Scout the cat, whom I had seen exactly twice since the puppies came on the scene.

"He's sulking," I said. "He misses the puppies."

While we were dutifully washing our hands, Boyd came back into the kitchen.

"The priest is going to call Hermie." He held up a card. "I have her cell number here and just tried it. No answer."

I shook my head. Hermie had told me to have Tom call her, but she was in hiding? What gave?

Boyd went on. "And as far as that woman and the bald guy? The priest doesn't know anything. He can't even remember when he saw the two of them. About two weeks ago, he thinks. I'll call the bartender at the Grizzly, but it does get crazy busy in there sometimes. There's no surveillance, and if it was two weeks ago, the saloon isn't going to have a credit card receipt. Still, it's worth a try. Let me call Tom."

I was grateful that Boyd had brought us up to date but frustrated that he hadn't learned more. He returned to the living room while Yolanda told Ferdinanda about her appointment that afternoon.

"Oh, for crying out loud," Ferdinanda said. "I can skip one appointment."

"No, you can't," Yolanda replied with equal firmness. "He is the one doctor who will see you with your Medicare. You're going." I'd never seen Ferdinanda back down, but this time, she did.

When Boyd rejoined us, he said he hadn't been able to reach Tom, but he'd left a voice mail. He pressed his lips together, then said, "Give me some duties here." I handed him a printout of our prep schedule. I cited unnamed errands I had to do myself that afternoon—the exact nature of which I did not want to share—and said I wanted to be done by eleven.

"We can do this," I said, encouraging them. There was no grumbling.

The four of us got down to work. The focaccia dough had risen, so I spilled it into two sheet pans. With one hand, I pressed holes into the dough, while with the other I carefully dribbled pools of golden extra-virgin olive oil into the depressions. Then I sprinkled the top with crushed fresh rosemary, dried oregano, poppy seeds, and sea salt. These breads did not need another rising, so into the oven they went.

Yolanda drained the new potatoes and shocked the haricots verts in ice for the *salades composées.* "You have a vinaigrette you want to use?"

"Do something fun. Since we're having Navajo tacos, we'll call it a Mexican–Caribbean–Native American fusion."

She smiled. "No *problema,* babe."

We were due to arrive at the Breckenridges' place at four. We would set up before the guests arrived for cocktails and Rorry's assortment of fruit and cheese, due to start at five. If all went smoothly, we'd serve the salads around six, followed by the lamb chops, bread, and tacos. Folks could make their choice. Or they could have both. Once the snows started in Aspen Meadow, everyone became hungrier. For six whole months, there were no more swimsuits or tiny tennis dresses to mess with.

I was thinking about this as Yolanda, her brow corrugated, shook the vinaigrette she'd made.

"What is it?" I asked.

She whacked the jar down on the counter so hard, I thought it would shatter. "Maybe I should just move Ferdinanda away from Aspen Meadow. Too many bad things are happening. I don't want you and Tom and Arch to be targets." She tore off a paper towel and wiped up the splashed vinaigrette.

"Yolanda, don't. Tom will figure this whole thing out, and you can be safe and happy again."

She said, "I doubt it."

"Don't doubt it," Boyd said tenderly. "We're going to nab this perp."

After that, we checked off all the items needed for the menu, then moved on to labeling and packing our equipment and the foodstuffs. Rorry had told me she was using "The Abundance of Fall" for her decorating theme and would have gourds, hay, and bunches of flowers in a big arrangement for her centerpiece. I packed the ingredients for the fry bread batter, the meats, minced garlic, chopped tomatoes, chopped lettuce, grated cheese, guacamole, and sour cream, and schlepped it all into the walk-in. I was glad not to have to worry about the table.

There were those nagging questions I still had for Yolanda. She was labeling all the items for the salads. Maybe she didn't know any more about Ernest's investigations, but she hadn't talked much to me about Humberto or Kris. I wanted to know everything about them. If Humberto was really dangerous, why did she seem to be protecting him? And was it possible he had burned down the rental and somehow forced her to ask Ernest to take her in? I wondered.

And if Kris was truly stalking Yolanda, then we were all in danger. Some famous general—Patton, maybe?—had said, "Know your enemy." In this case, make that *possible enemies*.

Once we were done with the packing up, Yolanda announced she had to get Ferdinanda ready to go to the doctor. Since it was quarter to eleven, they would have to hustle.

"But when will you be back?" I called after her.

"Should I pack up the van for the Breckenridges' event myself?"

Boyd gave me a severe look. "You're not packing up anything by yourself."

I put my hands on my hips. "Whoever this bad person or persons are, I'm pretty sure it's not me they're after."

"We should be back before four," Yolanda said as she wheeled Ferdinanda back into the kitchen.

"I'm going with them," Boyd announced levelly. "And I need to know exactly where you're off to, Goldy, and when you'll be back."

"Just picking up a few things at the grocery store," I lied. "No big deal."

"Then I'm walking you down to your van. Where'd you leave it?" I told him, and while he checked the outside perimeter of the house, I rapidly packed up one of the guava coffee cakes I'd made that morning. I also pulled four shots of espresso and poured them, plus a judicious amount of whipping cream, into my thermos. Where I was going, it would help to have a food bribe.

Yolanda gave me a skeptical grin as I made these preparations. "Those people at the grocery store must love you."

I put my finger to my lips. She grinned at me. I had no idea where she thought I was going, and actually, I didn't have a completely clear idea myself. Yet.

Boyd accompanied me through the melting snow. The sheriff's department had finished investigating our garage, and the yellow tape was down, as was the garage door. There was nobody around. In Aspen Meadow, folks tend to cocoon after the first big snow. A county snowplow was working our street, spraying enormous wedges of white stuff onto the curb opposite us.

At my van, Boyd opened the driver's door. "I want you to be watchful, do you understand?" When I nodded, Boyd said, "All right. I'll set the alarm and close up the house." I placed the wrapped cake on my passenger seat and revved my van. Where was I going, exactly? I had to think.

I wanted to know who had burned down Yolanda's rental. I wanted to know who had done the same to Ernest's house. I wanted to know who had stolen Tom's gun and then decided to make calls or shoot video, or send texts, or whatever, right outside our own place.

Somebody or somebodies were pressing in on our boundaries, and I was *pissed*.

As I eased my van through the ice and slush on Main Street, I reflected. When had this chain of events begun? I had not the slightest notion where the puppies had come from, even less of a clue as to where the marijuana Ernest was growing had originated. At the start of all this, Ernest's dentist appointment had been changed. With Charlene Newgate now a definite person of interest, would Tom be upset if I tried to talk to her again? Probably.

I called Charlene Newgate's number anyway, and was rewarded with voice mail. She was involved in this, I was convinced—although the evidence wasn't there yet. Tom still hadn't called me back, unfortunately. I asked Charlene to return my call and gave my cell phone number. I doubted she'd leave her new rich boyfriend long enough to attend to messages, but it was worth a try.

I drove up past Aspen Meadow Lake, which was an icy gray—not yet frozen, but filled with melting snow. It looked forbidding. I chewed the inside of my cheek and longed for the coffee I'd packed up. Was the change in Ernest's dental appointment really the beginning of these horrid events? No, it wasn't. Ernest had had some clients with big problems, and the one I knew about was Norman Juarez. Tom had said he owned a bar down near the Furman County Sheriff's Department.

I called Information and, hoping against hope, asked for a search for bars called Norman's, or Norm's, on the state road that ran past the department. It was a long, hilly highway that eventually ended up in Boulder, although I certainly didn't want to go that far.

She came up with nothing, as I'd expected. I asked her to try *Juarez*.

"I have one called the Juarez Bar and Grill," the operator said doubtfully. "It's listed as being on the highway. Want the address or the phone number?"

"Both, please."

Twenty-five minutes later, I pulled into the parking lot of the bar, which, even though it was small, was strung with green, red, and white flags. MEXICAN FOOD OUR SPECIALTY! a handmade sign blared. I wondered how hungry I was. I couldn't just go in and start asking questions.

One of the things about being female is that if you go alone into an establishment that serves liquor, day or night, everyone assumes you're looking for a pickup. I pressed my lips together, pulled the diamond ring Tom had given me around so it was in plain view, and bellied up to the bar.

At half past eleven, there were close to a dozen males—no females—sitting and drinking. There were booths and tables, all empty. I wondered about the men. Tom had told me that criminals often drink at bars during the day, so there are always a couple of undercover cops in there imbibing with them. The cops are always hoping to get some inside scoop, and often they do. The downside, unfortunately, is that more than one out-of-uniform police officer has become an alcoholic in the pursuit of his duty.

The guys at the bar ranged from scraggly-looking, with long gray hair and beards, to ruffian types, with tight T-shirts and torn jeans. They eyed me, and I pressed my lips together in a no-nonsense manner.

A tall Hispanic male, his curly black-and-gray hair cut very short, left his work at the bar and came up to me. There was a twinkle of amusement in his eye. "Help you?"

"A Heineken and two cheese enchiladas, please." I tried to sound normal, but drinking beer and eating Mexican food when you have a big dinner to cater in the evening wasn't exactly what you'd call normative behavior. For me, anyway.

He brought the Heineken first, then said it would be a few minutes for the enchiladas, as his wife had just made a fresh batch of tortillas. I said that sounded fantastic.

I sipped the Heineken as slowly as possible, but I still had to order a second one, because the enchiladas were taking some time. Okay, I really *couldn't* have more than two beers before catering the Breckenridges' gig, or I'd fall on my face in their kitchen. *Maybe I should have ordered water,* I thought, but then realized that it was less likely the bartender, if indeed he was Norman Juarez, would talk to me.

I signaled to him after I'd had a few sips of the second beer. He ambled over.

"So, your wife makes the tortillas? I'm impressed."

He nodded. "They are incredible." He had a slight accent.

I went on. "So, are you from Mexico?"

He snorted. "I am from Cuba." He pronounced it the way Ferdinanda did, "Koo-bah."

"My goodness," I said, trying to think of how to engage him in a conversation. "I should have ordered a Cubano."

He was drying a glass with a dish towel, but stopped. "Do you *want* a Cubano with your enchiladas?"

"Maybe next time," I said cheerfully. "You know, that's so interesting that you're from Cuba, because I'm having dinner tonight with a Cuban man—I mean, actually, I'm catering a dinner where he will be a guest. His name is Humberto Captain? Have you heard of him?"

Norman Juarez's face darkened immediately as my question hit its target. He carefully put down the towel and glass, then gave me a penetrating look. "I hope Humberto has already paid you for the dinner."

I slugged down some more beer, then said, "Why would you say that?"

A short, pretty Hispanic woman appeared with a plate of steaming enchiladas and placed them in front of me. I nodded my thanks, and she smiled. When she looked up at her husband, she knew something was up. As she scurried away, I waited for Norman Juarez to give me an answer.

I said, "It's a fund-raiser for our church. Do you think we shouldn't have taken his check?"

"Humberto Captain is a thief." Norman Juarez emphasized each word. "If he ever comes in here, I will throw him out."

I opened my eyes wide in mock amazement. "Was there a time when he didn't pay his bill?"

Norman Juarez's laugh was bitter. "So this is a charity dinner? He does a lot of those, gets his picture on the society page with one girlfriend or another. He tries to convince people he is a good man." He eyed my half-empty beer glass. "You want another?"

I said, "Sure," because I wanted Norman to keep talking. The crowd at the bar had thinned, and after a cursory glance at the remaining customers, Norman sauntered to his refrigerator and pulled out another bottle. There was no way in hell I was going to drink it, but never mind. I forked in a mouthful of enchilada. It was out of this world. There is simply nothing as divine as freshly made tortillas baked with Mexican *queso* and homemade salsa.

Norman opened the new bottle and topped up my glass. "Is this for a church in Denver or Aspen Meadow?"

"It's for Saint Luke's Episcopal in Aspen Meadow." Norman looked at me expectantly, so I took the tiniest imaginable swig of beer. "With everything going south in the economy, we're having trouble meeting our budget. Two generous parishioners agreed to host the event at their house. Each of the guests is paying a thousand dollars."

Norman expelled breath again in a signal of disgust. "Make sure the church cashes Humberto's check first."

I took another teensy sip of beer, to appear companionable. "Now you've got me scared. Did he steal something from you?"

Norman looked away and sucked in his cheeks. At length he said, "A long time ago, he stole my family's entire life savings. In today's market? Worth about ten million dollars. Maybe more."

I choked. "Ten *million* dollars?"

"Give or take."

"How in the world did he do that?" I asked, then took a big bite of enchilada.

Norman walked away without warning, and I thought he was done talking to me. But he was only checking on the other drinkers. A couple needed refills, so after he'd tended to them, he walked back to me.

"How're those enchiladas?"

"Unbelievable," I replied truthfully. "I'm going to have to come back here. My husband works for the sheriff's department. He and his pals love Mexican food."

At the mention of the sheriff's department, Norman's face again grew gloomy. "What does your husband do at the department?"

"He . . . investigates serious crimes, like homicides."

"I had a friend who used to work for the sheriff's department." Norman turned over a paper napkin wrapping cutlery. "My friend was killed a couple of days ago. I hope the department does a better job investigating his death than it did looking into the theft of my family's savings."

I made the mistake of glancing at my watch. I really could not spend more time talking to Norman, at least not now. Norman, for his part, asked, "How does one get tickets to this dinner?"

"You, uh, call the church. But I already have the menu set and most of the food made—"

"We will bring food. You like the enchiladas? Isabella and I will bring a pan of them."

"That's very nice, but—" I looked around desperately, trying to think. I didn't want Norman Juarez to pay two thousand dollars to come to a church dinner where he might get into a fight with Humberto Captain. Plus, we already had too many guests at this dinner. Maybe some people would cancel. One could hope. How had I gotten myself into this situation? And of course I could hear Tom's voice in my ear: *You're always getting yourself into these situations.*

"You need to go?" Norman asked. "You want me to wrap up your food?"

"I do need to take off," I said. "I'm sorry, I can't take the leftovers. If you come tonight, though, I'll get to taste more enchiladas. But, please . . ."

"Don't stab Humberto with one of your kitchen knives?" He gave me a wry smile. "I won't."

I didn't drink any more beer. I thanked Norman and asked him to tell his wife she was a superb cook. Then I paid my tab and left a huge tip.

On the way back up the mountain, I reflected on my conversation with Norman Juarez. That poor guy. He'd worked his way to running his own business after losing a family fortune worth *ten million dollars*? I wondered how long ago he'd hired Ernest, how much Ernest had found out, and in particular, what it was that Ernest said he had recovered. Part of that ten mil, or did Norman even know?

Presumably, the cops had asked Norman these questions. From my perspective, the theft of his family's gold and jewels, plus Humberto's apparent desperation to find out how much Ernest had discovered about him, made Norman a good person to know about. Maybe at some point he'd tell me more about his loss. And despite Norman's assurances, I was still worried that he and Humberto might get into a fight at the party that night.

As my van strained up the interstate, I tried once more to go back to the question of when all this mess had started.

Okay, there was the fact that someone may have been peeping in the windows of Yolanda's rental. Then the house had burned down, and not by accident. The presence of the oil can and accelerant at the scene pointed conclusively to arson.

Yolanda had told me that the owner was Donna Lamar. Had the police talked to her since Ernest's house had burned down? I wondered.

The van crunched through ice as I pulled onto the interstate's shoulder. I called Information again, got Donna's number, and punched buttons.

"This is Donna Lamar, owner of Mountain Rents," her recorded voice announced. Honestly, did anyone answer their own phone anymore? "I'm with a client now, but if you care to leave a message, you may. Or you can come visit me at my beautiful new office, suite two hundred in the Captain's Quarters."

"This is Goldy Schulz," I said in as authoritative a tone as I could muster. "I absolutely must know about a rental as soon as possible." I gave my cell number, hung up, and hoped that would do the trick.

I stared at the phone. The Captain's Quarters? Holy cow. I remembered when Donna—a renowned cheapskate who was also, for better or worse, the Saint Luke's treasurer—had operated a tiny storefront, Mountain Rents, on Main Street, above Frank's Fix-It. I'd just learned from Yolanda that Donna actually owned many of the houses she rented. And now, in an economic downturn no less, Donna was operating out of the swankiest new office building in Aspen Meadow? What was with *that*?

Determined to find out, I pulled the van from the shoulder back to the highway. Ten minutes later, I was signaling to turn into the parking lot of the Captain's Quarters, a stunning stucco and red tile–roofed office building that overlooked manmade fishing ponds. Beyond was a sweeping vista of Flicker Ridge. The Captain's Quarters was gorgeous, and leasing an office in there must have been mega-expensive. Even with one of Donna's properties burning to the ground, dealings in rentals must have been great.

I hopped out of my van and took a deep breath. The melting snow gave the chilled air a bracing scent. Still, I wanted summer back. This was September, for crying out loud, not January. I blinked up at the Captain's Quarters.

No expense had been spared on roof tiles and copper trim. I'd never been inside and was curious to see it. Back when business was booming all over Aspen Meadow, I had occasionally catered breakfasts and lunches for law firms and stockbrokerage businesses. But most of the stockbrokerages had gone under. The few remaining law firms had cut their staffs in half, and all catered meals had been canceled for the foreseeable future.

Donna Lamar, though, well . . . who knew what was going on with her? There was only one car in the lot, a late-model silver Saab station wagon with the license plate MTN RT. It looked as if Donna—who'd always used that vanity plate—had traded in her muffler-dragging, once-red Saab station wagon so in need of paint it looked like a used pencil eraser, for a new one, with no muffler in sight. She was parked in front of an oversize sign: CAPTAIN'S QUARTERS—PREMIER OFFICE SPACE TO LEASE. Under that was DEVELOPED BY HUMBERTO CAPTAIN.

Well, well. In addition to his import-export business, Humberto Captain was dabbling in real estate. I wondered how many of the offices he'd leased. With only one car in the lot and the economy in the tank, I doubted he'd leased many.

As I put the cake, thermos, and paperware into my all-purpose catering tote, I wondered if Donna would spill any details of her office-rental arrangement to me. I took the inside steps two at a time. At the top, I bumped into none other than Donna Lamar.

I blinked. In her late thirties, Donna had a very attractive face that I'd seen impeccably made up, as it was

today, only at Saint Luke's and at parties. Gone were the
jeans and sweatshirt. Now she wore a beautifully cut
chocolate-brown business suit. Instead of sneakers, she
had on heels that were so high I would have fallen over
putting them on. Her thick, puffy blond hair, instead of
being pulled back in a raggedy bun, was cut attractively
and curled in layers to the tops of her shoulders. Her
skirt was short and not what I would have called busi-
nesslike. Still, I'm sure it helped when her business was
with males. She was leaving her office in a hurry and
was fumbling with a bunch of keys.

"Gosh, sorry," I said. "I was just coming to see you. I
called?"

She narrowed her eyes at me in confusion, then
clanked her keys. "I'm sorry, I'm just not remembering a
call from you, Goldy."

"Well, I did," I said with exaggerated patience. "It's
important. A business matter."

I held out my hand, and she shook it limply. Then she
eyed me up and down, which gave me the chance to do
the same to her. I was again struck by how spiffy she
looked. New clothes, new car, new digs. As with Charlene Newgate, I wondered, *Where is all this sudden
wealth coming from?* She was probably wondering,
*What kind of business matter could Goldy the caterer
want to discuss?*

She still regarded me with puzzlement. "Did my *assistant* set up an appointment for you?" she asked. "She's
new, and she doesn't quite understand my business."
Donna looked longingly down the steps, as if they could
pull her away from me.

"I called because I want to talk to you about a rental."
I assumed an anxious look. "I'm pretty desperate."

"All right," she said with a sigh. "Let's go into my office."

"Did you not realize I was coming?"

"No, I didn't." She put a hand on my arm, and I
noticed beautifully manicured, scarlet-painted nails.
"Wait. Goldy. Okay, we can discuss a business matter, if
you want, but don't you sometimes get involved in solving crimes?"

"Actually, yes—"

"I wish you could help me solve one particular kind
of crime," she said fiercely.

"Do tell," I said, a mite too eagerly.

She ignored this, let go of me, and headed to her desk,
where she slapped her brown leather purse onto a stack
of papers. She put her hands on her hips, again lost in
thought.

I didn't want to step into whatever stream Donna's
consciousness ran in, so I looked around. The office
was sparsely decorated, but on one wall was a letter
framed with a photograph and a newspaper article. I
inched over to the wall, to see what Donna had found
suitable to hang. It was a thank-you note from a local
elementary school, in gratitude for Donna coming in to
talk about businesses run by women. The students surrounding Donna had given bored looks to the camera,
but Donna herself was beaming. A *Mountain Journal*
article accompanied the letter and photograph. The title screamed, LOCAL AGENT/OWNER SUCCESS! There
was no byline, and the laudatory paragraphs sounded

suspiciously as if they had been written by Donna herself.

I moved some brochures from an uncomfortable-looking side chair and sat down. "Donna, you really are an achiever. I'm so impressed with how well you're doing!"

"Yes." Her smile was frigid.

"So, do you want to talk about a certain kind of criminal activity?"

She assessed me. "Did you say you were looking for a rental?"

"I *am* looking for a rental," I lied. "That's why I'm here. I just thought, since you mentioned it, if you needed me to help you with something, I mean, like something with a property, a problem that might hurt your reputation as a female entrepreneur—"

Donna Lamar took a seat and flipped her blond hair off her shoulders. "Do you have an area or price range in mind?"

I cleared my throat. "I have two women staying with me. They need a place. We can't go on, all in the same house together, much longer," I said ruefully, wondering if the pity angle would work where the flattery one hadn't. "It's just too much for all of us in one place."

"Price range? Location?"

"In Aspen Meadow," I replied thoughtfully. "It needs to be inexpensive, and it needs to be all on one story, because one of the women is in a wheelchair."

"Oh, Jesus Christ," said Donna Lamar. She shook her head and gazed at the ceiling. "As if I didn't have enough problems. Don't *tell* me it's those two Cuban women."

"Hmm." As she glared at me, I said quietly, "Discriminating against potential renters based on their ethnic background is against the law. Not to mention that Father Pete wouldn't approve."

She tucked in her chin. Her shadowed eyes widened. "I don't care about ethnic whatever! Father Pete can think whatever he wants. That crazy old woman drove me nuts! She was always going on about how she was in Castro's army. You'd think she single-handedly turned that island into a haven for commies. Plus, if Cuba was so wonderful, why didn't she stay there? I *ask* you."

"I think you'd have to ask *her*."

This time, Donna hunkered down under her blond hair, as if it were a hood. She said, "Are you accusing me of something?"

"No, I'm gently reminding you that you can't refuse to rent to people just because they're Cuban-Americans."

Donna enunciated each word carefully. "I. Am. Not. A. Racist. I don't care if they're from Mars. The last rental of mine they lived in burned to the ground. Correction: Somebody burned it to the ground, and dropped a Cuban oil can nearby."

"But," I replied thoughtfully, "the police didn't blame the women for the arson, right? I mean, that's what the women told me. Have you . . . had any other rentals burned by arson?"

"Of course I haven't." A piqued, lost expression washed over her face. "I'm sorry, I don't have any one-story houses available."

"Donna, please." I knew that expression: It was the way a *hungry* person looked. "Let's start over." I reached into my bag and brought out the coffee cake, which I placed in front of her. It looked rich, buttery, and oh-so-inviting under its glistening plastic wrap. "This is a recipe I'm testing. You seem extremely hassled, and I'll bet you haven't had lunch."

She slumped back in her chair. The combative lioness became a kitten I'd just pulled out of the lake. She placed each of her hands on her cheeks and stared at my offering.

"Donna," I said softly, "would you like some espresso and cream? I brought a thermos—"

"Well, actually, could you make me some . . . instant cocoa?" Her voice was meek as she continued to stare at the cake.

"Absolutely," I replied, although I never used the word *instant* in the same breath as *cocoa*. Be that as it may, Donna needed comfort and sustenance, stat. Plus, my curiosity was aroused. She'd gone from a ramshackle storefront to a plush office—leased to her by a Cuban-American, but I hadn't pointed that out—and the place even included a kitchen. Instead of traipsing around in jeans and sweats, she now had the air and the car of a high-priced defense lawyer. All this transformation had taken place since the last time I'd seen her. Yet, as was usually the case, money hadn't bought happiness. In fact, *something* was making her miserable. I was hoping I could discover what.

In the kitchen, I found a small pot, filled it with water, and turned on what looked like a brand-new, unused stove top. I discovered paper cups, paper plates, and packets of instant cocoa, freeze-dried marshmallows conveniently included. Her office fridge didn't smell too good, so while the water heated, I decided to help Donna out, with the hope that she would do the same for me. You could be an Episcopalian and believe in karma, especially given our proximity to Boulder.

I discovered random packages of fur-bearing cheese and moldy crackers, along with two boxes of leftovers bearing stickers from expensive Denver restaurants. The crackers and leftovers I dumped. I removed the cheese, then scrubbed the refrigerator's small interior with wet paper towels and disinfectant. I washed my hands, trimmed up what turned out to be a chunk of cheddar, and placed a good-sized wedge on a plate. I stirred the boiling water into the powdered hot chocolate for Donna and put out two paper plates. I wanted to share a bit of cake with Donna and be sociable, even though I'd just plowed through two beers and most of a plate of enchiladas trying to do the same thing with Norman Juarez.

Back in her office, Donna was still staring at the cake. I began to wonder if she needed medical attention.

"Donna? Are you all right?" I asked softly. When she didn't reply, I unwrapped the cake and sliced an enormous piece for her plate. I placed her makeshift meal in front of her, along with the steaming cocoa, its tiny marshmallows bobbing about merrily. "Eat something. You'll feel better."

Startled out of her reverie, she nodded thanks, then sipped the cocoa and nibbled the cheese. She forked up a hunk of coffee cake, and as is often the case when one is sugar deprived and stressed out, the carbohydrates provided a jolt. "Thank you," she said. "This is good." Tears actually filled her eyes. "I've been trying to answer calls all morning, and I haven't—"

"Hey, I'm the caterer, remember? No excuses needed." I sliced myself a small piece of cake, then sat down and took a bite. The guava gave the cake a pop that I would have enjoyed even more had I some decent coffee—but wait, I did. I pulled out my Thermos, poured myself a cup, and sipped.

As we ate, I sent as many smiles Donna's way as I could. I remembered what my father had told me, back when I was young, feisty, and driving my teachers crazy by talking back. Good old Dad had said, "You can catch more flies with honey than you can with vinegar." Being vinegary by nature, I took considerable time to learn the lesson, if I ever had. But when I remembered Dad's advice, I tried.

"You know what?" I said kindly. "We really don't have to find a rental for Ferdinanda and Yolanda today. With the sudden storm, you must have tenants calling every two minutes." Actually, the phone had not rung since I'd been there, but never mind. And where was the assistant? Maybe driving around looking for takeout. "Tenants are probably driving you nuts," I babbled on, "because they can't find snowblowers, or snow shovels, or they don't have heat. Over a foot of white stuff in September has discombobulated everyone, me included. Isn't it bizarre?"

"Yes, it is." She sipped her cocoa and gave me a wary look. "But it's not my tenants who are driving me crazy."

"Um," I said thoughtfully, "not your tenants?"

"No, it's the people who *aren't* my clients who are doing that."

"You know what?" I said, leaning forward in what I hoped was conspiratorial confidence. "Six people just got added to the dinner I'm catering tonight. And there might even be two more. None of these people were regular clients, either, but—"

"I mean"—she interrupted me—"I like sex as much as the next person, but why do you have to ruin somebody's business because you won't go to a hotel?"

"Has the economy gotten *that bad*?" I asked. "I thought they had nooner rates down in Golden—"

"Oh, these people have money," she said conspiratorially, taking another bite of cake.

"The nerve!" I had no idea what she was talking about, but I sure wanted to find out. When she continued to eat cake, I asked hopefully, "Why would *anyone* ruin a business because someone refused to go to a hotel?"

"I know how they do it, too," she said without explaining the ruining-business part. She put down her fork and pointed a scarlet-painted nail at the ceiling. "One of them poses as a potential client. They ask for the cheapest rental houses available in the mountain area. Then they get my assistant to let them into the property, and then he or she says they're not interested. My assistant even thinks they're using disguises now."

"You've never seen these people?"

"No. I usually just show the high-end homes."

"Can your assistant describe the—"

"No. Believe me, I've tried to get her to tell me what

they look like. But she needs new glasses, and she says I'm not paying her enough so that she can get them. When I say, 'Well, then, how can you drive?' she says she probably shouldn't be driving, but anyway, she says these people are sort of young, sort of thin. As if that's going to help me." Donna shook her head and stopped talking.

"I promise you," I said, "if my friends rent from you? They will be as pure as the driven—"

"I have to catch these two," Donna said, interrupting me again.

"These two . . . ?"

"That's the only way. I've offered rewards to the neighbors of every single one of my unsecured listings. I mean, if the neighbors call me in time so I can catch the squatters."

"What are unsecured listings?"

But she lapsed back into her reverie. Eventually, she uncurled herself from wherever her mind had taken her. She looked at me as if she were again trying to remember who I was. When she did, she took another bite of cake and nodded her approval. "If I tell you about this, you can't tell the *Mountain Journal*."

"I wouldn't tell the paper. But it sounds as if you can't tell the paper either, because you don't know who *these two* are."

"No, I don't." She drained her hot chocolate and clapped the cup on the desktop. "But I *do* know when they sneak into my rentals and have sex. Sometimes I don't know right away, but I know, because they don't clean up after themselves. It's part of their, what do you call it, their MO."

I said, "Donna, breaking and entering is against the law. What did you mean by unsecured listings? Don't your rentals have security systems?"

"Only high-end homes have security systems. This couple prefers cozy little cottages, preferably deep in the woods. They break a window, open the back door, and let themselves in. They bring along their food and wine, and one time, two sleeping bags that could be zipped together. How *cozy*. I wanted to get the bags tested for DNA, but the cops wouldn't do it. They said it was too expensive and sleeping bags that I had handled would not be evidence of a crime. Then I wanted to have the genetic testing done on my own. But when I heard how much it cost, I didn't."

I thought about the couple who'd showed up at my door the other day, along with their real estate agent. Had they been casing Jack's place? It wasn't a rental. Then again, it didn't have a security system.

I said stubbornly, "You really should talk to the police again about the break-ins. If you have sleeping bags, they might be able to trace back—"

She waved this away. "I just wanted them to do DNA testing. I don't want the breaking-and-entering part to get out. You know how the sheriff's calls always appear in the *Mountain Journal*. If I tell the cops I have squatters balling away in my rentals, then everyone will want to do it. And nobody, but nobody, wants to rent a place where squatters have broken a window and left wine bottles, plastic wineglasses, cracker crumbs, and cheese wrappers. Those things attract rodents. Nobody is going to rent a place where there are rodent droppings, and my assistant and I can't check every single listing every day to make sure they're clean." Donna shivered. "The whole thing is disgusting."

"You could hire a private detective."

She shook her head again. "Actually, a nice investigator did come to see me. He had a client who was trying to track down a couple having an affair. His client thought the adulterers might be meeting in vacant rentals." She took a bite of cheese. "But last night, on the news? I heard the guy died. So I have no idea if he discovered them."

I felt as if I'd been slapped. "The detective? It was Ernest McLeod?"

"You knew him?"

"I did." I omitted the part about Yolanda and Ferdinanda living with him, fearing she might jump to conclusions. "Do you . . . know who his client was? The one trying to track down the people having the affair?"

"He wouldn't tell me." She rubbed her hands together and stood up. "Thanks for the cake. My assistant is showing a couple of properties and was supposed to bring back sandwiches, but who knows where she is now. Anyway, I was just going off to one of my listings, a small A-frame, when you showed up. A neighbor reported seeing a strange car there, so I was going to check. Whoever it is, they're probably gone now."

I stood up, too, but was reluctant to leave. "Why don't you let me do it? Ernest McLeod was a friend of mine, and I'd like to help you catch these people. Also, if you have some old cheese wrappers and plastic glasses they left, I might be able to figure something out. I *am* a food person."

She pointed one of those red-painted nails at me. "I don't want this in the paper."

"I won't call the paper," I promised.

"You'd better not." She stared at me.

What was with this woman? I wanted to ask her if she'd seen a stocky bald guy. I wanted to know what her relationship to Humberto was, if he gave her the office rent-free, if he had access to her rentals, and if he paid her to have that access. But Donna was both suspicious and hard to keep on track. Even though I was frustrated, I didn't want her to become distracted again.

"Um, Donna? If I have a list of your unsecured rentals, I might be able to do a better search."

She rifled through the papers on her desk and came up with a single sheet. "Ten listings without security systems."

When I asked, "Which one had the neighbor who called you?" Donna leaned down and put a red check mark next to one address. I said, "Did she get a description of the car, or a license plate, maybe?"

"All this neighbor saw was a dark SUV in the driveway. I'm telling you, all this couple likes is cabins far from everything. Wait here a sec." She went to a closet and pulled out a bag. "I don't know why I kept this stuff, but I did. There are two sleeping bags in there, plus plastic glasses, some cheese wrappers, and an empty box of crackers. You ask me, these people are pigs."

I opened the sack and immediately closed it. Like in the refrigerator, the scent of moldy food was overpowering. I stood up to wrap the cake. "Would you like the rest of this?"

"I'd love it, but I think it would just sit in my refrigerator, where I already have a bunch of old stuff. A cleaning crew was supposed to come through, but they didn't. One more thing I have to deal with."

An assistant. A cleaning crew. A gorgeous new office. "Oh," I said, as if it had just occurred to me. "Humberto Captain built this office space? It's gorgeous. I know Humberto," I added.

Suspicion flared in her eyes. "Yes, he built this beautiful building. You see, I'm not prejudiced against Cuban-Americans."

"This place is really top-notch. I used to cater in offices like this."

She lifted her chin in defiance. "Well, he gave me a really good rate, so that somebody would be in here, you know, occupying the place."

How could I ask her if he had access to all her files and keys without her clamming up? How could I find out if Humberto was the one who'd been looking in Yolanda's rental windows? Was it possible that anyone besides Tom suspected that Humberto might have burned down Yolanda's rental so that she would have to make other arrangements, like living with a private investigator who was getting close to discovering the gold and gems Humberto insisted he'd never stolen?

"Well, if you're going out to that cabin, I guess I'd better make some calls," Donna said. She gave me a solicitous look. "Actually, I'm thankful you're doing this."

"Oh, you're welcome." I put the rest of the wrapped cake, my thermos, and the list of unsecured rentals into my tote and tried to think of a way to take advantage of

Donna's sudden gratitude. "Humberto? Does he show the offices that are available?"

"Goldy? You can*not* put those two women into this office building. It's against the law for people to live in an office building. And anyway, Humberto's been great to me. Very generous. He would never agree to put them in here, and I would never ask."

"You don't understand," I said patiently. "Humberto adores Yolanda and Ferdinanda. He came over first thing yesterday morning, when he heard they were living with me. He wanted to help."

"Of course he did."

"They told him they were fine. And, uh, Yolanda is making money, by helping me cater tonight."

Donna shifted her weight to one foot and put her hand on her hip. Alas, the distrust was back. "I thought you were desperate to get these women out of your hair."

"I'm just trying to do the right thing. If any one-story rentals come up, I'd love to hear about them." I hoisted up the plastic bag, then picked up my tote. "I don't mean to delay you, but you know the party we're catering tonight?"

"The fund-raising supper. Thank you for doing that, Saint Luke's really needs the money."

"Well," I said, continuing blithely, "there are going to be some wealthy people at the dinner. Sometimes clients ask me questions, like 'Do you know if there are any good deals on offices in town?' And I thought, since Humberto will be at the Breckenridges' place tonight, I could introduce him to—"

"*I'll* be at the dinner tonight, so if anyone wants to

know about office space at the Captain's Quarters, *I* can introduce them to Humberto." Donna moved around her desk to give me the bum's rush out of her office.

I stood my ground. "Does Humberto himself show the offices? I mean, what if someone wants to lease an office right away? Does he have keys to all the offices?"

Donna *clip-clopped* to the door. "Yes, he has keys, yes, he shows the offices. He's got big offices and little offices in this building. I do appreciate your going out to help me with the people breaking into the rentals."

"Don't worry, if I find out anything, I'll call you. Maybe I'll even figure out who your squatters are."

She didn't offer a reward, but she did open the door for me. I smiled as I left, as if we were old pals and I really would call her if I figured anything out.

Which, of course, I had no intention of doing.

Chapter 13

Outside, the sun was shining, but the air was still cold. The plows had rammed dirty walls of ice onto the roadsides. Even so, the pavements were still swathed with thin blankets of snow. Driving would be treacherous, and I had enough problems without ending up in a ditch. I opened the side door of my van and carefully flung in my tote, followed by the plastic bag of detritus from one of Donna's rentals. Maybe this evidence wasn't technically from adulterers, maybe it was just from sort-of-young, sort-of-thin people, teenagers even, seeking a thrill. But it was something, and if Ernest had been investigating this couple, the evidence might be connected to his death.

Once inside my van, I turned on the engine and wished I'd worn gloves. It was twelve forty-five, and I was unaccountably hungry. The enchiladas were a memory and the coffee cake was calling. I unwrapped it, broke off a hunk, and chewed thoughtfully while staring at Donna's list. The one rental she'd checked, the one where the lovebirds had made their most recent nest, was way out by the Aspen Meadow Wildlife Preserve. I wasn't sure I had the time, the tires, or the tolerance to find a house in that area. Worse, there was no way to find out if the plows had been through the vast labyrinth of dirt roads that lay around the preserve.

I rewrapped the cake, poured myself some coffee, and stared again at the address. I knew Tom would be furious if I drove out there and poked around in an empty house, *alone*. But Donna had been on her way to do just that, right?

I could hear Tom's voice in my head saying, *You're not Donna.*

Wait a minute, I thought. I had a friend who lived in that area, not far from the rental, if I was judging distances correctly. Sabine Rushmore was a librarian whom I had known for years. I'd catered the retirement party she'd held at her house. She was sixty-five, but you'd never guess it. Except for her long, frizzy gray mane, she didn't look a day over forty. My theory was that she kept herself youthful with her work as a peace activist, her long treks to remote parts of Colorado and the Mountain West to hunt for dinosaur bones, and of course—*of course*—the labor she put into growing organic vegetables. To me, it all sounded exhausting, but Sabine thrived on the activity.

Unfortunately, I didn't know Sabine's home phone number. There was no way the privacy-obsessed staff at the Aspen Meadow Library would give it to me, even if Sabine needed a kidney and I had one on ice in the van. And anyway, I thought, as I punched the buttons for Information, what if Sabine's number was unlisted? What if she lived so far off the grid that she didn't even have a phone?

Well, glory be. There was a Rushmore listed on the same county road as the rental. I punched in the number and couldn't believe it when Sabine answered.

"Goldy, wow, I can't believe you're calling," she said, out of breath. In the background I could hear crunching noises, and I guessed she was digging out her driveway. "It's so good to hear from you. Gives me a chance to give up on clearing snow."

I pictured her steep, rutted dirt driveway. "Don't you have anyone to help you?"

"Not at the moment. Greg's taken the four-wheeler into town for supplies for our horses. I wanted to surprise him. Anyway, I'm almost done." She took a deep breath, then said, "Good thing I brought my phone outside in my pocket, huh? Maybe I subconsciously wanted an interruption. What can I do for you?"

I explained that I was hoping she could come with me on a bit of a hunt, sort of like one of her fossil-seeking expeditions.

"It's really exactly like looking for dinosaur bones. Only easier," I said.

"Goldy the caterer. Making the link between pastry and paleontology, eh?" she asked, a smile in her voice. "Sounds more like one of your crime-solving capers. I remember you found a body in the library once."

"Hey," I said in protest, "it wasn't my fault the guy was murdered there."

"And," she continued, "you said the perpetrator of another murder was in the library at the same time."

"Aspen Meadow Library is a popular place."

"So what I'm asking, Goldy, is this: Are we going to need to be armed when we go on this expedition of yours?"

I thought of Arch using the weeder on our would-be intruder. "Well, it might not hurt if we took some sharply pointed garden equipment. Just kidding. I think the perps have fled." I rushed on to give details that she would have to promise not to tell the paper: that apparently, a couple had broken into an A-frame near her, to have sex, most likely, and I wanted to see if there was anything left that would help me aid the real estate agent in figuring out who they were. "The agent was on her way out there when I volunteered to make the trek," I told her.

"I know the house," Sabine said. "The owner's home-based business collapsed. He had to move his family back in with his wife's parents down in Denver, where he's working in a restaurant. Their house has been for rent for a while. People don't like to commute to Denver from way out here." She took a deep breath. "Yeah, sure, come on ahead."

I said I would see her in less than half an hour and turned the van in the direction of the Aspen Meadow Wildlife Preserve. I knew there would be no wrath equal to Tom's if I did not tell him what I was up to, so I put in a call to his voice mail. I informed him of everything Donna had told me and added the caveat that he couldn't put it into the sheriff's calls in the paper. And, I said, I had a friend who was going to go into the empty house with me. By the way, I concluded, had he been able to question Charlene Newgate? And did he have the canvass, time of death, and ballistics and accelerant results back from Ernest's murder and the arson? "Just curious," I said, "trying to help." I could imagine Tom shaking his head.

I drove down to Aspen Meadow Lake, which blazed with sparkles from the afternoon sun. Vestiges of snow laced the water's edge. There was no traffic, so I pulled over. Something was niggling at the back of my brain after the call to Tom. Oh, yes, the informal dinner gathering at the Bertrams' place on Thursday, so everyone could remember Ernest. I wanted to help.

I dialed SallyAnn Bertram's number and put the phone on speaker. As her number rang, I turned right onto Upper Cottonwood Creek Road. When my tires skidded to the left, I inhaled sharply. Slowly, I started up the winding road. I needed to be on the lookout for black ice as well as snow that might have blown over it. An innocent-looking swath of white stuff could conceal a hazard that flipped your vehicle.

When SallyAnn answered, I identified myself and said I wanted to help out with the potluck supper on Thursday night, when the department was going to gather to remember Ernest. What did she need me to bring?

"Oh, Goldy, you're a dear! I don't know what to tell you, because I haven't even started to organize this thing, but I do know somebody is bringing hamburgers, because John wanted us to have this outside, so we can grill. But now I worry that it will snow again, or even rain, and if it rains or snows, everyone will have to come inside. That's really terrible, because this place is such a wreck, I hate to imagine what everyone's going to think when they walk through our doors. I think John has that disorder, you know, where someone hoards stuff? He built a six-car garage on our property, and it has one truck in it, plus a bunch of junk, including the lawn furniture that we never did bring out this summer. But John, you know? When he can't find something in the garage? He buys a new tool or other thingamajig, and puts it into one of the closets in the house. So our closets are all spilling over with stuff. What's supposed to be our living space is now filled with junk, and we don't have room for these people that he invited over here without even telling me—"

"SallyAnn, wait a sec." I had to interrupt her, because not only was she having a panic attack, she was about to give me one. And anyway, I'd just cleaned out Donna Lamar's refrigerator. That was all the mental space I could give to decluttering in one day. "One thing at a time," I said slowly. "Can you get a pen and paper?" When she rummaged for those, I heard what sounded like pots falling onto the floor. Maybe John wasn't the only one with a hoarding disorder. "First of all," I said, "let me bring something hot, because the weather has turned cool. If one of the guests is bringing hamburgers, then how about if I bring homemade cream of mushroom soup? Everyone seems to like it, no matter what the weather."

"Okay, but I don't know what to do about all the mess—"

"No problem there, either. I've already arranged a cleaning lady who owes me a favor to do some extra work. *I'll* pay *her* to clean up your house Thursday. How about that?"

"Oh, would you?" SallyAnn's stressed-out tone went from agony to relief. "Does she have a whole team? 'Cause that's what we're going to need."

"We'll work it out. How many people have said they're coming?"

"So far, about twenty, although I haven't been keeping a list. I suppose that I should, now that I've found the paper, although I'm having to use an old tube of lipstick to write down what you're telling me. But listen, we'll probably have double that number, at least. I don't want to run out of food, and if everyone decides to bring salads, then we'll really be in a mess. . . ."

A new worry. Could SallyAnn's doctor prescribe her a tranquilizer?

"Find a pen and keep it, with the paper, by the phone," I said sternly. "When people call, write down their names. Ask them to bring potato salad or dessert. Everybody loves those dishes with hamburgers, and if you want, I can bring a large tossed green salad with the soup."

"Omigod, Goldy, you're saving my life, thank you so much." Her breath caught. "I suppose I shouldn't be going on about my own hostess problems when Ernest . . ." She couldn't finish the thought.

After a pause, I reassured her. "The sheriff's department will figure out who did this, don't worry."

"But he's gone," she wailed.

"I'm sorry, SallyAnn, I didn't realize you were close."

"We weren't—I mean, we used to be, but after he had

to leave the department, we sort of drifted apart, even though his house is up the hill. . . . Now I feel awful."

"Well, let me ask you this. Did Ernest seem sick to you?"

"Sick, you mean, like the cancer? We didn't even know he *had* cancer until he was dead. You see, after he became a private investigator, we didn't get together with him too often. But come to think of it, last time we saw him, he looked a little thin. He said it was getting sober, you know. But don't most people eat *more* when they're recovering from alcoholism? Well anyway, I guess he didn't, because the last time we saw him, he said he was hiring someone to fix dinners for him a few days a week. I offered to bring food over, but he knows my cooking, so he, you know, declined. Nicely, but still. Anyway, the last time we saw him was a couple of weeks ago. He really seemed to like that gal—oh, you're not supposed to call anyone a gal anymore, but anyway, he was excited about having her cook for him. He liked her, and that seemed to brighten up his mood, you know?"

"He liked her?"

"Well not like he was falling in *love* with her, but then again, maybe he was, and he just didn't tell us, the way he didn't tell us about the cancer. Wait. Is this the woman who was living in the house when it burned down? The one whose aunt or whoever she is whacked John with her baton?"

"Yes, but—"

"Are *they* coming to the party?"

"Not if you don't want them to, but the women have

been through hell. Boyd has been staying with us, to . . . provide extra protection for them, since someone torched Ernest's house. Tom and Boyd don't think they're safe anywhere else. So, if you want Boyd at the party, the women will have to come. Yolanda caters with me, and her great-aunt really is a lovable old bird, once you get to know her. Tough, but not without charm."

"Well, I *do* want Boyd at the party," SallyAnn said, sounding uncertain again. "Ernest really liked Boyd. Everyone likes Boyd. So I suppose we have to have the women, too."

"Great." I slowed before a hairpin curve. "I'll send the cleaning lady over. We'll be there with soup and salad. Say about six?"

"Thanks, Goldy, thanks. Sorry to be so disorganized about all this, it's just that Ernie's death threw us for a loop."

"Ernie?"

"Well, Ernest. In the department? John was the only one Ernest allowed to call him Ernie. Ernest called John 'Bert,' so they could be Bert and Ernie. It was their little joke. You know how cops need their humor."

"Indeed I do."

We signed off, and I carefully negotiated the turn. Once again my wheels skidded sideways. I wanted to call Penny Woolworth, the spying cleaning lady, to talk about this new gig. But I didn't want to be distracted.

I turned right onto the long dirt road that led to the Aspen Meadow Wildlife Preserve. The byway had been plowed once, but now snow, mud, and ice had combined into a frozen sludge that my tires chewed through sometimes and skidded through other times. I sighed. It was already just past one. I absolutely had to be home by three at the latest, so Yolanda and I could pack up for the Breckenridges' dinner.

I was startled when a car raced up behind me and then overtook the van. It was a silver BMW that must have had four-wheel drive and snow tires worthy of a Sherman tank. Snow spewed over my windshield, and I was forced to slow.

I turned on the wipers and shouted, "Thank you very much," but of course the driver couldn't hear me.

As the wipers swept snow from the glass, I saw something. Or thought I saw something. It was a bumper sticker, a familiar one. Had it been *Secretaries Do It Behind the Desk*? I hurried up and sent the van into a one-eighty skid that left me cursing. I hadn't been able to see who was driving the BMW, but it had taken every bit of growing-up-in-Jersey driving to keep from landing in the snow-covered pasture that lay to my right.

I turned back around with the idea that maybe I could catch up with Charlene's vehicle, if that was what it had been. But the driver was zipping along at a clip my van would have had trouble managing going downhill, on dry pavement. And anyway, now the road was headed uphill. Where could the BMW have been going? That was the question, and not an easily answered one.

Before Furman County bought the enormous ranch that made up the preserve, people had built everything from gigantic houses to log cabins on the property surrounding the ranch. Either the rich had wanted the mountain view or folks wanted to farm or ranch. Taking into account Charlene's fur, car, grandson in parochial school, and altogether new lifestyle, I would have guessed her boyfriend was in that big-house-with-a-view category.

When I crested the hill, the BMW had disappeared. I motored along past five dirt roads going right, left, and sideways, with no clue as to where the silver car had turned. Unlike Sabine, I was no expert at tracking, and numerous vehicles had left their tire prints in the snow. I cursed silently and encouraged the van along to the turnoff for Sabine's.

She met me at the bottom of her driveway. Tall, with a commanding presence, she wore a cap that I was sure she had knitted herself, from wool she'd spun from her own sheep and dyed using vegetables she and Greg had grown. She wore thick, unfashionable specs with shades she flipped down when she needed sunglasses, like now. Her frizzy hair radiated like a gray halo from a ponytail at the nape of her neck, and her ankle-length olive-green overcoat looked as if she'd bought it from an army veteran who'd survived the Nazi assault on the Ardennes forest. She'd apparently taken seriously my quip about using sharply pointed garden equipment as weapons. At arm's length, she held two long-handled garden spades. Sabine Rushmore, pacifist, prepared for battle.

"There you are!" she said brightly when I hopped out of the van. She eyed me up and down. The skin at the sides of her eyes crinkled with worry. "You need boots and gloves? I've got some up in the house."

Knowing her home lay half a mile up the murderous incline behind her, I demurred. "But thank you for setting out on this expedition with me. Do you want me to get the address, or do you know exactly where this place is?"

"I know it."

I set off behind her. She insisted on carrying both "weapons," as she called them. Even though I was wearing sneakers and lighter clothing, was bearing no arms, and was more than thirty years younger than my compatriot, she left my butt in the dust. Or in this case, in the snow. I huffed along and finally called to her to stop.

"Is it much farther?" I panted, bending over to deal with the stitch in my side.

"Just around the next bend. Are you all right?"

"I'm not sure."

"It's all that high-fat-content food you make, Goldy. It's slowing you down."

Since the last thing I needed at this point was a nutrition lecture, I said merely, "Lead on." She smiled before trotting away.

After a few more minutes of muscle-squealing agony, I followed her up a driveway that had not been plowed but that had a set of tire prints in it—going in and coming out. I wondered if the lab at the sheriff's department could or would trace them. I doubted it. Tom had more serious crimes to investigate at the moment. And anyway, if the break-and-enterers were also adulterers, Father Pete would have pointed out that adultery wasn't a crime. It was a sin.

Ahead of us, tucked into a stand of lodgepole pines, stood a tiny red one-story A-frame. The deck out front needed paint. On either side of the small front door, white crisscrossing on the windows plus black shutters with cut-out heart shapes indicated the house had been built in the seventies, when trying-to-be-Swiss style was all the rage in Aspen Meadow.

No one had shoveled the walkway to the deck. The place looked forlorn.

"Following the tire tracks," Sabine called, "it looks as if your lovebirds broke in around this corner." She disappeared, and I was suddenly worried. What if something happened to Sabine? Tom would have my neck.

The sound of breaking glass brought me quickly around to the side of the house. Why hadn't I had the presence of mind to ask Donna Lamar for a *key* to this place? Sabine had used her garden implement to shatter what remained of the second window in the back door. The original breakers-in had smashed the first pane in the door. Sabine reached in and opened it.

"I didn't know if your husband would want fingerprints from that other windowpane," she said by way of explanation.

"Wait," I said, pointing down. "They parked, then walked through the snow to this door, instead of the front door. They broke one pane of glass, and you broke the other. Why come back here?"

"They must have thought their vehicle would be out of sight," said Sabine. "Hello?" she cried into the interior, which echoed.

"Sabine, wait," I said. Again thinking of Tom and my fragile neck, I hustled ahead of her to make sure the place was empty.

"*You* are not going anywhere," Sabine said, holding out an arm like a crossing guard. "I am strong, fearless, and sixty-five years old." She reached back through the door and picked up her garden spades, which she had leaned against the house. "*Nobody* messes with me."

Sabine ordered me to stay put while she traipsed through the two bedrooms, her gardening spades at the ready. She checked the two bathrooms and the closets while I pretty much stayed in the living/dining/kitchen area. At one point, I sneaked over to the kitchen and checked the cabinets and refrigerator. They were empty, except for an opened box of baking soda in the fridge.

Back in the living/dining/kitchen area, we looked around for clues as to who could have broken in before we broke in. The place was cold and dark, as A-frames tend to be. There was a solitary skylight, which let in some sunshine as well as water. Either Donna or the owners had put a bucket on the shag-carpeted floor to catch the trickle from the leak, and the melting snow made irregular plops.

"Looks like they had a fire," I said, eyeing the tiny, bleak fireplace.

"You know Sherlock Holmes would go through those ashes," Sabine announced. She put down her spades, picked up one of her bags, and hustled over to the hearth, where she got down on her knees. She began methodically sifting the gray dust, bit by small bit, over to one side of the hearth.

I looked around. What was missing? Something, and I couldn't quite put my finger on it. Wait: the fire.

"Where do you suppose they got their wood?" I asked

Sabine, who was still intent on the cold ashes. "Could they have brought in an armful from their vehicle? Or several armfuls? I didn't see any pieces of dropped bark between the driveway and the back door." I remembered the sleeping bags and cheese wrappers. Was it possible these folks backed a truck full of supplies into each of their love nests whenever they went for a roll in the hay?

"The home owners used to chop their own wood from their land," Sabine said. "We do, too. All of us out here cut down some trees, to keep the fire danger down. That big wildfire out in the preserve? It started less than a mile from here."

"But . . . when we came in, I didn't see a pile of firewood beside the house."

"Check out back," she said without lifting her eyes from her ash sifting. "The owners' store of wood should be covered with plastic. Up here, we tend to get more snow than in town. You have to keep the logs dry, in case you lose power and are completely dependent on your fire to keep you warm."

Off I went. Sure enough, once I rounded the back wall of the house, I saw a block the size of two cars—the woodpile. It was covered with green plastic. Huh . . . what would Sherlock Holmes do? He'd look down.

The fresh snow had filled in old, deep boot prints, so I carefully followed them. The prints went to the woodpile, then back to the *front* side of the house, to the deck, where there was another door. Bark and kindling littered the path. So they had parked, smashed a window to get inside the back door, and then gone in and out of the front door with firewood.

At the woodpile, I followed their trail to a spot where there was a showering of chips. The snow was tamped down with boot marks. I pulled back the plastic and saw where an entire section of logs had been depleted. Unfortunately, the thief had not left a sweatshirt with his name on it.

And then, from deep in the woods, there was an eruption of gunfire.

Damn it.

I dropped to my belly, with the woodpile between whoever was shooting and yours truly. "Sabine!" I screamed. "Did you hear that?"

She had come out the back door with its two broken windows and was looking for me. "Don't worry," she called. "We hear shots fired all the time. It's not even hunting season. The bastards!"

"You hear shots fired all the time," I muttered, as I got to my knees and brushed snow off my clothes. "Great."

"Still," she yelled, "we should probably leave. We *are* technically trespassing." As if to punctuate her words, another round of gunfire, closer this time, went off.

"Crap!" I hollered as I fell on my stomach again. Was my yelling more or less likely to rain bullets on us? Wait a minute. I'd seen something. Where? Not on top of the woodpile, not beyond it, but . . . below it. I inched sideways.

From this angle, between the snow and the bottom of the woodpile, I saw that something silvery had become wedged. It wasn't a coin. It was too flat. As my frozen fingers tugged on the tiny gray corner of whatever it was, a third round of gunfire went off.

"Goldy?" Sabine cried. "You're not in the best of shape, and I don't want us to try to outrun those shooters, whoever they are."

"Okay, okay." I pushed hard on the lowest log close to the silvery gray thing. The wood moved a tiny fraction. I slammed my shoulder into the woodpile. Nothing. "Sabine!" I hollered. "Duck down and come help me!"

"With what?" Bent at the waist, she trotted toward me. She was covered with ashes from the fireplace.

"Help me push this woodpile over," I said when she arrived.

"Are you mad?"

"Not mad, not angry, and certainly not insane. On three, push." We set our arms out straight against the logs. I counted, and Sabine and I heaved and groaned. The woodpile crashed over.

"You really must have hated those logs," said Sabine, brushing off her gloves. "And now we need to get going."

I bent over and scooped up a credit card that was partially covered with snow. Once more, gunfire exploded, closer still. Even though I was consumed with curiosity, I couldn't indulge it. My heart was pounding with the amount of effort it had taken to upend the logs, and I was worried about getting away from the shooter. I shoved the card in my pocket without reading the name.

Sabine motioned for me to follow her. Still bent at the waist, she jogged to the house, retrieved her gardening tools, and started trotting up the driveway. I raced after her, slipping and sliding wildly, as eager to get away from that A-frame as I'd wanted to get anywhere in my life. But I had, as they say in Tom's business, a clue.

Sabine, bless her sweet heart, waited for me at the end of the A-frame's driveway. Worry creased her face. "Are you going to make it?" This, from a woman three decades older than yours truly, propelled me the rest of the way to her house.

Once we were inside Sabine's hand-built log cabin, I pulled out the credit card. Printed at the bottom was the name *Sean Breckenridge*. I showed it to Sabine, who raised her eyebrows.

She said, "This calls for some hot herb tea."

I built a fire in her hearth and swathed myself in a homemade crocheted afghan. As I began to warm up, I wondered about Sean Breckenridge.

I didn't know him, really. He and Rorry had been living in Aspen Meadow for only a few years, and when Rorry had parties, Marla told me, she hired a Denver caterer. Rorry and Marla had become friends at the country club pool, where Rorry took her son for swimming lessons.

I knew Rorry from church, but only a little. Sean and Rorry's son, who I guessed was now in kindergarten, came to the altar for a blessing when his parents took communion. The little guy was dark haired and adorable, and possessed an amazing collection of checkered shirts and cowboy boots. He seemed to be wearing a new pair of boots every time I saw him, but always the same cowboy hat. As the mother of a son, I knew enough to tell him his outfit was "really cool" but to stop there. The little boy had looked at me with serious eyes and actually tipped his hat. He'd said, "Thank yeh, ma'am." I'd managed not to laugh.

Sabine returned with a tray and two hand-thrown pottery mugs, from which a steam emerged that smelled like lawn clippings. She said, "Maybe it's not as big a deal as we think it is." She settled into a rocking chair and blew on her tea. "Maybe Sean and Rorry just have so much money, and such a big house, that they go out looking for, you know, adventure while their son is in school."

"Adventure. Right."

"Well, Goldy, you don't *know* he was up to something else. *With* someone else."

"You're right, I don't." I took a deep breath. "What do you suppose that person or those people were shooting at? Do you think they saw or heard us?"

"I can't imagine they did," she said. Her nose and cheeks were smudged with soot. "I wish I'd found something. May I just see the card one more time?"

I placed the credit card on the coffee table Sabine and her husband had made, she'd told me when I did her retirement party, from a door salvaged from an abandoned church.

"It could have been stolen," I said. "Or, if he's the one who dropped it, he could have done it when he was lifting logs," I said, remembering how he'd dropped his keys when he was trying to carry his camera. "Credit cards are weird that way. They can work their way out of your wallet. Any man who was exerting effort like that, back and forth to the house, if he had a wallet? The card could have just fallen out. Then the guy's boot wedged it under the pile."

Sabine shook her head again and handed me the card. "I notice the expiration is in two years. So it's a current card." That information settled over us for a few minutes. "Well, old friend," she said, standing up, "I have to go take care of the horses. Hay, water, stuff like that. You're free to stay as long as you want, but I need to get out to the barn."

I scrambled to my feet and checked my watch. One-forty-five already! I had no idea our little escapade at the A-frame had taken so long. "I have to skedaddle, too. But, wait. Sabine, are you the one who called Donna about someone at the A-frame?"

She shook her head. "No. But there are other people who live out here. It's just hard to see their houses with all the trees."

"Has there been any other, you know, suspicious activity in the wildlife preserve? Some reason for people to be shooting?"

Sabine divided her ponytail just below the rubber band, then pulled it in two sections to tighten it. "Well, there's Hermie."

"Not Hermie Milkulski."

"The very same. She's an animal-rights activist, do you know her?"

I sighed. "Yes."

"Did you know she lost two fingers a couple of months ago, when she was trying to close down a Nebraska puppy mill *by herself*? The owner shot her hand."

I shook my head. "So that's how it happened."

"Unfortunately, yes. And since she was trespassing, the owner was within his legal rights. I heard she promised her son that she wouldn't go out of state anymore, nor would she go into places alone. Now, apparently, Hermie only acts locally. When she suspects some kind of abuse is happening, she just calls Furman County Animal Control."

"She doesn't go out of state, and she doesn't go alone," I echoed. Hermie had done more than call Animal Control. She'd hired Ernest to do her dirty work. It wouldn't help to tell Sabine this, and I knew Tom would not appreciate my sharing this tidbit.

Sabine shrugged. "Whenever the Animal Control people don't find what Hermie thinks they should find, she raises a stink. She was here once, asking me a bunch of questions. Some guy near here has a legit breeding operation on his farm. But Hermie claimed this was cover. She actually used that word." Sabine sighed. "Anyway, someone who bought a puppy from this breeder called Hermie and said the puppy got sick and then died. According to Hermie, the buyer said it was the veterinarian *himself* who suspected a mill. Also according to Hermie, Animal Control went out and couldn't find anything. Hermie insisted that the mill, or mills, were hidden in sheds, or kennels, somewhere on the breeder's property. Now, wait for it. Hermie thought this breeder knew she was onto him, words she also used. So, even though she's left-handed, and she'd lost those fingers from her left hand, she learned to shoot a pistol with her right."

"You're kidding."

"I wish I were. And she told me she was 'withdrawing from society.'"

I thought for a minute. "So . . . Hermie thought illegal

breeding was going on out here? Would that occasion gunfire? Or could Hermie be the one shooting?"

Sabine shrugged. "When Hermie showed up at my door, she was acting half crazed, asking if I knew back roads in the preserve that would lead onto private property. I told her, I don't. Plus, you know how it is out here. There really aren't good maps."

"So . . . she never found the place?"

Sabine said, "I don't think so."

"Do you know if she had any evidence of deplorable conditions?"

"I don't. But then I began to have suspicions. At the feed store, I ran into a bald guy, a very smarmy character, buying lots of bags of puppy chow. I held the door open for him—"

"*What?*"

Sabine closed her eyes and shook her head. "I mean, I have nothing to go on, but he put out bad vibes. When I asked him if he was raising puppies, he told me to get out of his way. After Hermie visited, talking about all her suspicions, I found myself wondering about that guy. Yes, Hermie *is* very excitable. She told me she was thinking of hiring an investigator to find the secret kennels, and get proof of the abuse for Animal Control. But listen, I really need to go feed the horses. Does that answer your questions?"

"All but one, Sabine. Did Hermie say the guy she suspected was raising beagles?"

Sabine's forehead wrinkled in puzzlement. She said, "How did you know?"

Chapter 14

I said, "Thanks for all your help," then hugged her and hustled out to my van.

On the way back to town, my cell phone began beeping. I had three messages. Three? Why hadn't my cell rung?

Tom's voice said, "Miss G.? Where are you? I'm just getting back to you now, sorry, it's been a firestorm at the sheriff's department. Please call me."

Then Yolanda announced, "Hi! We finished at the doctor's office. I'm driving back up from Denver now. When we get to your place, I'll check your schedule to pack everything up. See you soon."

Once again, Tom's voice implored me: "Miss G.? I know I didn't answer your earlier message, but now I'm getting worried that you haven't called me back. Are you all right? Please call me as soon as you get this message. This morning I had meetings, and then I was out of cell range."

I called him back immediately, and he picked up on

the first ring. "Sorry, Tom," I burst out. "I was out at Sabine Rushmore's place. She lives near the wildlife preserve."

"Goldy, what in *hell* were you doing out there?"

"Tom, look. I was just trying to figure out who broke into—"

"Miss G., we've been having reports of shots fired out there for weeks. It's what I was working on when Ernest was killed. And in case you didn't know, it's not hunting season—"

"I know, I know! Sabine and I heard gunshots—"

"Oh, Christ." Tom groaned. "You weren't out in that area where we had the big wildfire a couple of years ago, were you?"

"But . . . that's less than a mile from where we were. Why?"

"Please listen." Tom's tone turned guarded, as if someone were hovering nearby. "I don't want you out there anymore."

"Listen, Tom! Sabine saw a bald guy who might be running a puppy mill. I didn't see him, though, and Sabine didn't know where he might be—"

"Goldy! Will you please not go out to the preserve?"

"Oh, Tom. Sabine and her husband live right—"

"Please? We have a big problem in that area that I'm not at liberty to discuss. In fact, I don't want you going to any remote locations at or near the preserve."

Okay, somebody really was standing right next to Tom. I asked, "Will you tell me later?"

He said, "Maybe," and then announced that he had to go.

"But I need to talk to you! Did you reach Hermie Mikulski? Did you talk to Charlene Newgate? Because I thought I saw—"

"You're breaking up," said Tom through static. Then his voice was gone.

Damn it. I hadn't been able to tell Tom about how Hermie had lost her fingers. Nor had I shared the details of Hermie's suspicions of a guy running a puppy mill on his property, with a legit breeding operation as cover, a guy Sabine might have encountered, who was bald. And then there was that car that I thought had been Charlene Newgate's BMW, also on its way out to the preserve.

Speaking of which, what was going on out in the preserve that Tom had been so secretive about? And how was I going to discover more about these privacy-loving adulterers—presumably the very married Sean Breckenridge and his girlfriend—if I couldn't trek to remote cabins in the woods?

I called information and got the Mikulskis' home number. Like Tom, I was connected to voice mail. I identified myself and said I didn't know any more about the investigation into Ernest's death. I said I really would like her to call me on my cell, as soon as possible, about a puppy mill situation. I left my number and closed by saying I hoped Brad was recovering from hurting his nose.

It had been a long afternoon, with lots of frustrations. The formerly poor Charlene Newgate had struck some kind of gold with her new boyfriend. I was almost positive that one of them had been driving that silver BMW out by the preserve. Where had he or she been going?

And if the boyfriend had a big fancy house and I didn't know his name, how was I going to find out?

Donna Lamar was also suddenly rich. How had *that* happened? She was having trouble with a lustful couple that was breaking into her unsecured rentals. How could anyone catch such wily sinners?

As I was coming up on Aspen Meadow Lake, my mind said: *Wait.* There was more than one way to catch people with their pants down. I didn't have the DNA of Sean's lover. But I had their *garbage.* And I knew Sean would be attending the party that night. Maybe his girlfriend would be, too. If there were wrappers in their trash, I could figure out what food they liked. It might be like one of those algebra problems where you know the values of two variables, and an equation puts them together. With food, I was definitely in the putting-together business.

I checked my rearview mirror. No one was following the van, for which I was thankful. My mind was soaking up Tom's and Yolanda's paranoia. Plus, Tom's words had unnerved me. Someone was shooting guns out in the preserve? Why? People *hiked* out there. What if a stray bullet hit one of them? Was that what had happened to the bleeding beagle puppy brought in by a hiker to a local veterinarian?

I set this troubling thought aside. The rubbish, *their* rubbish, was what I needed to concentrate on.

There was no shoulder on this part of the road, only a high stone wall on the far side. Next to my lane, stretching as far as the eye could see, was a deep, snow-filled indentation. I pulled the van over to the edge of this ditch. The van still stuck out a bit into the road, but drivers in Aspen Meadow were used to swinging around horses, cyclists, and runners. With luck, they could steer past a caterer's vehicle. I eased the van up to a trash can, just in case I needed to explain myself to a roving sheriff's department deputy or worse, a state patrol officer. The sheriff's department tended to indulge me, but the state patrol was something else altogether. I mean, I'd gotten in their way in one or two traffic accidents. They had not been amused.

As I dug into the smelly plastic bag of trash that Donna Lamar had collected, I tried to look like any tourist wearing catering clothes who decides to dump camping detritus while standing ankle-deep in snow. I turned a pair of sleeping bags inside out. They were somewhat mangy, but a woman's pair of underpants dropped out of one. I picked it up. *Donna,* I thought, *you really do need a detective.* The panties were from Victoria's Secret, black and lacy, size four. She was either small and slender or medium height and skinny. Well, I couldn't exactly ask to see women's underclothes when they came through the door at the Breckenridges' place. But it was a start.

There was nothing in the other sleeping bag, so I set them both by the side of the road. I picked up first one, then a second plastic glass and held them to the sunlight. One had a semicircular tinge of mauve lipstick, but not enough to be able to tell what the exact color had been. The other just had the vague, vinegary scent of old wine.

Donna had put the cheese wrappers into a separate paper bag, and the stench when I opened that sack practically sent me into the ditch. I dumped the litter onto the snow and examined it carefully.

There were shreds of scarlet and gold foil from a package of an expensive Camembert I knew: Le Roi et la Reine. My king and queen of romance had fancy tastes. A red wax globe held a bit of moldy Gouda with the brand name 's-Gravenhage. I knew that Dutch word meant "the Hague," but I wasn't familiar with the brand of Gouda, although I probably should have been . . . unless Sean and his girlfriend got them from mail order? Maybe. The box of water crackers was Carr's, found in most supermarkets.

There was only one thing left in Donna's bag: an empty wine bottle. I didn't recognize the brand, but it was a Riesling *Auslese Kabinett,* with the further indication that it was a *Qualitätswein mit Prädikat,* the highest grade given to German wines. A partially missing price tag indicated the bottle had come from— hallelujah—Aspen Meadow Liquors. Would Harold at the liquor store be as privacy-conscious as the library, the schools, the church, or doctors' offices? I certainly hoped not.

I stuffed the sleeping bags, undies, wine bottle, and all the wrappers back into Donna's big plastic bag. I'd store it in the garage for Tom, just in case he needed it for evidence, although there was no chain of custody, and my fingerprints were all over everything. But having something tangible sometimes helped in interrogations, if things got that far. I cleaned my hands with disinfecting wipes from the glove box, wheeled the van away from the shoulder, and gingerly pressed on the accelerator. In catering terms, it was getting late, and I really, really didn't want Yolanda stuck with all the packing.

As I drove back toward town, I tried to unwind from the cabin incident by concentrating on that night's dinner. The cooking was largely done, except that I had to arrange the composed salads on whatever china plates Rorry wanted us to use. The lamb chops could easily roast over at Rorry's. Yolanda had volunteered to make the Navajo tacos, which would involve deep-frying pieces of dough—what the Navajos call "fry bread"— then quickly splitting these flat rolls and stuffing them with prepped ingredients. I was dreading serving something at a catered party that I had never actually prepared before. But Yolanda had said she knew how to make them, and I trusted her. Plus, if the tacos didn't work out, they didn't work out, period. As Julia Child had been fond of saying, "Never apologize."

My cell phone beeped with a message, probably sent while I was outside the van checking through the lovers' garbage. It was not from Tom, as I hoped, but from Rorry Breckenridge. She'd announced to my voice mail that the Hanrahans and the Bells were snowed in and had canceled, but that Father Pete had added two guests. Some people, apparently, felt guilty about coming at the last minute, so they would be bringing platters of extra food. If that was all right, she'd added. She was apologetic. One person had already brought over some caviar and put it in her refrigerator. Another was bringing enchiladas, and someone else was bringing several bottles of champagne.

I shook my head at the irony. The church wasn't managing to make its budget, but guests were outdoing themselves bringing goodies. Go figure.

Plus, *enchiladas?* Did this mean the Juarezes were coming? Oh, I *so* didn't want a scene between them and Humberto at the party.

I didn't call Rorry back, because really, what could she do? It sounded as if this party was becoming more and more like a potluck, anyway, albeit a fancy-schmancy one. How far this all was from the simple but elegant dinner we had initially envisaged, back when the party was going to be outside in the Indian summer air, on the Breckenridges' enormous deck.

My cell rang: Marla.

"Okay, so I'm bringing beer to this shindig tonight," she said without preamble, "and now I'm wondering, if we're having Navajo tacos, should I bring Mexican beer? Wouldn't you rather have the Dutch variety?"

"It doesn't matter," I said. My friend's voice warmed my heart. "Any kind would work."

"Where are you?"

"On my way to Aspen Meadow Liquors."

"Not to buy beer, I hope."

"No, I need some more white wine. German white wine, in case you're wondering."

"Why German white wine?"

"If I tell you, you can*not* tell anyone."

"About German white wine?"

"Marla? I need information, the kind you can often get. But you can't tell anyone what I've found out."

"Okay, okay. But satisfy my curiosity. Does this big secret refer to Riesling or Liebfraumilch?"

"Riesling." I took a deep breath. "Donna Lamar told me a couple is breaking into her rentals to have sex. So I went out to a cabin where they'd supposedly been. Get this—*one* of our lovers is Sean Breckenridge."

"Oh my God. Poor Rorry."

I summed up the trip out to the cabin and finding the credit card, which, I admitted, might have been stolen from Sean. I told her about hearing the gunshots and going through the bag of evidence. "And now I'm going to buy the stuff that our loving couple had to eat and drink. I'm hoping that if Sean did indeed drop his own card out at the cabin, his girlfriend will be one of the guests and they'll both indulge tonight."

"I simply cannot *wait* for you to expose these people. Should I have some of each of those cheeses, so it'll look like it's no big deal?"

"What you *should* do is act uninterested."

"Uninterested? All right, all right," she said to placate me. "Speaking of tonight, I'm already ravenously hungry. Now, don't worry. My cardiologist has given me a bunch of rules, and much as I'd like to, I'm not going to pig out."

I said, "Uh—"

"Oh," she said dismissively, "you know how it is with your parties. As long as one of the people at the dinner is cooking, like a hostess, guests hold back from gorging themselves. But when we have to buy a ticket or pay for the meal ourselves? It's full speed ahead on the stomach stuffing."

"You're right in your observation, I'm sorry to say. That's why I never, ever sell tickets to an all-you-can-eat buffet. Folks will come to that kind of meal pulling a cooler."

"What do you suppose the guests at the Brecken-ridges' will be wearing?" she asked. "I mean, it's a church event, but does that mean folks will wear churchy clothes?"

"The way I've seen it work, the more swish the locale, the more people tend to get dressed up, even in Aspen Meadow, which is Denim Heaven."

"Maybe," Marla said thoughtfully, "but we also like to be authentic, you know, to the theme of the party. So if there's going to be a hayride or anything involving straw bales, folks will pop five or six hundred for cow-boy outfits, right down to the red and white bandanas and Billy the Kid fringed leather jackets."

"The decorating theme is Abundance of Fall. You could come as a cornucopia."

"Are you making fun of my *size*?"

"No, silly. I'd say this will be more fancy-pants, be-cause the Breckenridges are loaded and their house is huge."

"Excuse me," said Marla knowingly, "you're wrong, the Breckenridges are not loaded. *Rorry* is wealthy, re-member? I heard they live on her money. That's why Sean doesn't have to work, although he calls himself a professional photographer, which is bull. Do you know anyone who's ever hired him?"

"Nope." I pulled into the parking lot of Aspen Meadow Liquors, where tire tracks crisscrossed in the slush. "Listen, girlfriend, I have to hop." I parked and threw on the brake. "Say, do you know Hermie Mikulski, from church? She used to be in charge of the Altar Guild, but I don't think she is anymore."

Marla sighed. "Oh, yes, now she's into making sure people take care of their animals. There was a woman in my neighborhood who was renting a house that was for sale. According to Hermie, this woman was keeping too many cats. Hermie got her evicted, and the cats were put up for adoption. I still don't think they've sold that house. They couldn't get rid of the, you know, scent."

"Thanks, Marla. See you tonight."

"In my abundance outfit. And much as I'd like to, don't worry, I won't say a word about Sean."

I ducked into Aspen Meadow Liquors. When I was starting out in catering, I'd bought wines and liquors from Harold, the beefy proprietor. But then Alicia, my supplier, had been able to get me better prices on everything, so I'd switched. I didn't know if Harold would care or even remember me. He'd been known to dip quite extensively into his own stock.

"Well, speak of the devil!" Harold, white haired, red nosed, and stooped, cried when I came through the door. My heart plummeted when I saw he was talking to Humberto Captain. Humberto was still wearing his duck suit, but the sartorial effect was ruined by the mud on his trouser hems. And then I noticed that Humberto, who was probably in his early fifties, was accompanied by a young woman, a svelte, top-heavy platinum blonde who couldn't have been more than twenty-two. She didn't look like his daughter. And anyway, she was wearing a skintight silver unitard that didn't exactly say *I'm out with Daddy doing errands.*

"Humberto's buying Dom Pérignon to serve at your dinner tonight!" Harold called to me. His speech was slurred, and his head waved slightly on his neck, as if a breeze were blowing in the store. "Aren't you lucky?" Harold asked, his voice petulant now. "Don't you feel fortunate?"

I smiled at Humberto and hoped it did not look fake. "I'm thrilled. I feel like, well, like ten million bucks!"

Humberto did not bat an eyelash. Nor did he introduce me to the woman, who turned away from me. Her face in profile, though, seemed familiar. Who was she? I didn't know any young women in Aspen Meadow who would purposely dress in a silver unitard while doing anything except trick-or-treating. And anyhow, I had the feeling that what this young woman did was, actually, turn tricks.

I moved up to them and offered my hand to the young woman. "Don't I know you? You seem familiar. Do you live here in town?"

"This is Odette," Humberto interjected. He put a protective arm around the young woman's waist. "Is she not beautiful?"

"That she is," I replied. And smart, too, I remembered distantly. Very smart, but without much money. How did I know her? "Do you have a voice, Odette?"

"Zat I do," she said, winking at me. When she did so, I noticed long fake black eyelashes. Her eyelids were dusted with silver.

All right, enough was enough. I reached into my pocket, felt for my cell phone, and squinted at it. Somehow, I managed quickly to maneuver over to Take Photo. "Smile!" I commanded, holding up the phone.

Humberto pulled Odette even closer, and grinned widely. Odette again turned away, so all I could snap was her profile. What was with this mystery woman? She whispered something in Humberto's ear. He blushed and shifted his weight. Dang! Too bad my cell phone couldn't pick up sexual tidbits on distance audio.

"We need to go get ready," Humberto said, his cheeks still red. "We'll see you tonight," he added.

Good, I thought. Maybe I'd be able to get a cell phone photo of Odette's face.

Harold heaved up the case of Dom and waddled out to Humberto's black Mercedes, which he'd parked illegally at the curb.

"Say, Harold," I said when he returned. "For this party tonight? I've had a last-minute request."

Harold's rheumy eyes regarded me unhappily. "I hope it isn't something weird, because I didn't get a delivery today. The truck driver was afraid of the snow. My wife's coming to get me early, too."

I certainly was glad his wife drove him to and fro, as I didn't want more drunk drivers on the Aspen Meadow roads. But I kept mum about that. Instead, I repeated the words I remembered from the bottle of white wine.

Harold relaxed and nodded. "No problem."

"You have any chilled?"

"Yeah, sure." He headed toward the wall of refrigerators. "Who's giving this party? The Breckenridges?"

"One and the same," I said. "Is it Sean or Rorry who likes this wine?"

Harold faced one of the cold doors. "How many bottles?"

"Three ought to do it. So, is it Sean or Rorry who buys this from you?"

"Uh, he buys it." Harold hugged the bottles to his wide chest as he trundled ahead of me to the cash register. "But maybe she sends him to the liquor store to get it for her."

"Did he say he got it for her?"

"He never says much, Goldy."

"Ah."

I paid and had him staple the bag shut, then placed my load into a cart and maneuvered through the slush to the grocery store next door. In the deli section, I noticed someone else I knew, a longtime deli worker named Lena. She was heavy and wore lots of makeup, including formidable black eyeliner. It didn't look quite as good on her as it had on "Odette," but never mind. Lena had dyed her hair black at the roots and blond on the ends, which gave her kind of a "Jersey summer" look. Maybe when my hair turned gray, I'd have to think about doing something similar.

"Goldy!" Lena cried. "Long time no see. We've got some smoked turkey on special." She changed plastic gloves.

"Thanks, but no thanks. Actually, I have to ask you about one or more of your customers."

"Well, could you at least buy something, so my manager doesn't get suspicious?"

"Absolutely. I need two more cheeses for a dinner I'm doing tonight. One's a Gouda, 's-Gravenhage. The other's a Camembert, Le Roi et la Reine. Do you have either one?"

Lena rocked her head back and laughed. "I have both of them, you sly dog. And I know what *you're* up to." She moved to the cheese section of the case and pulled out the Gouda first, then the Camembert. "How much of this would your clients like?"

"A pound of each, thanks. Could you please slice the Gouda? All right, I confess. I'm being a busybody and I need to know who usually buys this."

Lena's fifty-year-old face wrinkled as she placed the cheese on the scale. "Don't you know?"

"Not exactly."

Lena grinned. "Sean Breckenridge comes in and buys them. About two or three times a week, and never with his wife. He doesn't buy a pound each, though."

I feigned confusion. "So how much does he usually buy?"

Lena moved the Gouda out of the way, tucked it into a plastic bag, and slapped on the price tag. Once she had the Camembert up on the scale, she said, "He usually buys a quarter to a third of a pound each time. I told him he should buy more, so he'd have it in his home fridge when he wanted it." She measured out the Camembert and handed me the second plastic bag.

"And what did he say?" I asked.

"That's the weird thing," Lena said. "I've asked him a couple of times, and it's like I told him his fly is down."

Well, it is. I said, "Maybe his wife has him on a cheese-free diet, and he's sneaking it."

"Goldy, please. A cheese-free diet? Sean's skinny. And if he's lactose intolerant, he shouldn't be eating cheese at all."

"Is he ever with somebody when he buys the cheese?" I asked. "Somebody who isn't his wife?"

Lena wagged an index finger at me. "You think he's fooling around, and I think you're right. And that's, if you'll pardon the expression, cheesy."

"Lena, come on. Has he ever come with someone or not?"

Lena exhaled as someone called to her that they wanted to taste Braunschweiger. "I've never noticed anyone with him. Just the acting-ashamed routine."

"Keep this under your hat, okay?"

"Keep what under my hat?"

"Don't kid a kidder, Lena."

"Rorry is worth millions, Goldy."

"Well, then, once we know what's going on, you can sell your story to the tabloids."

Lena rested her large body against the glass on her side of the case. "But I don't know anything," she whispered.

"Neither do I," I protested, as I gathered up the bags of cheese. "But I'm hoping to be able to find out."

"Will you tell me, when you know?" she asked breathlessly.

"No," I said.

Lena harrumphed and quick-marched over to the person wanting liverwurst.

I raced back to the house. It was just after three, and I was consumed with guilt for being so behind our schedule. But when I came inside, it was Boyd who was placing foodstuffs into boxes. Yolanda was spooning the ground beef with seasonings into a container, and the house was filled with the heady scent of a Mexican restaurant. Zippered bags of chopped tomatoes, shredded lettuce, chopped scallions, and grated cheese stood in rows on the kitchen table.

"Sorry I'm late," I said. "How's Ferdinanda?"

Yolanda gave me an exasperated expression. "When the doctor told her it would be Thanksgiving before she was done with her cast, she pulled out her baton and was on the verge of popping it open when Boyd yanked it away from her. The doctor told us not to come back! He insisted he was done with us and that we needed to get another orthopedist. Ferdinanda said she wouldn't come back if he paid her to. Then she made loud quacking noises all the way out through the waiting room. She didn't stop until we got to my van."

"Where is she now?" I whispered.

"Sleeping. She said that quack tired her out." She hesitated. "I might need a recommendation to another orthopedic surgeon."

"No problem. Are we ready to start loading the van?"

She nodded, so I went back outside, where the weather was beginning to turn chilly. I was in the process of reversing the van up the driveway, so that it would be as near as possible to the deck next to the kitchen door, when my eye caught on something. Cursing under my breath, I threw the van into Park and walked quickly to the curb.

Snowmelt had caused a rapidly rushing stream on either side of our road. Without my willing it, I looked up. There were brown curtains hanging in the front room of my godfather Jack's house. The cold, moist afternoon air closed in on my heart. I tried to take a deep breath, but couldn't. Even though I hadn't seen a moving van, someone was either living in Jack's place or fixing it up before occupying it. That would mean he really was gone.

I chewed the inside of my cheeks to get feeling back into them. Soon, someone else would be living in Ernest McLeod's place, or at least on his property, whether or not the will held up. First we'd lost Jack, then Ernest had been shot and killed. I blinked, tried again to inhale, and felt a moment of dizziness. I turned and walked slowly back to my van. I pulled the sack of lovers' detritus out of the back, opened the garage door using the code, and tossed the bag of trash inside. Then I closed the garage door and walked back up to the house.

In the kitchen, I helped Yolanda finish the packing. Rorry was providing her table linens, china, crystal, and silver, all of which she had told us her live-in maid would wash the next morning, and that we were not going to have to bother with it that night. She'd also told me the Abundance of Fall flower arrangements would be delivered that afternoon.

When I'd talked to Rorry, she'd said Etta, her live-in maid and factotum, had a set of paring knives, but she had only one roasting pan. I stuffed my knives and several pans into one of our last boxes. The big problem, equipment-wise, was a deep fryer. Once everyone in the country had decided not to eat fried chicken anymore (unless it was from takeout), I'd donated my electric frying pan to the church rummage sale. But Yolanda had told me it would be helpful if she could use one, to make the Navajo fry bread. I'd put in a call to Rorry that morning, and she had said she would ask Etta if they had one. If not, we would make do with some kind of pot, of which Rorry assured me they had plenty.

Once everything on our list was checked, I was in the mood for an espresso, as was Yolanda. Boyd announced he had to find an outfit suitable for catering, so I pulled Yolanda and myself double shots. She doused hers with sugar, I did the same to mine with cream, and we sipped amiably until Boyd returned to the kitchen.

I had to suppress a smile at his impeccable black pants and freshly ironed white shirt. When had he gotten hold of them? Had he gone back to his house? When I asked, he confessed that he had taken to keeping clean catering clothes in the trunk of his car, just in case Tom wanted him to come help me with an event—one where I might need protection.

I said, "Oh, for crying out loud."

Poor Boyd. He hated catering. But he clearly was head over heels for Yolanda. Bless his heart, I was sure he'd do whatever it took to make sure no harm came to her.

I wondered if that desire would be enough to keep Yolanda safe. Then I shook that thought away, too.

The Breckenridges' long, meandering driveway rose from Flicker Ridge's main road to a palatial estate that was perched on an east-facing granite outcropping. This made for a breathtaking view of Denver. But the drop-offs were so steep, I couldn't even look down as we got close to the house. I wondered how Sean and Rorry had been able to train their son to keep away from the edge of the cliff.

The answer was plain enough when we pulled into the driveway. Surrounding the large, flat, sodded yard was a ten-foot-high fence made from sections of thick plastic. If I was not mistaken, this was the same kind of plastic used to fabricate doors in newer upscale houses. The plastic for the doors is stained and painted to look like wood, and it is free of the upkeep wood requires. But here it was clear, like the edge of an infinity pool. Hmm. I wondered if the fence acted to deter strong-minded elk from jumping into the yard to eat the Breckenridges' flowers, shrubs, and grass.

The yard boasted an expansive wooden swing set and slide, a sandbox, and a metal jungle gym. At one edge of the property was a brown playhouse with the word *Saloon* painted over the doorjamb. I smiled and wondered if Sean and Rorry's son would be allowed to attend the dinner.

Several cars were already parked in the driveway. I checked my watch: It had just turned four, which was when we were due to start setting up. Was this like a kids' birthday party, when the invitees were so excited they often showed up early?

I couldn't remember Rorry telling me if our catering team was supposed to come in through a side door or the front. With guests already arriving, a side door would have been preferable. I found the side door and knocked on it. There was no response. Rorry was probably busy entertaining her early arrivals.

We marched to the front door and rang the bell.

A long singsonging echoed into the interior. After a few moments, Rorry appeared to usher us in.

"Sorry, so sorry." She smiled, but she sounded wretched. Fortyish, short, dark haired, and very pretty, Rorry nonetheless had dark circles under her brown eyes. She hid her wide hips under a flared, embroidered purple skirt and a puffed-sleeve white blouse, which gave her a designer-homemaker kind of look. Marla said Rorry was one of the nicest, most generous people in the church, but that she kept her munificence quiet. She'd kept the misery she was undergoing quiet, too . . . although perhaps not from Ernest McLeod.

"People have been coming in and out all day to bring food," Rorry explained as we hauled our first boxes across the threshold. "It's been like a train station. I'm so sorry I didn't have a chance to open the side door for you." She eyed me apologetically. Rorry's accent was elegant, only slightly distinguishable as southern. Having attended boarding school in Virginia, I've had a pet peeve over the years at how Hollywood folks trying to portray a Southerner affect an ear-grating, bumpkin-from-the-farm style of speech. Those actors make me wish they'd actually *visit* the places whose accents they're trying to imitate. Listening to Rorry speak in her genteel, soft voice, one would know she was the real deal.

"You must be an incredible cook!" she said now. Perhaps she knew she was projecting unhappiness, so now her smile was wide and sincere. "I've never had *so many* extra people decide they have to come to an expensive dinner at the last minute. We even advertised for this supper in the *Mountain Journal,* with no takers except church people. It's lucky we had cancellations! Folks seem to have gotten wind that you were doing the cooking. The people Father Pete and Sean and I talked to? When they asked if they could come? They all asked if you were catering."

"Well, that is flattering," I replied. I wasn't *that* popular, was I?

Rorry led the way across the large, marble-floored foyer. The tawny walls were lit by brass and crystal sconces. A cherry bench upholstered with gold brocade stood between a pair of dark cherry cabinets. Both brimmed with pink-and-beige Limoges china, French crystal, as well as polished silver platters and bowls. It certainly did not look like any of the contemporary mountain homes where I usually catered, which were uniformly stuffed with heavy lodge-type furniture and cabinets. In the dinnerware department, I usually saw only stainless-steel cutlery and nondescript dishes.

Rorry said over her shoulder, "Sean's entertaining four people already. First to arrive were Father Pete and Venla Strothmeyer. To bring an elderly widow like that? He is *such* a sweet man. He even said Venla bought the tickets for them both."

I could hear voices, Father Pete's low rumble, Venla's occasional gravelly comment. Even Sean's high-pitched voice was sometimes audible. They must have been outside, or in a section of the house so well upholstered that all sounds were muffled. I said that Father Pete was indeed a wonderful man, even though Yolanda rolled her eyes.

"And to think it snowed last night," Rorry said. "Our son is in heaven. Etta took him up to our condo in Beaver Creek to spend the night, even though the lifts aren't open. They'll be back early tomorrow. Remember, I don't want you cleaning up tonight! Etta would have a fit if you put things where they didn't belong. Anyway, Seth was so excited about seeing snow. Those ski resort owners must be hoping the blizzards never stop."

"They must be," I murmured.

Rorry said, "Follow me," and turned. Her leather flats made soft clopping noises on the part of the foyer that was floored with stone and not Kirman rugs. Rorry seemed hassled, but not so self-centered that she didn't want to make us feel welcome. I appreciated that.

When Boyd, Yolanda, and I entered the kitchen, I gulped. The ceilings were at least twenty feet high. I bet someone had to build a scaffolding to change the lightbulbs. The decorating scheme of the enormous space was yellow cabinets with brass pulls; blue and yellow tiles on the island, countertops, and backsplashes; and a tiny flowered print of blue, yellow, and red for the matching wallpaper and curtains. I was pretty sure the kitchen table and chairs were solid cherry. The whole effect was like something you'd see in a fifties magazine for living in the South, not Colorado in the twenty-first century.

"This is a *gorgeous* kitchen, Rorry," I said as I put my box on one of the counters. *Especially for someone who doesn't cook,* I added mentally.

Rorry blushed. "It's an exact replica of our kitchen in New Orleans. Sean thought I was crazy, but I missed home so much, I wanted it to be the same." Tears appeared suddenly in her eyes, but she blinked them back. *She still misses home,* I thought. *Maybe she'll go back there, if and when she gets rid of Sean.*

"I'm going to get another box," Boyd announced.

"Shall I get the plates out, the way I usually do?" Yolanda asked me. When I nodded, Yolanda said to Rorry, "Do you want to show me which ones you want to use?"

Rorry waved toward one of the cherry cabinets in the front hall. "Just the pink and gold Limoges in there. There should be plenty."

When Yolanda left, Rorry cleared her throat. "Sean's also talking to a couple I don't know. They signed up today, through Father Pete. The man's first name is Norman, and I think his last name is Juarez, but I didn't catch his wife's name. They're Catholic, so I don't know why they're here."

My shoulders slumped. *I* knew why they were there. Church dinner notwithstanding, I prayed again for no fireworks between Humberto Captain and Norman Juarez. When Boyd returned with his box, I made a mental note to tell him we might be having an altercation that night.

Rorry waved her hand over the island and toward the kitchen table. "When people came by today with more food and wine, I told them to put it over there and in the refrigerator. That foil-covered pan is enchiladas from the Juarezes. Venla brought a homemade cheese ball with crackers. And then earlier, Humberto brought champagne, which he put in to chill. Kris Nielsen, who's bringing a date, brought caviar, which is also in the—"

She didn't get a chance to finish. Yolanda, precariously carrying the Limoges china into the kitchen, heard Kris's name and dropped the china she was carrying. The dishes hit the tile floor with a deafening clatter.

I thought, *Oh, hell*.

Chapter 15

M y Lord!" cried Rorry as she raced to Yolanda's side. "Oh, my dear, are you all right? Did you cut yourself?"

"Where's the bathroom?" asked Boyd. He'd deposited his box and was holding Yolanda's elbow. That was the only part of Yolanda's body that wasn't shaking.

"Let me show you," said Rorry, and she *clip-clopped* efficiently down the hall.

I looked for a broom and dustpan. I finally located the cleaning closet, grabbed the necessary tools, and started sweeping. Kris was coming. He was bringing a date. Upon hearing the news, Yolanda had broken what I estimated to be about a thousand dollars' worth of china.

While Boyd and Yolanda were in the bathroom, I swept the shards into a pile. Father Pete had said Kris was *so* generous to the church. Really? Was that the actual reason he was coming to the dinner tonight, bringing caviar and a date?

I looked for paper towels and could find none. Worse,

I was so addled I couldn't remember which of our boxes contained our stash. Desperate, I searched under the sink, where two new, large sponges had been tucked into zipped, labeled plastic bags. One said *Floor,* the other, *Counters.*

As I wet the floor sponge, I swallowed hard and reminded myself that I couldn't be sure of everything Yolanda had told me about Kris. But since I was thinking about Kris and had an actual sponge in my hand, it wasn't too much of a leap to place Kris—fairly or unfairly—into the sponge category. Father Pete had told me how Kris had paid for all the Sunday school rooms to be painted and carpeted, even though he didn't attend church services. And I'd just found out from Father Pete that in June, Kris had sought to secure the priest's help in getting a woman who sounded a lot like Ferdinanda involuntarily committed to an institution. That movement from generosity to demand was the way of the sponge. *I'll spend a couple hundred bucks on paint and cheap carpet, so you'll owe me.*

Call me a cynic, but I'd seen a lot of sponges in the church. They gave in expectation of receiving something, usually something much larger than their initial gift.

Using Rorry's damp sponge, I briskly swept the bits of broken china into the dustpan.

I washed my hands savagely in the sink and hoped I *wasn't* becoming a cynic. Still, just ask one of these sponges to teach Sunday school, or visit a handicapped parishioner in a nursing home, or bring meals to a family that had been in an automobile accident. Forget it. I'd catered for sponges; I'd had their checks bounce; I'd lived in a state of rageful humiliation when they refused to do the right thing unless they got a reward. Unlike actors with the fake southern accents, human sponges were difficult to detect.

I dumped the broken bits of china into the trash. I wasn't sure I had gotten them all, so I rinsed the sponge, got down on my knees, and wiped the floor with careful, even strokes. Then I threw the floor sponge in the trash.

Boyd and Yolanda returned to the kitchen. Yolanda's complexion was still pale, but she wasn't shaking anymore. Did she know that Kris had tried to have Ferdinanda—if that was who it was—involuntarily committed? Was that why she had reacted so negatively toward Father Pete in the grocery store? Or had she been so much on edge that an accidental brush by our preoccupied priest in the pickle aisle had made her lose her cool? I suspected the latter, and I didn't want to upset Yolanda any more than she already was by asking about the former.

Boyd was still holding Yolanda's arm. "Rorry's out with the guests. Yolanda says she slipped on something." He eyed the damp kitchen floor.

"Sorry, I just wiped it."

"Give Yolanda something to do, then."

I said, "No problem. The rest of the guests should be arriving soon. How about if you two open some red and white wine from this lot here? I'll put together an appetizer tray and start ferrying stuff out to the porch."

While they busied themselves lining up the bottles people had brought, I put together the cheese, fruit, and cracker trays. Rorry had said she would do it, but I felt so guilty about the broken Limoges, I wanted to do it myself. Besides, I had a bit of an ulterior motive in being in charge of the cheese. Venla's walnut-covered cheese ball, surrounded by crackers, went on one tray. I placed the Gouda—part of my trap for Sean and his girlfriend, if she showed—and a large wedge of sharp cheddar, a peppered goat cheese, and a block of Gruyère around a tumble of red and green seedless grapes. I carefully cut the Camembert, which had turned creamy, into four wedges. Around it, I carefully spread different types of crackers.

"Christ," said Marla when she popped into Rorry's kitchen. Yolanda was startled again; this time, though, she dropped only the keys to my van. Marla, who wore a shimmery gold-and-brown dress and shawl, looked around the kitchen in astonishment. She lifted the ruffles of the café curtains and smoothed her hand over the flowered wallpaper. "Who decorated this kitchen, Betty Crocker?" Then she caught a look at Yolanda's pale face, disheveled hair, and shaking hands. "Uh . . . did I come at a bad time? Hey, Boyd, how're you doing?"

Boyd gave a single shake of his head.

"Goldy?" asked Marla. "Do you need me to help with anything? I think some guests are already here."

I'd moved on to spooning Kris's caviar into a soft nest of crème fraîche that I'd brought just in case we needed it. I adore crème fraîche, as does Marla, who plucked a spoon out of a drawer and helped herself to a small mouthful.

"Mm-mm. Don't tell my cardiologist," she said. "So, do you need me to take stuff out?"

"Yes, thanks." I handed her the platter with Venla's cheese ball and crackers. "You can help by asking Rorry if she has more dishes. Also, please look at place cards, if Rorry's filled those out, and see exactly who's coming." I added in a low voice, "Don't mention Kris Nielsen. We didn't know he would be here, and now Yolanda's very fragile."

Marla took out another spoon and ate a second dollop of caviar with crème fraîche. "Take out cheese ball. Check on dishes and place cards. Got it."

She returned a few minutes later holding a sheet of paper. "Had to take notes, sorry. Including me, there are sixteen. And there *are* some folks who are here already. Rorry introduced me to some new people. They're Norman and Isabella Juarez. Isabella offered the information that she brought homemade enchiladas, so you better serve me some of those before anybody else gets any! Humberto Captain is coming, and the name of his date is Odette, no last name. Father Pete is already here with Venla Strothmeyer. Tony Ramos from CBHS is coming, along with his wife, Franny. Last, there are Donna Lamar and yours truly. Plus there's the couple you mentioned," she said in a low tone, "and Sean and Rorry and Brie and Paul Quarles." Marla made a face. "Paul Quarles always looks as if he swallowed a canary six years ago and has yet to digest it."

The doorbell gonged, and Marla disappeared. I moved over and closed the door to the kitchen. High-pitched voices, clearly eager for a party, filtered in from the foyer.

"Crunch time," I said under my breath, then cursed silently that there was no open wine out on the patio yet. "Keep her here," I ordered Boyd, who nodded once. Yolanda looked at the floor.

The guests would be coming through the house. That meant I had to go around it. I tucked the open bottles into a canvas grocery bag and hightailed my way through the now-unlocked side door in an attempt to make it to the patio before the guests all arrived. The grass was icy in spots and wet right through my sneakers, which I wore to all catering gigs, regardless of their fancy factor.

I gritted my teeth and ignored the discomfort. The party absolutely *had* to be a success. The great sucking sound I imagined was not so much the noise my sneakers were making in the glacially chilly mud but the crash of the church budget if people stopped payment on their checks and we lost the thousands being raised by this little shindig.

And then my eye caught on something—not footprints, but something shiny, slim, and metallic. It was a wrench. Without thinking, I picked it up and dropped it in my pocket, intent on leaving it in the kitchen. I was pretty sure neither Sean nor Rorry did any home repairs, and some hapless handyman was bound to come back asking for it.

The party was being held on the winter porch, which boasted a gas fireplace that was flickering merrily when I squeaked open the screen door. I looked around, disoriented. I had no idea where the Juarezes, Father Pete, and Venla had gone. Maybe they were welcoming the new arrivals. The room's tobacco-colored upholstered couches, plus an assortment of chairs, flanked the door I'd just come in. A long wrought-iron table surrounded with cushioned wrought-iron chairs stood in front of the fireplace. Dinner plates that Rorry had somehow located to replace the broken ones, silverware, napkins, and serving spoons were arrayed on a rolling tea cart. The main table itself sported three cornucopiae filled to bursting with gold, orange, and white mums, plus white roses and gold alstroemeria. When Rorry did a party, she did one.

I walked quickly to the table and was grateful to see that someone had already placed gold-rimmed crystal wineglasses, more napkins, and salad plates by each place card. Hallelujah. I squinted at the crystal and held it up to the light. It was the real deal, and Rorry was using it on her porch. I swallowed. No more accidents.

I rapidly moved one of the centerpieces over to the tea cart. I carefully plunked the bottle of white wine into an ice bucket labeled for that purpose, then placed both it and the bottle of red near the center of the table. As the rumble of voices approached, I scampered out the way I'd come.

I heard the unmistakable nasal voice of Paul Quarles. "Really, this is the time to invest. You have to believe me. What did you say your name was? Norman? Juarez? What kind of name is that?"

Really, sometimes people's insensitivity surprised even me, and I'd often been the butt of tactless folks as well as sponges. But Norman was a big boy; he'd just have to handle it. Maybe, like me, he'd even be able to make jokes about it later.

When I came back into the kitchen, Marla was already regaling Yolanda and Boyd with tales of Paul Quarles.

"I'm telling you, Paul Quarles hadn't taken two steps into the foyer before he found somebody he hadn't yet hit up to buy stocks. He said everyone should be putting money into the market, because it's so low. The mouths of the Juarez couple actually dropped open, as in, *We just paid two thousand dollars to come to this dinner, and now somebody wants to talk to us about investing?* They must think all Episcopalians are obsessed with money, which is more or less true, but never mind."

"Guys," I said, "we need the rest of the food from the van. Boyd, can you go out there?"

"Kris just arrived," Marla said to Yolanda, her voice low.

"It's all right," said Yolanda without looking up from the bunch of keys in her hand.

"He's brought a tall brunette," Marla said. "Do you want to hear about her?"

"Marla," I said, warning her. "Maybe this isn't the best—"

Yolanda's eyes flared as she gave me a steady look. "What, you don't think I can handle it, Goldy? Tell me, Marla. Tell me about Kris's new woman."

"Well, she's pretty," Marla said, "but not nearly as pretty as you. When Paul was going on to Norman Juarez about investing in the stock market, I asked Kris's date if she knew what it meant to short a stock. She said, 'Does

that mean you buy a stock from someone who isn't tall?'
So one thing we know about Miss Dumb About Dough
is that she probably isn't an Episcopalian."

"What's this woman's name?" I asked.

Marla raised her eyebrows. "Harriet. While Rorry
was ushering everyone out to the porch, I asked Harriet
if she had a job. She said she did modeling and odd jobs.
Of course, I think modeling is an odd job, but nobody
asked me. I guess in the current economy, you'll do just
about anything to make money."

I tried to give Yolanda a compassionate glance, but
she had turned resolutely to the sink. While she washed
her hands, Boyd caught my eye and shrugged. I asked
him, "Did you bring in the box with the lamb chops?" I
turned my attention back to Marla. "Listen, girlfriend.
How are your puppies?"

"Cute as can be. And yapping all the time."

"Great. Listen, could you see if you can get the conversation over to Hermie Mikulski? See if anyone has
heard anything about a local beagle puppy mill."

Marla, who had discovered the pan with the enchiladas, gave me a skeptical glance. "You want me to change
the subject from investing to *dogs*? How do you propose
I do that?"

"How about this," I said. "Tell people you've just
adopted three beagle puppies. Then see if you can move
the conversation over to whether you can make *money*
breeding dogs. If so, what breeds work best? And has
anyone heard about any mills in the area?"

Marla was still skeptical. "I thought you gave away
all the puppies."

"What I want you to do is see if anyone has heard any reports of rescuing abused beagles in this area. If so, from where?"

Marla placed the enchiladas on the counter. Then she ducked back into the refrigerator and hauled out two bottles of Humberto's Dom. Doggone it. I'd remembered the other guests' wine, but not Humberto's. "Know what, Goldy? People do better with sudden shifts in topic when they're well lubricated." She peered at the bottles. "These were leaning against a bowl of salad in the refrigerator. Does that mean someone knocked them over?"

I sighed. It could indicate that, which could in turn lead to an explosion of bubbly in the kitchen, which was not what we needed at this point.

At that moment, Humberto himself slithered into the kitchen. He wore a pale blue sport coat and yellow pants. "Ah, my countrywoman," he said silkily. When Yolanda ignored him, he drew himself up and gave me an expectant look. "I brought my champagne over myself, this afternoon. Would you please serve it?"

I said, "Yassuh," before I could stop myself. Humberto trundled out. I wondered where Odette was.

Marla raised her eyebrows and opened drawers. "I'm looking for a cloth dish towel to put over this thingy they use to stop up champagne. Where in hell does Rorry keep things?" She slammed a drawer shut, frustrated. "I met Odette, Humberto's date, or whatever he's calling her. More like paid escort, I'd say. She's a cute, busty blonde who looks less than half his age."

"Yeah," I said, "I saw her this afternoon. Does she seem familiar to you?"

"Never having worked for an escort agency myself, I have to say no, she does not look familiar. I'm going to go ask Rorry where her dish towels are."

I cursed silently. "Don't. We'll find some." I began pawing through Rorry's drawers, as well as the supply closet. Where would she keep cloth dish towels? She, or her cook, Etta, had hundreds of kitchen utensils and cleaning tools. They were clean and looked new. But they were in no discernible order.

Marla said, "So you want me to turn the conversation from cash to canines while you open the champagne?"

"Yes, please."

"The things I do for you, Goldy, I swear." She disappeared as Boyd reentered the kitchen hauling the box containing the lamb chops and Navajo taco ingredients. I asked him to start opening the shrink-wrapped packages of chops.

Yolanda, meanwhile, was bent on a new task: rolling out the balls of dough that would become the fry bread.

"If I can ever get this champagne open, I need to start the lamb chops," I said to her. "And I was hoping you could get going on the Navajo tacos. We're getting behind." When Yolanda threw a ball of dough on the counter, I said, "No, scratch what I just said. Go home. Take Boyd. I can handle this dinner."

Her face softened, and when she looked at me, her eyes were wet. "Oh, Goldy, no, thank you. No. I asked you for this job, and you're paying me to do it. I'm fine. It's just that . . . I haven't really seen him since our breakup." Her full mouth pulled into a tight smile. "There's a first time for everything, and this is it. And besides, you don't know how to make the Navajo tacos."

"Didn't I just hear you say there's a first time for everything?"

She barked a laugh. "You don't want to be learning how to make fry bread when you have a whole party to serve it to."

"O ye of little faith. Just help me find some dish towels, would you, please?"

It was stupid, really. How could you have a retro kitchen but no cloth towels? Boyd offered to help, but I said it was more important to get the racks of chops open.

"You've checked the cupboards?" Yolanda asked.

"Yup." I began to look along the walls, where Rorry, or Rorry's architect, had put open shelves. There were no linens anywhere. "I should drive out and get one," I said.

"I'd say to use towels from the guest bathroom, but all she has in there are monogrammed paper guest towels," said Yolanda.

"Just give me one more minute," I said, "and then I'll go look for a linen closet. Sergeant Boyd, could you go out to the porch and make sure people's glasses are filled?" He nodded and disappeared. I preheated the ovens for the lamb, then looked up the walls of the kitchen.

Over the center island, Rorry's architect had used chains to suspend one of those heavy oval rings, the kind that cooks hang all their pots and pans on. Rorry's were all copper, and polished to a high sheen. A metal net filled with dish towels dangled from the far end. I thought, *Finally,* then walked over and reached for it. I couldn't quite see how to unhook the net, so I tugged on it gently to see where it was attached.

And then the whole ring of pots, pans, and dish towels crashed down on my head.

Later, I judged that at least twenty pots came cascading down, along with the heavy metal oval, the screws, even chunks of the ceiling. Two tubs for poaching fish hit me on the head and shoulders, and I careened sideways on the floor. The banging and clattering mixed with the sound of Yolanda screaming. A corkscrew caught the side of my face. When the skin on my cheek tore open, I cursed vociferously and struggled to get up, but could not.

"Goldy!" Yolanda shrieked. "Goldy, are you all right?"

"Listen to me," said Boyd calmly. When had he returned to the kitchen? He leaned close to my face. "You're cut. Do you think any of your bones are broken?"

"No," I said curtly. "I'm fine. Just pissed."

I blinked back blood and could just make out Sean Breckenridge as he raced into the kitchen. "What the hell was that?" he hollered. He caught sight of me on the floor. His wide eyes fixed on my bloody face. At that point his mouth dropped open, his eyelids fluttered closed, and he keeled toward me.

"Damn it!" I screamed, but it was no use.

"Oh, for Christ's sake," Boyd said as he reached out in an effort to catch Sean. With blood dripping into my eyes, I could make out only enough of Sean's trajectory to hold out my arms.

"Oof," I cried as he landed more or less on top of me.

Rorry's voice sounded faraway, I realized, because blood was streaming into my left ear and Sean was blocking my right one. "Sean!" Rorry screamed. "Get off of Goldy! Did he see blood?" Rorry demanded.

As Boyd, Yolanda, and Rorry yanked and tugged an unconscious Sean off me, I wondered how often Rorry had had occasion to holler at her husband to get off a woman to whom he was not married.

Five minutes later, Rorry had revived Sean, although he still lay on the kitchen floor. Rorry kept pellets of ammonia salts in every room and in the car, she told me when I returned from the guest bathroom, pressing a wet paper towel to my cheek.

Yolanda gestured to one of the kitchen stools. "Sit down, Goldy. Let me clean that up for you."

"I'm okay."

"Sit *down*." She ran water over one of the searched-for dish towels and squirted dish soap onto it.

I took a seat. "You sound like Ferdinanda."

"Stubbornness runs in the family." She gently dabbed my torn skin.

"Sean?" I asked. "How're you doing down there?"

He groaned. Rorry said, "When Sean was in middle school? He thought he wanted to be a doctor—"

"Honey, don't tell this story again," Sean said, his voice just above a whisper.

"—right up to the point when a friend accidentally sliced his thumb with a knife in biology," Rorry said, continuing. "When the friend's blood spurted out?"

"Sweetheart," Sean whined, "you're going to make me sick."

"When the blood spurted out," Rorry said, her voice

raised a notch, "Sean passed out and hit his head on the lab counter." The look she was now giving her husband was somewhere between disgust and sympathy. "He got a concussion. He dropped biology, studied physics, majored in business in college, then became an accountant."

"And are you still one, Sean?" I asked as Yolanda carefully rinsed my cheek. "I mean, do you keep up with your certification, or whatever it's called?"

When he didn't answer, Rorry said tersely, "He doesn't." At this point, Sean, looking dazed, sat up and leaned against one of the cabinets. "He did people's taxes for a while, hated it, and wanted to become a professional photographer. He, um, *we* decided to travel around the world after we got married, so he could take pictures. Then we settled here, so he could take more pictures. He never went back to being an accountant. Am I telling the story properly, Sean?"

Sean did not look at his wife. He said, "Yeah, that about sums up the life of Sean, according to Rorry."

Could this marriage be saved? Somehow I doubted it. I glanced around the kitchen. "Where's Boyd?" I asked Yolanda.

"While you were in the bathroom," Yolanda said in a low voice, "he asked Rorry if he could get a ladder from the garage. He wants to take that whole metal oval and all the pots and pans and whatnot into evidence."

"Evidence of what?" I whispered.

"He wouldn't tell me," she murmured. "He asked Rorry for permission to take it, and she said yes. He also asked her who had access to the kitchen today, while she was getting ready for the party."

"And?"

"Just about everybody, apparently, except for Tony and Franny Ramos. They all brought food, wine, even beer, which was from Marla. According to Rorry, it was because they all felt guilty about adding to the dinner party. Except for Venla, of course, who says she always brings her cheese ball. For all these food donors, Rorry said she was either out on the patio setting it up or upstairs getting ready. Etta had already taken off for Beaver Creek with their son. Rorry said she was only in and out of the kitchen from time to time."

I tried to count. That meant that Kris and his girlfriend, Harriet, Marla, Donna Lamar, the Juarezes, the Quarleses, and Humberto and his young blonde had all been in here. I shook my head.

"Sean?" Rorry put her face in front of her husband's. "Are you ready to go back to our guests?"

Sean cleared his throat, tried to get up on his own, and couldn't make it.

"C'mon, Sean honey," Rorry said, pulling on her husband's elbow. "Let me help you."

"I don't need you!" Sean said fiercely. He jumped to his feet, wobbled, then stopped, perplexed, at the sight of Boyd walking in, carrying a stepladder with one hand. Boyd ignored him and opened the ladder under the hole in the ceiling.

Rorry turned back to me. "If you're up to it, could you bring Humberto's champagne out to the porch? He's been asking about it. And could somebody carry out some more white wine? We've finished what we had. And white wine usually helps Sean."

I nabbed a spare cotton apron I'd brought, placed it carefully over the stopper in the Dom, and cautiously turned it. But it was no use: the champagne had become shaken up in the refrigerator, and the stuff spurted everywhere. Well, tough tacks. I opened the second bottle, which also exploded. I cursed vociferously, if silently, and put both bottles on a wooden tray. Next I looked around for the bottles of Riesling I'd brought.

"I already moved the box with the bottles of white wine out of here," Boyd said. He was perched at the penultimate step of the ladder and was gazing at the ceiling. "How they survived all that metal crashing down on them, I do not know." He lifted his chin in the direction of the foyer. "It's out there."

"In the foyer?" I asked, gingerly touching the bandage Yolanda had taped to my cheek.

"That front hallway, yup." Boyd plucked his cell phone out of his back pocket and began taking pictures of the jagged opening overhead. When he was done, he pocketed the phone, came down the ladder, folded it up, and disappeared.

In despair, I looked at the jumble of pots and pans, plus the damn metal net with the dish towels that had been the cause of all this drama in the first place. Boyd was going to take all this? When he returned, he had paper bags under his arm—from the garage?—and was pulling on latex gloves. He began picking up the pots and stowing them in the bags. I wondered what Etta would think of a cop checking all her cooking equipment for signs of sabotage.

"Wait," I said to Boyd as he methodically clanked pot

after pot into the second bag. "Take this." I reached into my apron pocket and brought out the wrench.

"Where'd you get this?" Boyd asked.

"It was outside, on the ground. If this was a case of sabotage, I think our saboteur dropped it between the locked side door and the porch."

"Thanks," said Boyd as he placed the wrench into a bag. "Too bad you touched it with your bare hands."

I wanted this party to be over, but there was still work to be done. I asked Boyd to get the wine from the foyer. Then I gently picked up the tray with the Dom and made my way to the porch via the living room.

The space was lovely, filled with chintz-covered sofas and wingback chairs. On the cream-colored walls, enormous gilt-framed posters showed the evolution of marketing for Boudreaux Molasses: girls holding bottles of the dark liquid, bottles next to palm trees, bottles in meticulously kept kitchens, and yet more bottles next to piles of molasses cookies. Well, I thought, at least Rorry and Sean could have a constant reminder of where all the money came from.

I wondered what Sean thought of that.

A mirror in the living room reflected back to me how unappealing I appeared, even with Yolanda's expert bandaging job. Part of the supernova of champagne had landed on my arms, hair, and face, and the expensive slick was hardening like splattered glass. I forced myself to glance away, then quietly took the tray out to the porch. I asked Father Pete—who looked at me with concern—if he would please pour the champagne. He nodded. I didn't make eye contact with any of the other guests.

I walked quickly back to the kitchen and began opening the Riesling. Boyd was faster at the job than I was,
so I cut slits in the lamb chops, stuffed in minced garlic,
and popped them into the oven. Yolanda asked me to
heat up the taco meat while she worked on the fry bread.
With the pots and pans gone, though, she had nothing in
which to actually fry the bread. But Rorry or Etta had
left an old-fashioned electric skillet on the counter by
the sink, so Yolanda poured the oil into that.

She said, "Do you want to serve the tacos along with
the lamb chops?"

"Sure, right after the salads. It'll work," I said, reassuring her. "Thanks for thinking of that."

"I should be thanking you," said Yolanda as she
turned up the heat on the oil. "I'm going to have to dump
this oil when I'm done . . . do you suppose Rorry has an
empty coffee can around somewhere?"

"I couldn't find something in this kitchen if it was
right in front of me," I replied.

"I'll find a can," Boyd said as he handed me the bottles of Riesling. "And don't worry about the salads," he
said to me. "I know how to make one, so I can make
sixteen. Yolanda's already done the dressing, so all I
need to do is give it a quick shake."

I thanked him, too, then hustled out to the porch to set
my Riesling-and-cheese trap. The guests were speaking
in a bit of a forced tone, which I'd noticed is the way it
often is at parties where people don't really know one
another from work, or golf, or whatever. Marla gave me
a helpless look: Clearly, she'd been unable to change the
subject to puppy breeding. Maybe more booze was in

order. The champagne bottles were empty, but there were four open bottles of red wine. Rorry was right; they needed the Riesling.

I began to circle the table, asking people if they preferred red or white wine. I couldn't help but notice something odd, though, and it had nothing to do with Kris. What conversation there was was dominated by Donna Lamar, who, in addition to being the church treasurer, had clearly had way too much to drink. Not only that, but she was dressed in a manner that would have made my mother and her set back in New Jersey cringe: a way-too-low-cut bright red dress that revealed to what extent her cups were running over. She'd changed the place cards around so that she was sitting across from Humberto, at whom she aimed her cleavage and her voice, which had turned high and flirtatious. I looked at Odette, who was arching an eyebrow at her presumptive rival.

"Oh, Humberto," Donna was saying, as if he were the only one at the table, "you should have been there." She placed her hand suggestively on his forearm. "I wowed them. I told the teachers that they should aim to have three-fourths of their math students *above* the school median."

"That's not possible," Odette said coolly.

"Oh," said Donna, her voice huffy with indignation. "I suppose you are the one who was asked by the teachers to come give a motivational talk. Well," she said, directing her comments and her boobs at Humberto, "then I spoke to the science teachers, and goodness knows, they need a pick-me-up, with all the budget-cutting that's going on. They just loved me—"

"If you see eleven sunspots one day," interjected Odette, "and eight the next, and then three the next, what do you think the median will be? Eight," said Odette. "It's not possible to have—"

"What's not possible," shrilled Donna, "is to get rid of sunspots so quickly, dummy! You have to use makeup or concealer—"

She was interrupted by a laughing Odette. Everyone else looked dumbfounded except for Donna, who was furious. Her face was flushed with that horrible mixture of rage and booze that I'd seen on far too many wealthy clients' faces.

"Odette!" Donna squealed. "What in hell do they teach you at that escort service of yours?"

"I'm just correcting a common misperception," said Odette, unmoved by Donna's insult. Odette, still sheathed in her silver unitard, sent a twinkly smile at Humberto. Much to Donna's dismay, the entirety of the guests were now staring openmouthed at Odette.

"My dear little smart girl," said Humberto, patting her knee.

Marla said, "Remind me to give you a call, Odette, when I'm doing my taxes."

Donna's tone turned snarky. "Perhaps you'd like to take over as church treasurer, Odette. I mean, if that's your real name."

Father Pete murmured, "My dear Donna, no one could replace you."

Donna Lamar's eyes flashed in Odette's direction. For my part, I was still getting that I-know-you-from-somewhere feeling from this young woman in the shiny unitard. I slipped my cell phone out of my pocket and took a quick picture of her. I'd already known she was brilliant, but how did I know? I also knew she lived in Aspen Meadow, no matter what escort service she was working for. I slid my cell back into my pocket, frustrated that I could not pull the context of my acquaintance with this young woman from the recesses of my mind.

"Well, you're right about that, Father Pete," said Donna. "I have worked hard on the church budget, and that, Odette, takes considerable math skill."

Odette said drily, "Really? Then how'd you get the job?"

Humberto again patted Odette's knee, but this smart girl wasn't finished.

"And hey, computer guy?" she said, addressing Kris. "If you've spent most of your life in California, how come you have a Minnesota accent?"

Kris blushed deeply, right to the roots of his pale hair. "Well, I—"

"Let me ask you something about computers, then," said Odette, patting the top of her blond curls as she gave Kris a penetrating stare. "I want to upgrade my laptop so that I can plug in my external hard drive, a printer, a separate scanner, a custom keyboard, and a microphone. How could I expand my number of USB ports?"

Kris, dumbfounded for once, gaped at her. "That wasn't my area—"

"How 'bout this, then," Odette said, continuing. "Right now, I've got a dual-core processor, and—"

"Stop this!" squealed Donna. "You're boring!"

Kris, his cheeks still flushed maroon, had definitely not expected a technical interrogation at a church fundraising dinner, from a young woman who was clearly a prostitute.

"Sweet one?" said Humberto, once again patting Odette's knee. "Back off a bit."

"I am not boring," said Odette in protest. "And anyway, I was wondering if Donna, when she was talking to the science teachers, talked about medical isotopes—"

"Isotope?" said Donna loudly. "I know that's some kind of frozen dessert. You can't use it in medicine."

"Actually," interjected Kris, still smarting from his lack of computer knowledge, "medical isotopes are used for—" But just as quickly as he'd started speaking, he stopped.

Donna sniffed proudly and glanced around the table. It was clear she was looking for a new topic of conversation, something that wouldn't make her appear quite as drunk or stupid as she already did. When her eyes lit on me, my stomach turned over. I couldn't remember the difference between the median and the average, but I had heard that sunspots were related to business cycles. Had they predicted the current recession?

Donna raised her brows and pointed a red-painted fingernail in my direction. "Aha, Goldy! Maybe you can bring us up-to-date on the investigation into the murder of our dear fellow Aspen Meadow resident Ernest McLeod! I'll bet Odette doesn't know anything about *that*."

Odette exhaled and looked down. Father Pete turned

redder than Donna's nails. But he was not one to tell people to back off.

"Oh my goodness," I said. To cover my embarrassment, I picked up the wines and began circling the table again. "I, well, I don't know anything. Uh, Tom doesn't tell me that much. Tom Schulz is my husband," I said to Norman and Isabella Juarez, who so far had seemed completely at sea over the entire conversation. "He's an investigator at the sheriff's department?" I said with a stern look at Norman. *Please don't indicate we've talked about Ernest.* He seemed to get it.

"Goldy's a real detective," said Donna, wagging her finger at me.

That reminded me. I stared at the cheese platter. It was about half-denuded, but at that moment, I saw both Sean and Brie Quarles exchange a look. He reached for the Gouda. First he cut her a slice, placed it on a cracker and a napkin, then handed it across the table. Then he cut himself a wedge. With their eyes locked, they put the cheese into their mouths simultaneously. And Brie, I noticed, was wearing a lilac silk outfit and mauve lipstick. I thought, *Well well well. Is this a* gotcha *moment?* I glanced over at Tony Ramos, who, in typical Calvin Coolidge style, hadn't said anything during the dinner. What did he think of Brie and Sean's locked eyes? The last time I'd seen him, Brie had been showering her attentions on *him.*

"Are you going to pour Brie some of that Riesling, Goldy," Kris asked, "or are you waiting for an engraved invitation?"

"Sorry," I mumbled, and poured the Riesling—the

adulterers' Riesling, their favorite—into her glass. Again simultaneously, they picked up their glasses and made just the slightest movement, a silent toast to each other. Yup. *Gotcha.*

"Oh, yes," Donna said in a loud, querulous voice. "I know *all about* Goldy's detecting skills. In fact, I sent her on a mission! And it had to do with illicit sex!"

Father Pete choked on his cracker. Venla Strothmeyer's cheeks turned pink. But the rest of the table turned toward Donna. She preened. I thought, *Doggone. She didn't want me to talk to the paper, and now she's making a public announcement.*

"Do tell," said Marla. Showing remarkable forbearance, she did not look at me.

"So here's the scoop," Donna hissed conspiratorially. "People wanting to have sex have been sneaking into my rentals. It's a couple, always the same couple, judging by the glimpses from neighbors. Except now they might be using disguises. At least, that's what my assistant says. Anyway, these two are always looking for places without security systems. In remote areas. It just pisses me off! Oh, sorry." She glanced at Father Pete, who was trying to wash down the aberrant cracker with some red wine. "Anyway, one day, a neighbor who lives not far from one of the places—out by the Aspen Meadow Wildlife Preserve?—called to alert me. Then she shouted at them that the cops were coming, which wasn't true, unfortunately," Donna said, continuing breathlessly. She slugged down some wine. "But the pair had to skedaddle. They left behind their sleeping bags, wine bottle, cheese wrappers, and other trash. So I just handed it all over to Goldy. I suppose she wanted to help, since her husband works for the sheriff's department, and they won't do jack to help me. I said, 'You get 'em, girl!'" This was not what she'd said, but I knew by now that Donna was in the embellishment business. "So," she said to me expectantly, "did you figure out who they were? Did that stuff I gave you yield any *clues,* Sherlock?"

I was painfully aware of all eyes turning to me. Sean's and Brie's mouths dropped open. Brie blinked, turned away, and moved her wineglass several inches from her place setting. Sean gave me a malevolent, accusing stare.

"I didn't find anything," I lied. "I have no idea who they are. Between getting ready for this party and all my other work, I didn't really have time to investigate."

"But you went out there, to the cabin," Donna said, protesting. "What kind of detective are you?"

"Not a very good one, apparently," said Kris Nielsen, who up to then had said nothing. "Why, just yesterday, Goldy barged into my house, on false pretenses, mind you—"

Whatever it was he was going to say got lost as an unearthly series of screams issued from the kitchen.

Chapter 16

I whacked the wine bottles onto the porch table and raced back to the kitchen. Rorry trotted along behind me, muttering worriedly about what other thing could have happened now. The rest of the guests were clearly curious, but I heard Father Pete, bless him, tell everyone to just stay put and let Goldy and Rorry handle this, whatever it was.

Rorry and I ran into Boyd, who was carrying a shrieking, flailing Yolanda. "Bathtub!" he yelled at Rorry. "I need a bathtub and ice cubes! I've called nine-one-one."

"Upstairs, first door on the right," said Rorry, her voice cracking. She wanted to lead Boyd, but he was too quick for her. He dashed up the spiral staircase, his arms tight around Yolanda. Rorry stumbled up behind him. I ran into the kitchen to get ice cubes.

The place was a mess. Several pieces of cooked fry bread had scattered across the floor, next to parts of the electric skillet. The handle was upside down under the island, while the skillet itself had slid underneath the kitchen table. A thick, shiny layer of oil lay all over everything. What had happened?

I shimmied around the oil slick, mercifully found a large glass bowl in one of the cupboards, and filled it with ice cubes from Rorry's side-by-side refrigerator. Holding one hand over the top of the bowl and the other underneath, I moved as quickly as I could up the stairs.

Boyd's low voice and Rorry's high-pitched one led me to an opulent bathroom done in blue tiles and brass fixtures. Yolanda sat in a deep tub. She was sobbing inconsolably as Boyd ran cold water over her legs. She still wore her catering uniform. I handed Boyd the bowl. He upended the ice over Yolanda's thighs.

Rorry, kneeling beside the tub, took Yolanda's free hand. She murmured reassurances to Yolanda, whose sobs had turned to whimpers. Tears still flowed freely down my friend's face.

I said, "Can someone tell me what happened?"

"She was moving the frying pan," Boyd said. "I was right there." He shook his head. "I was holding a coffee can for her to pour the boiling oil into. The handle to the electric skillet just, it just, came off. The hot oil poured all over her."

"Oh, God, Yolanda," I said, my heart constricting. "I'm so sorry." I swallowed. "I just, I don't . . ." I didn't know what to say. "Boyd?" I asked finally. "Did any of the oil get on you?"

"Not that you'd notice," he replied, keeping his attention on Yolanda. "I'm going to need somebody to get me more ice."

"I'll do it," Rorry said. She grasped the bowl and stood up. Then she stopped. "It was an electric skillet?" asked Rorry, puzzled. "I thought Etta said we didn't have one after all."

Neither Boyd nor Yolanda answered. As Rorry and I walked back to the kitchen, I found myself transfixed by a trio of gold-framed photographs on the wall beside the stairs. They were of baskets of *beagle puppies.*

"Rorry?" I asked. "Where did you get these?"

Rorry looked up. "Those are pictures Sean took. They were supposed to be part of his *professional portfolio,* as he insisted on calling it. I said he should advertise as Fun, Furry Photos! He didn't find that amusing. So I framed his little doggy prints and put them in the bathroom. He didn't like that, either, so I put them in this hallway. We should get that ice."

I asked, "Do you know where he found the beagle pups to photograph?"

Rorry shook her head. "I don't. There was a guy outside of town who was breeding. Sean took the pictures with the agreement that they were going to be used in advertisements for the breeder, but then he and Sean had a falling-out, which is what usually happens between Sean and other people."

Outside, a siren blared. *That was quick,* I thought. Maybe emergency services responded more speedily if a cop called.

"Rorry," Boyd called, "could you let them in? Goldy, can you get us more ice?"

Rorry opened the front door. I filled the bowl with ice and sprinted back up the steps. Yolanda had stopped crying. As gently as possible, I sprinkled the cubes over her legs.

"Goldy," Boyd said sternly, "listen." He took his keys out of his pocket. "Get some latex gloves out of your van and put that skillet and the handle into a paper bag. Then put it into my car next to the bag of stuff from the pot hanger. Got it?"

"Of course."

"Then call Tom stat and tell him to get over here, to be with you."

"I'm fine," I said in protest. "I don't need—"

"I didn't ask your opinion," Boyd said harshly. "Just do it!"

Within moments two paramedics were at the bathroom door. They told Boyd to move but keep the cold water going. Once they were beside the tub, they checked Yolanda's vitals and commanded Boyd to get more ice. I said I would do it and raced to the kitchen, cursing inwardly.

After delivering the new batch of ice, I ran back to the kitchen, did as Boyd had directed with the pan and its handle, and locked it inside his car. When I returned, the paramedics were bringing Yolanda expertly down the stairs. Boyd clomped purposefully behind them. He wordlessly took his keys from me.

I went out the front door and pulled out my cell as the ambulance and Boyd's car rolled down the driveway. I called Tom and gave an executive summary to his voice mail as to what had happened.

Back in the kitchen, I noticed Rorry had grabbed a pile of terry-cloth bath towels. On her knees, working on the oil mess, she told me she'd announced to the guests that there had been a kitchen accident and that dinner would be slightly delayed. Together, we swabbed the kitchen floor with her towels, which I noticed were monogrammed. I felt guilty about the broken china; the fallen pot ring; the fancy towels, now ruined; the dinner . . . but most of all, I was worried about Yolanda, who was in excruciating pain from burns. . . .

Sean's face floated into view overhead. He asked if he could help.

"Yes. You can entertain our guests," Rorry replied without looking up.

"Well, we're out of food. Uh, can you give me a few more details as to what happened? Looks like more than a little kitchen accident."

I got to my feet and said only that some hot oil had spilled. Then I washed my hands and asked him to do the same. Puzzled, he followed my lead. Rorry continued to work on the floor. Quickly, I taught Sean how to follow me, assembly-line style, as we put together the *salades composées*. As he was putting the last ingredients on each salad, I wrapped the focaccia in foil and put it into the oven. Then I whisked Yolanda's dressing one last time and drizzled it onto each salad.

"You can manage four at a time on the trays," I told Sean as I loaded him up. "Don't stop to answer questions, don't give them any details. Just serve."

"People are going to ask me to tell them more," he whined, "especially after the pot hanger came down."

"Just tell them we had a mishap." I was so angry with him over his affair with Brie, I felt no compunction about ordering him around. "Don't embellish. Come back for more salads after you serve these four. I'll try to salvage the Navajo tacos. Uh, Sean?" I asked. "Do you happen to remember who requested these tacos?"

He gritted his teeth and blinked. After a moment, he said, "I don't remember. Sorry."

"How about this," I said. "Which breeder did you visit to get the beagle puppies? The ones you took pictures of?"

He colored deeply and looked away. "I don't recall." Then he hustled off.

You sure have one hell of a bad memory, I thought, but didn't say. Instead, I looked at all the ingredients Yolanda had placed neatly on one of the counters: seasoned beef; chopped tomatoes, lettuce, and green onions; grated Mexican *queso;* a big bowl of sour cream. I counted out the pieces of fry bread that had not fallen onto the floor. I shook my head and said aloud, "We don't have enough to go around."

Rorry had squirted a degreasing disinfectant onto the floor and was starting in with more towels from her load. "I don't need one, I know Father Pete would be more than willing to forgo his, and Sean can go without." She concentrated on wiping the floor and did not look at me as she said quietly, "You know, don't you? About him."

"I, I—"

"That's why you brought that white wine and those cheeses, isn't it? They were for him, and for . . . her."

"Well," I said, anxious to conclude the conversation before Sean returned, "yes, okay, I figured it out. But it wasn't because I was nosy, Rorry, or because I give two hoots about Donna and her rentals. I was just trying to find out who Ernest McLeod was working for. He'd been hired to find two adulterers."

Rorry stood up and gave me the full benefit of her round brown eyes. "He was working for me."

Before I could respond, Sean returned. He looked from Rorry to me and back again, then loaded up more salads and whipped out of the kitchen.

"Do you think Sean knows that you're aware of what he's doing?" I whispered.

"At this point, I don't care." She picked up all her monogrammed towels and tossed them down a laundry chute. She washed her hands and smoothed her wrinkled, slightly oily embroidered skirt. "I knew Sean was up to something, but he denied it and acted hurt when I asked him if he was having an affair. He kept asking if I had any *proof* for my suspicions. He acted like I was impugning his integrity. He insisted that he loved me, blah, blah, blah."

I rubbed my temples. The Jerk had done the same thing, turning my doubts about his fidelity into my problem, my insecurity, my paranoia. He had not, however, insisted that he loved me. He'd said if I loved him, I wouldn't be so suspicious.

Rorry said, "I only hired Ernest to get me proof. Ernest promised that if he discovered Sean with a mistress, he would take pictures of them. Last week he said he'd been following Sean, that he was sure Sean was cheating on me, and that he, Ernest, was sure he could get some photos. But he never got back to me."

Sean had not returned, so I said quickly, "Why did you even hire Ernest? Don't you have a prenup that allows you to file for divorce no matter what your husband has done?"

"I do," she said sadly. "We do. My daddy made sure one was drawn up. He never trusted Sean. Turned out, he was right." Tears welled in her eyes, but she shook them away. "I don't care about the money, to tell you the truth. But that was what I wanted: the truth. I wanted *proof* Sean was lying. Before I filed for divorce, I wanted to show him that evidence. I pray to God I didn't cause Ernest to be killed." Here she broke down. Unlike Yolanda, who'd sobbed loudly when her legs were burned, Rorry wept almost soundlessly.

"What's going on?" asked Sean when he returned to the kitchen. "Sweetheart? What's wrong?"

"She's upset about Yolanda," I said authoritatively. "She feels responsible, because it happened in her kitchen." I loaded up four more salads on Sean's tray, then put the last four, along with the warm focaccia and two sticks of butter, onto my own tray. "Let's go, Sean. People are waiting."

Sean stared wordlessly at his crying wife. Rorry kept her back to him.

"C'mon, Sean," I said, urging him on. "The guests are hungry. With Yolanda on her way to the hospital, the one thing Rorry wants is for you to step up and help with the food." I pushed his left arm a bit with my loaded tray. He gave me an exasperated glance, then turned with his culinary cargo and headed out to the porch.

Once we arrived, all eyes turned toward me. "Yolanda's fine," I lied. "A skillet handle broke. Just to be on the safe side, Yolanda's on her way to the hospital with the *policeman* who was helping us." I gazed at Kris Nielsen, who glared at me, then ran a hand through his white hair. I turned my attention to Humberto, who had his eyes fixed on one of the centerpieces. Was he avoiding my look, or was I imagining it? "That same policeman is keeping the skillet, just in case he needs it later."

"Goldy?" asked Father Pete. "In case he needs it for what?"

"Oh," I said mildly as I began to circle the table, placing a salad in front of each guest, "I don't know. He just said he wanted to take it with him." I was getting good at this lying business.

Father Pete said, "Your friend certainly seems accident-prone."

I had come to Kris Nielsen, and I hesitated slightly before lowering his salad in front of him. He said in a low voice, "Yolanda should be more careful."

"Speak up, Kris!" I said immediately. "I don't think the rest of the table heard that comment of yours."

"Yeah, Kris," said Marla. "I want to hear what you said."

"Goldy's making a mountain out of a pile of manure," he said, his tone again mild.

"I'm sorry," said Norman Juarez, addressing both the table and yours truly. "I do not know this expression." When he was nervous, his voice betrayed a tinge of an accent.

I said, "Father Pete?" And then I gave our priest a slit-eyed look that I hoped said, *Be pastoral, why don't you?*

"Don't worry about expressions," Father Pete said to reassure Norman Juarez. "I don't understand most of them myself. And, uh, where are you and Isabella from?"

"I already asked them," Paul Quarles put in. "They said—"

"You mean, before we came to Colorado?" Norman Juarez calmly interrupted Paul. Norman gazed at Humberto, who hadn't had the forethought, this time, to keep his eyes on the centerpiece. Humberto blushed. "Miami," said Norman. "I worked in restaurants there."

I rolled my eyes heavenward, hoping the Lord would somehow intervene. And He did, in the appearance of Rorry, who materialized holding aloft a tray of Navajo tacos that she had assembled herself. She'd also wrapped the lamb chops in foil and placed them next to the tacos. I set down my own empty tray, then relieved Rorry of hers. "Please sit," I begged her.

"I want to help," she said fiercely.

"You *have* helped," I said. "But in the catering biz, I've noticed that most people don't want to start eating unless the hostess is in her chair."

"You're right," she said before sliding into her place at the head of the table. I was beginning to like Rorry more and more. If Etta ever failed her, I hoped she'd call me to fill in.

Father Pete cleared his throat and directed his attention to Norman and Isabella. "I am of Greek ancestry myself. My grandfather and grandmother both came from Athens, but they did not know each other there. They only met in New York!"

"My father and mother came from Cuba," Norman said. He had not touched his food, and his gaze was still trained on Humberto Captain. "Our family was wealthy there, but someone took all our money."

Marla piped up. "That commie bastard, Castro—"

"Oh, it was not Fidel who stole our wealth," Norman said heatedly. I noticed Isabella putting a restraining hand on her husband's thigh. It didn't work. "No. Our father gave our gold, gems, and a valuable necklace of my mother's to a man he thought he could trust. His name was Roberto Captain. Roberto died, and since then, only one person has been able to find our wealth—"

Humberto stood up so swiftly his chair fell over. "It is time for us to leave."

"—and his name was Ernest McLeod," Norman said, his tone becoming more ferocious. "He had found something, and was about to tell us about it when he was murdered. Maybe by someone in the Captain family?"

Humberto took a deep breath, which puffed out his chest like a rooster's. "I will not stay and allow the name of my family to be impugned. Odette, come."

Odette, who was holding her taco and had just taken a big bite, reluctantly got up.

"Thank you, Sean and Rorry," Humberto said in a formal tone, pulling himself to his full height, which wasn't tall in any event. He rummaged in his pocket, pulled out a pristinely white handkerchief, and wiped his eyes, as if he had to deal with this type of accusation all the time. Then he cleared his throat. "Up to a few minutes ago," Humberto declared, "we have enjoyed being part of your party for the church." He turned to Norman and Isabella and raised his voice. "I do much good in this community. Many people appreciate me." He turned, took Odette's elbow, and made as if to lead her out.

Odette lost her balance momentarily on her high heels, then let Humberto right her. Directing her attention to Rorry, she swallowed her food and mumbled, "Yeah, thanks. Great food. Lotta fun. 'Bye, everybody."

Sean offered to see them out. When the three of them were on their way off the porch, Marla called across the table, "So, Norman! You think Humberto stole your stuff?"

"I know he did," Norman said.

"Let's hear the juicy details," Marla demanded.

"No," he said stiffly. "I should not have said anything. I am sorry. I do not want to ruin this dinner party."

Yeah, yeah, I said to myself as I skirted the table, pouring more wine. *Let's not ruin this dinner party! Ha! Ha!*

Marla scowled at Norman, then wrinkled her forehead at me, as if she were trying to remember something. "Say!" she said suddenly, causing the guests to jump. "Does anybody know anything about breeding puppies? I mean, like an investment?" When no one answered her, she plunged on with, "Has anyone heard of a puppy farm in Aspen Meadow? I did hear a rumor about one, where a guy was breeding beagle puppies, that ended up being—" With all the curiosity about Ernest, I did *not* want to talk about this now, after all. When Marla saw my black look, she stopped. "Well anyway," she said, "I took three of the puppies that had been . . . abandoned, let's say. So did my cleaning lady, Penny Woolworth. Has anybody heard anything about abandoned puppies?"

Everyone looked puzzled.

"I took three of the beagle puppies," said Father Pete into the uncomfortable silence. "The odd thing to me, though, is that they were all female, and they'd all been spayed."

"But that was true of mine, too!" Marla exclaimed. "Why would you raise beagles that you hoped would be passed off as American Kennel Club purebreds and then spay them?"

I busied myself slicing the lamb chops. After placing them on a platter, I rounded the table with them, trying to look as if I had no idea what it was Marla was talking about.

"Maybe you didn't want someone to breed them," Isabella Juarez said. It was the first thing I'd heard her say all evening. "Maybe your clients didn't want to have to deal with puppies, if they came along. Something like that."

"Wait a minute," said Kris Nielsen, suddenly interested. "They were all *female,* and they were all *spayed*?"

"Yeah," said Marla. "Why? Are you going into the dog-breeding business, Kris? Puppies would make a mess out of your Maserati, I'll tell you that."

As Harriet, Kris's date, snuffled with laughter, the doorbell gonged inside the house. I put down my empty platter and headed toward the front door. Once more, Rorry accompanied me.

"You should just let me get this," she said.

"I think it's my husband, Tom."

"Tom? Why would he come?"

"Oh," I said, working to appear offhanded, "Boyd wanted me to call Tom to get him to help me out in the kitchen."

"Dear me," said Rorry. "I should have helped you. There's no need for your husband to come all this way—"

But I had already opened the front door, and there was Tom, looking even more commanding and suspicious than usual. He said, "Show me the oil spill."

"I cleaned it up," said Rorry. "I'm so sorry you had to come all the way over here." Tom held up his hand for her to be quiet, and she immediately stopped talking. I was used to Tom's air of authority having that effect on people.

"Let me make the coffee," Rorry murmured as she led us into the kitchen. She busied herself with water, a bag of ground beans, and the pot. "I suppose I should find out if people want regular," she said, flustered. "Well, no, I'll just make all decaf."

"Rorry, I can do this," I insisted. "It's my job. Please go entertain the guests. That's *your* job."

As soon as she was gone, Tom huddled next to me at the coffeemaker. "Tell me what happened to your head."

"The pot hanger came down." I pointed to the ceiling. "A corkscrew caught me in the face. Do you know how Yolanda is?"

Tom shook his head. "They're not at the hospital yet. Boyd gave me the outline of what happened. He said the handle just came right off the pan."

"I wasn't here. Still, Rorry says she thought Etta told her they didn't have an electric skillet. They were supposed to have lots of other pots we could use." I felt distracted. "I supposed Etta could have gone out and bought one for us, but I would have thought she would then tell Rorry she'd done that. I'll tell you something else: I *was* out here when the pot hanger came down. And I found a wrench outside." I stopped what I was doing and pointed at the ceiling. "This house is decorated in an old style, but it's practically new. It's like the whole damn place was sabotaged."

Tom moved away and peered into the hole in the ceiling. "It was. Question is, who was the target? Maybe it was you, Miss G. Maybe it was Rorry. I'll want to talk to her about who had access to the kitchen and when."

I inhaled. "Boyd already did. Everyone here, practically, came during the day, to leave food." Tom tied on an apron, stepped to the sink, and washed his hands. "A couple of guests have already left. Humberto and his 'date,' if that's what you call a stacked girl in her twenties wearing a skintight silver outfit. Here, I have her picture." I pulled out my phone and queued up the pictures of Odette. "Does she look familiar to you?"

"Nope." He eyed the kitchen, including the two covered flourless chocolate cakes. "You need me to serve these people dessert?"

I checked my watch. Incredibly, the guests had had the main course for twenty minutes. I said, "First we have to clear the dinner plates." The coffeepot was gurgling merrily, so I led Tom out to the porch.

There was a general reaction of surprise at Tom's appearance. Yes, he was a member of the church, but he was not a dinner guest. So why was he there? And was it my imagination, or was Sean Breckenridge suddenly twitching nervously in his chair?

Donna was once again trying to command the floor. Without Humberto, she directed her remarks to all the guests, who appeared to be drooping with boredom. "And then I got my license, and what with my success as treasurer of St. Luke's, I was honored by the Aspen Meadow Chamber of Commerce to be the Businesswoman of the Year—"

"Oh, yes," Marla said, interrupting her. "The fire department loves you, too, right? I heard one of your rentals burned to the ground—"

"Marla!" I cried. Kris, Harriet, and Brie and Paul Quarles snickered. Marla pressed her lips together so she wouldn't laugh.

Venla touched the white hair in her bun and turned to Father Pete. She asked, "What did Marla Korman say that was funny?"

Rorry shook her head, while Sean's face was racked with misery.

The Juarezes looked as much at sea as usual. The Ramoses continued to ignore everyone.

"I will not be insulted by you, Marla Korman!" Donna Lamar cried. She whirled in her seat. "And not a word from you, either, Tom Schulz!"

"That's *Investigator* Schulz to you," Tom said as he balanced a pile of the new dinner dishes Rorry had brought out. I gulped and looked away as Tom made a beeline for the kitchen. If we had one more accident tonight, I did not want to witness it.

Quickly gathering up all the soiled silverware, I deposited it onto the remaining tray and hurried out to the kitchen.

"What in the world were you correcting Donna Lamar for?" I asked Tom as he carefully sliced the flourless chocolate cakes into eighths. "Odette, or whatever her name is, has already made mincemeat out of her in the science and math departments. And you heard Marla make fun of her. I'm actually beginning to feel *sorry* for Donna."

"Oh, don't. *Somebody* needed to puncture Donna Lamar's good opinion of herself," Tom said nonchalantly. "Without Humberto Captain, she'd still have that hole in the wall on Main Street and be renting wrecked houses to even more wrecked people."

"Goodness gracious!" Marla appeared at the kitchen door. "This is something I didn't know! So, *what* did Humberto do for Donna Lamar?"

"Brought her business up to a whole new level," said Tom as he gently placed slices of cake onto gold-edged dessert plates. "Gave her that office rent-free for the first year," he said, continuing as he scooped even spoonfuls of crème fraîche onto each piece of cake, "just so it would look as if someone was leasing the place. He said he was hoping that would attract more tenants. It didn't."

"And you know all this how?" asked Marla. She plucked a fork from a drawer and began eating a piece of cake.

"From Humberto himself," said Tom as he placed a tray holding eight plates on his shoulder. "We talked to everybody after the fire at Yolanda's place, to see if Donna could have set it. She owned the place and so was the beneficiary of the policy. We were thinking that if we dug into her financials, we'd find a debt on her own rent or something like that."

"And did you?" asked Marla breathlessly.

"Tom," I said, warning him. Did he really want any information he gave Marla fed into the town gossip machine?

"Oh, this was all in our report, which we made public," said Tom. "Goldy, can you bring sugar and cream with the coffee? I didn't see any out there."

Marla blocked his way out of the kitchen. "Tell me what you found out about Donna Lamar and her finances. I've endured her singing her own praises this entire evening. I'm desperate for a dose of Schadenfreude."

"Let's see," said Tom as he placed his tray on a counter. "Schadenfreude, rejoicing in bad news about others. I'll tell you what isn't in the report but was a result of my male intuition, how about that? Donna has the hots for Humberto. He gave her that office rent-free, and she thought, *I've found myself a meal ticket.* But alas, Humberto's taste doesn't seem to run to women who are close to being his peers, that is, in their thirties, forties, or fifties, no matter how good-looking they are. Does that make you rejoice?"

"Not really," Marla declared. "I could have told you Donna was making a play for Humberto after the first five minutes of this party. Goldy, load me up with the rest of the dessert plates. I'll take them out."

I obliged, then stood in the kitchen, thinking. The coffee wasn't quite done, so I made a quick call to Southwest Hospital, to see if Yolanda Garcia had arrived safely. They wouldn't tell me anything, so I paged Boyd. He called from outside the hospital. He said Yolanda was in the ER, waiting to be seen, which should be in the next five minutes. I asked if he'd called Ferdinanda, and he said he had.

"Was she a wreck?" I asked, immediately worried.

"Yes and no. She told me I should have arrested Kris Nielsen. She's sure he did this."

"Tom didn't even consider Yolanda the target. He thought maybe it was an attack meant for me or Rorry Breckenridge." I felt suddenly queasy at the thought that Yolanda might have been the target.

"I don't know," said Boyd. "I gotta go. They're taking Yolanda back."

"Call me later!" I hollered into the phone, but he'd already signed off.

Somehow, we got through the rest of the party. As soon as the last bite of cake had been downed, the Juarezes stood and told Rorry how much they had enjoyed the dinner. They hoped she and her husband would come down to their restaurant soon. I broke out in a sweat, just then realizing that with all the commotion, I'd completely forgotten to heat their enchiladas. They'd undoubtedly noticed, and I bumbled through an apology. They graciously said it was no problem, that I'd had my hands full with other things. Rorry assured them both that she loved Mexican food and would enjoy the enchiladas for the rest of the week.

Marla piped up and said, "I'm claiming a few for myself, if that's all right," whereupon Father Pete said, "Me too!" and everyone laughed.

At the beginning of the evening, Rorry had been adamant that the guests turn off their electronics. When Father Pete said he'd have to at least have his on Vibrate, in case a parishioner died suddenly, Rorry relented, but only for him. She hadn't noticed when I'd used mine to take pictures of Odette, thank goodness. But hostess's instructions or no, I always, always kept my cell phone on, in case Arch needed to reach me. He knew it, I knew it, and I didn't care if anyone else knew it.

In any event, once the Juarezes left, folks at the table pulled out their gizmos and turned them on. Soon all manner of beeping and buzzing caused people to start making their excuses, thanking Rorry and Sean, and leaving.

In the kitchen, I wrapped Father Pete's enchiladas up first, as he needed to get Venla home. Marla had been hot on my heels, eager for gossip as well as enchiladas, no doubt, but before we'd even started to chat, her cell phone began beeping urgently.

"Damn it," she said. "This is from my home phone. Penny came over to take care of my puppies, and hers, too. I'm paying her. . . . Hello?" Penny's voice came through loud and insistent. "Calm down!" Marla yelled into the phone. "Start over!"

"I'm telling you one of your puppies is sick!" Penny shrieked, near hysteria. "Really sick. I don't know if she's going to make it."

Marla unleashed a string of curses, then told Penny to call Twenty-Four-Hour Urgent Animal Care. Marla said she'd race right home to take in the ailing canine. "Tell Rorry to keep the enchiladas," Marla said as she hurried out. "And tell her thanks, too. Good Lord, one of the puppies is sick and might not make it? My heart's already racing. My cardiologist would say—" But then she stopped and gave me an anxious look. "Is this what it's like to have children? You worry about them all the time? And then something happens, and you worry even more?"

I said nothing, only helped her into her Mercedes and shut the door. As she maneuvered down the Breckenridges' driveway, I whispered, "Yes. This is what worrying about your child is like."

So I called Arch, who was at home.

"I'm here with Ferdinanda," he said in a low voice. "She's really upset about what happened to Yolanda." He shifted to a whisper. "She says a guy Yolanda broke up with *burned* her. I don't mean he stole money from her, he actually burned her. Is that true?"

"We don't know, hon. He wasn't anywhere near the kitchen when the accident happened."

"Well, is Tom there with you?" He could not hide the anxiety in his voice.

"Sweetheart, I'm fine."

"Is Tom with you?"

"Yes. We'll be home soon."

That worrying stuff? It worked both ways.

Chapter 17

Rorry prohibited Tom and me from doing more than washing and drying the dishes and silverware, which we carefully placed on the large table at the far end of the kitchen. Rorry again insisted that Etta was the only one who knew where everything went, and she would go ballistic if the caterer and her husband tried to put stuff away in its proper place. When Rorry laughed, it was sincere, not condescending. So I acquiesced. On a more serious note, she made me promise to call her with an update on Yolanda. Furthermore, I was absolutely, positively supposed to forget about the broken china. She and Sean had received it as a wedding gift, and she was glad it was gone.

Tom, meanwhile, was pacing around the kitchen like a fearsome jungle cat. He trusted Boyd, but I knew Tom, and he wanted to make sure his associate hadn't missed anything. He opened cupboards, asked Rorry questions, lifted up pans, crouched on the floor to check for proof that nothing had been overlooked. When he was satisfied, his team would begin to sprinkle black graphite fingerprint powder all over everything. I began gnawing my fist, desperate to tell Tom all I'd learned that day. But with Rorry coming in and out of the kitchen, I had to keep my mouth shut.

And then there was Yolanda. To keep myself from going crazy with worry—that worry again—I called Boyd, because I knew the privacy lovers at the hospital wouldn't give me a nano-update on Yolanda's condition. Boyd, who luckily was outside checking messages on his cell, said tersely that a nurse had told him Yolanda had first-, second-, and a few third-degree burns on her legs. Nothing was bad enough to warrant a hospital stay, the nurse had said. I rolled my eyes. *Welcome to managed care.* They were bandaging Yolanda up now, the nurse said, and she would be in pain for a couple of days, probably not able to work, although Yolanda kept insisting she *had* to work.

"That's ridiculous," I interjected. "We don't have catered events for the next week."

"She thought you had mentioned something about Saturday."

I sighed. "It was canceled. Part of the wave of clients deciding they couldn't afford to have parties."

"All right, I'll tell her." Boyd's tone was relieved. "How's Ferdinanda holding up?"

"I'm still at Rorry's. Arch said Ferdinanda is sure Kris Nielsen is behind this." When Boyd didn't reply, I said, "What do you think?"

"I have to look at the evidence, of which we do not have much." Now his voice was terse. "What's the big

guy doing?" I cleared my throat. I did not want to tell
Boyd that Tom was prowling around the kitchen checking for evidence that Boyd might have missed. I hesitated just long enough for Boyd to say, "Oh, I get it.
He's checking my work."

"Uh—"

"That's all right, I'm used to it. Tell him we'll talk
when I bring Yolanda home."

We signed off. Tom, crawling around on Rorry's
kitchen floor, reminded me of Sabine Rushmore hunched
over the rental cabin's fireplace, sifting through ashes.
But there was no way I was ever going to tell him *that*.
Finally, Tom's team arrived. He gave them the go-ahead
to start with the fingerprint powder. I skedaddled into the
foyer.

I gave Rorry the promised update on Yolanda. She
shook her head and said she was going to start bringing
her crystal in from the porch. Since she clearly did not
want me to touch any more of her stuff, I dialed Marla's
cell to ask about the puppies.

"The sick one is in surgery," she said, her voice low.
"But a nurse or assistant—I don't know what she does up
front here—took a call from the doc. He said to ask me
if this was a rescue dog. I said, 'Why, is he prejudiced
against rescue dogs?' She didn't like that, so I said yes.
Then she wanted to know, or I guess it was the veterinary surgeon who wanted to know, if there were more
rescue dogs who'd been adopted with this one. I said yes
again. So her eyebrows went up. I thought, *What in the
hell is going on?* Finally, she said that all the other rescue dogs who were adopted along with this one needed

to be brought in immediately. I said, 'What, do they all have rabies or something?'"

"This is not making any sense," I said.

"Maybe not, but don't worry, Penny is bringing her dogs and the rest of mine. I then had the unpleasant task of calling Father Pete and asking him to saddle up and bring all his new pups over to Twenty-Four-Hour Urgent Animal Care. Since he'd just gotten back from taking Venla home, then had settled the dogs for the night and poured himself a glass of ouzo, he was not a happy camper. But he's coming. I asked him to bring me some ouzo."

"Not a great idea."

"If you saw the tiny plastic chair I'd been sitting in for the last hour, you'd think it was a superb idea."

"Marla," I said in protest, "you've had a heart attack."

"And I'm going to have another one being anxious about these puppies. Oops, here's Father Pete. And Penny, too! Gotta go."

I glanced at my watch; it was quarter to nine. Tom's team was still hard at work when he appeared in the foyer. He asked, "Could you go get Rorry for me?"

She was not on the porch, where she'd moved all the crystal to the wheeled tea cart. Back in the foyer, the sound of voices raised in anger emanated from upstairs. I crept back to the kitchen.

"Tom? They're arguing. What am I supposed to do, interrupt a domestic quarrel?"

"You want my gun?"

"Oh, ha ha." Of course, there was no way Tom would ever loan me his firearm.

"I'll get her," he said. He stood up. I watched him make his stealthy way up the spiral staircase. My stomach clenched and prickles broke out on my skin. If anyone had interrupted the Jerk when he was howling at me, that person would have risked physical attack. What if Sean hurt Tom?

A door slammed. Sean Breckenridge, his face blazing, stormed past Tom. He raced down the stairs and into the foyer. Tom signaled for me to stop him from entering the kitchen. In the kitchen entryway, I raised my arms like someone about to be crucified. Sean seemed not even to notice me. He sprinted sideways in the foyer and went through a door, which he slammed behind him. It probably went to the basement, where, presumably, there was a guest bedroom.

Tom said to me, "Okay, come on up. I need you now."

Oh, peachy, just what I wanted—to deal with a woman whose unfaithful husband had just stalked away. Nevertheless, once upstairs I went to the closed door Tom pointed toward and knocked gently. Rorry, her eyes filled with tears, opened the door so suddenly I was taken aback. The enormous room behind her featured a four-poster mahogany bed and oodles of lace.

"Is everything all right?" I asked. I felt like a dolt asking, but I couldn't pretend I hadn't heard their argument.

"No, but that's all right. What's up?"

"We . . . wanted to check on you. And Tom needs you in the kitchen, please."

She shook her shoulders, as if to bring herself back to full awareness. "Just a sec." She went to a mahogany dresser that was the size of my catering van, pulled open a drawer, and said, "Oh, *damn* him." She grabbed a batch of keys and disappeared into a closet. When she emerged, she was holding a considerable wad of cash with the keys.

"Rorry, you've paid us," I protested. "You've tipped us. There's no need to—"

"This isn't for you," she said matter-of-factly. "My husband took . . . he emptied—" Then something occurred to her—decorum, maybe—and she clammed up. "Let's go downstairs." She closed the bedroom door quietly, moved past me toward the staircase, and held the large roll of bills aloft. "Does Yolanda have health insurance?"

"Yes."

Tom had returned to the kitchen and had gotten down on his hands and knees again. The two-man fingerprint team was working at the far end of the room. They were making an unholy mess. Rorry ignored all of them as well as the chaos. She took my hand and pressed the clump of cash into my hand. "This is four thousand dollars. Those insurance companies don't cover everything, so please let me know if Yolanda's medical bills are more than that, would you? This happened in my kitchen, and I feel responsible."

"Rorry, really, you don't—" But she marched up to Tom. "Thank you," I said to her back, then stuffed the money into my apron pocket.

"What can I do for you, Officer Schulz?" Belatedly, Rorry looked with despair around her kitchen. In addition to every cabinet being open, Tom's team had spilled the fingerprint powder on the cabinets and countertops.

Rorry cocked her head at Tom. "How long will the kitchen have to be like this?"

"I've gotten what I need to have analyzed. Sorry about the black powder. Do you and Sean have Colorado driver's licenses? I'm wondering if your prints are on file."

"We do and they are. Don't worry about the mess." She frowned at the open cabinet doors. "What are you looking for inside all these?"

"Space. You said earlier the electric frying pan wasn't yours, correct?"

"That's right."

"And, Goldy?" Tom asked. "You brought your own roasting pans, correct?"

"Yes."

Tom pointed at an empty area in a cupboard that held shiny top-of-the-line pots. "Rorry? There's space for an electric frying pan here."

Rorry ducked down, peered into the cabinet, and wrinkled her brow. She shook her head. "I just wish I knew where Etta kept everything. Do you want me to phone her?"

"Yes, please."

Rorry put in a quick call to Beaver Creek and explained the predicament to Etta, who replied quickly. Rorry closed the phone. "That's where she keeps the double boiler."

Tom picked up his notebook and read through it, flipping pages. "No double boiler in the inventory I've taken."

Rorry, genuinely puzzled, turned to me. "You couldn't have packed it up with your things, could you?"

"She did not," Tom said decisively. "I've already inventoried every single item in her van."

"But," said Rorry, again scanning the kitchen, "where is it?"

"My guess," Tom replied as he got to his feet, "is that whoever put the electric frying pan onto one of your counters wanted to make it look as if it really was yours."

Rorry slumped into one of her kitchen chairs. "Oh, my God. Why would someone do that?"

Tom peeled off his gloves. "To make it look as if *you* had put what we're assuming was a sabotaged electric frying pan on the counter."

Rorry shook her head. "Who would do such a thing?"

"That's what I'm going to find out," said Tom. He crossed his arms. "I've only gotten a few fingerprints, but I'm going to check them out. Still, I'm guessing those belong to Yolanda, Goldy, and my man Boyd. Whoever did this, and I'm guessing again here, wiped everything down." He paused for a moment. "Mrs. Breckenridge, you and Mr. Breckenridge have children?"

Rorry blushed. "We have a little boy, Seth. He's five."

"I'm not being judgmental here," Tom said soothingly. "I just want to know who inherits your money if something happens to you."

Rorry put her finger to her mouth as she got up and closed both doors to the kitchen. "It was Sean. But I had my will changed about a month ago," she whispered. "Sean doesn't know. If something . . . happens to me, my money goes to Seth, with my cousin as executor. Thirty-five million dollars."

I swallowed hard. That was a *lot* of money.

"You're *sure* Sean doesn't know?" Tom asked, his voice just above a whisper.

"I flew back to Louisiana last month, ostensibly to visit old friends, but really to see our family lawyer. He drew up the documents himself." She hesitated. "My husband and I are not getting along. I'm hoping we can straighten things out, but I wanted to be covered. Just in case." She hesitated. "Did Goldy tell you I hired Ernest McLeod to follow Sean, to see who he was . . . having an affair with?"

Tom hitched his eyebrows at me. I said, "I didn't know until tonight that Ernest was working for her. I also found out tonight that the person Sean is fooling around with is Brie Quarles."

Tom said, "Anything else you're not telling me?"

"I found a credit card belonging to Sean out at that cabin I went to this afternoon."

Tom shook his head. "Have you still got it?"

My cheeks reddened. In fact, I did. I pulled it out of my pocket. "Do you want it?" I asked him, then turned to Rorry. "Or should she—"

Rorry held up her hands to stop me. "Don't give it to me. I'll just cancel it and then cut it up."

"I'll take it, please," said Tom. He turned to Rorry. "I'd feel better if you went to a neighbor's house for the night. It's possible you weren't the target of the pan ring falling or the skillet accident. But we want to cover all the bases. We'll wait here while you pack. Then call us when you get where you're going, and let us know where you are. Then phone Etta and have her bring Seth to you in the morning."

"There's no need for you to wait." Rorry moved toward the foyer. "That 'just in case' I mentioned? I always keep a packed suitcase in the trunk of my Mercedes. I'll drive up to our Beaver Creek condo tonight and change the security code so Sean couldn't get in even if he wanted to. Seth and Etta and I will be fine," she said, reassuring me. She glanced around at the chaos of the kitchen. "Will your people clean this up?"

"I'll ask them to," Tom promised.

Rorry thanked us both again, turned on her heel, and walked quietly away.

Tom packed up his evidence kit and placed his notebook in his coat pocket. "Miss G., are you ready to go?"

"The sooner the better."

Tom spoke quietly to his team. Then we left.

The snow clouds had unraveled. Pinpricks of starlight filled the night sky. If Arch had been with us, he would have pointed to the Milky Way, now a river of brightness overhead. Away from Colorado's metropolitan areas, the glorious fields of stars on clear, moonless nights was breathtaking. I did not want to have my breath taken away, however, and once out of that godforsaken house, I greedily inhaled lungfuls of fresh, cold air that tasted like ice cream.

I followed Tom home. Knowing that once we arrived, Ferdinanda would fill the house with her rage over Yolanda's accident, I called Tom on my cell. There were things I needed to tell him.

"I need to bring you up to date on what I've been doing," I said.

"There's more?"

"I wanted to let you know *why* I was out by the Aspen Meadow Wildlife Preserve. I tried to tell you about it, but you cut me off."

"My captain was standing right next to me. I still don't want you going out to the preserve. Especially not alone."

"Why don't you want me going out to the preserve?"

Tom heaved a sigh. "Miss G., can't I just ask you not to do something, and you don't do it?"

No, I thought, but said reluctantly, "All right, whatever. But remember, Ernest was taking care of Yolanda when he was killed. She has been a dear friend for ten years. I want to *help* her. I want to find out who murdered Ernest. And now you know about Rorry hiring him."

"Right. Okay, go back. Where were you, exactly?" I told him about Donna, the evidence she'd collected, and the cabin in the woods. Tom said, "Whose house was this? I'm supposing you dispensed with the usual formalities, like search warrants?"

I decided not to tell him about Sabine breaking a window next to the one that was already broken. "The owners are long gone." Tom muttered something under his breath, and I plunged on. "I found Sean's credit card under the woodpile out there. Donna had given me a bag with evidence from one time when they'd broken into one of her rentals, and inside it were cheese wrappers and a wine bottle. So I bought the same kind of everything and observed Sean and Brie indulging in the—" Well, how to put it, exactly?

"The food trap. Anything else?" I told him about possibly seeing Charlene, or her BMW, anyway, on the way to Sabine's. And after Sabine and I ran away from the abandoned love-nest, she told me about seeing a suspicious bald man at the feed store. She'd thought perhaps he was Hermie's beagle breeder, whom Hermie thinks is running a puppy mill hidden behind a legitimate operation, I concluded.

"Back up," said Tom. "It was while you were trolling through the cabin, presumably, that you heard the gunshots?"

"Well, yes."

"Christ, Goldy."

A silence fell between us. I felt terrible, unable to speak. Unfortunately, any disagreement between Tom and me reminded me of the many arguments the Jerk and I had had, conflicts that had ended with him beating me up.

We were passing Aspen Meadow Lake. The sparsely placed streetlights reflected in the icy water's surface. I was suddenly aware of how exhausted I was. The fatigue from catering, the shock of Rorry's china breaking, the pot holder crashing down, the boiling oil burning Yolanda, and now Tom's extended silence—all these threatened to pull me under.

"Miss G.," Tom said at last, "I just worry about you." When I said nothing, Tom asked, "Did Rorry tell you whether she had a prenup? I mean, we can find out, but she *could* just divorce him. She doesn't have to prove he can't keep it zipped."

"She has a prenuptial agreement, Tom. Her father made her get one drawn up. He didn't trust Sean, smart fellow. Rorry did. Plus, she's religious. She loves the church and she thought she loved Sean. So before she divorced him, she wanted proof of the affair. Sean knew he'd have to keep his dalliance secret. Don't you think the DA might be interested in the fact that Rorry hired Ernest McLeod to get the proof for her?"

In front of me, Tom braked at the Main Street red light. He said, "The DA might find that interesting. But the grand jury might want to have more than an empty wine bottle, some cheese wrappers, and Sean's credit card with your fingerprints on it."

I sighed.

We hung up so as to negotiate our icy street. The van's tires crunched noisily between the plowed and frozen snowbanks. Tom parked by the curb and pointed for me to take the driveway. I moved slowly along the slippery drive and managed not to slide into Arch's Passat, which was outside the garage.

"Oh my God, how glad am I to see you!" Ferdinanda cried when we came through the front door. She'd been parked out in the hall, apparently, waiting for our arrival. Behind her, Arch gave me a helpless look. Clearly, he'd tried to soothe Ferdinanda, to no effect.

"I'm so sorry about what happened to Yolanda—" I started to say, but Ferdinanda interrupted me.

"This didn't happen to her." She wagged a wicked-looking finger in my direction. "Kris did this to her. Tom!" she said reprovingly as he helped me off with my coat. "You gotta do something about this man. He's going to kill my niece unless you kill him first."

"Let's go into the kitchen," Tom replied softly.

Ferdinanda didn't budge. "I want to go down to that hospital."

"Sergeant Boyd is bringing Yolanda back here," Tom said evenly. "He just phoned me and they're leaving now. If we take off, we'll miss them."

Ferdinanda crossed her arms. "And Boyd and Yolanda are just going to walk right up the sidewalk to the house? With Kris living across the *street*?" My mouth must have fallen open, because Ferdinanda looked bitterly triumphant. "Yeah, he came today in that loud car of his. Then a truck with furniture arrived. Kris drove out again and returned with a girl who had two suitcases."

"A girl?" I said, confused.

"A young woman," Ferdinanda replied, dismissing this person with a wave. "You know. A whore."

I said, "*What?* Arch, would you please go upstairs?"

Arch groaned but *clopped* upstairs anyway. Ferdinanda wheeled herself around in a tight circle, then pushed herself toward the kitchen. "Tom!" she cried over her shoulder. "Come out here, please, without Goldy, so I can talk to you without her asking stupid questions."

Tom patted me on the shoulder and whispered, "She's just upset. Why don't you look at those pictures you took again? Maybe you'll remember how you know Humberto's girlfriend. I'll go calm Ferdinanda down."

I sat on the living room couch and scrolled through the photos I'd taken. I had seen this young woman in some other context, not one associated with catering. I was having a hard time making a withdrawal from my mind's memory bank, though, because Ferdinanda's shrill voice still emanated from the kitchen. Tom's calm replies were like a low rumble. I placed the cell phone on the coffee table, plugged my ears with my fingers, and stared at one of the images.

School, I thought. *I know her from some academic context.* And just as surely, I realized that she had some connection with Arch—not as a hooker, thank God. She had helped him. But doing what?

I took the stairs two at a time and knocked on Arch's door. When he let me in, his face was racked with worry.

"What is it?" I asked. "Is something wrong?"

He went back to his bed, where he sat down and crossed his arms. "Not really. What do you need?"

"Arch, is something—" No, I'd already asked him that. I inhaled sharply to steady myself. Whatever was bothering him, he'd tell me in his good time. Or not. "It's just that I'm trying to place a guest from tonight's dinner party. I took a picture with my phone." I cued up the best image and handed him my cell.

Arch turned his attention to my phone. His brow furrowed as he paged through the pictures. Then he smiled and shook his head. "She sure looks different from when she was helping me with my math homework."

"Who is it?"

"Gosh, Mom. I can't believe you don't recognize Lolly Vanderpool." He handed the phone back to me, a glint of triumph in his brown eyes.

"Your old *babysitter*?" I squinted at the picture. "The one who had a full ride at Elk Park Prep? You're kidding."

"Nope. You used to say she was the smartest person you'd ever met, don't you remember?"

"Not really. Well anyway, I thought Lolly went to college."

"So did I."

"It doesn't look as if that worked out." Mentally, I added, *And if she's really smart, why hasn't she made a better career choice?*

Arch grinned mischievously. "So what's she doing instead?"

I pressed my lips together as high-pitched Ferdinanda and low-toned Tom continued their dialogue downstairs. To Arch, I said, "Did you get your homework done?"

"Good old Mom." Arch heaved himself up off his bed. "As soon as the conversation gets interesting, you find a way to make me do something else."

"I'm not making you do anything else." Although, of course, I was.

"Math homework's done."

"Good. Thanks for staying here with Ferdinanda. And for helping figure out the puzzle with Lolly."

"No problem." Arch walked me to the door of his room. "Do you think Lolly's available to come over tomorrow night, to do some tutoring with me? She could wear that same outfit."

"Very funny, buster."

Reluctantly, I went back down to the kitchen. Ferdinanda wailed at Tom, "But I don't understand why you can't arrest him. Look at what he's done!"

Tom rubbed his chin for a moment. "Let's put it this way. Do you like the fact that Fidel Castro promised elections within a year of taking over the country but, in all the fifty years since, has never held free elections?"

"Of course not!" Ferdinanda retorted. "I believe in democracy. I believe in freedom of speech. He wouldn't allow either. That's why I left."

"Presumably, then," Tom said patiently, "one of the reasons you came to this country is that we are a nation of *laws* that we *enforce*."

Ferdinanda waved this away. "Kris peeped in the windows of the house we were renting. Or he hired somebody to do that. Then he burned the place down."

"Ferdinanda, we have no proof—"

"So we moved to Ernest's house. Then Kris killed Ernest and burned down *his* house. Today he moved in across the street. He's crazy, Tom! Now, tonight, he tried to kill Yolanda. Aren't any of those things laws that have been broken?"

"Breaking and entering, arson, murder, and attempted murder," Tom said, still calm, "are *all* against the law. But Kris has an alibi for every single one of those events, and we do not have a shred of evidence that he was involved in any of it."

"Isn't stalking against the law?" asked Ferdinanda. "He stalked her."

"If we could prove it, it would be," Tom replied. "I understand what you're saying." It was clear to me, and no doubt to Ferdinanda, that he may have comprehended the older woman's accusation, but he was by no means certain of its veracity. And yet, he trusted Yolanda and Ferdinanda, liked them, even, as I did. If he didn't, he wouldn't have allowed them to come live with us.

Ferdinanda held her hand up to her ear. "You know I'm partially deaf. Why can't I hear you?"

Tom got up. "Ferdinanda, you know Goldy and I want to help you and Yolanda. I don't know why someone would target one or both of them or even somebody else, in the Breckenridges' kitchen. As I've said here several times, it sounds as if all the guests were in and out of that kitchen during the day. So I can't just go and arrest one person, can I? As I keep telling you, we actually have to have *evidence*. On the other hand, you could tell me more about Humberto Captain than you have. Did he know about Ernest's investigation of him?" Ferdinanda muttered under her breath. "Speak up, Ferdinanda! I can't hear you." The older woman fixed Tom with a baleful stare. Tom, unheeding, changed the subject. "Boyd will be home soon with Yolanda. Do you want one of us to stay here in the kitchen with you until they arrive?"

Ferdinanda, who was already wheeling away, stopped. "No. I'll tell you what I want. When they get back, I want you and Boyd each to stand beside Yolanda and bring her into the house. She needs to be protected."

"All right," said Tom. I could hear the fatigue in his voice, but he pressed buttons on his cell to tell Boyd how they were going to bring Yolanda into the house. Ferdinanda, satisfied, rolled herself into her makeshift bedroom without, I noticed, a word of thanks to Tom.

I shook my head. "Tom, I have something to tell you." I related Arch's news about his former babysitter, Odette, aka Lolly Vanderpool. "She's more than smart. She's brilliant. You should let me talk to her about Humberto."

Tom's sea-green eyes were full of skepticism. "You're going to interrogate a prostitute about a john who's a murder suspect, between your catering events?"

"Please, listen. First of all, it's much more likely she'll talk to me than she would to someone at the sheriff's department. Second, we're having dinner at this murder suspect's house tomorrow night—"

"I'll be wearing a weapon—"

"And third, I don't actually have catering events this week. Just the dinner at the Bertrams' place on Thursday night, and for that I'm making soup."

He shook his head. "I don't want you talking to Humberto alone."

"Humberto? No way. I only want to talk to Lolly."

"Couple things, then. You have max two days to talk to her before we do. And you have to tell me immediately whatever she says."

"Oh-*kay.*" I moved toward the walk-in. "Have you eaten? I'm famished."

"Yeah, I did. Wait, let me talk to Ferdinanda for a minute." He knocked on the swinging door between the kitchen and the dining room. When Ferdinanda roughly told him to enter, he asked her questions in a low tone. Again, Ferdinanda's querulous reply made me wonder what was going on, but when Tom said, "Thank you," I was even more curious. When he closed the dining room door, he said, "I'm going to fix you dinner."

"Tom, please. Don't. I can do it. And besides that, I don't think we have anything ready—"

"You do enough, Miss G.," Tom interrupted. He peered into the depths of the walk-in. "I came out to the kitchen yesterday and found Ferdinanda rummaging through the freezer."

I sighed. I'd found her in our pantry. Tom had found her searching through our freezer. In spite of the fact that I'd said *mi casa es su casa,* Ferdinanda's proprietary attitude toward our kitchen was getting a little old.

"Anyway, she asked me if she could thaw a package of ground pork. I said yes, and I just got her permission to cook one of her recipes that she was telling me about." He flipped through some papers by the computer. "All right, here we go."

I was too tired to argue. "Sounds great."

"I'm also putting together a salad for you," he said, his head back in the walk-in. He emerged carrying the pork, a container of cooked rice, and a bunch of fresh cilantro, which he placed on the counter. "Now, where is that balsamic vinaigrette I was making. . . ."

"What you're making is a mess," I said. But I found the sauté pan and brought out the olive oil for him.

"I have an ulterior motive," Tom said.

"Yeah," I replied, "you don't want me to get grouchy because I'm hungry."

"That, too," he said as he washed his hands to prepare for cooking. "Not another word until I have the food in front of you."

He poured me a glass of an expensive sauvignon blanc that Marla had given us, set the table for one, and went about his tasks. Twenty minutes later, he placed a heavenly scented platter on the table, filled with ground pork in a steaming orange-lime sauce. Next to it he put two bowls: one filled with fluffy heated rice topped with chopped fresh cilantro, the other brimming with a salad of baby field greens, grape tomatoes, toasted pine nuts, and tidbits of blue cheese, all cloaked in Tom's new dressing.

"This is enough for at least four people," I murmured. "But thanks."

"Don't worry about too much food," said Tom as he pulled a chair up close to mine. "If I know Arch, he'll have smelled something in the air, and he'll be banging in here in a couple of minutes, wanting a second dinner."

"So what's your ulterior motive?" I asked.

"Have some salad first," he said.

I obliged. "Great dressing. What's in it?"

Tom's smile was so akin to the Cheshire cat's that I became nervous. "Oh, mayonnaise, Dijon mustard, balsamic vinegar, garlic, olive oil, fresh basil. It's what I'm calling it that reveals my ulterior motive." He opened his eyes wide. "That's Tom's Love Potion."

"Tom," I said as I took my first bite of the pork. It was velvety and scrumptious. I would have to ask Ferdinanda for the recipe. "This is out of this world. And in the love potion department? I'm a sure bet. You needn't have gone to all this trouble—"

"I want us to have a baby," Tom blurted out.

I swallowed hard to avoid choking. "*What?*"

At that moment, my current baby, sixteen-year-old Arch, whacked the kitchen door open. "Aha!" he exclaimed. "Food! And does it smell great!" He looked from Tom to me. "What's the matter? Mom, you look as if you saw a ghost or something."

"I, uh, yeah, well," I said. "Let me get you a plate and silverware." I pushed my chair back, but Tom held up a hand.

"I'll do it," he said in that commanding way he had.

"Mom?" asked Arch. "Are you okay?"

"Oh, yeah," I said. "I'm just peachy."

Chapter 18

Twenty minutes later, I stood under a very hot shower. Tom was downstairs cleaning up. I thought, *Maybe I should make this shower cold. And while I'm at it, I could pull Tom into it.*

A baby? Tom wanted to have a *baby*? Why?

What would Arch think of the idea? What did *I* think of it? Was it selfish for me to wonder what would happen to my catering business if I went back to changing diapers? Besides, wasn't I too *old* to have a baby?

Thirty-seven was not that old, I reminded myself as I dried off. I loved Tom. But this thought, the very idea of having another child, was not something I had expected from him. And I felt exhausted just thinking about the prospect of doing the whole infant thing all over again.

There was a tapping on the door and I jumped.

"Miss G.? You coming out?"

"In a sec." I wondered if I should put on my cotton pajamas, if that would be seen as a signal that I did not want to—

Tom opened the door to the bathroom. "Come on, let's talk about this like normal married folks. In bed. Make that sitting on the bed, since I have to wait for Boyd and Yolanda. In fact, maybe that's where I should have broached this subject in the first place."

"I'll be right there." I pulled on my PJ's and walked quickly across to the bed, where I sat down.

Tom followed and pulled me in for a warm hug. "I'm sensing you don't like my idea."

Putting my arms around the man I had come to love so much, I thought, *I have to give him what he wants.* Then I thought, *No, I don't.* Through all the years with the Jerk and then post-Jerk, I'd come to see that my own opinion about what was right was the most important one. "What made you think of this all of a sudden? I mean, why do you want a baby?"

"I don't know," Tom replied. "It's been sort of building in my mind. I love you, and I love Arch. At work, I see death and pain and cruelty, all day, every day. And I just like the idea of making our family bigger, and spreading more joy into the world."

"Can I at least turn it over in my mind for a while?" I whispered.

"You can turn it over in your mind as long as you want," said Tom. Did I detect a note of disappointment in his voice, or was my imagination making me paranoid? He kissed me . . . and then his cell went off. He blinked at the screen. "Oh, Christ, it's Boyd already." Tom talked briefly into his phone. "They'll be here in a few minutes. I'm going out to the driveway, and then we're going to help Yolanda inside."

"Wear your service revolver," I said.

"Don't worry."

I shimmied off the bed, slid into a bathrobe, and for reasons I couldn't quite name, turned off the lights in our bedroom. I pulled open our curtains covering one of the windows facing the street.

Soon Boyd's car drove into view and crunched over ice in the driveway. Tom waited for Boyd to come around the front of the vehicle, then opened the passenger door. The two of them flanked Yolanda and helped her, slowly, into the house.

Again my skin broke out in gooseflesh, and my glance darted across the street. On the second floor of Jack's old house, new bedroom curtains there, too, were parted. Was my imagination making me paranoid again? Was somebody, or were somebodies, looking out the window at Yolanda coming home?

Was it Kris? Harriet? Were they watching us? Watching for Yolanda?

I raced downstairs, opened the front door, and waited for Boyd and Tom to bring Yolanda over the threshold.

"Oh, Yolanda!" I cried, seeing the thick white bandages that covered her thighs. "What can I do for you?"

Yolanda's russet hair was pulled back in a rough ponytail, and her skin looked as if it had been blanched. The wheels of Ferdinanda's chair squeaked as the elderly woman rolled into the hall. Seeing all of us there, Yolanda said, "I'm fine now. I've got my family, my friends, and my painkillers. What else do I need?"

After assuring us that the only thing she wanted was

the ladies' room, Yolanda allowed Boyd to carry her in there. Ferdinanda followed, yelling to her niece in Spanish that she was coming to help. A moment later, the bathroom door closed, water ran, and Boyd reappeared, shaking his head.

"Poor girl," he said. "I know she's in a lot of pain." He pressed his lips together and looked at Tom. "Learned anything yet?"

"The pan that fell apart didn't belong to the Breckenridges."

"Interesting," said Boyd. "Although I have to say, I figured as much. I called one of our teams. They came to Southwest Hospital and took the evidence I had, the broken pot rack, the parts of the frying pan. I uploaded the pictures I took of both 'accidents,' so our guys could look closely at them."

"Good work," said Tom.

"I also gave the team the names of every single dinner guest. Our guys are out interviewing them now. The one thing I've heard so far? Nobody confesses to owning the electric frying pan. It just appeared. I called Rorry on her cell, to find out who could have had time to loosen the pot rack with the cloth dish towels. She said folks were in and out of the kitchen all day. When I asked her who had requested the Navajo tacos? She said she was pretty sure the request had come through her husband. So I called him. The son of a bitch said he couldn't remember." Boyd ran his thick fingers over his black crew cut. "He's lying."

"Good job." Tom shook Boyd's hand.

The door to the bathroom off the dining room opened,

and Boyd nodded at both of us, said good night, and moved off to help Yolanda into bed.

When Tom and I were back in our bedroom, I stared at our alarm clock. I didn't need to set it, because as I had reminded Tom, I did not have a party to cater the next day. Feeling oddly helpless, I walked over to close our curtains. "Tom? I could have sworn Kris, or someone, was looking out the upstairs window over at Jack's place. Whoever it was was watching for Yolanda to arrive back home, all bandaged up."

"Miss G." Tom took his clothes off and slid into bed. "The only way to solve this crime and all the other crimes Ferdinanda mentioned is to work the case. We find out who killed Ernest? Everything else will fall into place."

"What about Yolanda's house burning down? And Ernest's? The attempted break-in here, at our place? You think they're related to Ernest being shot?"

"I do. I'm just not sure how." He pulled me to him. I did not resist.

"But *how* are you working the case?" I whispered.

"Miss G. You heard Boyd. We're interviewing people. We're analyzing evidence. Our canvass of Ernest's neighborhood didn't turn up much. The shell casings are being analyzed. Maybe somebody else had been out there on that service road, shooting off a weapon, but I doubt it. Maybe the casings will come back to a gun we can prove belongs to one of the people we're looking at for this crime."

"People you're looking at," I repeated.

"Someone had a big motive for killing Ernest and

burning down his house. Our theory is that Ernest had
looked under one rock too many, and somebody wanted
to destroy him and the evidence."

"Okay."

I did not feel as confident as Tom that we were, in
fact, going to find out who murdered Ernest. Hermie
Mikulski's face popped into my brain. Had *she* seen the
same man as Sabine Rushmore? Was it too late to call
Hermie?

I slid away from Tom and reached for my cell phone.

"Miss G., what are you doing?"

"Just making one more call," I said quickly, then hustled into the bathroom.

As I suspected would happen, I was immediately
connected to voice mail. Either Hermie behaved like
most civilized people and refused to answer the phone
late at night, or she was still not home.

When I slipped back into bed, Tom did not ask me
why I'd been making a call late at night.

Okay, so: I'd spoken to every person that Tom,
Yolanda, or anyone else had mentioned in connection
with Ernest and his investigations. I'd come up short. If
anything, I realized painfully, I'd made things worse. I'd
confronted Kris, and, after finding out from Penny
Woolworth where Yolanda was staying, he'd bought the
house across the street from us. If you had a lot of cash,
you could do a real estate deal pretty quickly. Even if
Kris hadn't closed yet, he could have worked out a deal
with Jack's son to rent the place until he did. Maybe, as
at the dinner party, Kris only wanted to flaunt to Yolanda
that he had a new, pretty girlfriend. People reeling from

a breakup could do weird things. Spending a lot of money on a house definitely fell into the rich-people-doing-crazy-stuff category. But was this a rich person doing a crazy thing, or was the rich person actually crazy? I sighed.

I'd questioned Charlene Newgate. If Charlene had been up to something, now she knew she needed to cover it up. I'd used Donna Lamar to help me dig into Sean Breckenridge's extramarital activities, and she had inadvertently let *him* know what I was up to. I closed my eyes. I'd questioned the Juarezes, and they'd bought tickets to the fund-raising dinner, where Norman had confronted Humberto. If Humberto really did have the gold and jewels, did he now know to hide them? I wondered.

Tomorrow, I would go talk to Lolly Vanderpool, aka Odette. But I didn't hold out much hope of that turning into anything substantive regarding the theft of the Juarezes' gold and jewels. What would a tutor-turned-hooker know?

All the faces involved with Ernest and his cases swam up before my mind's eye: Humberto, Sean, Brie, Kris . . . I was trying to figure this all out, how the people were connected. . . .

I felt like a failure.

Tom sensed I was still awake. He moved toward me and kissed my forehead. "Stop worrying."

"If only it were that easy." I paused, then said, "Thanks for dinner."

"You're welcome."

"Do you mind talking about Ernest's murder for a

couple of minutes? Arch is in his room, and I can't use his computer."

"Go ahead."

"Okay . . . so, Ernest picked up nine puppies, probably because he'd found the illegal mill that Hermie Mikulski had hired him to find. Right?"

"Okay."

"A bald guy burned down Ernest's house. Maybe the same bald guy tried to burn down our house, or to break in, before Arch stabbed him with your weeder. But . . . remember Sabine Rushmore had an encounter with a menacing bald guy at the feed store? He was buying a lot of puppy chow. When Sabine tried to be polite to him, he cut her off."

"You told me," he said patiently.

"You can talk to Sabine. But did I tell you that Father Pete saw Charlene Newgate, the temp service lady, with a bald guy at the Grizzly Saloon? How many bald guys are there?"

Tom reached over and turned on the light. He made a couple of notes in his trusty book, then firmly closed it and flipped the switch on the lamp. He said kindly, "It's good to cover everything. I'm glad you brought these things up, Miss G."

What I had not brought up was our conversation in the kitchen. Still, I'd fully expected that he would want to talk further about his desire for progeny, or, even better, make love that night. But he merely hugged me again, said he was tired, and turned away.

Great, I thought as I fluffed my pillow. A good marriage takes open communication and a willingness to give, the advice givers were always saying. Apparently, this was one more area where I'd failed.

The next day's dawn brought a deep blue sky and brilliant sunshine. Melting ice gurgled and dripped down our gutters. With any luck, Indian summer's lush grass would soon be poking through the snow. I lay in bed and realized that we hadn't even had the first day of *fall* yet, much less winter.

I felt with my left hand to where Tom's body had left an impression in the sheets. The linens were cold.

"Miss G.," he said cheerily, startling me. He had showered and dressed, and now placed a steaming cup of latte on my night table. "Aren't you the one who told me sloth was one of the seven deadly sins?"

"Thanks for the coffee and for reminding me of my wicked nature." I smiled at him and glanced at the clock. Quarter to seven? "Where are you going so early?"

"Remember that thing I told you last night, about working the case? That's where I'm going. What are you up to?"

"About a dollar fifty." I grinned again. "How's Yolanda?"

"Still in bed."

I took a deep breath. "Well, we have Humberto's dinner party tonight. I don't suppose Yolanda and Boyd will go. But Ferdinanda promised to make spinach quiches." I sipped the latte, which was delicious. "Do you remember that?"

"Yup," said Tom. "She's banging around in the kitchen already, making the rice for the crust, grating Gruyère, and who knows what all. I'll tell you one thing,

I cannot *wait* to see the inside of Humberto's house, either. He must have a security system that rivals a nuclear installation."

"You said his place was broken into a while back?"

"Last week," said Tom, sitting on the bed. "Or so he claims."

"What did the burglar take?"

"He won't say. He demanded that we analyze his guards' rum bottles from that night. We said we would if he would pay for the analysis." Tom shrugged. "He agreed, and we found traces of temazepam on the bottles' glass."

"Rum bottles, plural? How many guards are we talking about?"

Tom inhaled. "Three. These are the same guys who alibied Humberto for the time of Ernest's murder. Remember I told you about our guys smelling rum on their breaths? They couldn't be very good guards if they drank on duty."

"When Humberto was broken into . . . was there a security code, like an electronic burglar alarm, too?"

"Yup. It had been turned off, then on again, while the guards were asleep. So somebody came in, we just don't know who. Humberto is strangely silent on who had the code."

"And he won't tell you what was missing."

"He will not. But I do have an interesting bit of information. The casings on the gun that killed Ernest? The same weapon was used two years ago, to kill a gas station attendant."

"What? Where was this?"

"Outside of Fort Collins. The kid was a graduate student at Colorado State. He was just working shifts to make money."

"Is there any connection to the people around Ernest?"

"Not that we can find."

I shook my head. Another person killed, and for what? It was all too much. We stopped talking.

Finally, Tom said, "Anything else, Miss G.?"

I looked at him in puzzlement. He gave me such a hopeful look, I couldn't imagine what he meant by it . . . until I did. The *anything else* was asking if during the night, I had come to a positive response to his surprise request.

I opened my mouth and then closed it.

He brushed my hair off my face and touched my cheek. "Please don't go into a panic. We're going to be married for a long, long time, and we can discuss this any time while your biological clock is still ticking. Okay? And no matter what we decide, we're going to be happy together. Got it?"

"Yeah. Thanks, Tom."

He left. I did my yoga routine, then showered, dressed, and made my way to the kitchen. There, Ferdinanda was checking under the lid of a pot of rice, Boyd was hovering over a sink full of soapy water, and Arch was stuffing himself with thick-sliced bacon and pancakes smeared with guava preserves. Sitting beside Arch, Yolanda seemed to be in a daze. She was tilted sideways, with a faraway look in her eyes. A full cup of coffee in front of her looked cold.

"Yolanda, how are you?" I asked.

Arch, his mouth half full, glanced sideways at Yolanda. Then he swallowed and said, "She's in a lot of pain, Mom, that's how she is. Even I can tell that."

"Arch?" Yolanda came back to earth. Her rusty-sounding voice carried a note of reproof. "I'm capable of talking to your mother myself, thanks."

"Yeah," said Arch as he picked up his empty dish and took it to the sink. "You can talk, but you never complain. I'm just telling my mom the real situation."

I said, "Arch? Do you have all your homework?"

Boyd rinsed off the plate and silverware and handed it back to Arch to put in the dishwasher. My son shook his head. "There you go again, Mom, sending me off when you don't want to talk about what's really going on."

"Arch!"

"Mom!" When he tossed his silverware into the dishwasher, the metal clanked explosively. "I'm worried about Yolanda, too, you know! First some guy tries to break into where she's sleeping, then somebody tries to burn her."

I said softly, "Arch, please."

"I'm just saying what we all know." His tone was stubborn.

"Tom, Boyd, and the whole sheriff's department are working on it," I replied, keeping my tone even.

Arch muttered something under his breath and stomped out of the kitchen. I was about to holler after him to come back and apologize when Boyd held up a soapy hand.

"Goldy?" he said. "He's been traumatized. Give him a break."

"You're right," I said. "I overreacted."

"Sit down, Goldy." Ferdinanda poured batter into a sizzling sauté pan on the stove. "I want you to eat some of my pancakes, tell me how good they are with guava jam. And what your son said before he left the kitchen? He told me how much he liked my pancakes."

I was quite sure that was *not* what Arch had said under his breath, but I was touched by hard-of-hearing Ferdinanda wanting to cover for him. When she placed a plate with three steaming pancakes—each with a dollop of melting butter sliding sideways—in front of me, I thanked her.

"I make them with sour cream. Now spread guava preserves on top. I'll make you some espresso."

Boyd took the frying pan from Ferdinanda and placed it in the soapy water.

"Eat, eat!" Ferdinanda commanded me. "You want them to get cold?"

I obliged. The featherlight cakes had a heavenly tang that was perfectly complemented by the sweet, thick preserves. I groaned with pleasure. "I'd forgotten how good food tastes when it's made by somebody else. Thank you again. Ferdinanda," I added, "you're great."

"Not so great," she said darkly. "Cooking I know. How to get rid of Kris I don't know."

"Okay, ladies, that's enough of that kind of talk," said Boyd.

Yolanda sighed. "Are you staying home today, Goldy? Or going out?"

I rubbed my forehead. How was I supposed to say

that I was off to look for Humberto's girlfriend? Oh, yes, and that I intended to keep trying to talk in depth to one of Ernest's clients, Hermie Mikulski?

"I still want to talk to Hermie Mikulski some more," I said, deciding for now to omit any mention of Humberto.

Boyd, still drying dishes, turned to me. "I'm telling you, Goldy, Mrs. Mikulski is in the wind. We've left messages for her and cannot find her. The location Father Pete gave us was a bust."

I made my voice placating. "Fine. So is there any harm in *my* attempting to talk to her about Ernest? She's a fellow CBHS parent, and I saw her son get his nose whacked when a kid opened a locker. Maybe I just want to check up on him."

Boyd shrugged, wiped the now-clean pan, and put it away. "Ready for a trip to the ladies' room, Yolanda? You want Ferdinanda with you?"

"Naw, she's okay with just you there," said Ferdinanda, waving toward the dining room. "I only get in the way. Just wait outside the door till she's done."

Yolanda scraped her chair back, then put her arm around Boyd's wide shoulders. He delicately lifted her around the waist and carried her into the adjoining room.

"Listen," hissed Ferdinanda. "I gotta talk quick. I told Yolanda she can't go tonight to Humberto's, on account of her burns."

"I figured—"

"But I've been thinking," Ferdinanda interrupted. "Maybe it's not Kris doing all this. Maybe Humberto's the one who put that broken 'lectric skillet in the Breck-enridges' kitchen."

"Why would you think—"

"Humberto came over," Ferdinanda said, interrupting me again. "To the rental, after Yolanda lost her job at the spa. He said he wanted to help her. She said she didn't need him. Right after that, our rental burned down. Humberto came back. He took Yolanda aside, said he wanted her to spy on Ernest—"

"We know this," I said. "Humberto paid her seventeen thousand bucks, which burned up in the fire. And by the way, what are you going to do without that money? Rorry Breckinridge gave me four thousand in cash for you—"

"Let me finish, Goldy!" Ferdinanda said, interrupting. "So Yolanda took Humberto's money, and we moved in with Ernest. But Yolanda liked Ernest so much, she didn't do it. Spy, I mean. So she told Humberto she was reneging on the deal and that he could have his money back. He was furious!"

"Have you told Tom—"

Ferdinanda waved this away. "I told him last night. But when I got onto the cot, I was thinking, maybe Humberto burned down the rental, *and* maybe he paid someone to burn down Ernest's house. Yes, to destroy the files, but maybe to destroy Yolanda. And maybe he sabotaged that kitchen last night, too. As punishment, for not doing what he wanted. That would explain why whoever burned down Ernest's house waited until Yolanda was back there. It would explain the hot oil ac-cident. If you saw what I saw in Cuba? You would say,

'It could happen.'" From the dining room, Yolanda called for Ferdinanda. "Listen, I want to go shop for groceries today. Alone. Boyd will help me get into Yolanda's van."

I said, "That's a *very* bad idea. Why don't you tell me what we need, and I'll do the shopping—"

Ferdinanda shook a gnarled finger at me. "Don't you try to stop me! I've got my baton. I can take care of myself! If I want to shop, I'm gonna shop." She wheeled smartly away.

"For God's sake," I said to the air. I felt the same blankness I'd felt in bed the night before. Tom had checked out Humberto's alibi for Ernest's death and the two fires, and Humberto was in the clear, even if the guards were more blitzed than fraternity boys at Mardi Gras. Lacking an eyewitness or some forensic evidence that pointed to Humberto, this theory of Ferdinanda's was dead in the water. Still—

"Mom?" said Arch. He had entered the kitchen so quietly, I hadn't noticed. "I'm sorry I got angry this morning. I'm just bummed out, with Yolanda getting hurt so badly at your dinner last night."

"We're all bummed out, hon—"

"Look, I have to go. Tom said I could drive the Passat, and that the tires were okay. Boyd's going to watch me back out." He handed me a slip of paper. "This is Lolly's cell phone number and address."

I stared at the piece of paper in my hand. "How in the world did you get this?"

Arch rolled his eyes to the ceiling. "I entered 'math tutor Aspen Meadow Colorado' into Google, and she was the first name that popped up. I'm surprised she's here, though. She was the first person to get into MIT from Elk Park Prep in a long time. She should be back there now."

"I don't know why she's here. But thanks, Arch. Listen, one more thing. Could you send her a text from your phone, asking for an appointment today at"—I glanced at the clock—"ten? Say you're having trouble with calculus and was wondering if she was free."

"She's going to wonder why I'm not in school."

"In the message, tell her you have the day off from the Christian Brothers High School, but you have a calc test tomorrow."

Arch exhaled impatiently but maneuvered his thumbs at light speed to send the text. "Lolly's smart," he said when he was done. "She's going to know it's you." He glanced at his cell. "Oops, here she is. She says she's full up with tutoring clients, sorry."

"Tell her you're desperate and that you're coming over anyway."

Arch shook his head. "She's going to know it's you." But again his thumbs flew. A nanosecond later, Arch showed me her reply: "Tell yr ma 2 go f herslf." Well, great. From behind me, Arch said, "You know, Mom, *you* could call her, to let her know you want to see her, or that you're coming over, or whatever. You keep this up, I'm going to be late for school."

"Not to worry, kiddo, you can go. And thanks for—"

But Arch was already gone. He still had that ability to appear and disappear silently.

Which was what I was going to do, I thought, as I put

my own dishes and flatware into the dishwasher. Or at least, that was what I had wanted to do: to show up at Lolly Vanderpool's without making any noise. I hadn't planned on letting her know that I wanted to see her, or come over, or, as Arch would say, whatever.

Still. Apparently, she already knew I wanted to see her. I would have to think of some way to win her over, some way that did not involve surprise. I would, in investigator parlance, need to find a way to flip her.

Fifteen minutes later, Boyd stepped onto our porch and looked in both directions, then carefully scanned the area across the street. For a few moments, he glared at the house I still thought of as Jack's. There was no sign of Kris Nielsen, his Maserati, or his girlfriend.

"I'm walking you to your van," said Boyd. It was not a suggestion. He wore his service weapon outside his clothes, just so anyone watching would get the hint. I couldn't remember any time I'd ever had an armed escort.

"Thanks," I said as I stepped into my van a few moments later. "Listen, Ferdinanda wants to go shopping today. She's adamant."

"Christ, you women," said Boyd. "I'll try to talk her out of it. But I'm staying home with Yolanda," he said, his gaze on the street. "Don't worry, I'll keep the security alarm on."

"Okay, good. And here." I reached into my pocket and pulled out the wad of bills Rorry Breckenridge had given me the night before. "This is from Rorry. It's to cover any extra bills Yolanda might have."

Boyd stuffed the cash in his front pocket. "Anybody

snapping pictures is going to think we're doing a drug deal."

"Oh, don't get paranoid on me."

I thanked him again and scooted my van in the direction of the inexpensive Aspen Meadow apartment building indicated by the address Arch had scribbled. I had a moment of panic: What if Lolly wasn't there? If she was Humberto's girlfriend, wouldn't she be living with him? Somehow, I didn't think Lolly Vanderpool was Humberto's girlfriend. Clearly, neither did Arch.

Like all the other vehicles out that day, my car splashed through waves of water and slush. On Main Street, tourists who'd come to see the aspens turning yellow delicately picked through the blackened walls of snow the plows had churned onto the sidewalks. Unfortunately for these visitors, a major early snowstorm stripped most leaves from our deciduous trees. Town merchants who made big bucks off aspen-leaf-shaped pendants, earrings, and charms were not going to be happy.

Nor was I happy when my van encountered a bank of snow at the far entrance to Lolly's apartment building. Any plans I'd had to slip surreptitiously into a parking space were for naught. I drove around to the other entrance, slid into a spot, and hopped out.

I glanced up at the windows that overlooked the lot. Lolly's apartment was on the fourth floor. Was she watching me, or was I becoming delusional?

Rock music echoed through the door to her apartment, which I had reached via an ice-glutted outdoor staircase. It was not the kind of building to have a door-

man, or even keys to the hallways, but each door did
have an eyehole. When Lolly did not answer, I pounded
on the door. A slippery sound indicated someone approaching. And then she must have reached the peephole.

"Aw, shit, I knew it!" her muffled voice exclaimed.

"C'mon, Lolly, let me in," I called through the door.
"I really, really need to talk to you. It's about a friend of
mine who was killed."

After a moment of throwing bolts, she opened up.
Instead of the blond wig, she had a severe pageboy that
she'd dyed black with blue streaks. She wore an MIT
sweatshirt with the sleeves cut off and faded, thread-
bare jeans. I blinked. And then she really surprised
me.

She opened her eyes wide and said, "I didn't know
Ernest McLeod was a friend of *yours*."

I swallowed. "May I come in?"

She said, "Crap." But she pushed the door open anyway and headed into her small living room.

The place was spartan and meticulously clean. A
faded orange garage-sale rug adorned the brown lino-
leum floor. A small, sixties Danish-style sofa, covered
with a wrinkled bedspread of much-washed madras, had
been pushed against one wall. In front of the couch was
a glass-topped coffee table that might have come from
the same garage sale. Against the other wall were two
mismatched chairs, one wicker, the other a maple lad-
derback. A large chipped black desk, red desk chair,
plus a variety of old wooden bookshelves took up the
rest of the wall space. A laptop, a cell phone, and a neat

pile of sheet music sat pristinely on the desk. No musical instrument was in evidence.

I craned forward to read some of the titles on her bookshelves. There were chemistry and math texts, plus a number of books on something called string theory. I had a vague notion that this fit somewhere into the realm of quantum physics, although where, I'd been told, the quantum physics people couldn't exactly say.

In this as in all else, Lolly had her own strongly held opinions. For the clutch of string theory volumes, in the place where a Library of Congress number would be, Lolly had made her own labels. On one: *Crap*. On another: *More Crap*. (Apparently this was her favorite word.) For the theory of super strings, careful printing on the label read, *Super-Dooper Crap*.

"So how do you like my place?" she asked as she disappeared. "Before you answer that question," she called, "tell me if you want some coffee. I'm trying to be a hostess here, even if you are an uninvited guest."

I said, "I'd love anything caffeinated, thanks."

The kitchen was actually a kitchenette, I realized, just around the corner from the living room. Lolly had covered the entrance with another madras bedspread, hung from a wire. Water ran and microwave buttons beeped. I could not imagine the reason for Lolly's "new crib." Once again, I perused book titles. *Accelerated Calculus. Neurological Science. Hydronics.*

Maybe she'd flunked out of MIT. Somehow, I doubted it.

The microwave beeped again, and Lolly reappeared, holding two cups of steaming instant coffee. "I know it's not your kind of drink, but my espresso machine is on the blink, sad to say." She handed me a chipped mug and offered a wry smile. "Just kidding, I don't have an espresso machine. I don't have any milk, cream, or sugar, either, sorry." She looked around her cheaply furnished apartment. "You haven't told me how much you like my place."

"Lolly—"

"Sit down," she said, interrupting me, using her free hand to wave toward the bedspread-covered couch. "Here's what happened. I got a four-point-oh at MIT first year. Since I was on a full ride, my parents were thrilled. So was I. And . . . I celebrated a bit too much when I came home. Got a DUI right on Main Street, next to Frank's Fix-It. How come nobody ever busts him for smoking weed? Well, he wasn't driving. Anyway, with me charged with DUI? At this my parents were *not* thrilled." She put down her coffee and ran her fingers through her black and blue hair. "First they refused to pay for my lawyer. Not that they would have had that kind of money anyway. But then they kicked me out of the house. So here I am, taking a semester off, 'for financial reasons.'" Her black-painted fingernails hooked quotation marks. Her blue eyes pierced me. "I was lucky, though. A friend gave me a loan. I mean, what bank is going to lend money to a drunk scholarship student, right? With that money, I paid my lawyer, got new tits, and started to work for an escort service. I'm gradually paying back my friend—"

"Lolly—" I said again.

"You're interrupting me, Goldy," she scolded, wagging a black fingernail in my direction. "But still. That's the end of the story of how I became Humberto Captain's whore."

I said, "Oh my God."

"I know what you're going to say, because I've heard enough of it from Father Pete." She put her hand on her chest in mock seriousness. "'You shouldn't go from drinking to prostitution, Lolly!'" Her dead-on imitation of Father Pete's voice and manner made me smile, even though I was trying to be serious. "At least," Lolly said dolefully, "he's still talking to me. Which my parents aren't."

"You have a nice friend, to have loaned you all that money," I said conversationally as I leaned back on the couch.

"Why do you think I decided to open the door for you just now?" she asked. "I figure I owe you. This friend? He used to work for you. Julian Teller."

I started at the sound of Julian's name. I hadn't seen him since Jack's funeral. Julian had inherited a packet from his biological mother, who'd given him up for adoption, then tracked him down before she died. In spite of having money for the first time in his life, Julian continued to hold down jobs. He'd been going part-time to the University of Colorado while cooking at that vegetarian bistro in Boulder where the owner took August off. The restaurant had survived the recent downturn, thank goodness. When Julian had told me this, he'd also insisted that I hire Yolanda to fill his place as my assistant. She needed the money and he didn't, he said. So here was Julian again, reaching out to women with financial difficulties and asking nothing in return.

"I know what you're thinking," said Lolly. "Julian shouldn't have loaned me that kind of cash."

"I was thinking no such thing," I said huffily. "And if you're so good at mind-reading, why aren't you in Vegas?"

"I tried gambling," she said matter-of-factly. She sipped her coffee. "But you have to have a team. If you're going it alone, there's more money in whoring."

"Good God, Lolly."

She squinted at me. "Hey, I'm trying to redeem myself here! I'm going to repay Julian. I'll go back to school. My parents and I will eventually work things out." She frowned and looked out the dirty living room window. "But Father Pete said I had to do more."

"Do more?" I felt completely at sea. "Do more what?"

"Do *good,* Goldy! Jesus, wake up! How do you think I got involved with Ernest McLeod in the first place?"

"Because . . . Father Pete told you to?"

Lolly heaved a large sigh, as if my inability to comprehend her leaps in thinking were beyond her ken. She said, "As far as I know, Father Pete and Ernest don't— didn't—even know each other. But after our good rector gave me a lecture on doing something for the good of humanity or whatever, I said to myself, 'The next person who comes to me for help—unpaid help, that is—I gotta do something for them.' The next day, Ernest McLeod showed up at my apartment door. Just like you, except he didn't pound on it and demand to be let in."

"When was this?" I asked sharply.

"Couple of weeks ago. He'd sorta been watching Humberto for some clients—"

"The Juarezes."

"Those people who were at the party last night? That man who confronted Humberto? Omigod, I figured they must be. . . . But no, Goldy, Ernest didn't tell me their names, and I didn't want to know. So Ernest had seen me with Humberto. He'd followed me. When he came here, he talked about how Humberto had stolen a big whack of dough from these people, or rather, from the man in the couple. Ernest said it wasn't actually money, it was gold and gems. I didn't believe him until he showed me a picture of a diamond necklace that had belonged to the guy's mother. It was from a photo in a Havana nightclub, and the newspaper was all yellowed and raggedy, plus it was in Spanish." Lolly paused, shaking her head. "But I could see the picture, and the necklace." Lolly gave me another of her fierce looks. "I'd *worn* that frigging necklace, Goldy." My throat turned dry. Lolly went on. "Humberto had loaned it to me to wear to a charity shindig we went to. We had sex in the afternoon, and afterward he told me he wanted me to wear a very special piece of jewelry to the posh dinner. He clipped it on my neck and said it had belonged to his aunt. Since he'd already told me neither his mother nor his father had had siblings, I thought, *Duh, I just caught you in a lie, Humberto.* So I believed Ernest's story. And I decided to help him."

Abruptly she stood and raced to the bathroom. I rubbed my arms, trying to get the feeling back in them. When Lolly came back, her eye makeup was smeared. Somehow I felt that she would be damned before she let anyone see her cry. After a moment she cleared her throat and again took up her story.

"So I said to Ernest, 'What do you need me to do?'

He told me it wasn't really legal. I said, 'That's okay, neither is prostitution.' He smiled, you know? And then he said, 'This'll be prostituting yourself for a good cause.'"

I took a sip of coffee, now cold. I could hear Tom's voice in my ear. If Lolly had engaged in an illegal search, then any evidence gleaned from that search would be tossed out of court. Still, if all this helped lead to Ernest's killer . . .

Lolly said, "Ernest told me Humberto didn't have a safety deposit box, 'cause he'd been following him for weeks, like a Rocky Mountain tick stuck to his skin, he said. And Humberto had never once gone to a bank. But Ernest *had* followed Humberto to New York City, to Forty-seventh Street, to be exact. The Diamond District. And that's where Ernest found out Humberto sold a couple of diamonds. So, Ernest said, he was convinced that Humberto got them from somewhere in his *house*. Ernest asked me to look around for a safe. I did. There wasn't any safe, at least not then, but I'll get to that. For Ernest, I looked under pictures, tapped on the floor, checked the backs of closets. Stuff like that. I'm no investigator, but I couldn't find anything remotely suspicious. I'm not talking about the *necklace*. That was different; he kept it in a jewelry box, the dummy. But a cache of gold and gems? No." She shook her head again. "One thing's for sure. Humberto is not the brightest bulb in the box. So I was sure I'd be able to find the rest of what Ernest was talking about, since I *am* a pretty bright bulb myself."

"You're a supernova, Lolly. But are you telling me

Humberto doesn't have a safety deposit box and doesn't have a *safe*?" I asked, incredulous.

When Lolly shook her head, the black and blue hair moved like wings. "Not that I could find. Of course, that doesn't mean it's not in some place I didn't find. All he has is his place. But the house does have security. There are two sets of codes, one for the front gate, one for the house itself. Of course, the third time I went over there, I opened my compact and used the mirror to watch him enter the codes, and I memorized them. What you learn in Vegas does not stay in Vegas. Anyway, I watched him do this several times. And Humberto is too stupid or too lazy to realize you need to change the codes from time to time. Furthermore, I'd done enough nose-powdering for him to think I only cared about my appearance. Not only that, I'd faked enough orgasms for him to think I was only in our relationship for the sex. When he paid me, he always said, 'This is for you to buy yourself a little something.' I always acted surprised and grateful."

"Two sets of codes, and that's it?" I still couldn't believe what she was telling me.

"No, no, no, that is not it. As I said, there was no hiding place that I could *find*. But Humberto has his four cars, and his office building. He also has three thugs who guard his house and grounds. They're all Spanish-speaking, and I don't speak Spanish." She sighed. "I did tell Ernest about the necklace, and that it was kept in an *unlocked* jewelry box. I felt terrible admitting I hadn't been able to find the cache of stolen stuff Ernest insisted must be there. So I searched again. I went through the bureaus one more time. The closets. I scoured the cars. I looked in the freezer, under the mattress, and in every item of Humberto's clothing. I checked the seams on all the pillows and upholstery. There was nothing hand-made or hand-sewn. While Humberto slept and the guards drank themselves silly out in the gatehouse, I went through every box in the basement and the attic. One day I even took the toaster apart. No diamonds. I figured all I had to say if I was caught was that I'd lost something."

"But that didn't happen," I said.

"Nope."

I said, "Damn it. But why did you get upset a while ago? It's not your fault that Ernest was killed."

"Just let me finish my story, will you, Goldy? I want to get through this. Next time Ernest came over, I told him I'd failed. He said he had a new plan and gave me some of his temazepam. Know the drug?"

"Sleeping pills."

She pointed a black-painted fingernail at me. "Correct. He asked me to open up the pills and sprinkle the powder into new bottles of the guards' rum. He said to pour a little rum out of each bottle first, so it would look as if the guys had started drinking them and just forgot they'd opened them. Ernest assured me the dose I was putting in wouldn't be enough to kill the guys." When she shrugged, the torn-out neck of her sweatshirt fell off one shoulder, revealing the ratty strap of a bra. She pulled the sweatshirt back into place and went on. "The guys kept their bottles of rum in the refrigerator, so I knew I could do it. Ernest asked for the security codes, and I gave them to him. He also furnished me with a disposable cell and told me to call him the next time Humberto and I were going out on a date. That's what Humberto always calls them: 'dates.' What a joke."

She rubbed her eyes. I waited.

Finally, she said, "So then Humberto invited me to the opera. He always wanted to show me off to people, like he was such a stud, he'd been able to land a young girlfriend. And he wanted to appear cultured. Yeah, like yogurt, I always thought. Anyway, when he was on his way over here to pick me up, I called Ernest. Then I put the phone into my purse, to throw away at the opera, the way Ernest had told me. When I told Humberto I needed to stop at his place for a jacket I'd purposely left there, I threw away the guards' open bottles of rum and put the doctored ones in their place."

"Then what?"

"Down in Denver, I tossed the cell, the way Ernest told me. When the opera was over, I was so nervous we'd surprise Ernest while he was robbing the house, I told Humberto the music had moved my soul. I wanted to make love in the car. He complied." She ran her hand through her hair.

"And when you got back to Humberto's house?"

"The guards were all fast asleep. Humberto woke them up, yelling at them like there was no tomorrow. He insisted they search the house. That's when they discovered the missing necklace." She sighed. "Humberto called an ambulance for the guards. Then he phoned the police. But I think he was afraid of getting caught telling them about a piece of jewelry *he* had stolen *being* stolen, so he clammed up. As soon as the cops left, those son-of-a-bitchin' guards hollered that *I* had to be the one who had stolen the necklace." She lifted her chin, indicating the tiny apartment. "They came over here and tore the place apart." Her right hand patted the couch. "I had to put this bedspread over my sofa, because they ripped through the old fabric, looking for the necklace. They went through the trash, inside my apartment and out in the parking lot, so I was glad I had dumped the cell in Denver. Then the assholes broke into my *parents'* house and ransacked *it*. But wait, this is the good part."

"There's a good part?" I said faintly.

"My mom and dad get back from a church meeting? They surprise the guards. My dad blocks their car in our driveway. He calls the cops on his cell, then takes a crowbar out of his trunk and treks to the front door to threaten whoever's in the house. So much for 'Blessed are the peacemakers.'"

"Oh my gosh, Lolly—"

"Next thing I know, Humberto's tooling over there, with me beside him. He's giving my parents five K in cash, in exchange for them saying the guards were their friends who'd come to a party on the wrong night. No charges were brought. Arrests or no arrests, I was furious and told Humberto he had to give *me* money for new furniture and tell the guards to leave *me* alone. Otherwise, he could find himself a new"—she hooked her fingers to indicate quotation marks again—"'girlfriend.'"

"Good Lord, Lolly."

She closed her eyes and shook her head. "The guards backed off. Humberto gave me ten thousand dollars, do you believe that? I called Julian, told him I'd come into some cash, did he want part of his money back? He laughed and said he'd take repayment after I got my degree and a jobby-job. So I bought this spread and those two chairs"—she pointed across the room—"at the Aspen Meadow Secondhand Store. My bank account got fattened up, and Humberto and I got together." She stopped, and I waited while she summoned the will to tell me the next bit, which I knew was coming. "Next thing I knew, Ernest McLeod had been shot and killed."

She rubbed her eyes furiously to keep herself from becoming upset. When she finally began to weep, I figured it was better just to let her have her cry.

Chapter 19

After she'd cried her way through a roll of discount toilet paper, she calmed down. I asked, "Did you tell the cops all this?"

Her bloodshot eyes gave me that look again, like I was hopelessly dense. "No, Goldy. I did not tell the cops that while I was working as a whore, I conspired to steal a valuable necklace and then drugged three guys so that my coconspirator could break into the house where the necklace was. I didn't even want to tell *you*. But then when you knocked and knocked and knocked on my door, I had this vision of Father Pete shaking his head and of Julian looking disappointed, and I couldn't stand it. Your husband's a cop, isn't he? Can't *you* tell him, and keep me out of it?"

I blinked. "I've already told him I was coming to see you."

"Oh, Christ."

"I don't think Tom will arrest you for prostitution if you tell him all you've told me."

She exhaled. "The cop who arrested me for DUI wasn't exactly empathetic."

"Nor would I expect him to be. But this is murder and is therefore different. Humberto had motive—Ernest had discovered and taken the necklace—and he probably had opportunity. Or he could have hired one of his guards to do it."

"But how would he have found out about Ernest in the first place?"

"When Ernest was a cop, he had worked Norman Juarez's case. Humberto or his people had put together that Ernest was investigating him. Humberto had even hired Yolanda to spy on Ernest. Maybe he had someone else watching Ernest, someone we didn't know about."

"Oh, Christ. Who?"

I shook my head. "You know I can't talk about that. But here's the big question: Did Ernest tell you where the necklace was? Because he didn't give it to the Juarezes."

"He didn't?" She raked her blue-black hair behind her ears. "Holy crap. I *wondered* why Norman Juarez acted so angry last night. But no, after the break-in, I didn't call Ernest. I was afraid if I called Ernest on my regular cell, Humberto and his guards might find his number on my 'calls made' list. Ernest had told me very specifically not to phone him. And I'll tell you something else. The very day after Ernest took the necklace? Humberto began a huge redecorating campaign. He stripped the rooms to the bones and started over. They're almost done, too, which is amazing."

"Who's doing all the painting and whatnot?"

"The guards. They installed new appliances, new draperies, new lights, you name it. But they weren't allowed in the bedroom when I was there. The furniture was replaced; there are new pillows, new fabrics on everything. And all the materials were brought in by the guards."

"Why would he do all that?"

"I have no idea."

"And you don't have a clue what Ernest did with the necklace?"

"None."

Another dead end. No necklace, no gold, no gems, and no key as to who had killed Ernest. *Wait; keys.* I asked, "Do you know if Humberto has access to the houses Donna Lamar rents out?"

Lolly rubbed her forehead. "You mean, Donna that rental agent who was at the party last night? All I know about her is that she has an office in the Captain's Quarters."

"I'm aware of that," I said patiently. "But do you know if Humberto has access to her keys, or security codes, for her rentals?"

Lolly shook her head. "I only see Humberto when he wants to see me. But he owns the Captain's Quarters, Goldy. And even though it's not fully leased, Ernest said he followed Humberto very carefully and then broke into the building. He was sure the gold and gems weren't anywhere in there."

"But keys to the rentals that Donna handles?"

"If he told Donna he wanted some keys, he'd probably get them, especially if they were to empty rentals. Still, if Ernest was stuck to Humberto's ass, don't you think he would have seen Humberto going into one of the rentals, and found the gold and gems hidden there?"

"I don't know."

When Lolly saw my disappointed look, she said, "I'm sorry. But I can't ask Humberto anything, or he'll think I had something to do with the stolen necklace."

I thought of Yolanda's rental burning down right after Humberto had said he wanted her to spy on Ernest. I did not want to burden Lolly with any more, though. "Don't apologize, Lolly. I'm the one who should be sorry. I didn't mean to upset you, coming over here and talking to you about Ernest." I hesitated before getting up to leave.

"What?" she said.

"Well," I said hopefully, "my husband always asks if there's anything out of place. Anything at all, he always says. Anything besides the redecorating that's aroused your curiosity?"

She wrinkled her forehead. "Humberto is getting a delivery later this week. Friday, he told me. But he wouldn't say what, only that it needs to be 'installed'—his word—and I can't come over that day."

"Anything else?"

"Well, he keeps a pretty tight hold on his wallet."

"I thought you said he'd been generous to you and your parents."

"I don't mean it metaphorically, Goldy. I mean when he's dressed, he keeps a really tight hold on his *actual wallet*. He's always checking to make sure he has it. One time when he was asleep, I went through it. All I found for my trouble was a couple hundred bucks plus three or four receipts. BFD."

"Three or four receipts for what?"

"I don't know. I didn't look at them that closely."

I had no idea what these might be, but even the slenderest of clues could offer something. "Does Humberto have a photocopier?" When she nodded, I said, "Could you copy the receipts for me? *Don't* steal them. I'm coming to Humberto's tonight, for dinner."

"I know."

"Will you be there?"

When she nodded again, I said, "Got any of that temazepam left?"

"I have one left. Oh, Christ, Goldy, don't tell me you want me to drug somebody."

"Are you and Humberto getting together this afternoon?"

She let her head drop back. "Yes. He says if we make love first, he has a better siesta. And before you ask, yes, we usually have a drink first."

"So, you open up the pill and sprinkle a little bit in each of your drinks. Okay? Then you pretend to drink some of yours while he drinks his. When he's asleep, you get the stuff out of his wallet, copy it, fold it up, and save it for me, just until tonight. Then you have a tiny bit of your drink and lie down next to Humberto, until you fall asleep—"

"Know what?" Lolly interrupted me. "I already saw *Romeo and Juliet*. As I recall? That dual-poisoning thing didn't turn out so well."

"This will have a happy ending," I insisted. "He'll

wake up, and then he'll wake you up, and even if he gets suspicious and sends the drinks off to be analyzed, you're in the clear. Listen," I said earnestly, "I need to see what Humberto's keeping in his wallet, Lolly. Maybe it'll lead somewhere."

She sighed. "Please don't tell Tom about my part in all this, okay?"

"I'm not even going to tell Tom what *I'm* doing. Hide the photocopy well, and don't swallow much of that drink."

"Yeah, yeah." She led me to the door. "Don't worry, I'm in the fix I'm in because of booze. I've learned my lesson."

In the van, I checked my watch. It wasn't even ten o'clock, but my stomach was rumbling. The Aspen Meadow Pastry Shop had survived the downturn, and I thought a buttermilk doughnut and a cup of brewed coffee would do the trick.

I still hadn't heard back from Hermie Mikulski. Then again, I hadn't been expecting her to be checking her voice mail. On the way to my doughnut, I decided to leave her another urgent message.

"Hermie Mikulski," she answered briskly. Her gravelly, serious voice startled me.

"This is Goldy Schulz." I coughed to hide my surprise. "Sorry." I maneuvered the van into a spot on Main Street not walled off with plowed snow. "My husband, the sheriff's department, e-everyone," I stammered, "we've been trying to reach you."

"Yes, well, I've been very busy, what with trying to keep this town safe for animals. Plus, my son's nose is very bruised and swollen. He can only have soup, and I have to make it for him."

"So, you're at your house? May I bring some homemade soup over to you and Brad?" I remembered the mushroom soup that I was planning on taking to the Bertrams' house. I could go home and make a double batch—

"No, thank you." Her voice scraped my ears, and I cringed. "I am perfectly capable of making soup."

"I understand." I tried to make my voice soothing, when in truth I was desperate to ask, *Where the hell have you been?* "Actually, Hermie, I'm calling because you said you were a client of Ernest McLeod's, and he was my friend—"

"Huh," she interrupted. "I left a message at the sheriff's department, saying Ernest McLeod was killed because he was in the process of helping me close down a puppy mill, which I am absolutely positive is hidden somewhere on the grounds of a legitimate breeding operation."

"*When* did you call the sheriff's department?"

She paused. "I reached your husband's voice mail this morning."

"Did you tell him where this mill was?"

"If I had known where the puppy mill was at that point, I would have told him. How stupid do you think I am?"

At that point? What did she mean? Not wanting to scare her into hanging up on me, I said, "Actually, I think you're very smart, Hermie. That's why I called you. You've been staying away from home—"

"I had been getting threatening phone calls," she said.

"You know, 'Mind your own business, you eight-fingered hag,' that kind of thing. I was scared."

I paused. "But why are you at your house now?"

She didn't say anything for a minute. Had she heard about Marla's puppy being sick? I wondered. At length she said, "I came home to get some clothes this morning. Along with all the other messages on my machine, there was an anonymous one giving me a number to phone if I wanted the location of the puppy mill. I called and got directions. The tipster said I shouldn't go right away, that I should wait until around ten. So I'm going out there as soon as I'm dressed. And no one is going to talk me out of it! The tipster also told me the puppy mill owner had a gun. The police don't care and won't protect me or the dogs. So I'm taking my own firearm."

"Hermie," I said desperately, "please don't—"

"If you wish to join me, be at the Aspen Meadow Lake parking lot in fifteen minutes."

"Hermie, this is not safe for you. This is a very bad—" But she had hung up.

I was less than five minutes from the lake. I called Tom, left a message on his voice mail saying I was meeting Hermie at the lake, that someone had told her the location of the secret mill on the grounds of a legitimate breeding enterprise. I asked him to please, please come, because Hermie was bringing a gun, which I'd already told her was a terrible idea. I sighed and hung up.

What should I do? I wondered. I pulled the van out of the parking space and raced up Main Street.

I was almost to the lake when I heard the *vroom-*

vroom sound that had so upset Yolanda and Ferdinanda. I braked hard. Luckily, no one was behind me. On my right, on the snowy sidewalk, Harriet, the lovely, tall woman who had been Kris Nielsen's date at Rorry's party, had just opened the passenger-side door to a white Maserati. Kris's Maserati. I squinted. She wore jeans, a black turtleneck, and a leather jacket.

Where was she going? The Maserati pulled out in front of me, which gave me a chance to look hard on my right. The only thing directly on my right was the two-story building that had held Mountain Rents. A red and white FOR LEASE sign hung in the upstairs window. Below, on the main floor, was Frank's Fix-It.

Maybe she was going in to drop something off? I shook my head as the Maserati moved up Main Street. You could leave a broken article with the potheads at Frank's Fix-It and it would be there for years, gathering dust and spiders as it deteriorated, and when you came back to claim it, they'd say they hadn't been able to repair it, after all.

I shook my head as the Mas made it through on a green light, while I got stopped by a red.

A few moments later, the van was chugging toward the lake. At the ramp that led to Upper Cottonwood Creek Road, I turned left, so I could get to the parking lot in time to meet Hermie Mikulski. Hermie Mikulski drove a large beige van that was like mine, only newer. When she pulled into the parking lot, I jumped out of my vehicle and waved to her.

Her window powered down and I hurried over. Hermie's pale, wide face was heavily made up, but the foundation and powder did not conceal the dark circles under her eyes. Her short gray hair, curled in complex whorls, had not been brushed. She wore a purple silk dress, a string of large pearls with matching earrings that pulled down her large lobes, and a purple boiled wool coat embroidered with green crewelwork. She looked like she was going to a meeting of my mother's New Jersey bridge club.

The remaining fingers of Hermie's left hand gripped the steering wheel. On the passenger seat lay a gleaming .22. This was not something you'd see at a bridge club meeting.

"Hermie," I said, my voice full of concern, "I just think it is a very, very bad idea for you to go out to this place, much less take a weapon. I've called the sheriff's department and asked my husband to meet us—"

"I don't have time to wait for him. He'll have to get a warrant and by then the breeder may have cleared out his mill kennels and hidden the evidence. Those puppies could die."

"But if you'd just talk to him first—"

"Look, Goldy," she said brusquely, "you don't have to come with me. I invited you and I can disinvite you."

Damn it. When Tom was in a meeting or en route to a scene, he rarely checked his voice mail. "Where are you going, anyway?"

Her powdered face broke into a wide smile. "Out by the Aspen Meadow Wildlife Preserve. My tipster told me how to get in the back way. You see, this man, the breeder, claims to have a legitimate operation. I've seen it. It's a spanking-new red-painted barn that you can view from the dirt road that leads to his house. That's what Animal Control sees when they come out. But according to the tipster, the mill operator has several sheds where he actually breeds puppies in the most deplorable conditions. Oh, that son of a bitch! I'm sure Ernest found the sheds, and then he was killed. But now my tipster has marked the precise way to get there!" She patted binoculars and a digital camera on the seat beside her. "I'm going to get the evidence I need."

"May I know where we're going, please?" I asked. She shook her head vigorously and exhaled with impatience. "Hermie, please wait for the sheriff's department."

"No, no, no."

"Please, please, *please* don't take a gun out there. If this person is armed and expecting trouble—"

"I know this person is armed, Goldy." She wrinkled her brow. "That is why I'm taking my own weapon. And I know how to shoot, too; I took lessons. Nobody is going to deprive *me* of any more digits!" She glanced at a pearl-crusted watch. "Ten o'clock. Now, if you're coming, follow me. Otherwise, go home and make soup."

Damn it to hell, I thought as I jogged back to the van. *Don't people understand how dangerous firearms are?* If One-Handed Hermie got into a gun battle with the puppy mill owner, I had no doubt who would win, and it wasn't Hermie Mikulski.

She drove fast, so fast her van slung itself from one side of the two-lane road to the other. Occasionally she crossed the yellow divider line. I prayed that a state patrolman would stop her, give her a ticket for speeding, and then notice the gun. He would take her down to jail, and that would be that.

No such luck. Once we were several miles outside of town, I tried again to reach Tom on my cell. But fate wasn't smiling on me then, either. We were out of range.

I cursed silently when Hermie's van zoomed past the sign indicating the Aspen Meadow Wildlife Preserve was five miles ahead. The road turned from pavement to mud mixed with gravel. Hermie's tires sloshed through puddles and spewed up curtains of sludge and stones. To avoid having my windshield thoroughly spattered, I allowed my van to trail farther behind Hermie's, and cursed her again.

Our vehicles began to climb. The snow on either side of the road was deeper. Here and there, patches of sun-bleached grass dotted brilliantly whitened meadows that led up to hills thick with pine. Vistas of the ice-capped peaks of the Continental Divide appeared as the road rounded one hill, then another.

My inner ear echoed with Tom's words: *I still don't want you going out to the preserve.* And *Miss G., can't I just ask you not to do something, and you don't do it?* And I'd said yes.

Yet here I was, trying to follow crazy-ass Hermie Mikulski as she raced her van out to some godforsaken rendezvous with an armed puppy mill owner, in a place with no cell phone reception.

Hermie passed the left-hand turnoff that I was almost positive had been the one Charlene Newgate had taken when she'd been driving ahead of me, the last time I'd been out there. I still suspected Charlene of lying about providing any recent employees to Drew Parker, DDS. But, why would she do that? Money? Maybe. But given the way she'd pulled her fur around her and the proud note in her voice when she'd talked about her "boyfriend," I suspected another motive: love.

About a mile beyond Charlene's road, Hermie suddenly slowed and turned left. There had been no sign. A deeply rutted dirt road was lined on either side by thick woods. Occasional mailboxes indicated driveways that veered up out of sight. I didn't see a single house. This was not a place where builders had ventured to build minimansions; those owners wouldn't have been able to abide the difficulties of such a horrible dirt road. I surmised that we were in an area where there were a lot of summer cabins, not unlike the one Sabine Rushmore and I had gone through, although that one had had a fireplace and, presumably, some alternative kind of heat for the winter months. Once the first snows hit, the summer owners usually boarded up their places and headed south.

The road itself became narrower, barely wider than a lane. Pine branches brushed the sides of the van. Only an occasional sun-loving aspen, its yellow leaves mostly stripped by the snowstorm, broke through the gloom. I felt like Gretel following Hansel. Problem was, we weren't dropping stones to let anyone come after us.

At a tree with a rope twined around it, Hermie turned left again, onto a bumpy path that was not wide enough for our vans. Her vehicle bucked and rocked over stones, undergrowth, ruts. Bile rose in my throat and my skin chilled. I fought a sudden urge to stop my vehicle, do a fourteen-point turn in the woods, and hightail it back to town.

Before I could do that, though, Hermie abruptly halted. I braked too, and looked around. We were in deep woods. There was no discernible trail in front of us. I scanned the surrounding forest and again saw a rope tied around a tree.

I am beyond pissed off, I thought, jumping from my van. I was going to stop this right now. I raced up to Hermie's door, where I pushed hard to prevent her from opening it.

"What are you doing?" she screamed through the glass. She'd been leaning down to her right and hadn't seen my approach. "Move!" she screamed. Then she had the bright idea to buzz down her window. "Stop that this instant," she hissed. "And don't make any noise."

"We need to leave." I looked down to where Hermie had been leaning. She'd moved things around: two pairs of binoculars, plus the digital camera, sat on the floor below the passenger seat, the seat that now held the gun.

"Goldy, you are impeding my progress."

"That is exactly what I want to do. Hermie, we have to *get out of here,*" I said. "This is not safe. You followed the directions of some anonymous caller. How do you know this isn't a trap? How do you know the owner of the puppy mill didn't call you himself?"

She picked up the gun and tapped the inside of her windshield with it. I practically jumped out of my skin.

"Put that away!" I told her.

"Look there, Goldy. Down through the woods. Use these." She put down the gun, thank God, but used her good hand to pick up one of the pairs of binoculars and hand them to me. "Just below us is the shed the puppy mill owner uses to stow puppies in deplorable conditions. If you come all the way out here because you're answering an ad for beagle puppies, you only see a nice red barn and a new shed the owner's put next to the road. You don't see *that shed*."

"How do you know about these deplorable conditions?" I demanded as I focused the binocs first on the shed in question. About a fourth of a mile up from it stood a red-painted barn and a newer-looking shed. Across a meadow from the suspect shed stood a sprawling one-story house. I refocused the binoculars. In the house's driveway sat a dark sport-utility vehicle, its back gate open.

When Hermie didn't answer, I lowered the binoculars and stared at her. "How do you know?" I asked again. "Did someone have a sick puppy and complain?" I knew from Sabine that Hermie had said she'd gotten on this breeder's trail owing to a concerned veterinarian. But I wanted to see if she'd give me any other information about this commando operation she was dead set on.

Hermie's mouth was set in a tight frown. Finally she said, "There's a veterinary nurse I pay, here in town, to tell me about suspected abuse cases. She told me about the beagles after a puppy in bad shape came into their office. When Animal Control claimed they found no irregularities on the property and I couldn't find anything out on my own, I hired Ernest." She picked up the other pair of binoculars and stared through them. "Look now, will you? Check out the driveway. If the puppy mill owner is trapping us, why is he packing his car?"

I trained the binocs on the house and the driveway. I tried to make out the Colorado license plate: BHG 223? Or 228?

My skin chilled again when I saw a bald man. He looked to be about the right size and shape of the man who'd set Ernest's house on fire. I couldn't be sure, though. He disappeared and then came back into view carrying three suitcases, one tucked under his right arm, his hands carrying the other two. Trailing behind him was a woman. A sudden breeze made her pleas audible.

"But why? Why won't you tell me? What have I done? Are you just going to leave me here? Answer me!" It was Charlene Newgate. She wore the same fur coat she'd had on in the CBHS gym. "I love you!" She said his name then. Stony? Sony? Crony? "I love you so much, Stony!" she yelled. When Stony did not heed her, Charlene cried desperately, "I'll tell the police! I'll tell them everything! Everything you had me do—"

Stony, the bald man, methodically put the suitcases into the open trunk. Then he turned with startling swiftness and punched Charlene in the face. She fell hard. The bald man said something inaudible down to her inert form. Charlene did not move and did not make any reply that we could hear.

"You see!" said Hermie triumphantly. "You see how he even abuses *people*! What if he kills her? Like in the next few minutes? We have to go down there right now!"

I was so stunned by what I had seen, so unnerved by what Hermie was saying, that she was able to push her door open. The force toppled me backward and I collapsed on top of a small pine tree. I struggled to get balance, but found myself in a tangle of the binoculars and their strap, clumps of snow, damp earth, and pine needles. The needles were wet and shockingly cold. They pierced my cheeks and ears and snarled my hair. When I finally managed to stand, Hermie was plowing through the trees well ahead of me. In her right hand, she was holding her gun.

I cursed under my breath, pulled the binoculars and their strap over my head, and tossed them into the snow. I struggled through the woods, but bushes, branches, and spills of rocks slapped my face and arms and made me stumble. Hermie seemed to be on an actual trail, while I was cutting one. I smashed through the undergrowth to find her footprints in the snow, then followed them. She was about twenty yards in front of me. How far was she going to go? The woods went down a slope that opened onto the meadow that led back to the house. I tried not to think of how a .22, at this distance, would not even hit the side of the closest shed.

"Stop!" I called after her. "Just let him go! Hermie! You're going to get hurt."

She paused and glared back at me. "Shut *up*!" she snapped. "He'll hear you! Do you want that woman to be shot? Because that's what will happen. And he'll get away. That's what always happens with these people," she muttered, as if to herself, but I heard it anyway. Then she crashed onward at an even faster clip.

My sneakers were soaking wet and I was panting. I made myself trot. I was trembling with heat and fright.

For a large woman, Hermie was quicker than I expected. Maybe in addition to learning how to shoot, she'd been working out. My chest tightened with exertion. I prayed not to have a heart attack before I could stop crazy Hermie.

Soon we were out of the woods and in the snowy stretch of open land. I was losing Hermie, who was wearing sturdy hiking boots along with her pearls, her purple silk dress, and her boiled wool coat. She ran forward, about half a football field's length ahead of me. The tin-roofed barn lay the same distance from her. I cursed again and tried to pick up my pace.

Unfortunately, melting and refreezing snow had formed an ice crust on the meadow. No matter how hard I tried, I could not run. My shoes crunched and slipped, and once I fell headlong on the frozen surface. I got up quickly, ignored a searing pain in my knees, and checked the surroundings again.

Charlene still lay motionless in the driveway. The bald man appeared, carrying a box. Hermie, having broken through to an expanse of brown grass, rushed forward. I steadied myself and clomped heavily toward her back. She was about twenty yards from the house.

"Stop!" Hermie screeched at the bald man. "You horrible creature! Stop or I'll shoot!" Startled, the bald man dropped his box. Without waiting, Hermie raised her gun over her head and fired.

The firecracker explosion of Hermie's gun echoed in the chilly air. But then there was an even louder boom, and another. Had the bald man shot back? I heard Tom's voice in my ears, or maybe it was just my mind imagining Tom's voice, because there were no police cars, no other people, anywhere. *Get down! Get down!* the voice yelled. I fell forward onto the snow. Above me, the air splintered with another boom.

I scrabbled across the icy meadow, then began to roll downward. I had to get to Hermie and make sure she was all right. Once again I imagined Tom's voice: *Always make yourself a moving target.* My jacket, my clothes, my sneakers were soaked. Rocks ripped my sensible caterer's support hose. My mind scolded, *That's the only sensible thing about you.*

Suddenly I was on snow, behind a building. In the distance, a car drove away. I blinked and looked for Hermie, but could not see her. After a few moments, I was aware of sirens. I lifted my head and scanned the meadow. Hermie lay in an unnatural heap on the tan grass. Her gray curls hung in a limp mess; her coat and dress resembled a dark, wrinkled map. Had I seen her foot move? I thought so.

I hoped the shock of gunfire had only made her faint. . . . *Dear God, let her only have fainted, I don't want Brad to be without a mother, no matter how crazy that mother is. . . .*

I planted my face in the snow to try to shock my brain. Oh yes: the bald man, Charlene Newgate, Hermie Mikulski on a mission of mercy. Yet I could hear no human voices at all. In fact, the only noise I could hear beyond the incessant bleating of the sirens was the yipping and crying of what had to be fifty, no, a hundred little dogs. . . .

I scooted to the corner of the dilapidated shed. Next

to its outside wall was damp earth and dead grass. The whining of the dogs was bothering me so much that I shook my head and reached forward to pull open the door to the shed, just as darkness flooded my brain.

Some time later, a blustery foghorn voice stabbed my consciousness, saying, *Come out slowly showing your hands now. . . .*

Astonished by a sudden warm wetness moving back and forth across my cheek, then more moist warmth tickling my legs, I scrambled awkwardly to a sitting position. Beagle pups were whining and licking my skin where it was torn. I remembered teaching my Sunday school class about a dog licking Lazarus's wounds—

"Miss G.? Oh, Christ, Goldy? Are you all right? What the *hell* are you doing out here?"

Someone, a man, *Tom,* had put his hands under my arms and was pulling me gently upward. The air still broke into slivers: sirens, voices, car doors slamming, dogs whining and barking.

My mouth felt as if it were filled with flannel. "I'm sorry, I'm sorry. Is Hermie all right? Where is she?" When I turned to look, blades of sunlight reflecting off the snow blinded me. A frigid wind made my skin break out in gooseflesh. Tom pulled me close. I shivered against him. "Hermie?"

"She's fine. She passed out, it looks like." Still holding on to me, he spun and yelled, "Will someone bring this woman a blanket?"

Will someone bring this woman *a blanket*? Not *Will someone bring* my wife *a blanket*? Not *Will someone bring my nosy, meddling, intrusive wife a frigging blanket*?

Then he hollered, "And will someone please round up these damn dogs?"

I heard myself babbling, "Tom, please don't let them take the puppies, please don't round them up. That's why Hermie and I came out here, to save them, not to have them sent to a pound. Not to have them put where they'll be killed." My words were tumbling out too fast, but I couldn't help myself.

"They're not going to the pound." Tom's kind face finally came into focus in front of me. I realized his muscular arms were holding me up. "Don't worry," he said.

"I can stand on my own." Yet when he let go of me, I wobbled, and he grabbed me. "No, I'm okay," I told him. "I just—" I was looking at the driveway, where a tarp had been unfurled. It was the kind of tarp the sheriff's department used to cover a body.

Charlene Newgate, her tufted brown hair disheveled, her fur askew, was on her feet, bending forward. Policemen flanked her as she was put into handcuffs.

I was shivering uncontrollably. "Who, I mean, who's under that tarp—"

"It's a guy named Stonewall Osgoode," Tom said. "Animal Control already knew about him from when they came out to investigate Hermie's puppy mill allegations. But you know what? I think he's our bald suspect in the burning of Ernest's house. The same one we think stole my gun from our garage."

"Did Hermie, I mean, how did he—"

"We don't think Hermie shot him. No way was that guy killed by a twenty-two at that distance." He held me, then took a blanket a uniformed cop offered and wrapped it around my shoulders.

"Wait," I said as Tom put his arm around my shoulder and started to lead me to a patrol car. I pivoted awkwardly and pointed across the meadow, into the trees, where a sharp wind sent veils and chunks of snow off the pine branches and into the air. "My van's in the woods—"

"We know. I just got a radio call. Hermie's is there, too." We stood like that for a moment, but then he murmured, "We need you to come wait in one of our vehicles." Tom led me back to a patrol car, where the heat was turned to high, thank God.

I watched there while Tom commanded his team. Uniformed police and plainclothes investigators went into Osgoode's house and came out. The coroner's van arrived. I averted my eyes while they did their job. If Hermie hadn't shot Osgoode, and Charlene had been on the ground, then who *had* fired so unerringly? While I was rolling in the snow and Hermie had surprised Osgoode with her shot, had Charlene gotten up, taken Osgoode's weapon, and killed him?

After what felt like an eternity but probably was only half an hour, Tom, his expression grim, returned to the patrol car. Before I could ask him what they had found and how soon would it be before I could go home, he said, "Armstrong's coming. He needs to question you."

Chapter 20

I shook my head. "I can't do this now."

"Miss G., a man has been murdered. You don't have a choice." Tom softened his tone. "Do you want me to stay with you? I won't be able to say anything."

Did I want Tom with me? Hmm. Tom's colleague, Sergeant Armstrong, was going to question me. Maybe I would have a chance to question *him*.

I shouldn't have been surprised that the sheriff's department had gotten there so quickly. Last night, I'd told Tom what I'd learned from Sabine Rushmore. The Animal Control section of the department knew the location of the legitimate cover for the beagle-breeding operation, because Hermie Mikulski had complained to them about it. And then this morning, I'd left a frantic message with Tom about where I was going.

Still, oddly, it hadn't felt like more than a few minutes between the last explosion, a car maybe driving away, and the scream of sirens. I felt out of it and suddenly did *not* want to be questioned.

I reminded myself that I'd gotten into this mess because I was trying to help Yolanda, and that had led me into the quicksand of the Ernest McLeod murder. I had not been motivated to punish a puppy mill owner. But interrogations could take strange turns, and I didn't want to feel unprepared. So I said, "Yes, Tom. Please stay with me. Thank you."

We got into a patrol car parked behind Osgoode's SUV, which still had its rear hatch open. Since I'd known Sergeant Armstrong, he had lost about half of the thin brown strands that he still combed over his shiny bald spot. His complexion was as pasty as ever, and his thin frame was now marred by a pot belly. Odd hours, stress-based eating, and lack of exercise will do that to anyone, but cops are particularly susceptible.

"Thank you, Mrs. Schulz." Armstrong's tone was formal. He'd asked me to sit next to him, while Tom stayed in back. Armstrong took out a small digital microphone and clipped it onto a dashboard knob. Then he retrieved a notebook and pen. I didn't need to ask why he was using two modes of recording our conversation. Tom had complained relentlessly about the unreliability of the department's tech toys. That was why my husband now insisted that all police take notes in addition to using what might end up as a blank tape, disc, or other device.

"You know the drill," Armstrong said. "Start with when you got up this morning and bring us to you being here."

I thought of how I should begin. I didn't know what words I'd use to tell them about Lolly, without divulging what she'd done on Ernest's behalf. On the other hand, I knew I had to say *something* about how I'd spent the morning, or there would be a gap as long as the Eisenhower Tunnel in my narrative. But I'd promised to keep her out of it. As Lolly would say, crap!

I turned in my seat and asked if I could tell them something I'd found out without saying where I'd gotten the information. Tom rolled his eyes. After a moment, Armstrong told me to go ahead. So, without names, I related the tale of the theft of the Juarez necklace from Humberto Captain's place.

I looked in the rearview mirror and caught Tom's eyes. He said, "This is the diamond necklace that for years Mr. Juarez has been claiming Humberto stole from him?" Tom's tone was incredulous. "*That* was what the break-in at Humberto's was all about? Jesus, Goldy, how long have you known that Ernest stole the necklace?"

"I just learned about it! And after I heard the tale of the necklace, I had to deal with Hermie. Plus, I left you a message. So, give me a break, would you?"

Tom said, his voice peevish, "You said you were going out to the puppy mill with Hermie. No mention of a necklace or of Ernest breaking into Humberto's place to perform grand larceny."

"Well, I was *going* to tell you, once I got through the Hermie mess."

"Let's get on with the story of you coming out here." Armstrong struggled to keep his tone neutral. Clearly, he didn't want to get between his boss and his boss's wife.

I shivered and said, "Well, let me think."

Tom, in spite of his apparent anger, drew a thermos out of somewhere and poured me some black coffee. It was hot and strong and made me feel better than I had in several hours.

"Did Hermie say she was going to shoot somebody?" Armstrong asked.

"No. But you've seen her . . . left hand? When she tried to close down a Nebraska puppy mill, somebody fired at her. She lost two fingers."

Armstrong's face was impassive. "We know the whole story. She had a toy gun and she was trespassing. When the guy had finished moving a box of puppies, she jumped out of nowhere with her Kmart Kalashnikov and told him to put his hands up. He had a gun and he shot the toy thing out of her hands, which he was perfectly within his rights to do to a trespasser whom he thought was armed." Armstrong exhaled. "Did she tell you she'd taken shooting lessons? 'Cause that's what she told us she was going to do after the toy-gun incident."

I said, "Yes, she told me. But I really am sure she didn't intend—"

"Why did you bring two vans? Why not just come in one?"

"It was just the way it worked out. I called her, thinking to leave a message. She answered, which surprised me." I gave Armstrong a helpless look.

Armstrong's dark eyes were frighteningly opaque. "And why were you calling her today?"

"Because I thought she might talk to me, instead of the cops. Hermie was single-minded in her desire to close down the mill, which was housed in sheds hidden from view. She hired Ernest to get the exact location, which was somewhere on the property of what appeared to be a legitimate operation." Thinking of those poor, darling puppies, I shook my head. "One of the dogs Ernest adopted, adopted by my friend Marla, got sick. The veterinarian called Marla and said she had to phone the other owners of the adopted beagle pups and have them rounded up and brought in."

Armstrong said, "Do you know why?"

"I don't. Maybe while they were all crowded into that dilapidated shed, they got canine flu or something."

Armstrong glanced at Tom, which I caught in the mirror. Tom gave an almost imperceptible nod. Armstrong said, "The dogs didn't have the flu. They were being used to smuggle marijuana seeds."

"What?"

Armstrong raised his thin eyebrows at Tom, who again nodded. Armstrong handed me a Colorado driver's license. "First of all, just for the record, this guy out here, Stonewall Osgoode? He's the one you saw torching Ernest's house?"

Staring blankly from the license photo was the bald guy who'd tossed two Molotov cocktails into Ernest McLeod's greenhouse. "Yes," I said. "This is the guy. You might want to show this picture to my son, Arch. He stabbed Stonewall Osgoode with a weeder when Osgoode was trying to break into our house."

Armstrong said, "Anyway, Osgoode, our vic here, was running a full-service marijuana operation. In his house, we found a map. We've just had a radio report from a helo. They found his garden way in there." He wagged a thin hand toward the Aspen Meadow Wildlife Preserve. "When we had that big forest fire, followed by floods? Some service roads in extremely remote areas were never repaired. That's where Osgoode's growers set up camp. But you know hikers in Colorado, not afraid to go anywhere. The growers were armed. Any time hikers came near, there were shots. We've had quite a few reports of gunfire, but we didn't have the location of the grow operation until today."

"Wait," I said, "what does this have to do with the seeds in the puppies?"

There was quiet in the car for a moment, until Tom said, "When Armstrong says Osgoode had a full-service operation, it means that, at this point, our theory is that Osgoode grew some of it, probably hiring locals to guard it. You know guys around here. They shoot off a round if they hear wind in the woods. But the full-service part? Osgoode, we've discovered, flunked out of veterinary school. But he knew enough to do surgery. In addition to the map in his house, we found surgical instruments in that far shed, the one with the metal roof. He was smuggling some of the seeds he'd bought from who-knows-where to other growers. Somebody wants a regular beagle? They buy a puppy from his legitimate breeding operation. Somebody wants hemp seeds? They buy a spayed female pup from the shed. When he spayed them, he inserted canisters of seeds. *Those* are the puppies Ernest took, probably because he figured out something hinky was going on. Marla's puppy got sick when the dog's internal organs got tangled around the canister. Her dog's all right now, and they think the others will pull through. But the damage to them was done by Osgoode."

I said, "That son of a bitch." I rubbed my forehead. "Do you think Hermie knew about this?"

"She's denying it," Tom replied.

I took a deep breath and remembered Ernest's greenhouse before it was destroyed. "Listen. The day after Ernest stole the puppies? He put their chow next to his own medical marijuana plants. I think he was trying to send us a message, just in case something happened to him. "

Armstrong said, "Ah, that would qualify as reaching."

Tom said, "Most investigators tell other people what they're doing and why they're doing it. Or they leave a note. You know, like in a file?"

I recalled what Ferdinanda had said Ernest had told her, right before he left for town on foot. *If something happens to me, ask the bird.* It still didn't make sense. "Maybe he did leave a note somewhere," I said. "His files, everything, got burned up in the fire. But I found the puppy chow next to the marijuana," I repeated stubbornly. "It was after I'd searched all over his house for it. There was no *reason* for it to be there."

There was silence in the car for a few minutes. I'd lost the thread of my narrative, and my brain was too addled to pick it up.

Tom said, "Remember that hiker who brought a bleeding puppy into our town's veterinarian? Way out on a hiking trail? It was a female puppy that hadn't been spayed. She somehow managed to escape, lucky little thing. We figure Osgoode, or someone working with him, tried to shoot her, and that's why she was bleeding."

Armstrong said, "Back to Hermie. She didn't mention the weed. But how did she know to come in the back way to the puppy-mill shed?"

"She got a . . . oh, God." I sighed. "She got an anonymous phone call telling her where the secret sheds were that were housing the puppy mill. Whoever it was told her to come armed, because the mill owner had a gun."

"So that's why she brought a firearm today?"

"Yes," I said tentatively. I didn't want to betray Hermie, but she was probably giving a similar statement to the police right now. I rubbed my forehead. "We were set up."

Tom said, "Who else knew you were going to be here?"

"I told you, Tom. I called *you*."

"Right. But who else knew you were going to meet Hermie?"

"Nobody."

"Think," said Tom.

I closed my eyes and went over the events of the morning. "Okay. I mentioned to Yolanda, Ferdinanda, and Boyd that I was going to try to track down Hermie."

Tom said nothing. Armstrong took notes.

"How did you decide to park where you did?" Armstrong asked.

"Someone had marked the trail with rope. Hermie followed it. And yes, at that point I thought we might be walking into a trap. I couldn't get any cell phone reception, or I would have called you. But there was no way I was going to let Hermie go it alone against an armed puppy mill owner."

"Did you see anything?" Tom asked. "Someone hiding, or even something that didn't look right?"

I ran the scene through my mind. I'd been so intent on trying to convince Hermie not to shoot, I hadn't been paying much attention to Osgoode . . . or to Charlene, who'd trailed after him, whining.

"Charlene Newgate," I said. "His girlfriend. We could hear her when we were at the edge of the woods. She was screaming at him, begging him not to go. She threatened to go to the police. He . . . punched her hard, and she went down. It looked as if he knocked her out, but maybe he didn't."

"You never saw her move again?" Tom asked.

"No. Is she all right?"

"He broke her nose," Armstrong said. He inhaled. "Okay, so someone left markers saying where you should park. Why there?"

"I guessed it was so we could approach without being seen."

"It was a man who called her?" Armstrong said sharply.

"Hermie never said whether it was a man or a woman. She was focused on closing what she saw as a mill. I tried to keep her inside her car, once we were up in the woods. She pushed so hard on the door that I fell over. That's why I couldn't keep up with her," I said, my tone apologetic. "She was racing across the open meadow, right at Osgoode."

Armstrong said, "I need to know exactly what you heard."

"Hermie screamed at Osgoode, threatening him."

"Her exact words?"

I told them. "Then she lifted her gun, which was a twenty-two, and fired into the air. It sounded like a firecracker. Right after that, there was a boom, like a blast from another gun. I didn't see where it came from. It was just loud. I thought I could hear you in my ear," I said to Tom. "You were telling me to get down, so I fell and rolled in the snow. I heard two more of the same big explosions after that. I think I kept rolling, because I landed out in back of that shed. Oh, wait. I might have heard a car drive away."

"From where?" Armstrong asked.

"I couldn't tell. My ears were ringing from the gunfire. I was soaking wet and couldn't see Charlene or Osgoode. I opened the door to the shed, then blacked out. Next thing I knew, I heard your bullhorn and then all of a sudden beagle puppies were licking my face and my legs. That's it. I'm sorry I don't know more."

Neither Tom nor Armstrong said anything.

"What about Charlene?" I asked finally. "She threatened to go to the police. Was it because of the marijuana?"

Armstrong said, "She was conscious when we got here and sitting up in the driveway. Osgoode had a twenty-two, but it was in the car and hadn't been fired. There's no sign of another gun. And Charlene said she's not talking until she sees her lawyer. I doubt we'll get anything out of her anytime soon."

Damn it. "Look," I said, exasperated, "I'm convinced

Charlene is in this up to her neck. She's never had any money, and now, all of a sudden, she has lots of cash. She's got a new car, new clothes, furs, and she's put her grandson into a relatively expensive parochial school. Osgoode was getting *something* from her. So, where'd he get that kind of money? Did he have, if you'll pardon the expression, seed money?"

Armstrong said nothing. After a moment, Tom said, "We're checking his financials, seeing if he had a safety deposit box, that kind of thing. We'll be using law enforcement computers to see if he pops up. The Animal Control people and a veterinarian are checking out all the puppies. Our guys and DEA are out at the the marijuana grow now, cutting it all down. It wasn't mature, so he could not have made lots of money yet. Not on the seeds, not on the buds. The only thing we've been able to find out is that Osgoode only rented this house a few months ago, and he paid in cash. Our guess is he was just starting his operation."

"He flunked out of veterinary school," I said. "Where did he get the cash he had to start all this? Charlene's not attractive, she's difficult to get along with, and, from what I could see, she's quite a bit older than Osgoode. So what gives?"

"Miss G.," Tom said patiently, "we're working on all that."

"Do you remember the dinner party at the Breckenridges' house?" I asked. "Sean Breckenridge recently took photographs of beagle puppies. They could have been from here."

"Tell me about that," Armstrong said.

So I did. I added that Sean's wealthy wife, Rorry, had hired Ernest McLeod to prove that Sean was having an affair. My mind reeled. But then what? Would Sean have had the fortitude to shoot Stonewall, to cover things up? I wondered. Almost as an afterthought, I said, "All this that's happened out here? It might be connected to Yolanda."

"To Yolanda?" asked Armstrong. "Yolanda Garcia, the chef Boyd is protecting?"

"Look," I said, "isn't it possible that the same person who torched Ernest's house, stole Tom's forty-five, and was lurking outside our house, also burned down her rental?"

Armstrong said, "Do you think Yolanda knew this guy Osgoode?"

"I'm not sure."

Tom said, "That reminds me. We found a stab mark in Osgoode's back. Where Arch got him with my weeder. And his closet had size-eight shoes. But we haven't found my gun in Osgoode's house."

I said, "You should put pressure on Sean Breckenridge to tell you if Osgoode was the one whose puppies he photographed. If he won't answer your questions? Prick the back of your hand with a sterile needle and show him the blood. He'll faint, but when he comes around, if you threaten to do it again, he'll talk to you." Armstrong shook his head. I rushed on. "You could show Osgoode's picture to Yolanda, see if she recognizes him from anyplace."

Armstrong asked me for Sean's contact information. Then there was silence in the patrol car.

"So, are you going to talk to Arch?" I asked, but faltered, imagining Tom asking my son, *This dead guy? Is he the one you stabbed with a garden tool?*

Armstrong read my mind. "You can be there when we question your son, if we even need to do that."

"Osgoode was shot with a thirty-eight," said Tom, his voice matter-of-fact. "We found three shells near the garage, so whoever killed him was hiding back there. Also, Goldy, we can't be sure, but the shells look like the same ones we found last week—"

"Last week?"

"From the gun that killed Ernest McLeod. In addition to not finding my forty-five, we have not found a thirty-eight," Tom said.

"Are you saying Osgoode didn't kill Ernest McLeod?" I could hear the incredulity in my voice. All along, I'd thought, *The bald guy with the Molotov cocktails, the bald guy outside our house, he's the one who murdered Ernest.*

"I'm not saying he didn't kill Ernest," Tom replied. "I'm only saying the gun he had with him, in his car, is not the one used to shoot Ernest."

I slumped in my seat. I felt tired, cold, wet, and dispirited.

"Do you have your keys, Miss G.?" Tom asked me. I patted my pockets and shook my head no. "Let me take my wife home," Tom said, pulling a set of keys out of his pocket and handing them to Armstrong. "See if your guys can find her key ring in the meadow, and if you can't, use these for her van."

"We have Mrs. Mikulski's set, too," Armstrong said. "You want us to drive her van to her house? I think the ambo took her down to Southwest Hospital."

Tom said, "Yeah, call Hermie's son at CBHS." Tom turned to me. "What's his name, Brad?" I nodded. "Let Brad know what's up. If he has his own car, he can probably pick her up at the hospital when she's discharged. And, hey, Armstrong? Make sure you examine the markers where Hermie and Goldy turned off the main road. Call me if anything else comes up." He patted me on the shoulder. "Okay, Miss G., let's go."

I pulled the blanket close around myself and walked slowly toward Tom's Chrysler. I was dreading the bawling-out I would get from him. But then something caught my eye. In fact, it had been right in front of me all the time.

Osgoode didn't have the silver BMW he'd given Charlene out in the driveway. He'd been packing up a Jeep Grand Cherokee that was so dusty it was hard to tell it was black. In the passenger-side rear window were stickers: a ram, the mascot for Colorado State University; an NRA sticker; and a bumper sticker that read, *You can have my gun if I can have your bullet-proof vest*.

"Wait, Tom, look," I said, pulling on his elbow. "The car. Osgoode's."

"Yeah?"

"It's a black SUV. Just like the one that mowed down Ferdinanda in Denver."

Tom sighed. "Goldy, you're reaching again."

"You could do forensic tests—"

"That's the problem with TV," Tom said. "They make you think we can test for anything. Ferdinanda was hit, what, two, three months ago? This car had to have been washed numerous times since then. And now look at it. I mean, Osgoode lived on a dirt road, for God's sake."

"Please have your guys examine the Jeep carefully, especially the grille. Please? What if Osgoode is the one who mowed down Ferdinanda? Maybe someone wanted to send some other kind of message to Yolanda: *I can hurt your aunt, too.*"

Reluctantly, Tom called over a crime scene tech and asked him to process the Jeep very carefully. The tech, young, thin, and scarred with acne, said, "Don't I always?" Tom thanked him.

When Tom and I reached his car, he opened his trunk. "Once we're out on the road? Take off your wet clothes and put these on." He handed me a set of sheriff's department sweats.

My voice shook when I said, "Thanks."

Tom warmed up the engine, then pulled out of Osgoode's driveway and turned the heat to high. As soon as we were on Upper Cottonwood Creek Road, I peeled off my wet garments and pulled on the dry sweats. They were like heaven. But I was still shivering.

We'd gone about a mile before Tom said, "I need to talk to Lolly."

"Oh, brother."

"Goldy, this is not just a larceny case, in case you hadn't noticed. We now have two bodies. Ernest McLeod worked for the sheriff's department for years. Osgoode, okay, he was a scumbag. But neither one of them deserved to be killed. I have to know every single word Lolly told you about Humberto Captain. Why? Because Norman Juarez's case, with its missing gold, jewels, and necklace, was one that Ernest was working on. In case I have to put it together for you, that makes Humberto a suspect."

I exhaled. "I know he's a suspect. Just let me call Lolly, okay?"

Of course, I knew I'd told Lolly to drug Humberto that afternoon, copy the receipts from his wallet, and then drug herself. Still, I needed to appease Tom, and I did want him to be able to talk to Lolly eventually. So once we were back within cell range, I called Lolly's home number and left a message, saying Tom wanted to talk to her that night.

My stomach growled. With all the commotion, I hadn't noticed missing lunch. Now I did. Still, I needed to put in another call. I wanted to talk to Father Pete. I needed guidance, counseling, prayer, something. And I wasn't the only one.

"This is Saint Luke's," Father Pete answered.

"Father Pete, why aren't you out having lunch?" I asked, apropos of nothing.

"Goldy? The church secretary goes home for lunch. I think I can man the phones for an hour and a half. But . . . you don't sound good. Is everything all right? The veterinarian called to tell me it would be several days before I could have my puppies back. What's going on? How is Yolanda feeling?"

"Fair," I said, "thanks for asking."

"Is she home from the hospital?"

"Yes, she's recovering."

"And the dogs?"

Tom made slashing motions across his throat, so I quickly went on. "I don't know much about the dogs, except that everyone should have their adopted animals back soon. It's actually, I mean, this call is about . . . two parishioners who may need some pastoral care." I waited while he fetched pen·and paper. Apparently Father Pete didn't believe in tech toys, either.

"All right, then," he said, "who are they?"

"I can't really talk about their situations," I said guardedly, "but Hermie Mikulski and Charlene Newgate may need you to visit them. Hermie's fine, just shaken up, and she should be on her way home from the hospital this afternoon. Charlene Newgate has a broken nose. At the moment, she's down at the Furman County Jail."

Father Pete muttered something unintelligible. Then he said, "All right, I'll track them down. Hermie should be easy enough, but I haven't seen Charlene Newgate for years. I'm glad her secretarial service turned into a success. I just wish she'd check in from time to time. That poor woman was in need of pastoral support. People think once they have money, they don't need a *spiritual* safety net, and they do."

"Thanks, Father Pete."

"And you, Goldy? How are you doing?"

I said, "Not good at all, I'm afraid. I was in the mess with Hermie, but I'll let her tell you about it."

"I promise I'll try to reach them. I just have to be back late this afternoon for a counseling appointment. If I don't see the women before then, I'll keep trying. Thank you for alerting me to this, Goldy."

"You're welcome." I signed off with a promise that I would see him soon.

We turned off Main Street and up our street. Tom miraculously found a spot next to the curb. When I jumped out, a wave of fatigue, hunger, *something* rolled over me.

"I'm going to question Yolanda and Ferdinanda, if you don't mind," Tom said in a low voice as we made our way up the ramp that Boyd and Tom had built. It was surprisingly sturdy. "Please don't interfere."

"Question away. I'm ravenous, though. Can it wait until after lunch?"

"Let me get a feel for things here."

Tom opened the door for me. I groaned as the rich, luscious scent of eggs mixed with cream, cheese, and spinach ballooned out of the kitchen and enveloped us. In the hallway, Tom said he would give a limited recap of the morning's events to everybody while I took a shower. I thanked him and mounted the stairs.

From our bedroom windows, I saw a moving van pull into the driveway of Jack's old house. As I watched, a white Maserati pulled in behind the van. I didn't want to be caught looking, so I quickly pulled down the shades.

As the hot water cascaded down my back, my thoughts inevitably returned to the image of the sheriff's department tarp over the body of the person I now knew as Stonewall Osgoode. Why would someone want to murder him? Even eco-terrorists didn't target puppy mill owners. Had there been a dispute over the marijuana garden? Drug dealers had no qualms about killing one another. But why go to all the trouble of luring Hermie and me out there? Had Osgoode's murderer actually thought that silk-and-pearls Hermie Mikulski, with her maimed left hand, her little .22, and her course in shooting, would really kill someone? As Tom had pointed out, no matter what Osgoode had done, he hadn't deserved to die for it.

And the big question, as far as I saw it, was: If indeed the same gun had been used to murder Ernest McLeod, why would someone want both him and Osgoode dead? What was the connection?

My mind spun, a result, no doubt, of the morning's trauma. I toweled myself quickly and put on one of my own sweat suits. I was eager to get down to lunch, to hear what Tom was going to say. He had a remarkable way of providing clarity when all I could see was a jumble.

When I got to the kitchen, however, Boyd, Yolanda, and Ferdinanda were in a jovial mood, talking back and forth about where Yolanda and Ferdinanda were going to live after Ferdinanda got out of her wheelchair. Clearly, they didn't know about Ernest's will yet. Yolanda's burned legs were still bandaged up, and her face registered pain whenever she moved. But she seemed to be enjoying Ferdinanda's suggestions. Make enough money catering to rent an apartment. Live frugally and save up. Buy a little place on Cottonwood Creek. Have enough land to plant a garden to grow yuca. Be able to go out onto a deck and admire a view of snowcapped peaks.

Boyd grinned widely, then winked at me. He knew as well as I did that homes in the valley created by Cottonwood Creek would not have great views unless they were fifty stories high. The *Mountain Journal* had pointed out

that actually, very few houses in town were situated so as
to have a full view of the Continental Divide. And as far
as gardening went? The reason Ernest McLeod had built
a greenhouse was that Aspen Meadow's growing season
was too short for root vegetables. Most gardeners opted
for the perennial-and-rock variety. This was the kind
that Tom had put in our backyard. Still, Boyd and I
weren't about to spoil their planning fun.

Meanwhile, Tom was not joining in the discussion,
much less doing any questioning. He was slicing and
dicing something on a cutting board. Curious, I moved
over and saw garlic and fresh basil falling from his
knife. The scent was deliciously pungent.

"What are you doing?" I whispered.

"Making more of that salad dressing," he said, his
tone nonchalant. He did not look up from his task, which
was probably not a bad idea, considering he was holding
a very sharp knife. "Could you get the mayonnaise out
of the walk-in for me? Please? Also, I need some of your
best-quality olive oil and aged balsamic vinegar. If that's
all right."

"Sure," I said.

I fetched the ingredients while Boyd washed his
hands and set the table for five. Tom turned the blender
motor to its loudest buzz. Thank goodness. Such deafening noise meant I didn't have to mention the moving van
and Maserati across the street, much less my escapade
that had ended with the death of Stonewall Osgoode,
arsonist, gun thief, puppy-mill operator, and drug dealer.

Ferdinanda asked me to bring the quiches and rolls
out of the oven, which I did. As instructed, I put one
quiche on a rack to cool, for us to take to Humberto's

that night. The other one I placed on the kitchen table, next to a crystal bowl of field greens, pine nuts, grape tomatoes, and blue cheese crumbles. Tom had already tossed it with his new salad dressing.

The harrowing events of the morning had not diminished my appetite. Ferdinanda's luscious, cheesy quiche was melt-in-your-mouth fabulous, and Tom's dressing, the same love potion he'd made the night before, was out of this world.

"Need to talk to you all about a few things," Tom said casually when we had finished eating.

"Who's 'you all'?" asked Ferdinanda suspiciously as I got up to clear the dishes. No matter how gently Tom questioned Ferdinanda and Yolanda, I didn't want them to read my facial expressions.

"'You all' are you and your niece," said Tom.

"Espresso, anybody?" I asked. When Yolanda, Boyd, and Ferdinanda all replied in the affirmative, I put the sugar bowl on the table and began pulling shots.

"Goldy got into a bit of a mess this morning," Tom said.

"Oh, my," said Boyd. He grinned and looked my way. "Goldy? In a mess? I can't *believe* it."

Tom's voice was matter-of-fact. "The man who burned down Ernest's house, who is the same man we suspect of stealing my gun from our garage, the man who tried to break in here—all the same man, right? He was killed today. He had a puppy mill." Tom paused for a moment. "He was also running a marijuana grow operation."

Yolanda and Ferdinanda turned stunned faces in my direction. Yolanda said, "What happened?"

"Has either of you ever heard of a man named Stonewall Osgoode?"

They both shook their heads.

Tom pulled out Stonewall Osgoode's driver's license. Neither one of them recognized him. "Not any chance you saw him around Humberto at some point?"

Yolanda and Ferdinanda shook their heads again.

"Don't worry about it," Tom told them. "I'm just trying to cover all the bases." When Yolanda said she needed to take a pain pill, Ferdinanda insisted on wheeling into the dining room with her, and Boyd joined them. Tom's phone buzzed with a text. "I have to go down to the department. Are you going to be all right?" He glanced around the kitchen. "I hate to leave you with this mess."

"I'm fine," I said, but felt unconvinced. "I'll clean up. Are *you* going to be okay?"

"Absolutely."

"Would you approve of my driving Ferdinanda to Humberto's tonight?"

"Absolutely not." He headed toward the hall. "I've been invited. I'm driving you. We'll follow Ferdinanda."

"Wait. Tom? I always thought when you had a fresh homicide you worked it until you got a break."

He turned and gave me the full benefit of his sea-green eyes. "I *will* be working the case tonight, when I talk to Humberto and, separately, to Lolly Vanderpool. And anyway, if you think I'm going to let you go into Humberto's house without me, you are entirely mistaken."

Chapter 21

While Boyd, Ferdinanda, and Yolanda spoke in low murmurs in the dining room, I set about doing the dishes. This is always a caterer's least favorite task. In fact, the one good thing about going to Humberto's house for dinner was that there wouldn't be any cleanup.

Once every dish and pan was clean, an inner anxiety told me I had to cook. I didn't have the time to start on the soup for the Bertrams' party. Ferdinanda wouldn't be in the mood to give me her recipe for the luscious pork we'd had the night before. But I did peer into the walk-in and saw that Ferdinanda had replaced the meat she'd used with sliced grilled pork and pork tenderloin. *Mmm.* I could put together a marinade for an old standby of mine, Snowboarders' Pork Tenderloin. I'd marinate two, one for Boyd and Yolanda to have that night, and one to take to the Bertrams' house the next night, Thursday, when SallyAnn Bertram had said we'd be cooking out to commemorate Ernest's life.

Which reminded me! I put in a call to Penny Woolworth's cell. Once connected to voice mail, I gave the address of the Bertrams' house and told her about the dinner. Could she please clean the Bertrams' place when she finished at Kris's? I'd give her double her usual rate, I promised sweetly, before hanging up.

I gratefully went back to cooking. First I pulled out a pan and mixed together red wine, garlic, Dijon mustard, and herbs for the pork. As I reflected on all that had happened, I whisked in olive oil to make an emulsion. I eased the tenderloins into the silky mixture, turned them over to coat them thoroughly, and covered the whole dish with plastic wrap.

Once I'd placed the meat in the walk-in, I tiptoed up the steps to Arch's room, where I booted up his computer and reopened the file I'd begun. I stared at the questions I'd asked myself back then. The *messy divorce,* I now knew, belonged to the Breckenridges. At this point it didn't look as if Ernest had been following *Brie Quarles,* as I'd originally heard; he'd been following Sean Breckenridge. I changed that, but it seemed minor.

Ernest McLeod had had cancer and had been self-medicating with marijuana. Yolanda had been cooking meals for him before she and Ferdinanda moved in full-time. He'd decided to leave his house to her in his will.

The night before he was shot, he'd brought home nine puppies. The next morning, he'd told Ferdinanda, she of the encroaching deafness, that if anything happened to him, she should ask "the bird." Right. Then he'd left his house on foot for an appointment that had been faked.

He'd sensed—according to the department's theory, which put the time of death at about a half hour to an hour after he left his house—that he was being followed and turned down a little-used service lane. When he'd thought he was in the clear, he'd come out, walked back toward the paved road, and been shot in the chest by someone using the same weapon that had been employed to kill a service-station attendant two years before.

The next night, his house had been burned down by Stonewall Osgoode.

The night after that, Stonewall Osgoode had stolen Tom's gun and tried to break into our house before he was foiled by Arch.

Why would Osgoode steal Tom's gun? I mean, presumably he had his own weapons. Maybe he'd cased the garage, found the hidden compartment with the .45, and then taken it so that we couldn't use it on him when he broke into our place. Or perhaps he'd figured he'd use it to commit some other crime. I had no idea.

Two days after the incident with the weeder, someone had held what was probably the same gun that had killed the gas station attendant and Ernest McLeod, and killed Stonewall Osgoode.

I sighed.

From Lolly Vanderpool, I'd found out about the necklace belonging to Norman Juarez's mother, that Humberto had indeed had it and Ernest had stolen it back. Ernest had called Norman with the exciting news that he'd found something belonging to his family. But he'd been killed before he could give it to Norman. I had no idea who was in possession of the necklace now. But there was a much bigger problem than larceny: the first-degree murder of Ernest McLeod.

I was suddenly glad that Tom was accompanying me to Humberto's. Like Tom, I didn't trust him, no matter how glossy and smooth-talking he appeared.

I also knew what Ernest had been doing for the person Yolanda had known only as Hermie. Hermie Mikulski had been trying to close a puppy mill. I typed that up and added that I suspected I knew *why* Ernest had stolen nine spayed female puppies from Osgoode. Ernest must have come across the smuggling-seeds-in-puppies operation. He'd decided to steal some back. Because their chow was next to Ernest's own medical marijuana, I was convinced that he was trying to send a clue, in case something happened to him and his files.

I sat back in Arch's chair. Had Ernest run afoul of some surveillance equipment out at Stonewall Osgoode's place? Had Stonewall then found Ernest, killed him, and burned down his house to destroy the puppies, the files, and any other evidence that could incriminate him?

If so, then who had killed Stonewall Osgoode?

I blinked at the screen. Back to the larceny. I still hadn't found Norman Juarez's gold and gems, but given what Lolly had told me, I was convinced now that Humberto had indeed stolen them. Problem was, I didn't feel anywhere close to finding a big cache of anything. Tonight, Lolly was going to photocopy—surreptitiously, I certainly hoped—the contents of Humberto's wallet. Finding something usable in there seemed like a long shot.

Would I be able to do some surreptitious questioning of Humberto that night? Or would Tom want to have that honor himself, when he talked to Humberto about Osgoode?

I put these thoughts aside while I stared at the screen. There was Kris Nielsen, still a cipher. According to Yolanda, he had been obsessed with her. And of course, I *had* witnessed his repeatedly calling her out at Gold Gulch Spa. Had it been love, as Penny Woolworth insisted, or had it been stalking? Of course, when I'd been working at the spa, Yolanda had not told me about the venereal disease, the attack with the broom handle, or the strange events at the rental, before it was burned to the ground.

Did the disease, the attack, and the strange events at the rental house really happen? Much as I loved Yolanda, if I couldn't corroborate those facts, then I couldn't verify them. And what about at the ethnic grocery store, when Yolanda had reacted in such an overwrought way when Father Pete had absentmindedly bumped into her? I shook my head.

Humberto had brought champagne to the dinner. Any caterer worth her chef's whites knew you had to put a dish towel over a bottle of sparkling wine before you opened it. This was especially true if the wine—in this case, champagne—had been shaken or in any way disturbed. Had an unknown person sabotaged the metal ring holding pots, pans, and dish towels? I'd found a wrench out in the Breckenridges' grass. If someone knew what they were doing, it would have been easy to loosen the bolt from which the ring had been suspended.

According to Sean Breckenridge, an unknown guest had requested Navajo tacos to be served at the dinner. Making them, Yolanda had been severely burned by boiling oil. Afterward, Kris said she should have been more careful. But was I reading too much into that? Who could have known that Yolanda would be the one making the fry bread? Had I been the target and not Yolanda?

So, really, anyone connected to this case—Sean or Rorry Breckenridge, Kris Nielsen, Brie or Paul Quarles, even Humberto Captain—could have unscrewed the bolts on the frying pan handle and the overhead pot rack.

What had happened to the couple with a family who supposedly bought Jack's house, and wanted to meet me? Had the deal fallen through? Why had Kris bought the house across the street from us? I'd seen him today on Main Street. Harriet had been getting out of his Maserati. I tried to picture that section of the two-lane road that bisected our little town. Why had he been leaving her off there? Had she been withdrawing money from the bank?

I typed up what I knew about Charlene Newgate, who ran a temporary secretarial service in Aspen Meadow. She was an older, unattractive woman with a shrill voice and a resentful, angry personality. Yet she'd snagged a new boyfriend, Stonewall Osgoode, who had showered her with wealth. Was I being cynical in wondering what Stonewall had received from Charlene, in exchange for his attentions? Had Charlene made up the dental appointment for Ernest? It was entirely possible, I reasoned. Then she'd told Stonewall, who had killed Ernest.

I wondered if Tom would be better at getting information out of Charlene than I had been. Even if you wanted to see a lawyer before you said anything, having your nose broken by your boyfriend was a powerful incentive to talk.

My cell startled me out of concentration. It was Arch.

"We're all taking a pizza to Peter's tonight after practice." He was out of breath. "Is that okay?"

I smiled at the reverse order of this announcement. What ever happened to asking for permission, then doing the activity? "Do you have homework?"

"Not much, and I got most of it done in study hall. I can finish it at Peter's. Mom, I gotta go run up and down the stairs. That's what the coach is having us do now to get into shape."

"All right. Have fun at Peter's. Tom, Ferdinanda, and I will be out tonight, but Boyd and Yolanda will be here. Please call them before you pull into the driveway. I want Boyd to make sure you get into the house okay."

"Oh, *Mom.*"

We signed off. I saved what I had written and closed down his computer. I had no idea who had killed Stonewall Osgoode, much less what the motivation had been. But Tom's gun had not been found at Stonewall's house, and we had no idea why Stonewall had been trying to break into our house. Call me overprotective, but I didn't want any member of our family, or any of our boarders, to be going into or out of the house without someone watching over them.

Incredibly, my watch said it was half past three. I still felt shaken by the events of the morning, and my work in the kitchen and typing on Arch's desktop had not alleviated my sense of unease. I had to get dressed for the dinner. But I needed to do something. What? I realized I wanted to visit our church. Hopefully, that would help me feel more in control.

I quickly put on a black dress, flats, and a blazer. Downstairs, Boyd was sitting in the living room tapping out a text.

I said, "Do you know if the sheriff's department has brought my van back?"

By way of answer, he held up my key ring. "Out front."

"Could you walk out with me when I get into it? The morning left me a little freaked."

"I thought you were going out tonight with Tom."

"Not to worry. I'll be back by quarter after five."

Boyd pocketed his cell and accompanied me through our front door. Together we went down Ferdinanda's ramp.

I took a deep breath. During late-September afternoons in Aspen Meadow, insects whisper in the browned stalks of field grass, even when chunks of snow stud the ground. A sudden breeze thrashed the pines, shushing the bugs' chorus. The evening would be cool, verging into downright chilly. But at this moment, as I walked beside Boyd along our damp driveway, the deepening-to-cobalt sky, soft wind, and sinking golden sun made me feel a bit better. But not much.

Boyd helped me into my van. Across the street, the movers had left. The Maserati was not in evidence.

I turned the van around and headed toward Main Street. I had a call to make that I did not want Boyd even to have a chance of hearing. I punched the buttons for Penny Woolworth's cell and left a message on her voice mail. She'd promised to let me into Kris Nielsen's big fancy house while she was cleaning it the next day, I said. Did she remember? I'd also left her a message asking if she would clean up the Bertrams' house. Did she receive the message? I hated to make Penny work so hard, but with her car-thieving husband about to get out of jail, she could surely use the extra cash.

The Saint Luke's parking lot held three cars: Father Pete's old Ford, a black Saab that looked familiar, and a blue Lexus that I also thought I'd seen before—and recently, too. I checked my watch again: a quarter after four. These weren't enough cars for a meeting. Then I remembered that Father Pete had said he had a counseling session late this afternoon.

Well, I was not Marla and I was not about to barge into our rector's office and say, "Who've you got here that needs to talk?" Yes, I needed counseling and comfort, too. But if Father Pete was busy, there was something else I could do.

A vision of the rumpled tarp flung over Stonewall Osgoode's body made my throat close. I walked quickly through the narthex and down the darkened nave, then knelt at the intercession table. After a brief hesitation, I lit two candles: one for Ernest McLeod, who'd done much good in the world.

The other was for Stonewall Osgoode, who probably hadn't.

The sound of voices and the door to the rector's office

closing made my skin chill. I held perfectly still and willed myself to be unseen. I really did not want to chat with any parishioners at the moment. It could be embarrassing to them to be seen leaving a counseling appointment. I breathed slowly, deeply. There was no reason for anyone to look into the darkened church, was there? As the voices and footsteps down the uncarpeted hallway receded, I ducked into the opposite hall, which ran parallel to the nave. The closed doors to the Sunday school rooms made the narrow space dark. But after years of teaching the Bible to kids, I knew my way. I took off my flats and scurried forward in my stocking feet, stopping just before the opening to the narthex.

The heavy wooden church door squeaked as it opened. Father Pete bade a muffled farewell. I listened carefully. Both a man and a woman responded. *Wait a minute.* I knew those voices. Why were the two of them being counseled—*together*? I shook my head. *Hurry up, Father Pete, hurry up,* I commanded silently, and finally the door squealed closed. Once I heard Father Pete shuffling back down the opposite hallway, I raced into the narthex and peeked through the barred window in the wooden door.

Sean Breckenridge was trying to embrace Brie Quarles. She pushed him away. When he tried again to hug her, she shoved him hard. I eased the wooden door slightly open, less than an inch. I prayed that I would not get to the point where the hinge needed oil.

"Leave me alone!" Brie squealed. "You promised me! You lied!"

"Sweetheart, I didn't," Sean pleaded. "I said we

would get married. I just didn't know I wouldn't get any money *at all* from her. I never dreamed she'd stick to that crazy prenup."

"You are a *liar*. When I think of all I've done for you," Brie said bitterly, "it just makes me ill. You said you didn't love her anymore. You said we'd have a wonderful life, that neither of us would have to work, that we would be able to jet all over the world. When I think of everything you said to me, I want to slap you." Brie paused. "I don't want you to call me anymore," she announced loudly. "We're done."

"Brie—"

"Tony Ramos has money!" Brie's tone was cruel. "A national sporting goods company paid him a couple mil for the Pitch Bitch. He told me he's only continuing to teach because he likes to help kids with sports. He hates his wife and can't wait to dump her. Tony's a *real* man who would be able to take care of me. Unlike you."

"Brie, sweetheart," Sean pleaded. "How can you be so cruel? You're a lawyer. I thought you would *want* to work. Please don't go. We're soul mates. We were meant to be together."

"We were never meant to be anything!" Brie shot back. "No, wait. You were meant to be an *accountant,* and good luck with that after all these years of not keeping up with tax law."

"Brie, honey—"

"Watch me, Sean," Brie interrupted. I blinked and kept my eyes trained on her as she fumbled with something on her wrist. "See this antique bracelet you said you bought for me?" she cried. "I know you stole it from her. The initials *RB* are engraved inside the band. That's Rorry Boudreaux, in case you're too stupid to remember your wife's maiden name."

I remembered Rorry cursing when she opened a bureau drawer, looking for something—presumably cash for Yolanda that she perhaps kept with her jewels? Rorry had said, *Oh,* damn *him,* before stalking into the closet, where, I guessed, she kept a safe to which Sean did not have access. While she was searching in the drawer, though, I was willing to bet a batch of cream puffs that she'd discovered Sean had taken the bracelet.

"Watch me, Sean!" Brie shouted, grabbing my attention again. "One of the diamonds came out when I fell running away from that cabin. So now all that's left is a very sharp setting." Brie held her wrist with the bracelet to the top of her opposite arm, then dragged it down to her elbow.

Blood spurted out of the scratch. Sean keeled forward, passing out on the gravel of the church parking lot. Ignoring him, Brie took off the bracelet and dropped it on his back. Then she brushed the blood down her arm and got into the blue Lexus. The tires ground the gravel hard as she accelerated out of the parking lot.

I looked at Sean. He wasn't moving. *Should I call an ambulance, or go get Father Pete and ask if he has any ammonia salts? When he asks what happened, what should I tell him?*

Oh, for crying out loud. God was punishing me for eavesdropping, to put me in such a quandary. I sighed, slipped my feet into my shoes, pushed through the heavy door, and sprinted to Sean's side.

"Sean!" I said. Without ammonia salts, I resorted to shaking his shoulder. When he did not respond, I rolled him over. "Wake up, Sean." I brushed caked gravel off his face and gently slapped his cheeks. When he still made no sign of reviving, I picked up the antique bracelet, put it into his jacket pocket, then lightly smacked his temples. "Wake up or I'll call your wife!"

Finally, Sean blinked. "My— Who are you?"

"Goldy the caterer. You passed out." His eyes lolled from side to side. His face was totally drained of color. Was he okay to drive? Should I call an ambulance? I put my hand on his shoulder. "Sean? I put the bracelet in your pocket. Do you want me to get—"

"Leave me alone." He shoved my hand away. "You and your snooping. You've ruined my life. You and that—" He did not finish the thought.

"I and that *what* ruined your life? Fill in the blank for me, Sean."

"Shut up." Sean propped himself up on one elbow so that he was not facing me. He began to make an odd huffing noise. Oh, Lord, he was crying. He got to his feet, wobbled over to the Saab, started it up, and drove away.

You should have kept your pecker in your pocket, I thought as I raced to my van. When I turned the key in the ignition, Father Pete came lumbering out of the church. He caught sight of me and reared back, his expression one of puzzlement. I merely waved and spun my vehicle in a corona of gravel as I headed toward Main Street. At this point, I really didn't have time to stay and visit.

But on the quick drive home, I did want to *think*. Was Ernest McLeod, the private investigator whom Rorry had hired, the other person who had ruined Sean's life? Okay, Sean couldn't stand the sight of blood. So presumably, he could not have raised a .38 and shot Ernest—not without fearing he'd pass out and be found along with Ernest's body. But Sean could have hired someone to do the job. In fact, he could have paid Stonewall Osgoode, whose beagle puppies he had photographed, to do the job for him.

There was something else that confused me. Brie had said, *When I think of all I've done for you* . . . Apart from sex, what had Brie done for Sean?

Rorry Breckenridge's usual routine was to avoid cooking. But on the day of the church party, Etta was gone, and Rorry had been in and out of the kitchen as much as anyone. Say our saboteur had not been aiming for Yolanda or me, as I had thought. If Rorry had been hit with the ring of pots, or had been burned by the hot oil, then what? Did Sean think he would inherit Rorry's money if she died? Could Brie, a lawyer, have found out the terms of the previous will, which left millions to Sean, and then sabotaged Rorry's kitchen in an attempt to get rid of her?

Could Brie have found out about Ernest's investigation of Sean and killed him? Or perhaps *she* had hired Osgoode?

I had no idea how to find out. The sheriff's department had no murder weapon yet. And the problem with contract killings was that I'd never heard of there being an actual contract, as in, on paper.

I called Boyd. He said Tom would be waiting on the porch for me, gun drawn. *Very funny,* I thought as my van's engine groaned up our street.

Talking on the cell, then seeing Tom, arms crossed, on our front porch reminded me of something else. I had not heard back from Lolly Vanderpool. Oh Lord, I hoped nothing had gone wrong with our plan. Guiltily, belatedly, I realized the whole thing had probably been too dangerous in the first place. Still, Lolly had said she would be at Humberto's dinner party that night. Tom would not be happy to find out that I hadn't made contact with her.

And he wasn't. "Will I see her tonight?" he asked as he opened the front door for me. "Will she be there?"

"Gosh, Tom. Let me at least talk to her before you start berating me about her, okay?" I looked him up and down. He wore khaki pants, a dark brown sweater, and a shirt and tie.

"Doesn't he look handsome?" Ferdinanda crowed as she wheeled herself down the hallway. She had the covered quiche in her lap. "He's been so sweet to me, too. The monsignor says I have to forgive, so I forgave him."

"Only after I apologized profusely for asking you a few questions," Tom reminded her.

Ferdinanda shook a crooked finger at Tom. "You don't fool me for a minute. I've been interrogated by experts. And I've done some questioning myself, if you want to know the truth."

To our great surprise, the doorbell rang.

"I didn't hear anybody come up the steps," Tom muttered. He held his hand out to keep any of us from going closer to the door. When he checked through the peep-hole, he said, "Jesus Christ."

"So the Lord is here?" Ferdinanda asked gaily.

Tom's look was so somber that I shivered. "It's Kris Nielsen and a young woman. Boyd, why don't you come with me? This may look like a social call, but I doubt it is. Yolanda, stay put. Ferdinanda? You too."

Yolanda had her head in her hands. She had looked so happy, so at ease, when Boyd had had his arm around her. Now she looked as if, once again, she were falling apart.

"Hey, neighbor!" Kris called through the door. "I just wanted to say hello."

"Get behind that makeshift curtain," Boyd told Yolanda and Ferdinanda. He tucked his shirt in so that his service revolver was visible. "Tom, let's go."

"I'm coming out with you two," I announced as Kris knocked again. "Two cops and one caterer?" I added to forestall their objections.

Tom's shoulders slumped. "I wish you would not."

I shrugged. "I want to meet our new neighbor, in better circumstances than the last couple of times I've seen him."

"Don't goad him, Goldy," Tom warned.

"Me?" I said innocently. "Never."

Tom opened our front door just wide enough for the three of us to scoot through. When Kris tried to peer around Boyd into the house, Boyd paced forward aggressively, a get-out-of-my-space move. Kris backed up quickly and almost toppled off our porch. Harriet, surprised, merely stepped out of the way.

"I just wanted to talk to you about Harriet!" Kris said. He wore khakis and a long-sleeved orange and black rugby shirt. Harriet, as tall and statuesque as I remembered from the Breckenridges', had on an ill-fitting navy flannel dress and tattered sneakers.

"Let's take this parlay into the street," Boyd said with a smile that did not reach his eyes.

When we reached the middle of the road, Tom and Boyd stopped as if on cue. I halted quickly behind them, with a sudden mental image from *West Side Story:* The Sharks and the Jets were getting ready to rumble. Kris, also taken aback, grabbed Harriet's hand and glanced at our front windows. I shook my head but did not say what I was thinking: *You're not going to make Yolanda jealous, Kris.* It was then that I noticed out-of-place jewelry on Harriet. Despite her tatty clothing, she wore a thin diamond choker and dangling diamond earrings.

"So here we are," Tom said, lifting his chin.

"I was hoping we could—" Kris said, but then stopped and squared his shoulders. "I wanted you to know I'm moving on. Letting bygones be bygones, you know? Life is too short."

"Indeed," Tom murmured. "So I want to warn you very gently not to harass my wife or her friends."

Kris's tone turned steely. "I bought this house"—with his free hand, he gestured at Jack's place—"so Harriet can have a project—"

"Yes," Harriet interrupted energetically, "I'm good with my hands. I work at—"

"And as long as you're issuing warnings," Kris said,

interrupting right back and pulling Harriet closer while glaring at me, "here's one for you, Goldy. Sean Breckenridge is very upset that you snooped around in his business." He gave me a defiant smirk.

"His business?" I asked. "What business would that be?"

Tom cleared his throat and shook his head, one time. I knew better than to speak again. The five of us stood uneasily in the road for a few long moments, until finally Boyd said, "I'm going back in to check on Yolanda. Nice to meet you, Harriet."

Harriet, perhaps cowed by Kris's grip on her hand, merely looked down at the pavement and nodded.

Tom caught my eye and tilted his head toward our house. I sighed and followed Boyd back to our front door, with Tom right behind me.

Despite Boyd's warning to get into their makeshift bedroom, Yolanda was waiting in the hall. Her brown eyes were large and fearful, and when she spoke, her teeth seemed to be chattering. "What did he want?"

While Boyd gathered her in for a hug, Tom said, "To show off some jewelry he got his girlfriend. Goldy? Let's get ready to go to Humberto's."

Ferdinanda insisted on knowing what Kris was "up to now," but Tom merely repeated what he'd said to Yolanda. Ferdinanda spoke under her breath while Tom took the quiche. After a few minutes gathering up keys and whatnot, Ferdinanda rolled herself down the ramp, a skill at which she was becoming quite proficient. Then, over Ferdinanda's protests, Tom helped her into Yolanda's old van. He signaled that we were going in his Chrysler.

"Tom, what are you doing?" I asked. "She won't be able to manage by herself."

"She's fine," Tom said. "She admitted to me that even though she can't walk yet, she did just dandy driving to and from the store. Her weight-lifting exercises, which she has continued with cans from our pantry, make her arms strong enough to lower the wheelchair to the ground, open it, and then get herself into and out of it." He shrugged. "Or at least, so she says."

"Do you believe all she was doing was driving around town?"

Tom's face was inscrutable. "She insists she likes the feeling of freedom that driving gives her. Anyway, even with a GPS system, I don't know if I could find my way to Humberto's house. It's perched way up at the end of a private lane on a mountain circled all round with unmarked roads. So I have to follow Ferdinanda. And I want to talk to you alone."

I said, "Oh, great. About what? Our little parlay with Kris and Harriet?"

"No, that was just BS. But I did put a rush on the evidence from the Breckenridges' house. There were no fingerprints at all on the clamps and bolts that held up that hammered copper ring for the pots. That we could understand, if the house is kept sparkling and is regularly dusted with a cloth. But . . . besides Yolanda's, there were no distinguishable prints at all on the electric skillet. I mean, there was nothing, and *that* is weird. Say someone left the pan there for you or Yolanda to use. They wouldn't wipe their prints off unless they were up to something. And they were definitely up to something, because the screws on the handle were *new*. But they'd been stripped and were loose."

"So someone was trying to hurt her. Or me."

"Someone was trying to hurt *somebody*."

"Sean knew Rorry would be in the kitchen, which she usually wasn't, and he didn't know that Rorry had changed her will. Maybe he was hoping to kill her or scare her."

"It's possible. That's why I suggested she not stay in the house last night." Tom's voice was calm as he sped to catch up with Ferdinanda, who had turned onto a dirt road north of Aspen Meadow.

"Something else," I said. I told him about running into Sean and Brie at the church, and their acrimonious exchange. There had also been Brie's shrill reproach of Sean, left hanging in the air: *When I think of all I've done for you. . . .*

"Brie as Ernest's killer?" Tom's tone was doubtful. "She just sounds like a garden-variety gold digger."

We were still bumping over the gravel. I said, "And what do you make of Kris at this point?"

Tom shook his head. "He probably came over to our place tonight because we questioned him this afternoon about his buying Jack's house. He's very insistent to anyone who will listen that he purchased it solely as a renovation project for his new girlfriend, the lovely Harriet, and not because his ex is currently living across the street."

"Baloney. What more proof do you need that he is stalking Yolanda?"

"A lot more, as it turns out. She didn't report the assault with the broom handle; she just says when he gets angry, he becomes violent. She won't give us the name of the doctor who treated her for venereal disease. Not that that's a prosecutable offense, but don't you think she'd at least give us the doctor's name?"

"Not necessarily."

Tom drew up behind Ferdinanda, who'd stopped ten feet in front of a large iron gate. The entire property was surrounded by a tall fence composed of iron spikes nailed to metal rails at six-inch intervals. Two uniformed men came out of a guardhouse to greet Ferdinanda. Tom put down his window, and we could hear Ferdinanda merrily talking to the men in Spanish. She did not protest when they asked to see her driver's license. After that, they slid open the van's big door to examine the interior.

"There is no way I'm letting them into my trunk," Tom said. "We'll go home first."

"What about the gun? Does the department have any idea who killed the gas station attendant in Fort Collins?" I asked.

"Not yet."

I'd been convinced that Osgoode had killed Ernest, then burned down his house to conceal evidence. Every other person Yolanda had told us about or that we'd learned about—Kris, Hermie, Sean, Brie, Humberto—did every single one of them have an alibi for killing Ernest?

"And you haven't found the gun," I said.

"Again, Miss G., not yet."

"Are you rechecking—"

"Yes. Everyone's alibi for the time we think Ernest was killed."

Ahead of us, Ferdinanda had been let through the gate. Tom pulled up and got out of the car. He'd closed his window so that I wouldn't hear what he was saying to the guards, which I found very annoying. No doubt he was thinking of my habit of butting into conversations, or at least of eavesdropping on them. How bothersome to have a husband who knew you so well.

Tom showed his identification and talked to the guards. He then, apparently, asked for their identification. The guards' swaggering confidence turned to general consternation, a panicked search for wallets, and the handing over of cards. Tom held each ID up to the setting sun—what he was looking for, I knew not. Then he handed them back their cards, pointed to the gates, and made a sweeping motion with his right hand to indicate the spiked fence. The guards nodded seriously, then motioned for Tom to go through. There was no check of Tom's trunk.

"What in the world was that about?" I asked as Tom accelerated through the gates and waved to the guards.

"I told them they had an illegal fence," Tom said mildly. "The county permits them if they're six feet or lower. Humberto's spikes are about ten feet high. I told them I was sure they didn't want to have county officials driving up here tonight with jackhammers to take down a metal fence. Not while Humberto was having dinner guests. And, I added, sometimes county officers bring along representatives from immigration."

"There is no way any county official—" But then I caught Tom's grin. "You are mean."

"I'm not. Every single thing I told them was true." His tone was all innocence. "The fence is illegal. I was sure they didn't want county administrators driving up here tonight. Sometimes immigration officials accompany county bureaucrats. All true." His smile widened. "Most of the time it's damned hard to work for the government. That, on the other hand, was fun." Ahead of us, Ferdinanda began the steep climb of first one switchback, then another, to ascend the hill to Humberto's place.

I said, "Do you have anything else to tell me?"

"Yeah. There was a safe in Osgoode's house. Our guys finally drilled into it and found a hundred thou, give or take, in cash. No papers or files, unfortunately, and there was no checkbook conveniently placed in his desk. But the marijuana out at the grow hadn't been harvested. So what we're wondering is, how did Stonewall make money to bankroll his rental, purchase seeds online, buy dogs to breed, and support Charlene? That's what we're trying to figure out, without Charlene's help."

"Who's her lawyer?" I asked.

"Jason Allred," said Tom. "Aspen Meadow all-purpose attorney."

"Why does that name sound familiar?"

"Goldy, you've probably catered for him. He does lots of business in Aspen Meadow."

Allred, Allred. I asked, "Wasn't he the one who drew up Ernest McLeod's will, that left everything to Yolanda?"

Tom steered carefully around a hairpin turn. "Yeah, as a matter of fact. Why?"

"I'm just trying to connect the dots," I said as we drew into a paved oval where an old Toyota was parked next to a red VW bug. The VW had a window sticker that read, *Massachusetts Institute of Technology:* Lolly's.

Maybe Tom did need to call the county zoning officials. Why? Because if there was a law against out-of-style residences, Humberto's huge white Caribbean-style mansion would get the first citation. My mouth actually dropped open. The previous year, I'd seen two photos of the house in the *Mountain Journal,* and they had both been taken inside. How could anyone have a *white* stucco house in the mountains? The dust all summer, and snow all winter, would make it impossible to keep clean. *Oh, well,* I thought as Tom parked his car next to Ferdinanda's van. At least I didn't have to clean the place.

Tom hurried around to Ferdinanda's side, where the irrepressible older woman was already settling herself in her wheelchair. Tom pushed her up to the front door. I brought the quiche.

A silent, uniformed maid greeted us with a nod, took the foil-wrapped pie, and ushered us into the living room. It was the size of a small gym, but with a red tile floor. White marble fireplaces stood guard at each end. A bank of floor-to-ceiling windows filled the opposite wall. The western view featured a sweeping vista of the Continental Divide, where snowcapped peaks were tinted pink by the setting sun.

Tom said, "Wow. No wonder he bought this piece of land."

The smell of paint made my nostrils itch and my eyes tear up. I didn't know what kind of redecorating Humberto had done, because care had been taken to make everything look old. Gilt-framed oil paintings of hunters carrying dead game hung above the fireplaces. Armchairs on either side of the hearths were upholstered in tapestry prints featuring hunting dogs carrying dead birds in their mouths. Several couches set between mahogany tables were upholstered in dark leather. The walls were tan. Instead of crown molding, woodworked arches surrounded the room. Overhead, aged timber beams—like the arches, these performed no actual support function—gave a hacienda feel to the place, as did wrought-iron wagon-wheel light fixtures. The whole place was laughably over the top. Still, I was sure Norman Juarez wouldn't have found it funny.

"Hello, hello!" trilled Lolly as she rounded a corner teetering on silver stilettos. She wore a silver tube-type dress; her black and blue hair had disappeared under another platinum, wig. The hairpiece was on slightly crooked, I noticed with dismay. "Remember me? I'm Odette. I'm Humberto's, uh, date," she told Ferdinanda as she shook the older woman's hand. Lolly then cast her eyes downward as she shook hands with Tom, who looked at her suspiciously. Lolly quivered as she came forward to hug me.

"Can you show me the bathroom, please?" I asked, a bit too loudly. Again Tom's hawk's eyes missed nothing.

"Too heavy on the T," Lolly whispered as she led me down a hallway featuring more hunting pictures. "Photocopy is in bottom of tissue box in bathroom. Maid'll be in kitchen through dinner. New surveillance everywhere. Watch out."

"Tom wants to talk to you."

Her shoulders sagged. But after a few more teetering steps, she whispered, "All right, but you'll have to get rid of Humberto first."

"Your wig's on crooked," I whispered back.

She cursed and said she would fix it.

As surreptitiously as possible, I checked the white-tiled bathroom for a surveillance camera. A tiny red light, glimmering high up in the corner opposite the toilet, made me feel distinctly violated. I fake-sneezed once, then again, turned my back to the camera, and leaned over the sink. My fingers trembled as I dug down into the white tile tissue box beside the faucet. I pulled out several tissues along with Lolly's piece of paper. I sneezed once again for good measure, honked into the tissue, then slipped the folded paper and the tissues into my pocket.

When I returned to the living room, Humberto was making his entrance. His salt-and-pepper hair was swept back, as usual. He was impeccably dressed in a tan-colored suit, white shirt, and red tie. But his eyes were heavily lidded and he truly did look as if he'd just awakened from a too-deep nap. Too heavy on the temazepam, indeed.

"What may I prepare for you to drink?" he asked, bowing toward Ferdinanda and me. "Oh dear, and how is Yolanda? I should have asked after her welfare first."

"She is fine." Ferdinanda took hold of Humberto's proffered hand and tugged down on it. Humberto, who was having a bit of trouble maintaining his balance anyway, cascaded forward, nearly losing it altogether. Undaunted, Ferdinanda pulled on Humberto's hand again.

Only Humberto's grasp of a nearby table kept him from going ass-over-teakettle. "Yolanda is strong," Ferdinanda said menacingly. "Like me."

"Yes, Ferdinanda," said Humberto. He groaned as she maintained her iron grip on him. "I know you are both proud"—here he moaned—"uh, Cuban-American—ack—ah, women."

"Yes," said Ferdinanda, "we are. Last night, did your *puta* loosen the bolts on the electric skillet?"

"I, uh, agh! You're killing me! And I don't know what you're talking about."

"Don't hurt Yolanda, or you'll have me to answer to," said Ferdinanda, with her death-steel grip still on Humberto.

Humberto gasped with pain. "I, I wouldn't dream of it."

"Good." Ferdinanda let go of Humberto's hand so swiftly that he had to grab the back of one of the hunting-dog chairs to keep from falling into the fireplace. "As long as we understand each other."

"This is interesting," Tom said to me in a low voice. "I wouldn't want to tussle with Ferdinanda in a dark alley, wheelchair or no wheelchair."

I said, "Nor would I."

The silent maid came and bustled about pouring drinks. Ferdinanda asked for a Cuba libre. Humberto shook the hand that Ferdinanda had been squeezing to restore feeling in it. He said that he, too, would like a Cuba libre. Lolly said she would give booze a pass, thanks, and just have water. Tom and I opted for white wine. The maid filled the drink orders, then came through with appetizers on individual plates with tiny forks: hot Cuban sandwiches cut into tiny triangles, a myriad of olives on toothpicks, and squares of the heated spinach quiche. It was all delicious, and I made another mental note to ask Ferdinanda for her quiche recipe.

Ferdinanda and Humberto began to discuss Cuban politics, with Humberto blaming President Kennedy for Castro's getting a stranglehold on Cuba, and Ferdinanda blaming Castro for putting on the stranglehold in the first place. Lolly remained silent while Tom and I tried to make polite but nonpolitical comments. As the discussion turned into a heated argument between Humberto and Ferdinanda over whether any ruler should be allowed to suspend freedom of speech or the press, or restrict dissent in any form, I feared our dinner was in jeopardy. Ferdinanda had more examples at her disposal, while Humberto, full of bluster but intellectually lazy, seemed to become more and more frustrated by Ferdinanda's interrupting him. If push came to actual shove, I didn't doubt Ferdinanda's ability to arm-wrestle Humberto to the floor.

"Humberto!" I shrieked as I jumped up, startling everybody. "Tell me about your view here!" I walked over to the windows. "I remember seeing this in the newspaper. How did you find such a magnificent piece of property?"

Humberto, his face flushed, gave Ferdinanda a final fierce look, then attempted to smooth his expression. "Ah, thank you for asking. I looked a long time for this land. The whole thing was very expensive."

"I'm sure it was," I said, smiling. "Can you tell me which mountain is which?"

Of course I knew which peak was Mount Evans, which was Longs Peak up north, and how on a clear evening, which this was, Pikes Peak was visible way down south. Humberto, who seemed not to have memorized his mountains, gave me a confused look, so I said, "I know you're acquainted with my friend Marla. Did you know one of her puppies was very ill?"

Humberto rubbed his orangey-tan forehead. "I didn't know she had puppies."

"Yes!" I exclaimed, and Humberto jumped. "She got them from . . . a friend of a friend. But it looks as if the puppies came from a mill. Run by a guy named Osgoode? Does this ring any bells?"

Humberto frowned at me and seemed to welcome the maid ringing an actual bell, the one announcing dinner. *Dang!*

On the way into the dining room, which also faced the Continental Divide, I whispered to Tom, "You need to get Humberto out of here so we can talk to Lolly. Have your people interrogated him about Osgoode?"

"Yes, Miss G.," he said. He gave me a sideways smile. "Like you, they came up empty. But don't worry, I can get rid of Humberto." Tom excused himself to make a cell phone call, outside.

The dining room also smelled of paint. Like the living room, the floor was paved with red tile. Stone floors are hell on a caterer's back, and I was glad not to be cooking and serving, although I did feel sorry for the maid. When Tom returned, my heart warmed when he pulled one of the leather-tooled chairs from the long trestle table to make way for Ferdinanda's wheelchair. She loudly thanked him while glaring at Humberto.

Humberto proudly dimmed the lights on the chandelier, which he said he'd found in Paris on one of his travels. Like the ones in the living room, it was a ring of wrought iron topped with candle-shaped bulbs, but this one was at least more delicate than the wagon wheels. The dimmed lights gave the place a romantic feel. Lolly kissed Humberto's cheek and said everything looked fabulous, and wasn't he a smart fellow to find such beautiful decorations? He preened under her admiration.

The maid brought out a heavenly scented roast chicken surrounded with potatoes, carrots, yuca, and fried plantains. We talked and ate for twenty minutes without a single political comment from anyone, for which I was thankful.

We were halfway through luscious, creamy flans when Tom's cell rang. He apologized to the group, went into the hall, then came back looking rueful.

"Humberto," he said, "I'm sorry, but it looks as if there's a team here to take you to the department for more questioning."

"But we haven't finished our dinner!" Humberto sputtered.

Tom shook his head. "I know, I tried to put them off, but they've got three cars down at your gates, and it's the district attorney himself who ordered the interrogation. Some new evidence has come to light. And if *you* don't go with them, they're going to arrest your guards as material witnesses. We do have several interrogators who are Mexican-American, and they speak perfect Spanish. So unless you're willing to hire individual lawyers for your guards at this late hour, then I'm afraid—"

"No, no," barked Humberto. He waved his hands. "I will go. But I'm sorry, the rest of you will have to leave."

"Leave?" said Ferdinanda, her mouth full of custard. She swallowed. "Now?"

"Yes, I am sorry," Humberto said, his voice full of fury. "I cannot leave my house unguarded."

"Are you saying you don't trust us?" Ferdinanda demanded. "What have you got in here that's so valuable you can't allow your guests to finish their dinner?"

Humberto snarled something unintelligible. "Even the maid will have to go. Everyone must leave."

Lolly did not look at us. Instead, she pushed back her chair and mumbled that she would go get her things.

Ten minutes later, Tom had helped Ferdinanda into her van, Lolly had loaded her overnight bag into her VW, and Tom and I were seated in his car. The maid came bustling out, furious, and slid into her Toyota, cursing at Humberto the whole time. He ignored her, opened his garage door with a remote, and drove out behind us in a silver Mercedes.

We made an odd procession snaking down the hill. The maid's old Toyota belched exhaust. Ferdinanda fearlessly heaved the listing, rusted van from one side of the driveway to the other. Lolly followed cautiously in her lollipop-red VW, while Tom smoothly navigated his Chrysler and Humberto tailgated us in his ultraslick sedan. As we rounded the last turn, the commotion was apparent. Outside the illegal fence, three police cars, their lights flashing in the early dark, looked truly ominous.

"What did you have to do to get them here?" I asked Tom.

"Not much." He gave me another of his Cheshire-cat grins.

"But you said Humberto had to be interrogated because there was a new piece of evidence."

"No," Tom patiently replied, "I said he had to be questioned. I also said there was new evidence, which there is. I didn't say the two were linked."

"You are a dog that is sly, Tom."

The photocopied sheet was burning a hole in my pocket. Still, I thought it would look too suspicious to the guards if I turned on the interior light to read the sheet, which might, after all, contain nothing. I needn't have worried. At the bottom of the hill, the guards all looked as if the police presence was making them wish they could disappear.

Chapter 22

Outside the gates, Lolly swerved left behind Ferdinanda. But where Ferdinanda continued on Aspen Meadow Parkway to get to Main Street, Lolly turned on the road that would lead to her apartment building. I used the cell to phone Boyd, asking him to walk out when Ferdinanda arrived. I said we'd be along shortly and that he should tell her something that would sound plausible, like that we'd gone for ice cream since we hadn't finished dessert.

He chuckled and said it was no problem.

In her apartment parking lot, Lolly got out of her VW and came over to our car, where she climbed in the back. She'd taken off her wig.

"Nice do," said Tom, looking at her in the rearview mirror. "I've always wondered what it would be like to have black and blue hair."

"I could dye it for you," she replied, slamming the door.

"No, thanks." Tom killed the engine and turned

around to face Lolly. "Okay, Lolly, I want to hear it from the beginning."

"I don't want to be prosecuted for prostitution."

"Who said anything about prostitution?" asked Tom innocently. "That's not my department. Homicide is. So, tell me your story."

Lolly obliged. She gave a quick summary of the DUI, her parents, Julian's loan, her signing up with an escort agency, her liaison with Humberto, and wearing the necklace to a charity shindig. It wasn't until she got to the bit about Father Pete telling her to do good, and her helping Ernest, that her voice faltered.

"I got him killed," she said guiltily. "That damn Humberto."

There was silence in the car.

"No, you did not get Ernest McLeod murdered," Tom said firmly. "You helped him with a client's needs. That's all you did. So, you have no idea where the necklace is now?"

"Nope."

"Is there anything else you want to share?"

Lolly told him about Humberto being furious that the necklace had been stolen, his suspicion of her, his guards tearing apart her parents' house and Lolly's apartment, and the subsequent cash payments. Then her eyes strayed to my face in the rearview mirror. I looked straight back with as blank an expression as I could muster.

We were thinking the same thing. It was one thing for Ernest to ask Lolly to do unlawful acts, which she was now confessing. It was quite another thing for the wife of a police investigator to ask her to drug her mark, do an illegal search, and photocopy receipts in the mark's wallet. She knew she shouldn't mention what she'd done today unless I told her to.

I didn't. I figured, if I found something out from the wallet receipts, great. I'd tell Tom without mentioning my source. If I didn't discover new evidence, well, then, no harm, no foul, and I would avoid being soundly scolded.

"Anything else you want to tell me?" Tom asked, his voice nonchalant.

"How's this? Humberto still suspects me of something," she lied smoothly. "I don't know what. Earlier, I told Goldy that he'd redecorated, repainted, the works, after the break-in. He also installed security cameras, including in the bathrooms. I mean, that's illegal, isn't it?"

Tom sighed. "No, I'm sorry to say. It isn't against the law to spy on people in your own home. But it should be. Still, I want you to be extra careful. Humberto may be responsible for the murders of two, or possibly three, men. He may have killed them, or he could have had them killed. Has he ever mentioned anything to you about being in Fort Collins? One of the murders is of a gas station attendant up there."

Lolly shook her head. "He doesn't tell me that much about his life, except stuff that isn't true."

Tom shook his head. "Still, I'd feel better if you dropped out of sight for a few days."

"No can do," said Lolly, shaking the black and blue hair. "Humberto knows where my parents live, and even though I'm not on speaking terms with them, I don't want Humberto coming after them. Don't worry, I know how to handle Humberto."

Tom thought about this for a moment. "All right. I just want you to call me if you find out anything, or if you think you're in danger."

"Oh-*kay*." She sounded like Arch.

Tom grinned. "Is there anything else you can tell me that might be pertinent?"

"Your computer guy? Kris? He's a fraud."

I said, "You weren't too nice to him on that USB port thing."

"Nice?" said Lolly, her blue eyes wide. "Who cares about nice? A real data-processing geek would have known, in answer to my question, that I needed to buy a USB hub. That guy's a liar. I don't know how he made his money, but it wasn't starting a computer business in Silicon Valley, or any other valley, for that matter. He's from Minnesota. He knows something about chemistry, because he tried to jump in with an answer to the medical isotope question. But you could know that from high school, unless you're Donna Lamar. Still, I'll bet Kris built up his fortune selling farm equipment. It's just not as sexy as a Silicon Valley start-up."

"Lolly?" asked Tom. "You want to apply to work at the sheriff's department? I'm not kidding, we need a mind like yours."

"I'm flattered," said Lolly. "But I'm sure I make more money turning tricks. See you cats later." She got out of the car.

"Be careful, Lolly," said Tom.

"No worries."

When we got home, the streetlights indicated something different about our house.

"What the hell is that?" asked Tom. We both stared at one of the pine trees in our front yard.

A carved wooden mask was nailed to the trunk. Tom shook his head as he pounded ahead of me up the new wheelchair ramp.

"Hey, guys!" said Arch when we came through the door. He was sitting in the living room with Yolanda, Boyd, and a very smug-looking Ferdinanda. "Did you see the cool Santería mask that Ferdinanda made? I helped her nail it to the tree out front."

"What does it mean?" Tom asked coolly.

Arch's face dropped at Tom's tone. Yolanda looked at her hands, while Boyd, clearly in mental discomfort, straightened his shoulders. Ferdinanda lifted her chin.

"Tom!" Ferdinanda said. "You let me worry about what it means."

"It's our front yard," Tom replied evenly.

Ferdinanda sighed. "It's to ward off evil spirits."

"I thought that's why we all went to church," Tom replied.

"This is extra," Ferdinanda said.

"What is the significance of that mask?" asked Tom.

"The exact significance?" said Ferdinanda. "After all these years, I forgot. You know what? I'm tired." She yawned, stretched her arms over her head, and turned the wheels of her chair toward the dining room. "I'm going to bed." Then she stopped. "Hey! Where's the ice cream you were out buying?"

"I forgot," said Tom, before starting up the stairs. I bade everyone good night, then gave Arch a stern enough look that he nodded. Time for him to go to bed, too.

In our bathroom, I pulled out Lolly's photocopy. With Tom's mood turning foul after hearing about Lolly's dealings and seeing a Santería mask in our front yard, he probably wasn't ready yet to hear about Lolly doing an illegal search of Humberto's wallet.

Humberto Captain had kept several receipts, only one of which interested me: Aspen Meadow Printers, High Country Dry Cleaners, Frank's Fix-It, and Excalibur Safes.

Excalibur was delivering its premier model, the Deerslayer, on Friday. *Room for numerous guns and pistols,* the receipt said, *with anchor holes for bolting to the floor, an electronic/mechanical lock, and two-hour resistance to fire.* The Deerslayer was touted as their *best model for storing papers and valuables.*

Yeah, I thought. *I just bet.*

Say Humberto had figured out that Ernest had stolen the necklace, and either killed him or had him killed. He had put the .38, the gold, and the gems somewhere, until the safe could be installed. But Ernest had insisted that Humberto did not have a safety deposit box, and Lolly had searched the house. If Humberto had put the weapon and valuables into one of Donna's houses, I would be sunk. Yet Lolly had not said Humberto kept keys with him all the time. He kept his *wallet* with him. And the wallet had yielded these receipts.

Without a warrant, there was no way Tom or I or anyone could get access to a fancy safe after Friday. But I could visit the three local places the next day. Perhaps one of the receipts would lead to something.

I stuffed the paper back in my pocket and took a quick shower. Once in bed, I felt guilty about Lolly, about the photocopy, about things in general. I loved my husband. When he slid between the sheets beside me, his warm presence made me feel, more than ever, that I wanted him to be happy.

Well, I knew what that meant, didn't I?

I felt a quirk of emotional discomfort. Was I ready for this? Were we?

Was anyone ever ready to bring another being into the world? Probably not. But I realized suddenly, *Yes, I want this, too.*

I said, "Why don't I forget the protection tonight?"

He pulled me in for a warm hug. "Are you sure? You think it would be okay if our family got bigger? Should we talk to Arch?"

"If we do, it'll get his hopes up. He's always wanted a sibling. Better just to keep it to ourselves, I think, until we know something."

"Miss G., are you sure?"

Unexpected tears slid down my face. "Yes."

When the alarm went off at seven, I woke up, startled. Had I been dreaming, or had something occurred to me? Something had been wrong about Humberto's house. What was it? But the dream, or memory, was as elusive as sunlight flashing across the surface of Aspen Meadow Lake. I hopped out of bed and almost fell down. Exhaustive lovemaking had led to extremely sore muscles.

"Good God," said Tom, as he rolled over to bop the ringer on the clock. "I can't move."

"Me either. But we have to."

"How about a shower together?"

Well, I knew what *that* meant, and after twenty minutes of having sex in a hot shower, my muscles were screaming at me. But I felt great, and I moved through a slow yoga routine that eased the physical pain a bit.

In the kitchen, Ferdinanda said, "I already fed Arch. He left because he is meeting someone to review for a math test." She appraised me with a lifted eyebrow. "You made some racket last night."

"We didn't," I protested. In fact, we'd made a special attempt to be quiet.

"Yeah," she said as she rolled over to the espresso machine, "you didn't. But I could tell by that stupid happy look on your face that you made some kind of something."

My cheeks grew hot. Instead of responding, I bustled about feeding Jake the bloodhound and Scout the cat. Both animals were acting neglected. Jake had his own way of showing this: He came up close and gave me a long, mournful gaze. I patted him, whereupon he threw himself onto the kitchen floor to have his tummy rubbed. Scout, on the other hand, trotted away after eating, without so much as a backward glance. This feline behavior meant that only after he had gotten over his sulk would he twine around my legs and purr.

I let Jake outside. Ferdinanda chuckled and offered me espresso mixed with cream and ice. My face heated up again. Why should I feel embarrassed for making love to my own husband in our own house?

Boyd came into the kitchen. Maybe I was being paranoid, but it seemed as if he, too, was evaluating my expression. He smiled furtively but said nothing. There would be hell to pay from his boss if he so much as said a word about our personal life.

"Yolanda's going to help you with the soup today," Ferdinanda told me briskly. "I'm going to chop the mushrooms. You got chicken stock in your freezer?"

"Yup," I said, and moved with relief to the walk-in. Yolanda called to Boyd, asking for help making up the cots. He disappeared.

"I made you toasted pork sandwiches for breakfast," said Ferdinanda when Tom appeared in the kitchen, dressed for work. "Sit down and eat. You're going to need strength after that night you had with Goldy!"

Tom's questioning expression made me shake my head. Ferdinanda removed a cookie sheet from the oven and slapped it onto the table. English muffin sandwiches lay in neat rows, with sliced grilled pork steaming around the edges and melting cheese oozing onto the pan. Ferdinanda pulled a spatula out from beside her thighs in the wheelchair—one of these days, I expected her to retrieve a full-grown alligator from the wheelchair's depths—and began levering sandwiches onto our plates.

Boyd came back out and said Yolanda needed Ferdinanda to help her change her bandages.

"I'm going," said Ferdinanda, wheeling away. "You three eat, or I'm going to be angry."

Tom's cell rang as he was eating his sandwich. He said, "Schulz," then listened. When he hung up, he told Boyd and me, "Stonewall Osgoode was an army ranger who got a dishonorable discharge for dealing drugs. Then he went to veterinary school at Colorado State but was kicked out of *there* for dealing drugs. This is what we call self-destructive behavior."

"Colorado State?" I asked. "In Fort Collins, where the murder of the gas station attendant happened?"

Tom nodded. "That gas station attendant was a grad student in chemistry. Stonewall Osgoode probably had nothing to do with that, since he was definitely in his room when the kid was killed at the gas station. They found Osgoode's roommate, who's now a full-fledged vet, Dr. Hopengarten. Dr. H. had had the flu and remembers pulling an all-nighter that night, December twenty-third, because he had to turn in a paper on Christmas Eve, the twenty-fourth, or risk flunking a class. The two of them only had enough money for a studio apartment. Stonewall was there, asleep in the same room, so Dr. H. knows Osgoode never left." Tom ate his last bite of sandwich, then said, "Oh, and get this. Dr. H. suspected that Osgoode was dealing drugs to support himself in school. Dr. H. is also pretty sure Osgoode had a partner. Whenever the phone rang and it was for Osgoode, it was always the guy on the line."

Boyd put down his sandwich. "Did Dr. H. see this partner?"

"Nope," said Tom, discouraged. "And he has no idea who it was. But when Dr. H came back from turning in his paper, it was all over the news that shortly after midnight, this kid had been shot and killed at a local gas station. What Dr. H. particularly remembers, though, is that Osgoode went somewhere late that morning and came back in a foul mood. He said he was going to have to find a job to support himself, because he'd just lost the one he had. Dr. H. said, 'What job was that?' but Osgoode said, 'Some people have no guts at all,' then clammed up. The next week, the Fort Collins police pounded on their door and arrested Osgoode for dealing drugs."

"Somebody turned him in?" Boyd asked.

Tom said, "Yeah. Our guys got good information from the Fort Collins authorities. An anonymous informant called them and gave the names of people Osgoode had sold drugs to. The cops pulled in the users, and they all immediately confessed that Osgoode was their supplier."

I said, "Please tell me Osgoode gave up the name of his partner."

"Nope. But Osgoode wasn't as broke as he made out to Dr. Hopengarten, because somebody paid all his legal bills and court costs."

"Who?" Boyd and I asked in unison.

Tom shook his head. "Don't know, and whoever it was didn't visit Osgoode in jail, either. Only the lawyer came, and he was a high-priced criminal defense attorney who managed to wangle a plea deal. Osgoode got a ten-year prison sentence, suspended, and only spent eighteen months in jail. Apparently the DA figured all those drug users wouldn't make very good witnesses."

I shook my head. Tom stood, cleared our dishes, and said, "I need to get down to the department."

After he left, Boyd and I finished cleaning the kitchen. When he went into the living room to watch the news, I quietly pulled Lolly's photocopy out of my pocket. Ferdinanda and Yolanda were talking in low tones in the dining room, so I crept down to the basement and loaded pink and yellow photocopy paper into our printer, slipped in Lolly's paper, and let 'er rip.

Inspecting the result, I didn't know if they'd fool anybody. But as I scissored away to make the copies look like actual receipts, I resolved that I was certainly going to try.

As I walked back up the stairs with the fake receipts in my pocket, the memory that had disturbed me early that morning resurfaced. The part of Humberto's house that had been weird was an aspect of the décor.

Lolly had told me Humberto had redecorated the house at a fast clip. It had begun the day after Ernest broke in and stole the necklace. Why redecorate *then*? Okay, he wanted to put in surveillance cameras, but you could do that without painters and a whole bunch of new furniture.

That elusive memory was still flashing, but it was out of reach. I decided to make my first stop the Aspen Meadow Library.

I put four frozen homemade coffee cakes into my canvas bag. Food bribes usually worked if someone balked at helping me, and I couldn't let that happen. Then I asked Boyd if he would accompany me to my van. When we were walking down the ramp, he asked me where I was going.

Surprised, I said, "Just running a few errands." He lifted his eyebrows questioningly, but there was no way I was going to tell him what I was really up to.

In the van, I glanced across the street to see if Kris or

Harriet was anywhere around. Neither was. I realized I
didn't even know what kind of car Harriet drove. Would
Tom be able to find that out, if I didn't know her last
name? Or would he say if I continued to try to snoop
into Harriet's life, *I'd* be stalking *her*?

Ten minutes later, I breezed through the library doors
and headed right to the reference desk. I didn't know the
new reference librarian, a young, slender woman who
wore a khaki pantsuit and had black hair with red
streaks. Didn't anybody lucky enough to have black hair
just wear it au naturel these days? I guessed not.

I offered her a coffee cake for the librarians' break
room, and she gratefully accepted. Then I asked my
question, and she brightened. She said she loved a challenge, and I had the distinct feeling that she would have
helped me out, food bribe or no.

She moved with alacrity to the website archives of the
Mountain Journal. I certainly did not know how to
search for the articles I needed, the ones that asked,
"Can you guess whose view this is?" The following
week, the answer was given, complete with a picture of
the home's owner.

Miss Black and Red Hair found the answer by swiftly
pressing buttons, and soon I was looking at Humberto
Captain's view, which the librarian had put next to a
photo of Humberto proudly pointing to the vista. In fact,
I was interested in neither of these views. What did capture my attention was that memory that had been wrig-
gling out of reach. Above Humberto's head, there was
not a light fixture in the shape of a wagon wheel. There
was something else entirely.

I thanked the librarian and revved my van in the direction of Frank's Fix-It Shop, which I thought was the most likely of my receipts to turn up what I wanted.

Frank's Fix-It, next to Aspen Meadow Bank, looked as run-down as the bank appeared modern and immaculate. I made a U-turn, parked directly in front of the shop, then banged on the door until a heavy young man wearing torn jeans and a scruffy sweatshirt opened up. The scent of marijuana wafted out around him.

"We're closed," he said, looking at his wrist that was without a watch. He blinked and slowly turned his head to squint at the bank's clock, which indicated it was half past ten.

"Your advertisement says you open at ten," I lied smoothly. The guy looked around for a sign with his hours, but in fact he didn't have that, either. I figured it was better to play on his sympathies than to piss him off. And wait: If he'd been smoking grass, shouldn't he have the munchies wicked bad? I pulled another coffee cake out of my big canvas bag. "Would you like to eat a homemade coffee cake?"

The fellow eyed the cake greedily. "Well—"

"Here." I handed him the cake in its zippered bag. "And, please, please can you help me?" I pulled the pink receipt out of the bag and thrust it under his nose. "My boss says I have to get this today, as early as possible. If I don't, I'll lose my job."

Now the stoner stared at the receipt, his mouth hanging open. Drool trailed from his lower lip as he clutched the coffee cake to his chest. After a few long moments, he said, "We have this?"

"Please help me," I begged. "It's your receipt."

"Awright." He pushed the door halfway open and lumbered into the darkness of the store. I quickly stepped through and followed him.

The place positively reeked of weed. The wooden floor was worn through to concrete in a number of places, and Frank, or his son, or someone, had sprinkled sawdust on top. The counters were so dusty it was hard to tell if the glass cases actually held anything. But when the guy rounded the corner and ducked behind a curtain, I followed him there, too.

The fluorescent light he turned on did not help. He put the coffee cake on a cluttered table and again gaped at the fake receipt. With more clarity than he had mustered so far, he said, "I have no idea where in hell this is. Or even *what* it is."

"Oh, *I* know," I said cheerfully. "Why don't I find it?"

"I can't leave you here with the stuff," he said dully. "We'll lose our insurance if I do."

I almost choked at the idea of them even having insurance. "I won't break anything."

"Doesn't matter," he said stubbornly.

We seemed to be at an impasse. But a torn red plastic chair offered a solution to our problem. I said, "Why don't you sit down while I hunt? Then you can eat the cake and keep an eye on me at the same time."

"Well, I do got the munchies."

"Go for it. But may I have the receipt back, please?"

"Awright." He handed it to me, then made his way to the chair. He sat down heavily, opened the bag, and broke off a hunk of cake. Well, I didn't mind if he dispensed with the whole utensil thing. I just didn't want to watch.

I surveyed the vast, untidy storage room. Shelves at odd angles were filled to bursting with dusty articles. *Damn it,* I thought, *why can't anything be easy?*

Half an hour later, I realized I was hungry, too. All I had found in searching through the first two-thirds of the shelves was an assortment of toasters with frayed cords, pots missing handles, clocks without hands, and broken, functionless tchotchkes.

The stoner had finished half the cake, and now he was openly smoking a joint.

Well, great. This was another one of those situations where the fact that I was married to a sheriff's department investigator did not look so hot. I was unlawfully searching for something that I was pretty sure was valuable but that did not belong to me. Meanwhile, the man entrusted with the care of said article was huffing away on an illegal drug. If a reporter from the *Mountain Journal* came in, I'd be, as they say, screwed.

On the last set of shelves, my hands closed on a large, dirty plastic bag. Inside was what looked and felt like a bunch of dirty rocks. But the receipt number, oh, the blessed receipt number, was the same as the pink one in my hand. And the rocks, I suspected, had been carefully coated with mud, in order to hide what they really were.

"Got it!" I yelled. But the stoner had slipped sideways on the chair and appeared to be asleep.

I tiptoed past him with the bag going *clunkedy-clunk.* He seemed not to notice. I wrapped up the remains of the cake and stuffed it into my catering bag. I didn't

want to leave any trace of myself. Then I picked up both
bags and walked out the door, gently closed it behind
me, and heaved the bags into the back of my van.

Unfortunately, I caught a glimpse of Kris Nielsen's
Maserati in my rearview mirror. He was driving very
slowly up Main Street. I debated whether to stay in my
parking space or take off. Had he been watching me all
along? I put on my blinker and pulled out. I drove slowly
so as to make out what Kris was doing. He maneuvered
the Maserati into my empty space. Had he seen me? I
still wasn't sure.

Lovely, tall Harriet-the-model-with-odd-jobs got out
of Kris's car. She said a few words to Kris, then walked
into Frank's Fix-It. *Hmm.*

Ahead of me, the streetlight turned. If I didn't move
the van forward, it would attract attention. Still, I
strained to observe Kris in the rearview mirror. Was he
waiting for her, dropping her off, or what? I really
wanted to know, but had no way to find out just then. At
the moment, I did not think a return trip to Frank's Fix-
It was advisable.

I skipped the dry cleaner and the printer, because I was
sure I had found what I was looking for. But as I drove
home, I wondered *why* Humberto would leave the
diamond-laden chandelier at Frank's Fix-It, even covered with mud, even for a short time. Okay, the place
was a jumbled-up mess, like one of those garages full of
what the owner thinks is junk. So the owner has a big
garage sale, and a lucky customer pays a dollar for a
painting worth two million.

As far as I knew, Frank's Fix-It Shop was not planning on selling off its dusty merchandise anytime soon.

Not only that, but if Humberto knew, or suspected, that Ernest was on his trail, maybe even that Ernest was behind the theft of Norman Juarez's necklace, the last place he'd want to put something valuable was in a safety deposit box or other obvious storage place. He'd want to get rid of Ernest first and then wait for the heat of the murder investigation to cool.

The other reason he'd decided on Frank's Fix-It was that he'd needed to stash the diamonds somewhere unlikely, while waiting for the big Fort Knox–worthy metal safe to be delivered.

And what if Osgoode had been Humberto's partner? Maybe Humberto had wanted to hide the diamonds, just in case, and then get rid of Osgoode, in the event he knew anything about the Juarez fortune.

I called Boyd to ask for lookout duty as I returned. Unfortunately, this meant he would see me bringing in a large, unwieldy bag full of clanking stuff, which would mean questions. So when he answered, I asked if he could meet me in the driveway to help me carry in groceries.

"That's what you have?" he asked when I pulled in, opened the sliding door, and gestured to the dusty giant-size trash bag. "Somehow, it doesn't look like food shopping."

"It isn't. If you'll take it inside, we can both have a look."

He mumbled something about keeping his job as he humped the bag up the ramp. I thanked him pleasantly and said how much I appreciated his being a house-guest.

"Oh!" said Ferdinanda when we came through the front door. "What have you got there?" Yolanda, who was reading a cookbook, gave us a curious glance.

"I don't know yet!" I said more loudly than I intended. "Maybe I can tell you later." *Like when the police come to get it,* I added mentally. Even if Humberto and Ferdinanda had seemed to be at each other's throats the previous night, I didn't want our houseguests to glimpse the contents of this sack, just in case it contained what I hoped and feared it did.

"Let's go upstairs, Boyd." I scurried upstairs and stopped in Arch's room for a pair of wire cutters he'd used for one of his projects. Then I led Boyd into Arch's bathroom and stopped up the bathtub. "All right, lower it in there, as slowly as you can."

Boyd did as I asked, then untied the top of the bag and gently pulled out the light fixture by its chain. It was a gigantic chandelier that looked as if it had been sprayed with mud. Well, I thought, it probably had been. I wondered what kind of cock-and-bull story Humberto had used when he left it off at Frank's Fix-It. Probably something along the lines of, "We need to order parts for this from France, and we'll bring them in when they arrive, so you can do the repairs."

"Should I rinse this off?" Boyd asked patiently.

"Carefully." Once the warm water was running, I reached for a pair of cotton towels.

"Goldy?" said Boyd. "This thing is huge. Is it an antique or something? I don't want to know if you stole it, because I know you probably did. Is it worth a lot of money?"

By way of answer, I reached in and gently cut the wire holding one of the pendants in place. Interestingly, these teardrop-shaped pieces were not drilled through at their tops, but were in tiny individual nylon nets. Once I'd freed the stone from the wire and the net holding it, I held it up to the light.

The fire and brilliance of the gem hurt my eyes. I tried not to contemplate the magnitude of Humberto's theft.

"No, Sergeant Boyd, the chandelier is not an antique. But each of these sparkling pieces is a diamond. The whole chandelier is worth many millions of dollars. Humberto Captain stole these gems from the family of Norman Juarez."

"Oh, Jesus," said Boyd. "Time to call Tom, eh?" He punched in the numbers and was poised to talk but at the last moment pushed his cell toward me. "You tell him."

"Boyd?" my husband's disembodied voice said. "You there?"

"It's me," I said once I'd taken Boyd's cell. "I found Norman Juarez's gems."

Chapter 23

M iss G., what in God's name are you talking about?"

Ferdinanda's wheelchair was rolling along the hallway downstairs. "I can't stand it any longer!" she yelled up the steps. I motioned to Boyd. "Please don't tell her what's going on. No matter what," I added.

"No matter what *what*?" Tom said impatiently. "Can you tell *me* what is going on?"

So I did. I knew he would not be pleased when I informed him of Lolly's job for me, which I called "borrowing" Humberto's wallet. I told him about my manufacture of the fake receipts, my hunch about the photos that would be at the library, and finally, of retrieving the chandelier under false pretenses.

"And they didn't give you any trouble at Frank's Fix-It," Tom said disbelievingly.

"The guy was so trashed, he had no idea what I was doing," I said. "I could have gone in there and pulled the Hope Diamond out from under him, and he wouldn't have known."

"We've known about the pot for a long time," Tom said. "But we've never actually searched the place. I guess we could now."

"And you could find—oops!—a chandelier made of diamonds. Then you could charge him with receiving stolen goods—"

"Don't get too far ahead of yourself, Miss Detective. You've already broken enough laws for one day. I'm coming up there now, to get the chandelier from Boyd. Do not let our guests know what you are up to. I'll tell one of the guys here to get a judge to issue a search warrant for suspicion of drug dealing." He paused. "You better hope this works."

"It'll work," I said confidently. "Uh," I said painfully, "I have to meet somebody in a little bit and will probably miss you. Boyd can pack up the chandelier and help you with it."

"This is when I ask you who you're meeting."

"And this is when I tell you it's none of your beeswax."

"I'm so glad we have an open, honest, committed relationship," said Tom, "full of mutual trust."

"I won't steal anything valuable," I promised.

"That does not make me feel better," he said, and signed off.

Kris Nielsen's Maserati was parked in the driveway opposite our house when Boyd escorted me to my van. I shuddered and concentrated on getting behind my own wheel. Still, if Kris was at the house on our street, then he wouldn't be at his home in Flicker Ridge, which was my next stop.

I set off just before noon. I wished for another of Ferdinanda's pork sandwiches, but satisfied myself with a quick stop at the Aspen Meadow café for an iced latte, which I combined with a slice of one of my leftover coffee cakes. I polished both off as I drove through the entrance to Flicker Ridge.

The sky began to boil with dark clouds rolling in from the mountains to our west. A stiff breeze rocked the van and blasted my windshield with dust. Another storm was coming. I wondered if Arch had taken a jacket to school and if he kept a spare pair of boots in his trunk. The answer to both questions was *Probably not*. And what about his tires? Snow wasn't in the forecast, but I still worried about him in *any* bad weather.

Well, I hoped the math test had gone well.

My cell startled me. Penny Woolworth's scratchy voice said, "Goldy? Where are you? Are you coming over here or not?"

"I'm coming," I announced as I wound up the paved roads in Flicker Ridge. "What are you worried about?"

"I usually finish here around one. There's no check here, so he'll probably come over to pay me. I mean, that's what he ordinarily does."

"Is there a place for me to park where he won't see my van?"

"Try the dead end right below us. Just leave your car on the side of the road. Come straight up through Kris's property. I'll be at the door of his study. It opens to the outdoors."

"I'll be there in less than five minutes."

In the encroaching darkness, the huge gray houses in

Flicker Ridge took on a silvery glow. Expanses of window glass shimmied in the wind. I looked down at my sweatshirt and jeans. *I* hadn't even remembered a jacket. But once I removed the remaining coffee cake, I had an empty canvas catering bag. If I found something useful—like a receipt for work on an electric skillet—I would snag it. I would just have to be fast.

I grabbed the cloth sack, parked and locked the van, and took off on foot. Tom's and my energetic lovemaking that morning and the previous night had done nothing good for my leg muscles. But I trotted painfully up the hill anyway to where Penny stood, hugging herself in the sudden chill.

"Where have you been?" she asked crossly. "I could so lose my job over this. And it's not—"

"It's not what?" I asked as I slid inside the door.

Penny's shoulders slumped. "Nothing."

"It's not *what,* Penny?" I said with a sudden flash of anger.

She looked down at the wooden floor. "It's not the first time I've let somebody in here. Ernest McLeod was an old friend, from when I was a bartender. He said the same thing you did, that Kris was, you know, maybe going to hurt Yolanda. I thought Kris loved Yolanda. I mean, he kept saying he loved her. But Ernest, well, he was my friend."

"For God's sake, Penny. I wish you had told me this sooner." Yolanda had not been sure whether Ernest had started investigating Kris when he was killed. He had only promised that he would, eventually. I asked Penny, "Did you tell the cops?"

"With Zeke about to get out of prison? No way."

I shook my head as I moved into the huge study, which boasted scarlet red wallpaper and an oak floor.

A mahogany desk, bookshelves, and filing cabinets lined one wall. On the side opposite, where I stood, were a framed diploma—from Carleton, I noted—and various masks. They looked African, perhaps, or South American. Made of straw or wood and painted garish colors, they made me uncomfortable.

"He collects these?" I asked.

"Yeah, it's like his hobby."

"So tell me about what Ernest wanted," I said as I moved to the desk.

"Same as you," Penny said nervously. "To look at files, mail, stuff like that. There's a safe in Kris's closet, and of course I don't know the combination or what's in there. I kept asking Ernest, 'What are you searching for?' Ernest said he thought that since Kris was obsessing over Yolanda, which is what he called it, Kris might have drawn up a plan of what he was doing, or what he was going to do, or maybe he was keeping a journal. Something like that. He brought a handheld scanner." Penny exhaled and cocked her ear to the door.

"Did Ernest find anything to scan?" I asked as I pulled on file-drawer handles. A single lock at the top kept them all tightly closed.

"I don't know, Goldy. My job is to clean, get it? I just left him alone in here. Later, I felt really bad about letting Ernest in. So then when Kris told me how much he loved Yolanda, and that he just wanted to know how she was doing and where she was, I told him. I mean, Kris paid me. Ernest didn't, but as I said, he was an old friend."

I turned and faced her. "So I can't get into the safe. Does he keep the key to these files on a ring or fob of some kind? Or is it separate?"

"Actually," she said reluctantly, "I think it's separate, 'cause one time he came barging out of his study, where he'd been working on taxes all morning. He was hollering that he needed to go somewhere, and did I know where his car keys were?"

I rustled through the desk drawer. There was nothing except blank paper, index cards, and writing utensils. No key. "Please, Penny," I begged, "you need to help me find the key to this file cabinet. And I will pay you for your help here, plus at the Bertrams' this afternoon."

"Oh, hell, Goldy, I don't know how to find one little key."

"There's a recession on, Penny. And I pay in cash."

She grumbled something unintelligible, then yanked open another desk drawer, which revealed more pencils, pens, and another neat pile of paper pads. I asked her to run her hands over and behind the books on Kris's shelves. She sighed heavily but climbed up on the long desk and starting poking behind the volumes.

I did a visual survey of the room. The door I'd come through was in the wall with all the masks. There were about forty of them.

"So, Penny, did he say these masks were valuable?"

"Huh?" She was prodding the area behind the highest books. "Oh, I don't know. I don't think so."

Right, I thought. *Because if they were really valu-*

able, Kris Got-Bucks would have had cases built for them, right? A quick glance at my watch said it was half past twelve.

"Couple more questions, Penny. Do you know where any of these masks come from? I mean, does he tell you?"

"Uh, yeah. One is from Kenya." She wavered on the desktop and pointed uncertainly. "One is from Brazil. Can't remember which one that is. Oh, and the new one?" She pointed to a red-painted mask. "That's like, voodoo. He told me the word. Something like *San Rita.*" She pulled out her hand and inspected it with disgust. "I swear to God, I don't know why I've never dusted back here. There are dead bugs and all kinds of crap. And before you ask me, no, I haven't found a key."

"Was the word *Santería*?"

"Yeah, yeah, that's it."

"Could you point to it again?" She did, and I walked quickly to the new mask. I felt its sides. Nothing. Gently, I lifted it off its hook and placed it upside down on the wood floor. A key was taped to the back.

I peeled the key off the dry clay and said, "Okay, Penny, you can go finish your other cleaning. Call me if he comes."

"Oh my God," she said as she jumped down and slapped her palms together to dislodge dirt. "It's a good thing I haven't cleaned in here yet."

I said, "Thanks again." As Penny raced out the study door, I crossed to the file cabinet, inserted the key, and turned it. The drawers unlocked.

Quickly, go quickly, I thought. I needed to protect

Penny, Yolanda . . . and myself. The files were alpha-
betical. *Amenities. Boats. Board Notes.* The first two
contained pamphlets of things he apparently wanted or
was interested in; the third was notes from an alumni
board that he belonged to. *Media. Miscellaneous.
Mother.* The final drawer contained everything from
Northwest—a list of restaurants he wanted to visit or
had visited in Portland and Seattle—to *Taxes, Subscrip-
tions,* and *Warranties.*

There was no file on Yolanda. I didn't know if I was
happy or disappointed.

It was quarter to one. I leafed through *Media* and
found another batch of pamphlets for televisions, cameras, and laptops that Kris either had or was interested
in. *Mother* was a very fat file. Puzzled, I saw it contained numerous letters to and from an insurance company, police reports, and newspaper clippings. On one
police report, Kris's neat handwriting had penned *Jackass.*

Police reports? Jackass?

It was ten to one. I didn't have a handheld scanner, so
I stuffed the *Mother* file into my bag. This would warrant further study, and if I could get out of there quickly,
I'd be able to peruse it at my leisure . . . provided Kris
didn't notice the file was gone.

The *Miscellaneous* file was intriguing because it did
not, in fact, contain miscellaneous clippings, letters, and
other papers that one would expect. Instead it contained
neatly penned charts with numbers in columns. Each
line on the charts contained dates, with numbers and
initials.

Well, I thought as I crammed this file into my bag, too, *in for a penny, in for a pound. Penny Woolworth probably wouldn't appreciate that saying, but—*

"He's coming!" she screamed. "Get out!"

She didn't have to tell me twice. I straightened the now loosely fitting files, closed all the drawers, and re-locked the cabinet. Unfortunately, the piece of tape that had held the key in place was clogged with clay parti-cles, so I had to take a moment to find a new roll and retape the key behind the Santería mask. My hands shook as I replaced it on the wall.

I heard the Maserati's characteristic *vroom-vroom.* I swallowed hard and looked around the study. My mother had always checked the trash when she returned from shopping, sure that evidence of my misdeeds would have been chucked in there. Penny said she hadn't cleaned in here yet, so I stuck the used bit of tape in my pocket, emptied Kris's small garbage can into my can-vas tote, and skedaddled. Running back down the hill, despite slipping through patches of snow, proved easier than trotting up. Nevertheless, I was still huffing and puffing when I arrived at the van.

A diamond-studded chandelier, some stolen files, and another person's garbage. Not bad for a day's haul.

Five minutes later, still slightly out of breath and with my heart ceaselessly pounding, I piloted the van through the Flicker Ridge exit and called Boyd. This alerting him to my every arrival and departure was definitely cramping my style.

"Your husband has a lot of questions for you," he said.

I cleared my throat. There was no way I could tell Boyd what I had just done. Instead, I said, "Did they get the chandelier out okay?"

"Yeah. I told Yolanda and Ferdinanda they had to stay in the dining room while some sensitive police materials were being moved. Tom's guys brought in a large cardboard box and took the chandelier away in it. Tom still doesn't know how he's going to structure the search warrant for the fix-it shop."

"Well," I said dismissively, "I'm not a lawyer."

Boyd chuckled. "Oh, don't we know that! Still, Tom wants you to stay home until we go to the Bertrams' place *together.*"

I sighed. I had plenty of things to look at, plus soup to make. So this was a manageable constraint.

At the house, I waved to Yolanda and Ferdinanda. The two of them were sitting in the living room with a plate of cookies and cups of coffee. Boyd followed me through the door, then closed and locked it. He looked suspiciously at my canvas bag, but I kept the handles well tucked under my arm. Ferdinanda fussed so much over the fact that I hadn't had lunch that I almost lost my temper. But instead I placed a cookie in my mouth and thanked her for her concern.

Yolanda looked tired. The burns on her bandaged legs still made movement difficult for her, and standing was also a challenge.

"I want a bath," she said ruefully, "but, Goldy, what about the soup? Do you want me to—"

"What are you complaining about?" Ferdinanda said, chiding her. "Bath? Bath?" She dismissed this with a wave. "When I was a sniper in Castro's army, up in the jungle? We only got to wash in streams."

"Goldy," said Yolanda, ignoring Ferdinanda, "I want to start on the soup. I mean, if you do."

I glanced ostentatiously at my watch. "Why don't you have that bath now? You look exhausted."

"I had a restless night."

"You don't have to cook," I said.

"No," she replied stubbornly, "I want to."

"Tell you what," I said as I clutched the bag tightly to me. "Can we talk in the kitchen, just the two of us?"

She looked downcast, but followed me. I carefully closed the kitchen door.

I said, "Ernest had already begun investigating Kris."

She immediately looked away. "Oh, God—"

"Yolanda, please. Are you sure that Ernest never said anything about Kris? Or about finding something in Kris's house?"

Yolanda again began to tear up. "Ernest did tell me he was looking at Kris. I . . . didn't want to tell Tom, because . . . I was afraid," she whispered.

"Of Kris?"

"Yes, of course." Her voice was still low, as if she were sure Kris could hear her. "But also, Tom was so suspicious of me. Like he didn't believe me."

"In a murder investigation, Tom has to suspect everybody. So, did Ernest find anything at Kris's place?"

"He had a lead. That was all he told me."

"Is there anything else you need to tell me?"

"Ferdinanda told me she informed you that Humberto had hired me to spy and paid me the seventeen thou that went up in smoke. I never did any spying. I loved Ernest."

"I know. And Tom knows."

Yolanda shook her head. "We never should have stayed here."

"No, no, don't say that." I put down my bag. "You may feel crazy now, but you're going to be fine. Look, I went through this breaking-up thing with my ex. In spades. Come on, give me a hug." She obliged, and then I pulled away. "Tell you what. Could you go back out to the living room and tell Boyd what you just told me, about Ernest and Kris? Try to remember details. Then ask him to call Tom."

She nodded her assent, turned away quickly, and pushed through the kitchen door.

I tried to focus. When Yolanda had arrived at the house, she had not told me the whole truth. She had been afraid. And given my history, I didn't blame her.

In the living room, I could hear Boyd on his cell phone. I stared at our landline, which was blinking. I pushed the button for voice mail and was told I had one message.

"Oh, Goldy, thank God your machine picked up!" SallyAnn Bertram's breathless voice announced. "I don't have your cell number, or if I do, I can't find it. When is that cleaning lady coming over? I can't remember, and I can't find my calendar, and when I started tidying up, I realized that there was way too much for me to . . . well, actually, I feel overwhelmed. John promised he'd be home early, but he just called and said he thought we needed some more propane, plus he's borrowing a grill from somebody—" The machine cut her off. She'd called an hour ago.

When was Penny due at the Bertrams' place? In my current mental state, I could not remember. It seemed to me she'd indicated she was going straight from Kris's house. My watch said half past one. I did not dare call her cell, in case Kris was nearby and saw the incoming number. If I used Boyd's cell, Penny might answer. Even though she blamed the Furman County Sheriff's Department for all her husband's woes, with her husband getting out of jail the next day, wouldn't she pick up?

I was worried about her. That trumped everything.

I picked up my bag and found Boyd back in the living room. He was off the phone. Yolanda and Ferdinanda had retreated to the dining room.

"May I borrow your cell, Sergeant?"

"What happened to yours?"

"Just—please?"

Boyd said, "You have to stand right here while you use it."

"Thanks. A friend of mine cleans for Kris Nielsen, and I want to make sure she's okay." I added, "She's worked for him for a while. I don't think this is a big deal."

Boyd shook a carrot-shaped forefinger at me. "That's what you always say."

Penny answered on the first ring. "Zeke? Did they let you out early?"

"No, it's Goldy. Sorry."

"Christ, Goldy!" There was the quick crash of a door slamming. "I've been over at your friend's house for half an hour, and the place is a frigging rats' nest! You could take half the stuff out of here and have enough for *two* garage sales!"

"Well, I'm sorry—"

"Why are you calling me from the sheriff's department?" she asked curiously.

"I'm not at the department, I'm borrowing a phone. Did you finish at Kris's place okay?"

"Yeah, I suppose. He didn't seem to suspect anything. I was so nervous I thought I was going to pee while he wrote out my check. Did you put everything back just the way you found it?"

"Well, not exactly. But if he didn't notice, then we both should be fine. Listen. There was a message for me at home from SallyAnn, and I wanted to make sure you got there."

"When I got here, that woman was having a *major* meltdown. She kept following me from room to room, until I finally handed her a gigantic trash bag and said, 'Here, fill this with everything you haven't used in the last year. When you have one bag full, start on another one. When I finish here, if I ever finish here, I'll take them all to Evergreen Christian Outreach.' Do you know, that woman's on her *third* bag?"

"Good, then—"

"Listen, Goldy, I'm *here,* but I'm not sure I can get through all this. I think I'm gonna need *help.*"

"How's three o'clock? I'll try to bring helpers."

"Better than nothing." She disconnected.

I gave Boyd an imploring look. "Can we—"

"Yeah, yeah. Just remind your son to go over to somebody else's house for dinner. And to stay there until we call him."

I promised I would, then raced upstairs with my bag. I grabbed four hundred dollars from my underwear drawer, which was where I stowed emergency cash. I stuffed it into my wallet, for Penny.

I picked up my canvas bag and tiptoed to Arch's room, where I closed the door. I dialed his cell—which the CBHS kids were not allowed to answer during school hours—and left a message asking if he could please eat dinner over at Gus's and call me when he was done. Then I apologized and said I would explain it all to him later.

I nipped over to his desk, booted his computer, and pulled out the things I'd stolen from Kris's. I began with the *Miscellaneous* file, since it was far thinner than the one marked *Mother*. With any luck, I would be able to take good notes on the contents, then return both files to Penny that night, so she could replace them the next time she worked at Kris's.

The *Miscellaneous* file was indeed sparse: It contained only two pages, each with three columns. Had I dropped something? I certainly hoped not. Two pages I could photocopy and figure out later. I raced down to the basement, avoiding contact with Boyd and our house-guests, and copied both sheets.

Back upstairs, I did a cursory study of the pair of papers. Along the left side of each were dates. I blinked at the papers and told myself to concentrate.

The dates along the left side of the first page began in June and went through July; the second page covered

August and went through the previous day, September the sixteenth. Today had not been entered yet.

Every date in June was not noted, but there was one D, with a check mark. The far-right number corresponding to the D had four digits; the others all had three. July, on the other hand, contained many S's and two B's. Most of the S's had check marks, some had X's. The B's had check marks. In July, every date was noted.

It was the same for August, a pattern of S's and B's. All had check marks with three digits in the right-hand side. For September, there were also three I's, two F's and a K. The K corresponded to a five-figure number, and each F and I matched a four-figure number.

Back on the first page, I wondered why there was only one D there, and then I looked at the date: June the fifteenth.

Hadn't Yolanda told me Ferdinanda had had her accident in mid-June? Since I'd seen a black SUV over at Stonewall's, I wondered again if he'd been involved in the accident, and if so, *why.* I would have to get the exact date of the accident from Yolanda.

The dates and figures swam before my eyes. They could relate to anything in Kris's life. I for Investments, S for Sell, B for Buy. *Crap.*

In the back of my mind, I could hear Penny's voice saying she needed me to come help her clean up the Bertrams' house. We had a party to do that night, and I had no idea whether the pages in front of me—papers I had obtained illegally, no less—meant anything or not.

I opened the packed *Mother* file. It contained the last

will and testament of one Rita Nielsen. A coroner's report, dated the fifteenth of January, two years and eight months ago, indicated Rita Nielsen had died between the twentieth and the twenty-sixth of December, from carbon monoxide poisoning. I went through bank account slips and statements from mutual funds. It looked as if Kris Nielsen had inherited twelve million dollars, as he'd drunkenly admitted to Penny Woolworth. So the "making money starting up a computer company" was bunk, as Lolly Vanderpool had suspected.

I sifted through the many pages until I found the one that Kris had written *Jackass* across the top of. It contained a name, Joe Pargeter, and a number. I called it and was connected to the police department in Lake Bargee, Minnesota.

"Is Joe Pargeter in?" I asked.

"Oh, no, he's out on a job," a female with a midwestern twang replied. Then she probably remembered she wasn't supposed to give out information to a stranger and became suspicious. "What do you need him for?"

I gave her my name and cell number and asked if Joe Pargeter could please call me as soon as possible. I said I desperately needed to talk to him about the death of Rita Nielsen.

The woman clucked. "You're another insurance investigator?"

Insurance investigator? I said, "No, I'm not. But I really, really need to talk to him."

She said, "Yah, I'll pass the message on to Joe."

"Thank you."

"You betcha," she said, and signed off.

I had no idea whether Joe Pargeter would call me back. Ideally, Tom and the cops should talk to him if he did, but first I wanted to see if there was anything there, or if I was on another wild goose chase. Where was Lake Bargee, Minnesota? A place you could go on a wild Canadian goose chase?

I was due in the kitchen. I closed up both files and stowed them in my canvas bag. Yolanda, Ferdinanda, and I needed to make fresh cream of mushroom soup for the gathering at the Bertrams' to remember Ernest.

My heart was still pulsing so loudly from my day of burglaries, I was sure I could hear it. Cooking would help me calm down.

Boyd was in the living room talking on his cell. Ferdinanda and Yolanda were already in the kitchen working. Yolanda was heating up the chicken stock. Ferdinanda narrowed her eyes at me, but I kept my mouth resolutely closed.

"Nobody tells me anything," said Ferdinanda. She wheeled over to my portable CD player and slotted in a Tito Puente CD. Soon the first floor was reverberating with the sounds of Latin music.

I washed my hands. "The two of you started working without me."

"We wanted to," Yolanda replied as she melted butter in a huge stockpot. She kept her voice neutral, but she still wouldn't meet my eyes. "Why don't you help Ferdinanda chop ingredients? I poured boiling spring water over some dried mushrooms, because I figured you'd want them in addition to the fresh ones."

"And you were right," I said, equally neutral. I drained

the now-plumped mushrooms through cheesecloth and saved the water. Despite the upbeat music, Ferdinanda seemed angry with everyone. She muttered under her breath as she rolled herself into the walk-in. She emerged with the ingredients Yolanda had requested, then handed them to me. I gave her a cutting board with the plumped mushrooms and asked her to slice them.

Ferdinanda and I sliced and diced while Yolanda pulled out dry sherry and cream. Within minutes, I'd minced shallots and fresh mushrooms and scraped them into the butter. A scent that was both earthy and heavenly bloomed in the kitchen.

When the mushrooms began to release their liquid, Yolanda stirred flour into the stockpot. Once the mixture bubbled, she slowly poured chicken stock and sherry into the roux. She was not smiling. I wondered if our friendship would ever get back to normal.

What was normal when you'd just survived a breakup with a crazy-possessive ex-boyfriend, lost your friend and benefactor to murder, escaped an arson attack on your home, and suffered oil burns on your legs?

I blended glistening whipping cream into the soup and set it to simmer. Yolanda heated everything while I pulled out the remaining marinating pork tenderloin and slipped it into a zipped plastic bag. No matter what, it certainly was easier to cook for a big party when you had experienced chefs as houseguests.

Ferdinanda disappeared into the dining room to get herself ready for the party while I nabbed several packages of greens and Tom's Love Potion dressing for a salad. Yolanda, Boyd, and I packed up. It didn't take long. I had gotten to the point where I just wanted this party to be over.

After fifteen minutes of cleaning up and making sure we had everything, I puréed the soup and packed it up. Then I slipped upstairs to take a quick shower and change. I knew I'd probably need a much longer shower later, but hot water would help clear my head. I stowed my wallet with the money for Penny in the pocket of clean jeans and pulled on a polo shirt and a sweater. Then I heard an unfamiliar car stop on the street. I looked out our window.

It was a Furman County Sheriff's Department prowler, lights blazing.

Fright poured through my veins as I punched in numbers. At quarter to three, Arch was probably at his locker.

"Mom!" he said, exasperated. "I got your message, okay? After practice, I'm going to Gus's for dinner. You don't have to call me ten times."

"I'm sorry," I whispered. "And it's not ten times. Can you call me when you finish eating?"

"All *right*. Jeez, have a little faith, will you?"

I'm trying, I thought as he hung up. I walked quickly down to the front hall, where Boyd had placed all our boxes. He stood with his arm around Yolanda and Ferdinanda's wheelchair next to his legs. Ferdinanda's mouth was set in a determined, angry line. Yolanda, who had changed into a turquoise Caribbean-style dress, looked paralyzed with fear.

"I don't think we should go," she whispered. "I haven't been anywhere since my legs were burned—"

"I promised SallyAnn and Penny we'd help." My voice sounded rusty. "It'll be all right. It's a house full of cops! SallyAnn wants Boyd there, and he'll be able to guard you—"

"I'm driving all of us in Yolanda's van," Boyd announced. "The Maserati is back. Tom found something out, and he sent a police car to watch while I load the van and get you ladies out of here. We'll have armed officers escorting us all the way."

Yolanda looked at me in alarm. I took a deep breath and nodded to her, as if to repeat, *Everything will be all right.*

Boyd was as good as his word. The prowler lights flashed as we went out to the van, one at a time, with Boyd beside us. My mind worked overtime as I tried to figure out what Tom could have discovered. If he'd told Boyd, it was clear we weren't going to hear it.

Did this have to do with Kris, or was Tom concerned about protecting us from someone else?

As soon as we were on our way to the Bertrams', my cell rang. The caller ID read *Pargeter.*

"This is Goldy Schulz." My voice had somehow turned high and querulous.

"Joseph Pargeter, returning your call. The office manager took your name and number, but she didn't tell me who you were, where you were, or what your interest was in Rita Nielsen's death."

"I'm in Aspen Meadow, Colorado," I said quickly, "I'm an independent citizen. I was wondering what you could tell me about Rita Nielsen."

"And you are interested because . . . ?" he asked.

"Kris Nielsen is giving my friends and me some trouble."

At this, Ferdinanda and Yolanda began to speak rapid-fire Spanish. Boyd glanced at me in the rearview mirror.

"You've told the local authorities?" Pargeter asked.

"Oh, yes," I said breezily. "My husband, Tom Schulz, is an investigator with the Furman County Sheriff's Department. But—" My mind ran over recent events: the fires at Yolanda's rental and Ernest's house, the discovery of a marijuana grow, the murders of Ernest McLeod and Stonewall Osgoode, the chandelier with the stolen diamonds, the files I had found in Kris's house. I said, "Kris's ex-girlfriend is a friend of mine."

"Why don't you put your husband on the line?" asked Pargeter. "I'd feel more comfortable talking to him."

Chapter 24

I sighed. "He's not here at the moment. But I can put you on with a member of his team. His name is Sergeant Boyd."

Boyd shook his head but took the phone from me anyway. He identified himself, then gave his Furman County Sheriff's Department cell phone number to Pargeter.

"Careful fellow," commented Boyd, who handed me back my cell phone, then answered his own.

While Boyd listened to Pargeter talk, I reflected that I still did not know how everything connected. I didn't know what the connection, if any, was between Stonewall Osgoode and any of the suspects in Ernest's murder. Sean Breckenridge had taken pictures of puppies that might have been Osgoode's. Was Sean Breckenridge Stonewall Osgoode's investor? Had Sean been hoping for a big payday with the marijuana grow operation, a payday that would enable him to leave Rorry and marry Brie? If so, then why kill Osgoode? Because he knew too much? Had that been Ernest's problem, too, that he knew too much?

What about Kris? Had he somehow learned that Ernest was snooping around him at Yolanda's request? Or had he just not liked that she was living at Ernest's house?

Humberto had been the most directly threatened by Ernest's investigations, besides maybe Osgoode. Ernest had managed to retrieve Norman Juarez's long-stolen necklace, tying Humberto to the theft of the Juarez family fortune. Had Humberto followed Ernest and killed him, then retrieved the necklace? Or had he had one of his henchmen do it? Or had Humberto hired Osgoode? Who had changed Ernest's dental appointment, Charlene or somone else? I shook my head, feeling helpless, just as Boyd hung up.

"So what was that all about?" I asked.

Boyd did not answer me. Instead, he asked, "How did you happen to get Pargeter's number?"

Oh, crap. I said, "I can't tell you that," thinking of all the TV crime shows I'd seen, of how evidence got thrown out because it had been obtained illegally. *Fruit of the poisonous tree,* the defense lawyers always maintained. And out went *those* apples.

"I'll talk to Tom," said Boyd cryptically, and I thought of a prosecutor saying, *Inevitable discovery, Your Honor.* But inevitable discovery of what?

I shivered. We were driving along Main Street toward the Bertrams' house, which was less than ten minutes away. Behind us, the prowler's lightbar still blinked, which made me feel safe. I said, "Can't you tell us anything?"

Boyd said, "Joe Pargeter suspects Kris in what was ruled the accidental death of his wealthy mother, Rita Nielsen."

Yolanda gasped. Boyd said he couldn't tell us any more until he had talked to Tom. I hugged my sides, frustrated.

Boyd and our police escort carried our boxes into the house. Overhead, the clouds had cleared without our having a storm. The late-afternoon sun was shining. The weather was cool for just after three o'clock.

Some cops, undoubtedly those with the day off, had begun arriving. Despite all that was going on, I felt safe walking down the Bertrams' driveway. One of the investigators told me Tom would be arriving within the hour. *Good,* I thought. I had a lot to tell him, as did Boyd.

Beside me, Yolanda glanced up at the hulking ruins that constituted Ernest's burned house. Once her gaze had snagged on it, she couldn't take her eyes away from the place.

She was shaking, so I put my arm around her. Ferdinanda still looked grim.

Yolanda said quietly, "I wish Ernest could be here. I feel as if this is all my fault."

"None of it is your fault," I replied. "Let's go inside."

To my surprise, the first person I saw upon entering the Bertrams' house behind Ferdinanda was . . . Father Pete.

"The Bertrams invited me," he said hastily. When Yolanda drew back, Father Pete moved forward to embrace her. "I came early. I am hoping you will forgive me, Yolanda. I know you have been through a rough time, and I didn't mean to startle you in the grocery store. I am absentminded." He hesitated. "You have been a good friend to Goldy. I hope I can be a good friend to you."

Yolanda said, "That would be nice. And of course I forgive you."

Ferdinanda, unforgiving, rolled toward the kitchen. I wondered if, in the pastoral business, a 50 percent success rate was considered good.

"Do you know where Penny Woolworth is?" I asked Father Pete.

"In the kitchen. She has been working very hard here, cleaning, cleaning, cleaning. The last time I was in this house . . . well, never mind."

I glanced around the living room. The upholstered brown furniture was what the discount houses call "Early American." It was old but freshly polished, and the worn orange wall-to-wall carpeting had been vacuumed. There was no clutter. Penny must have performed a miracle.

SallyAnn, greeting guests, winked at me and then hustled over. "Thank you so much for sending your friend. I've thrown away more junk, and donated more out-of-style clothing and shoes, than I even knew I had."

"Did you find anything valuable?" I asked.

"My sanity," she replied, then left to say hello to more folks.

The kitchen was gleaming, and there was plenty of counter space. As Yolanda began unloading our first box of food, she opened a refrigerator that was half-full . . . and sparkling. Ferdinanda pulled drawers wide to find utensils. Penny herself, a bucket of soapy water at her feet, was washing the kitchen walls. SallyAnn was nowhere in sight.

"Penny?" I said. "It doesn't look as if you needed us after all."

Her face shone with sweat. "You're right. I was in a panic the first hour. Now I'm almost done. There are two clean bathrooms with new towels in them, and one clean bedroom, the master, where people can put their coats."

"Thank you so much," I said. I slipped the four hundred bucks into her jeans pocket. "You're the best. How many sacks of discards did SallyAnn end up filling?"

Penny stopped scrubbing and shook her head. "Five. They're in my pickup. I'll take them to Evergreen Christian Outreach on my way home. But get this: There are another five full garden bags stacked in their trash shed, out by their garage. When I go home, I'm sleeping for twelve hours straight, or until Zeke calls me tomorrow, whichever comes first." She lifted an eyebrow and lowered her voice. "What do you think of the décor?"

I looked around at mismatched but clean canisters, large wooden salt and pepper shakers, and a garage-sale rack with half-full bottles of spices and herbs that didn't look as if they'd been used in a decade. The pictures on the walls were decoupaged cards, pictures of tiny mice clinging to autumn leaves, kittens snuggling, puppies playing. I whispered, "Well, it's different from Kris's."

"And from Marla's, and from nearly every other house I do. But they have money. SallyAnn told me. She just hates to clean. So I'm taking them on, even after Zeke comes back."

"You are good," I said, "and I am so thank—" My eyes caught on something. "What is that?" I pointed to a framed print from *Sesame Street*. "They don't have kids, so what gives?"

"Oh." Penny's tone was offhand. "I didn't find it until we removed about a ton of stuff from that counter. It's a picture of Bert and Ernie, you know? I think John Bertram's old partner gave it to him. You know, the partner was called Ernie, and the cops call John Bertram Bert—where are you going?"

I dashed into the living room and looked around for Boyd. It really couldn't be that simple, could it? I hadn't even processed it when SallyAnn first told me about the nicknames. But when I saw the picture, it seemed to make perfect sense. "Where's Sergeant Boyd?" I asked a couple bringing in a covered casserole dish.

"Uh," said the man, a tall fellow whom I vaguely recognized. "On the patio, I think. Having a beer."

I thanked him and raced outside. Boyd, his right hand around a can, was giving advice to John Bertram, who was trying to start the propane grill. Boyd was laughing.

"Sergeant," I said, my voice urgent. "I need you. Please?"

Boyd's shoulders dropped, but he put down his beer and followed me. "Where are we going?"

"I need you to show me the crime scene. I mean, where Ernest was shot."

Boyd exhaled but moved in front of me. John Bertram's paved driveway was wide and long and led to the detached garage where he kept the numerous cars and trucks he was ostensibly working on. We walked down the driveway until we reached the field of boulders that stretched upward, to the left, between the Bertrams' place and Ernest McLeod's spread. Boyd turned and began climbing across rocks and over wild grass.

Finally he stopped. Nobody had followed to see what we were up to. For that I was thankful. This *was* a bit morbid.

"Here," said Boyd, pointing to the gravel service road used by the fire department to reach otherwise inaccessible stands of trees. "He'd come down from his house. He must have heard something, or was suspicious, so he detoured onto this road. Then, we think, he turned back up toward his house and came into this field of rocks. Still, whoever was tracking him found him anyway. The cancer had weakened Ernest, we figure, so he couldn't move so fast anymore. But he must have heard something and turned around . . . the killer shot him in the chest, then dragged him out of sight of the main road."

I turned in a complete circle. There were boulders and pine trees, the Bertrams' long driveway and big detached garage, their low-slung house, the main road, then uphill, to more boulders and evergreens, and the ruins of Ernest's house.

"Say he didn't detour down this road," I said. Boyd looked skeptical. "Bear with me. Let's say Ernest knew his house was being watched. So before someone could break in there, he put evidence incriminating Sean and Humberto into his backpack, with the intention of hiding it in John Bertram's garage. Then imagine that he said to Ferdinanda, 'If anything happens to me, ask Bert,' not 'ask the bird.' And then Ernest, aka Ernie, walked down here and hid something at John Bertram's place."

"Goldy," said Boyd, with doubt in his voice, "we don't think so. There were no footprints, and nothing was dropped—"

"But it rained, and then it snowed. Any footprints would have been rinsed away."

Boyd was still dubious. "Well, if there was anything hidden in John's house, it's probably in the bottom of a trash bag, if it's there at all. Your friend said she's been cleaning for several hours. John Bertram and Ernest McLeod were polar opposites in the let's-keep-things-tidy department."

I turned again, less sure of myself. My gaze swept across the vista. Ernest was neat; John was not. Ernest McLeod had left Saturday morning to walk into town. According to Ferdinanda, he had his camera, wallet, and other belongings in his red backpack. The backpack had not been found. SallyAnn hadn't mentioned it, and Penny certainly hadn't.

The detached garage was a quarter-mile away. Say Ernest *sensed* he was being followed, and wasn't sure he had the strength to escape whoever it was. But he went ahead and made his stop first, then wended his way back up through the boulders in the direction of home. . . .

Nobody had cleaned in the garage, or, as far as I knew, even looked in there for Ernest's backpack. It was too far away from the crime scene.

"May I search John Bertram's garage?" I asked Boyd eagerly.

"Goldy, no. It's a total mess. I don't know how John even finds his tools in there."

"Please?"

Boyd's shoulders slumped again. "All right, I'll come with you."

"I'd rather you stayed with Yolanda."

"Okay. I'm going to watch you go in there, though. We've got more cops here than a law enforcement convention. But don't stay long. I'm telling you, if we had hurricanes here, you'd say that garage got hit ten years ago, and nothing had been cleaned up."

"Thanks."

I scrambled down the rocks, huffing and puffing for the second time that day. When I stopped to catch my breath, I realized I could see down to Cottonwood Creek and the main twisting road into Aspen Meadow. I stifled a whoop when I saw Tom's car rumbling along behind a line of traffic.

Finally, finally, I arrived back at the propane grill, which John Bertram was still trying to light. Ferdinanda, who'd just whacked John with her baton a couple of days before, showed no hint of remorse as she gave John directions on lighting the grill.

"John," I gasped. "Ernest called you 'Bert,' right?"

He looked up at me. "Sure. We were Bert and Ernie. No big deal."

"May I look around in your garage?"

His cheeks reddened. "Well, it's kind of . . . chaotic in there. I mean, Ernest was always after me to clean it up. What are you looking for?"

"I'm not sure," I called over my shoulder as I walked

briskly down the pavement. I didn't see Boyd anywhere and I didn't want to wait for him. Yolanda needed him more than I did right now.

Behind me, Ferdinanda yelled, "Hey, Goldy! If this man ever gets this grill lit, we got to put the pork on. Where are you going?"

"I'll be back shortly," I called. "We don't need to cook the pork for at least another hour."

To my dismay, the sound of Ferdinanda's wheels squeaked along behind me. She called, "Come here, Goldy! I don't want you going anywhere without something I'm going to give you."

I stopped. Tom would be here soon, and I wanted to look in the garage before he arrived. But I dutifully waited for Ferdinanda. Maybe she would give me a Santería talisman, or—

"Take this," said Ferdinanda. She reached beside her hip and pulled out the baton. "You've made enemies out of Humberto and, it sounds like, Sean Breckenridge, and maybe Kris, too." She pointed to a button on the side of the baton. "You want it to extend, punch this."

"Okay," I said. I'd need both my hands if I was going to search through trash and who knew what all in the garage, but I did not mention this. "I'll be right back."

I raced off, but to my dismay I again heard Ferdinanda's wheels squealing along slowly behind me. Maybe she would find somebody else to give advice to along the way. I certainly hoped so.

The crowd was thick, and it took me more than five minutes to thread through it. With any luck, Ferdinanda would be held up much longer, and not bother me on my quest.

The garage door was a red wooden sliding entrance, more like the type you would find on a barn. I slid it open, felt along the right wall, and switched on overhead fluorescent lights.

As promised, the place was a wreck. I counted six trucks and two cars, each in varying states of disrepair. The hoods of most of them yawned. Like many Coloradans, John Bertram cannibalized his old vehicles for parts to put in newer ones. But that wasn't what interested me.

Which vehicle looked clean? Which one looked as if Ernest might have been in it?

It took only a minute. While the pickups were generally filled with rags, old cans, and all manner of detritus, there was one, a red one, over by the other side of the garage. I could see it well because daylight spilled in from the regular-size door on that side. The roar of traffic from the road below was clearly audible.

There was even a somewhat clear path to the red truck, as if someone—in my mind, Ernest—had tried to indicate where one should walk to get to the red truck, which looked as if it had been hastily wiped down by someone who wanted to indicate he'd been there. I walked quickly to it.

Someone—again, I was willing to bet it was Ernest—had dumped all the trash that had been in the back of the truck on the garage floor. I levered myself up to check the cab. It was empty. With my free hand, I pulled open one of the doors and felt along the floor and between the seats, but my hands came up with nothing. When I opened the glove box, a crumpled heap of old restaurant reviews spilled onto the floor. I checked through them quickly, but found not a shred of anything of interest.

Cursing, I slammed the door shut and climbed up one of the wheels, vaulted over, and landed with a soft thump in the back, which was empty . . . except for Ernest McLeod's backpack.

"I got it!" I cried as I lifted the backpack with my free hand. But then someone—a man, moving very quickly—vaulted into the truck bed behind me. And then something very hard, *very* hard, hit me across my shoulders. I screamed and fell, the baton slipping from my grasp. The big thing—the butt of a gun?—cracked against my back.

The pain made sickness shoot through my body. Then the butt of the gun hit me again.

I'm going to die, I thought. I imagined Arch motherless, Tom without a wife—

"Did you really think you were going to steal from me?" Kris Nielsen's menacing voice came close to my ear. His free hand grasped my neck. I stretched out my right hand, trying to find the baton. Once my fingers closed on it, I pulled it quietly toward my body. Kris said, "Did you really think you could just waltz into my house and take files, and I wouldn't discover it? The next time you burgle someone's house, don't run out the back door where someone in the house can see you. What's mine is *mine*. I am smarter than you, and I will destroy you. Now, drop the backpack, or I'll shoot you in the head."

I let go of the backpack but pressed the baton against my thigh. "Please," I said, "please stop—"

I torqued my head sideways and saw a glint of metal. Kris was indeed holding a gun. The whoosh in the air from his raising it again made me wince. I pressed the extension button on the baton and whacked backward with every ounce of strength I possessed.

Stunned, Kris tumbled onto the floor of the truck bed. The gun rattled away in the darkness, but Kris, using his superior strength, snatched the baton out of my hand before I could get my feet under me. He levered to a standing position while I tried to scramble away from him.

"Hey, Kris!" came Ferdinanda's unexpected shout.

Kris turned toward the front of the garage. I grabbed the side of the truck bed and pulled myself up to a half crouch. Ferdinanda sat in her wheelchair near the red truck, her hands in her lap. Light from the big doors created an aura around her.

"I should have had Osgoode run over you twice, you old bat!" Kris yelled.

"I'm not that easy to kill," she said, "so you better come get me now."

Kris raised the baton, his face flushed as red as the backpack dangling from his other hand. I estimated how far it was to the open side door if I tried to vault from the truck bed. But I couldn't just leave Ferdinanda here with Kris. What if he recovered his gun? If I screamed, would it carry to the house?

Before I could figure out what to do, I watched Ferdinanda pull something out of the recesses of her ever useful wheelchair. I had time to register that it was a

gun—Tom's .45 from our garage, I vaguely realized—
and heard Kris shout something. Then the woman who
had been a sniper, a *francotiradora* in Castro's army,
pulled the trigger and fired once, twice.

Kris Nielsen fell against me, sending us both back
down to the truck floor. I wiggled out from beneath him.
A cratered hole lay where his forehead had been. He
wouldn't be stalking anyone ever again.

At least twenty cops descended on the Bertrams' garage. I didn't see or hear much, because the sound of the
shots had once again temporarily deafened me. Kris's
blood was on my face, in my eyes, and dripping into my
ears. My whole body quivered uncontrollably. I wanted
to get away from Kris Nielsen's corpse as fast as hu-
manly possible.

But of course the whole place was now a crime scene.

Tom arrived and took his gun back from Ferdinanda.
She confessed immediately, saying that she'd been looking for a weapon from the first morning she'd awakened
in our house. That was what she had been doing in our
pantry when I'd come upon her so early. She had not
been looking for cans. She'd also searched in our freezer,
because she couldn't believe a law enforcement officer
wouldn't have a weapon hidden somewhere.

And after breakfast that first morning? Ferdinanda
had told Yolanda she was still scared, even with Tom in
the house. Ferdinanda had told Yolanda she'd had a terrible night. Even after Boyd and Tom built the ramp,
Ferdinanda insisted she didn't know if she'd ever be able
to sleep easily in our dining room. And when Yolanda

kept saying they would be safe sleeping under our roof, Ferdinanda had continued nagging, saying she didn't feel secure. Finally Yolanda had said they would be fine, because Tom kept a gun in the detached garage—a fact I had told her.

Then Ferdinanda, who was perhaps *not* as hard of hearing as she had claimed, had overheard me remind Tom of the code to our garage door. She'd had her work cut out for her.

"It was all for self-defense," the old woman told Tom.

Well, not quite. There was something else Ferdinanda had needed to do—arm herself. She had the baton; she got the gun. When Kris bought the house across the street from us, he had installed Harriet there. But really, Ferdinanda insisted, it was because he wanted to keep an eye on Yolanda, perhaps to kill her. I suspected she was right.

So Ferdinanda knew something, some event, some person associated with Yolanda—that would be yours truly—would pull the trigger on Kris's rage. That was why she gave me the baton. That was why she kept the .45 beside her in the wheelchair.

Kris had discovered my break-in at his house. This was what had frightened him into action. Because I had taken the number of Joe Pargeter, and Joe Pargeter knew quite a bit that the authorities in Colorado did not. When I'd handed the phone to Boyd, Pargeter had told him about the death of Rita Nielsen, whom Pargeter believed was murdered. After Kris was dead, I asked Boyd to tell me the story, and he obliged.

Johann and Rita Nielsen, Kris's parents, had been

flinty Scandinavians who'd built a farm, saved every nickel, and researched stocks in farming equipment and other companies. They'd savvily bought and sold the stocks according to their research—and made millions. Ten years ago, Johann had died and left everything to Rita. In his will, Johann said he wanted his son to make his own way, just as he had. Word around Lake Bargee, Minnesota, was that Kris was furious. His mother had inherited twelve million dollars, and he'd gotten nothing?

Three years ago that month, Kris had dropped out of graduate school in Colorado and returned to Lake Bargee. Rita still lived out on the farm. In the years since Johann's death, she'd sold the livestock and had only a small garden. But she was managing. Then Kris arrived and told everyone that he would be taking care of his mother from then on. People from the grocery store, the farmers' wives club, and the Lutheran church asked after Rita. He said she was fine, but he refused to let people come visit.

I sighed. This was a typical abuse pattern. Isolate the victim from everything that's familiar.

Boyd said that Kris was there for a few months. A grocery store clerk remembered him buying a turkey for Thanksgiving but not for Christmas. That year, beginning the nineteenth of December, they had their first big blizzard. Four feet of snow fell before Christmas Eve. Two days after Christmas, Kris Nielsen called the Lake Bargee police department from Colorado. He said he'd left his mother after they'd celebrated Christmas together, and driven back to his apartment. Now he couldn't reach her, and would somebody please go out and check on her? Two officers went out on snowmobiles and found Rita dead. The exhaust to her furnace was completely blocked with snow. The carbon monoxide had done her in.

Joe Pargeter's theory was that Kris had been waiting for a big snowstorm so he could block up the exhaust, kill his mother with the carbon monoxide buildup, and drive away before anyone could catch him. But there were no footprints, no physical evidence. Kris had no alibi, except to say that he'd left his mother on Christmas Day. He had no gas or hotel receipts. He said he learned thrift from his parents and always paid in cash. The Minnesota authorities couldn't prosecute him on the basis that he hadn't bought a Christmas turkey.

Pargeter had held up the death certificate for as long as he could. He flew out to Colorado to question Kris Nielsen. But Nielsen stuck to his story. He lived alone and worked hard as a chemistry grad student. *Of course,* I thought. *Actually,* he'd said in that flat Minnesota accent, *medical isotopes are used for—* And then he'd stopped. He hadn't wanted anyone to know he was well acquainted with chemistry; he was desperate for them to think he was a California entrepreneur. The one person who knew his secret was Stonewall Osgoode.

But then, Tom said, came the kicker. I was not the first person to call Pargeter about Nielsen. No, that would have been Ernest McLeod, who'd rifled through files at Nielsen's house, found Pargeter's number, and traveled the same mental paths as yours truly.

So. When Kris discovered I'd broken into his house

and stolen his file marked *Mother,* he guessed that I might have discovered one of his worst lies: that he hadn't earned his money starting a data-processing business in Silicon Valley. Lolly Vanderpool had figured that out: *A real data-processing geek would have known, in answer to my question, that I needed to buy a USB hub.*

Kris liked to be in control. He'd lost Yolanda. He'd gotten rid of Ernest and Stonewall Osgoode, who we later found out had been an accomplice of Kris's. Both victims knew too much or had crossed him. And then I became a threat. He had driven over to our place, where he'd watched us leave with the police escort. He'd followed us and climbed up to the crime scene via the back way. The last thing he wanted was for me to get Tom looking into the death of Rita Nielsen.

But then he'd overheard me talking to Boyd about the backpack and feared yet more evidence against him or Osgoode would be on Ernest's camera. He'd found his way via the back door into the garage . . . where he attacked me.

Ferdinanda had known to be ready. That was why she'd given me her collapsible truncheon; that was why she'd wheeled down to the garage. When Kris had come at her with her own baton, well . . . she was a *francotiradora,* and she knew what to do.

When Tom arrived at the Bertrams', he took charge. My knees buckled when he hugged me. He helped me sit on the grass outside the garage. I made a complete statement. Tom called Arch and asked if he could spend the night with Gus, as I was indisposed. Arch had asked if I was all right, and Tom said I would be.

Boyd, of course, felt terrible that he had done what I asked and stayed with Yolanda instead of accompanying me into the garage. But how could he have known that Kris would find his way in from the road below? He had followed the police escort, figured out where we were going, and climbed up the steep hill that led to the Bertrams' garage.

Harriet, whose odd jobs included being a handywoman, immediately confessed to being Kris's accomplice. She had done some odd jobs for Kris in the past year, including sleeping with him from time to time. She'd found a regular job working at Frank's Fix-It. In fact, she claimed she was the only one who actually did any work there. Kris had offered her room and board and money, promised to drop her in the morning and pick her up at night . . . if she would only sabotage an electric frying pan and loosen some bolts on a hanging pot rack at the Breckinridges' house the day of the dinner party.

But it was Charlene Newgate who had given Tom the key to the case. Faced with a possible charge for conspiring to grow marijuana—of which she was actually innocent—she confessed to being paid to provide Stonewall Osgoode with information about Yolanda, information that she gleaned as a temporary secretary. When she'd jealously asked Stonewall if Yolanda was some other girlfriend of his, he'd laughed and said Yolanda was the ex-girlfriend of his boss. Charlene had typed the new will for Ernest McLeod while working for Allred, the attorney. She'd worked for Drew Parker, the dentist, enough to know how to set up the fake dental appointment for Ernest McLeod, the trap that had gotten him killed.

She also admitted to acting on Stonewall's order to chat up Humberto Captain at the Grizzly. She'd stolen Humberto's cell phone at an opportune moment and handed it over to Stonewall later. He'd used it to call Ernest's house moments before torching the place, with us inside. Tom figured Stonewall was trying to throw suspicion for the arson onto Humberto.

In addition, Charlene acknowledged she had accompanied a real estate agent and Stonewall Osgoode to Jack's house, where they'd pretended to put an offer on it, then backed out. She and Stonewall had come over to our house, too—the "elderly couple"—to make sure they had the right place, the one belonging to Goldy the caterer, the one where Yolanda was staying.

And yes, Charlene also confessed—to avoid a conspiracy-to-commit-murder charge—Stonewall Osgoode had worked for Kris Nielsen. They'd hooked up in graduate school at Colorado State, where Stonewall was in veterinary school, because they were both interested in making money selling drugs. But it was dangerous, and could lead to unwanted attention from law enforcement.

What Tom and the department theorized was that after Kris killed his mother, he didn't need money anymore. He told Stonewall they should get out of the drug business. That was probably why Stonewall had been so upset when his partner had left the enterprise.

And then someone—probably Kris, the department again theorized—had anonymously turned in Stonewall, who'd been kicked out of veterinary school. Kris's files revealed he had paid a lawyer to defend Stonewall, who'd gotten the light sentence. *I can control you,* Kris's actions said. That control thing was the way his mind worked.

After Stonewall's stint behind bars, he had bummed around for several months, not doing much of anything, according to Charlene. Charlene said when Stonewall drank or smoked dope, he would tell her these things. That Kris had met Yolanda and was crazy in love, but then she had dumped him. And then Kris's real craziness had once again surfaced. He'd been obsessed with Yolanda, even though that obsession hadn't stopped him from sleeping around. Yolanda had gotten a sexually transmitted disease. She'd confronted Kris, who'd flown into a rage and hit her with a broom. Yolanda and Ferdinanda had moved out.

Stonewall's job for Kris expanded from trying to get rid of Ferdinanda—in June—to full-out stalking of Yolanda. The pages I'd taken from the files showed the payoffs to Stonewall, for surveillance, for looking in the windows of Yolanda's rental and our house, for arson, and for murder. Stonewall's bank account showed the exact amounts that Kris had paid him being deposited the next day.

Still, Stonewall hadn't been able to stay away from the easy money of drugs. He had told Charlene that there was "money to be made" in the drug business, but she insisted he hadn't told her about the puppies or the grow operation. He'd said, "You don't want to know."

Yet Kris had found out. He knew Marla's puppy, rescued from a mill, had gotten sick. We'd gotten the news at the Breckenridges' party. A dump of Kris's phone showed a call to the veterinarian's secretary. She said he claimed to be the puppy's owner, wanting to know what had been taken out during surgery. She said she wasn't supposed to say, because the veterinarian was calling the cops. Kris had driven over and, claiming he had adopted a sick beagle puppy, too, charmed the information out of her. She was so sorry, she told sheriff's department investigators, she just felt so bad for an owner whose puppy had been spayed so a container of marijuana seeds could be smuggled inside. . . .

Stonewall Osgoode had told Charlene it was all over. His "partner," as he referred to Kris, had fired him. He didn't want him growing weed, because it could attract too much attention to the two of them. "After all I've done for him," he'd grumbled to Charlene.

From us at the Breckenridges' dinner, Kris had found out about Hermie Mikulski. His phone log showed he'd called her, to tell her about the puppy mill, to set her up to be there when he hid beside Stonewall Osgoode's house until an opportune moment to shoot Osgoode. Kris had been hoping to frame Hermie for Osgoode's death. More important, he wanted to keep the cops from associating *him* with Osgoode.

Kris had used the same gun that he'd loaned to Osgoode, when he'd hired Osgoode to shoot Ernest McLeod. Tom said Stonewall had killed Ernest, on orders from Kris, using a gun supplied by Kris, the same one Kris used to kill the gas station attendant, the same one he used a few days later to kill Stonewall Osgoode himself. All this was confirmed by the files I'd taken from Kris's house . . . and the .38 they found beside Kris Nielsen.

Kris had used that same .38 to shoot a fellow grad student, who'd been working at a gas station outside of Fort Collins. That poor young man, Tom theorized, had seen Kris when he was driving back from Minnesota after killing his mother, by sweeping snow over the furnace exhaust pipe. The young grad student, working at the station, had probably accosted Kris, been glad to see him at that ungodly hour. Driving back from Minnesota days earlier than he later claimed, Kris had not wanted anyone to know exactly when he arrived back in Fort Collins.

"Such a waste," Yolanda said. "So many people died so he could have money. And power over others. But . . . why couldn't he leave me alone?"

That was the psychology of stalkers, Tom explained. They want their partner back, because without the partner, they don't feel whole. A piece of them is missing, and they're desperate to retrieve it. Father Pete had inadvertently given us the clue to Kris's behavior when he'd talked about his support of Charlene all those years. He'd said the church is a safety net.

Kris hadn't wanted Yolanda to have a safety net of any kind. That was the key to those papers with dates, letters, and figures that I'd taken from the file marked *Miscellaneous*. Kris had paid Stonewall to surveil Yolanda—"S." Stonewall Osgoode, whose files revealed a receipt for a Unifrutco oil can, had burned down the rental. That was "B." When Kris heard from Charlene that Ernest had left his house to Yolanda, he'd hired Stonewall to murder Ernest—"K"—then firebomb Ernest's house, while she was in it, just so she would know he could find her anywhere.

In addition to Kris being killed, the big news from my searching the Bertrams' garage was my discovery of Ernest's red backpack. Inside was Norman Juarez's mother's necklace, a digital camera showing Sean Breckenridge and Brie Quarles in various clinches, and the pages he'd photographed from Kris's files, which had set him on the track to find out about the suspicious death of Kris's mother.

Everyone had a lot to thank Ernest for, we heard, when we had the delayed party to celebrate his life a week later. People in AA expressed gratitude for Ernest's support. Norman Juarez, with the discovery of the necklace and the diamonds in Humberto's chandelier, was now a wealthy man. The gold, Tom speculated—when Humberto refused to confess—was long gone, spent on Humberto's land, cars, house, and lifestyle. Norman Juarez is suing Humberto for it, nonetheless.

In typical humble style, Norman said Ernest's tenacity had brought him new hope after years of trying to lock up that thief, Humberto Captain.

Yolanda apologized to me, again and again, for not telling me Ernest had told her he was investigating Kris. I told her it was fine; I understood the insanity that her life had become. Did I ever.

At the memorial party, Ferdinanda and Yolanda gave thanks for Ernest laying down his life for them. They have moved out of our house and into an apartment in

Lolly Vanderpool's building. Norman Juarez, with his wife's blessing, gave Lolly Vanderpool a diamond, for her bravery in helping Ernest recover his mother's necklace. She repaid Julian, returned to MIT, and is no longer working as a hooker.

Norman Juarez gave Yolanda and Ferdinanda another diamond. Yolanda squealed—with happiness? surprise? disbelief?—when she heard Ernest had left his land and house to her. She and Ferdinanda are drawing up plans for a new place. They're already squabbling over the size of the kitchen.

Rorry Breckenridge is divorcing Sean and moving back to New Orleans. Facing a charge of conspiracy to commit assault, Sean admitted to Tom that it was Kris who'd asked for the Navajo tacos at the church party and Kris who had told him Yolanda had hepatitis. Sean is looking for a job, but according to a gleeful Marla, no one is willing to hire an accountant who hasn't kept up with tax law for over a decade.

Brie and Paul Quarles are separated. Father Pete asked for, and received, the resignations of both Sean and Brie from the Saint Luke's vestry. According to Marla, Brie has moved to Albuquerque. Marla said, "Maybe *she's* working as a hooker."

Hermie Mikulski is very happy that Stonewall's puppy mill is closed. All the beagles have been adopted. She's now starting a drive to restore habitat for the wild birds that flock to Aspen Meadow. The avian population declined after the forest fire, and she wants to bring their numbers back up. All in all, that pursuit seems safer than trying to close puppy mills.

Norman Juarez offered Tom, Arch, and me a diamond. I was tempted, because if we do have a baby, we'll probably need more money. But the temptation lasted only a moment.

"I know someone who needs it more," I told Norman Juarez. "It's a kid named Peter at Arch's school. He has leukemia, and the family might have trouble with their bills."

Norman Juarez gave Peter's family the proceeds from the sale of three diamonds. At last report, Peter was getting better.

And Tom and I, well, we are trying to get pregnant. It's fun.

Acknowledgments

The author gratefully acknowledges the assistance of the following people: Jim Davidson; Jeff, Rosa, Ryan, Nick, and Josh Davidson, with thanks again to Rosa for help with the Spanish in the text; J. Z. Davidson; Joey Davidson; Sandra Dijkstra, Elise Capron, Elisabeth James, and the rest of the excellent and hardworking team at the Sandra Dijkstra Literary Agency; Brian Murray, Michael Morrison, Liate Stehlik, Carolyn Marino, Debbie Stier, Dee Dee De Bartlo, Wendy Lee, Joseph Papa, Megan Swartz, and the entire brilliant team at Morrow; Jasmine Cresswell, who offered the idea for this book, and the rest of our brainstormers' group, who helped hammer it out: Connie Laux, Karen Young Stone, and Emilie Richards McGee; David and Linda Ranz, for again providing the author with space to work in Nashville; for inspiration and support, as ever, the St. Anne's-Belfield School community, Charlottesville, Virginia, with special acknowledgment of the passing of our dear Emyl Jenkins; Jeff Joseph, Maserati aficionado,

Sarasota, Florida; Carol Alexander, a wonderful friend who tested the recipes, made suggestions, and then re-tested them all; Kathy Saideman, who read the text in numerous incarnations, always offering insightful comments; Richard Staller, D.O., who as usual addressed all medical issues; Julie Kaewert, kind as ever; the real John Burtrum, who bears no relationship to the character in this book; Triena Harper, who brings her sharp coroner's eye to all questions; and as always, Sergeant Richard Millsapps, who patiently addresses all manner of inquiries on police procedure, and like Triena Harper, now retired from the Jefferson County Sheriff's Department, Golden, Colorado.

Recipes in *Crunch Time*

Goldy's Caprese Salad

Crunch Time Cookies

Love Potion Salad

Tex-Mex Ham and Cheese Casserole

Goldy's Garlic Lamb Chops

Goldy's Guava Coffee Cake

Homemade Cream of Mushroom Soup

Breakfast Bread Pudding with Rum Sauce

Puerco Cubano

Ferdinanda's Florentine Quiche

Goldy's Caprese Salad

1½ pounds organic heirloom tomatoes, chopped if large, or you can use grape or cherry tomatoes, halved

8 ounces *ciliegine* (small fresh mozzarella balls), drained

12 leaves fresh basil, finely chopped

3 cups baby field greens (mâche), gently rinsed and spun dry

Dressing

¼ cup best-quality white wine vinegar

2 teaspoons Dijon mustard

¼ teaspoon granulated sugar

½ teaspoon coarse sea salt

¼ teaspoon freshly ground black pepper

⅔ cup best-quality basil oil (infused with basil, not with dried basil leaves in it; recommended brand: Boyajian)

In a medium-size bowl, combine the tomatoes, *cilie-gine,* and chopped basil. Place the dry greens in a medium-size, attractive glass or crystal salad bowl. Set aside.

In a jar with a screw-on lid, combine the vinegar, mustard, sugar, ½ teaspoon salt, and ¼ teaspoon pepper. Screw the lid on tightly and shake to combine well. Take off the lid, pour in the oil, screw the lid back on tightly, and shake very well to combine.

Place the tomato mixture on top of the greens. Shake the dressing again, and pour on about ¼ to ½ cup dressing. Taste carefully. Depending on the sweetness of the tomatoes, you may need a bit more sugar. (Do not use too much dressing. Store the remainder, still in its covered jar, in the refrigerator.)

Toss the salad and serve immediately.

MAKES 4 TO 6 SERVINGS

Crunch Time Cookies

1 cup pecan halves
1¼ cups all-purpose flour
½ teaspoon kosher salt
½ teaspoon baking powder
½ teaspoon baking soda
½ pound (2 sticks) unsalted butter,
    at room temperature
¼ cup softened cream cheese
1 cup dark brown sugar, firmly packed
¾ cup granulated sugar
2 large eggs, at room temperature
1 teaspoon vanilla extract
2½ cups rolled oats
8 ounces (1½ cups) semisweet chocolate chips
4 ounces (⅔ cup) toffee bits (Heath toffee bits or
    Bits o' Brickle)

In a large frying pan, sauté the pecans over low heat, stirring frequently, for about 10 minutes, or until the nuts begin to change color and emit a nutty scent. Turn the nuts out onto paper towels and allow them to cool, then chop them roughly and set aside.

Sift or whisk together the flour, salt, baking powder, and baking soda. Set aside.

In a large mixing bowl, beat the butter and cream cheese on medium speed until the mixture is very creamy. Add the brown sugar and beat very well, until the mixture is creamy and uniform. Add the granulated sugar and again beat very well, until you have a uniform, creamy mixture. Add the eggs, one at a time, and beat well after each addition. Stir in the vanilla.

Using a large wooden spoon, stir in the dry mixture just until combined. Then stir in the oats, chocolate chips, cooled nuts, and toffee bits, blending only until thoroughly mixed.

Cover the bowl with plastic wrap and put it in the refrigerator until completely chilled, at least three hours or overnight.

When you are ready to bake the cookies, take the bowl out of the refrigerator and allow the batter to warm slightly while the oven is preheating.

Preheat the oven to 375°F. Place silicone mats on two cookie sheets.

Measure the batter out by tablespoonfuls, two inches apart. Place no more than a dozen cookies on each sheet. Bake, one sheet at a time, for 9–11 minutes, until the edges of the cookies are very brown and the centers are no longer soft.

When you remove a cookie sheet from the oven, place it on a cooling rack for 2 minutes, so the cookies can set up. Then use a pancake turner to remove the cookies to cooling racks, and allow them to cool completely. Store in airtight containers or in zippered freezer bags. These cookies freeze well.

MAKES 4 DOZEN

Love Potion Salad

1 ounce pine nuts
4 cups baby field greens (mâche), gently rinsed and
    spun dry
1 pound grape tomatoes, rinsed, patted dry,
    and halved
½ cup blue cheese crumbles, or to taste

In a wide sauté pan, toast the pine nuts over low heat, stirring constantly, until they are lightly browned and emit a nutty scent. Turn out on a paper towel to cool while you make the dressing (see below).

When you are ready to serve the salad, place the greens and tomatoes in an attractive salad bowl. Toss with about ¼ cup dressing, and taste. (You may need to add more dressing, but do not overdress the salad.) Sprinkle the crumbles and pine nuts on top of the salad, and toss again. Serve immediately.

MAKES 4 SERVINGS

Love Potion Salad Dressing

- 1 teaspoon minced garlic
- 2 teaspoons minced shallot
- 1 tablespoon best-quality mayonnaise
- 1 tablespoon Dijon mustard
- 1 tablespoon finely chopped fresh basil
- 3 tablespoons best-quality aged balsamic vinegar
- 2 tablespoons freshly grated Parmigiano-Reggiano cheese
- kosher salt, to taste
- freshly ground black pepper, to taste
- 1 cup best-quality extra-virgin olive oil

Place first seven ingredients, plus salt and pepper to taste, in a blender jar. Blend to purée. Stop the blender twice, and with the blender off, use a spatula to scrape down the sides of the jar. When the mixture is a uniform color, remove the filler cap (the small plastic cap inside the large plastic lid), and while the blender is running, very slowly drizzle in the olive oil. (With your free hand, you may want to hold a paper towel over the filler cap opening between drizzling operations, to prevent spattering.) When the mixture is completely emulsified (less than a minute), stop the blender and pour the dressing into a pint-size jar or pitcher. With ¼ cup of dressing, dress the salad. Tightly cover the jar or pitcher with the remainder of the dressing and keep it in the refrigerator.

When you want to dress another salad, bring the dressing out of the refrigerator (where it will have separated), so it can come to room temperature. When it is at room temperature, use a whisk and quickly stir the dressing, so it can re-emulsify.

Tex-Mex Ham and Cheese Casserole

1½ cups grated sharp cheddar cheese
1½ cups diced ham, from which the fat
  has been trimmed
¼ cup prepared picante sauce
3 ounces diced canned chiles, drained
  and patted dry
5 pieces sourdough bread, buttered and cubed (you
  should have about 4 cups of cubes)
2 large eggs
1¼ cups whole, low-fat, or skim milk
¼ teaspoon cayenne pepper
½ teaspoon paprika
½ teaspoon kosher salt

Preheat the oven to 325°F (high altitude: 350°F).

Butter a 9-by-13-inch glass or ceramic pan.

Combine the cheddar and diced ham in a bowl and toss
well. In another bowl, combine the picante and chiles.

Place one layer of buttered bread cubes in the bottom of
the prepared pan; sprinkle with one half of the ham and
cheese mixture. Carefully spoon half of the picante

mixture over the ham and cheese. Place the rest of the bread cubes on top, sprinkle with the remaining ham and cheese mixture, then spoon on the rest of the picante mixture.

In a large mixing bowl, beat the eggs, milk, and seasonings together until well mixed. Use a spatula, if necessary, to break up any clumps of paprika. Strain this mixture evenly over the layered ingredients in the pan. Bake, uncovered, for about 25–30 minutes, or until the center is cooked and the casserole has turned golden brown. Serve immediately.

MAKES 4 SERVINGS

Goldy's Garlic Lamb Chops

2 racks baby lamb chops (about 1¾ pounds each)
2 tablespoons crushed garlic
olive oil
½ teaspoon sea or kosher salt, or to taste
½ teaspoon freshly ground black pepper, or to taste

Preheat oven to 425°F. Lightly oil the rack on a roasting pan.

Remove the lamb chops from their packaging. Rinse them, pat them dry, and place them on a cutting board. Using a very sharp knife, carefully trim a ¼-inch layer of fat from the area above the meat. Set this fat aside.

Still using the sharp knife, cut 8 evenly spaced, deep pockets in the meat itself. Stuff the pockets with the garlic. If you have garlic left over, spread it across the meat.

Pour enough olive oil over the chops to cover, then gently massage it into the meat. Sprinkle the chops with the salt and pepper, then place the reserved layers of fat over the pockets of garlic. Place the chops on the pre-

pared rack of the roasting pan. Carefully insert a meat thermometer in the meat.

Roast until the meat thermometer reads 145°F. Remove the lamb from the oven and carefully place a piece of foil over the chops. Allow to sit for 10–15 minutes. Serve, preferably with mint jelly.

MAKES 6 TO 8 SERVINGS (2 TO 3 CHOPS PER PERSON)

Goldy's Guava Coffee Cake

¼ pound (1 stick) unsalted butter,
    at room temperature

1 cup granulated sugar

2 large eggs

1 cup commercial sour cream

2 teaspoons vanilla extract (preferably Mexican
    vanilla; you may also substitute one teaspoon
    vanilla extract and one teaspoon vanilla-bean
    paste)

1 tablespoon finely minced orange zest (the zest from
    about one large navel orange)

2 teaspoons finely minced lemon zest (the zest from
    about one large lemon)

½ cup best-quality guava preserves, well stirred
    (recommended brand: Queensberry)

2 cups all-purpose flour (high altitude:
    add 2 tablespoons)

1 teaspoon baking powder

1 teaspoon baking soda

¼ teaspoon salt

Confectioners' sugar, for sprinkling on top of the
    cakes (optional)

Preheat the oven to 350°F. Butter and lightly flour two
9-inch round cake pans or two 8-inch square pans.

In a large mixing bowl, beat the butter with the sugar until very light and fluffy. Add the eggs one at a time and beat well, until very well combined. Add the sour cream and stir in thoroughly. Add the vanilla. Mince the zests together (or whirl them in a coffee-bean grinder dedicated to mincing zests). Stir in along with the preserves. Stir thoroughly.

Sift together the flour, baking powder, baking soda, and salt. Add the dry ingredients to the butter mixture and stir carefully until thoroughly combined. Do not over-mix. Batter will be stiff.

Divide the batter evenly between the two pans. Spread the batter to the edges of the pans.

Bake on Convect for 15 minutes, or on Bake for 20–30 minutes, just until the cakes pull away from the sides of the pans and a toothpick inserted in the center comes out clean.

Place the cakes, still in their pans, on racks. Allow them to cool 10 minutes, then invert the cakes and remove the pans. Allow the cakes to cool completely.

When you are ready to serve the cakes, you may sift the tops with confectioners' sugar.

MAKES 2 CAKES

Homemade Cream of Mushroom Soup

1 ounce dried wild mushrooms (porcini, cremini,
   or morels)
2½ cups spring water
4 ounces (1 stick) unsalted butter, plus an additional
   2 tablespoons, if needed
1 shallot, finely diced
8 ounces fresh button mushrooms, gently rinsed,
   patted dry with paper towels, and finely diced
7 tablespoons all-purpose flour
4 cups (1 quart) homemade chicken stock
2 cups heavy whipping cream
¼ cup dry sherry
sea salt or kosher salt, to taste
freshly ground black pepper, to taste

Place the dried mushrooms in a large heatproof bowl.
Bring the spring water to a boil and pour it over the
dried mushrooms. Allow to sit for 30 minutes. Remove
the reconstituted mushrooms with a slotted spoon, pat
dry, and chop finely. Set aside. Strain the mushroom
water through cheesecloth and set the water aside. You
should have about 2 cups of mushroom water.

In a large stockpot, melt the butter over low heat. Place the diced shallot and diced fresh mushrooms in the pot and allow to cook over low heat, stirring frequently, for about 10 minutes, or until soft. Raise the heat to medium, sprinkle in the flour, and stir constantly until the mixture bubbles and the flour is cooked, about 3 minutes. (If the mixture is completely dry, add up to 2 tablespoons of the extra butter. Stir the mixture until the butter is completely melted, then stir and cook until the flour is cooked.)

Using a ½-cup measuring cup, add the chicken stock and reserved mushroom water ½ cup at a time. Bring the heat up to medium-high, and cook, stirring constantly, until the mixture thickens and bubbles. Lower the heat and add the chopped wild mushrooms, the cream, the sherry, and salt and pepper to taste. Cook, stirring frequently, for another 15 minutes. Remove from heat.

When the soup has cooled slightly, spoon it in batches into a blender, and purée. Place the puréed batches into a large heatproof bowl. When the soup is completely puréed, pour it back into the stockpot, taste, and correct the seasoning. Bring the soup back to a simmer and serve.

MAKES 6 TO 8 SERVINGS

Breakfast Bread Pudding with Rum Sauce

1 teaspoon cinnamon

1½ cups granulated sugar

1½ pounds cinnamon raisin bread, torn up into bite-size pieces

4 tablespoons (½ stick) unsalted butter, softened

4 large eggs, at room temperature

4 cups half-and-half

2 tablespoons vanilla (preferably Mexican, or you can use 1 tablespoon vanilla extract and 1 tablespoon vanilla bean paste)

Mix the cinnamon into the sugar until well combined; set aside. Butter a 9-by-13-inch glass baking pan and place the torn-up bread into it.

In a large mixing bowl, beat the butter until it is creamy. Mix in the cinnamon sugar and beat until very creamy. Add the eggs, one at a time, and beat until well combined. Mix in the half-and-half and vanilla, and beat well. (The mixture will be thin and will not be completely combined; this is normal.) Stop the beater and use a spatula to mix as well as possible.

Pour the butter mixture over the torn-up bread. Cover the pan with plastic wrap and place in the refrigerator overnight.

In the morning, remove the pan from the refrigerator and discard the plastic wrap.

Preheat the oven to 350°F.

Bake the pudding for 30 minutes, then remove from the oven and stir with a wooden spoon. Place the pudding back in the oven and bake for an additional 30 minutes, until it is puffed and golden. While the pudding is baking, prepare the rum sauce (see below).

Place the pudding on a rack and carefully pour the rum sauce over it. Allow the rum sauce to soak into the pudding (2–3 minutes), and then serve. Pudding will be very hot.

MAKES 8 SERVINGS

Rum Sauce

    4 ounces (1 stick) unsalted butter
    1 cup light brown sugar
    ⅓ cup best-quality rum
    ¼ teaspoon freshly grated nutmeg
    1 large egg

In a medium-size sauté pan, melt the butter. Add the sugar, rum, and nutmeg, and stir with a wooden spoon or heatproof spatula until the sugar dissolves and the mixture is well blended. Remove from the heat and allow to cool slightly, still in the pan.

In a small bowl, beat the egg until it is very frothy. Beat the egg into the butter mixture until well combined. Place the sauté pan back on the stove and cook, stirring, over medium-low heat, until the mixture thickens.

Remove from the heat and immediately pour over the pudding.

Puerco Cubano

¼ cup (½ stick) unsalted butter
1 pound ground pork
2 tablespoons freshly minced or crushed garlic
2 teaspoons demi-glace de poulet or demi-glace de veau (chicken or veal demi-glace)
¼ cup all-purpose flour
½ teaspoon dried oregano
¼ teaspoon kosher salt
¼ teaspoon freshly ground black pepper
2 cups fresh orange juice
¼ cup fresh or organic, not-from-concentrate lime juice
2 teaspoons (or more) granulated sugar
1 cup chopped fresh cilantro

In a large (12-inch) nonstick sauté pan, melt the butter over medium-low heat. Add the pork and the garlic, and cook, stirring and breaking up the pork, until the meat is just cooked. Add the demi-glace and stir well.

Add the flour, oregano, salt, and pepper, and cook, stirring, until the flour is cooked and the mixture bubbles.

Stir in the juices and sugar and raise the heat to medium. Stir constantly until the mixture bubbles and is thickened. Taste and correct the seasoning.

Spoon the pork onto a large platter and sprinkle with the chopped cilantro. This dish goes well with hot cooked rice.

Serve immediately.

MAKES 4 TO 6 SERVINGS

Ferdinanda's Florentine Quiche

rice crust (see next page)
1 10-ounce package frozen chopped spinach
2 tablespoons unsalted butter
3 large eggs
2 cups small-curd cottage cheese
2 tablespoons whipping cream
1 teaspoon Dijon mustard
½ teaspoon kosher salt
⅛ teaspoon paprika
⅛ teaspoon cayenne pepper
⅓ cup best-quality Gruyère cheese, grated
¼ cup best-quality Parmesan cheese, grated

Preheat the oven to 350°F. Butter a 9-inch glass pie pan. Prepare the rice crust and press it into the pie pan; set aside.

Cook the spinach according to package directions. Drain thoroughly, pressing all the liquid out through a strainer. Place the drained spinach in a bowl and add the butter; set aside.

In a large bowl, beat the eggs until frothy. Stir in the cottage cheese, cream, mustard, seasonings, and grated cheeses. Stir until well mixed. Add the buttered spinach and stir again until well mixed. Pour the spinach mixture into the rice crust.

Bake about 40 minutes, until puffed, golden brown, and set in center. (Check the center with a spoon to be sure it is no longer liquid.) Allow to cool 5 minutes. Slice and serve. This dish goes well with sliced fresh fruit and hot rolls.

Makes 8 servings

Rice Crust

    1 large egg
    2 cups cooked rice, at room temperature
    ⅔ cup best-quality Gruyère, grated

Beat the egg until frothy. Add the rice and cheese and stir well. Spread this mixture in the buttered pie pan.

Welcome to the delectable world of Goldy Schulz!

Double Shot

Dark Tort

Sweet Revenge

Fatally Flaky

Crunch Time

DOUBLE SHOT

"Another fascinating mix of culinary delights, puzzling dilemmas, and foul play."
Greensboro News & Record

Caterer supreme Goldy Schulz has more on her plate than she can handle. Her ultra-charming, ultra-wealthy, and seriously psychopathic ex-husband, Dr. John Richard Korman (aka "the Jerk"), is free now that the governor of Colorado has commuted his prison sentence. And someone—the Jerk, perhaps—has taken great pains to sabotage Goldy's latest culinary endeavor, a post-funeral reception for a friend at a local lodge.

But even more than the anonymous threats, rumors, and violence that have lately been directed Goldy's way, it's her discovery of a fresh corpse that really spoils the stew—a murder that could tear her family to pieces, a murder that virtually *everyone* believes Goldy committed.

True, she's been efficiently framed, but at least she's still breathing—which may not be the case for long, if she doesn't track down a killer who's cooked up a very nasty repast for Goldy and the people she loves.

DARK TORT

"In the subgenre of foodie mysteries,
Davidson remains the master chef."
Booklist

Caterer Goldy Schulz's lucrative new gig, preparing
breakfasts and conference room snacks for a local
law firm, is time-consuming, but she's enjoying it . . .
until the night she arrives to find Dusty, the firm's
paralegal, dead. The deceased also happens to be
Goldy's friend and neighbor, and now Dusty's griev-
ing mother is begging Goldy to find out who murdered her daughter.

Just because the police are on the case doesn't
mean Goldy can't do a little snooping herself.
While catering a party at the home of one of the
firm's lawyers, she just happens to overhear an
incriminating conversation. She also discovers a few
tasty clues in the kitchen. Before long, Goldy finds
herself knee-deep in suspects. But one of them is
incredibly dangerous . . . and very liable to cook
Goldy's goose.

SWEET REVENGE

Goldy Schulz is thrilled to be catering a holiday breakfast feast for the staff of the Aspen Meadow Library.
But little does she know that on the menu is a large
helping of murder. While setting up at the library,
Goldy spots a woman lurking in the stacks who
bears a striking resemblance to Sandee Brisbane—
the Sandee Brisbane who killed Goldy's ex-husband,
the Jerk. But Sandee is supposed to be dead . . . or so
everyone believes.

Goldy's suspicions mount when the body of Drew
Wellington, a former district attorney, is found in a
corner of the library, with a map worth thousands
of dollars stashed in his clothing. Goldy is convinced
that Sandee, a confessed felon, is involved. But the
holiday madness is only just beginning for Goldy.
Soon she's drawn into the dangerous, double-
crossing world of high-end map dealing. And like the
ghost of Christmas past, Sandee keeps making an
appearance. Could she be out to prove that revenge
is oh-so-sweet?

FATALLY FLAKY

"Another winning entry in Davidson's
mouthwatering series."
Publishers Weekly

It's been a long summer for Goldy Schulz, who is
engaged in planning a wedding reception for Aspen
Meadow's nuttiest bridezilla. But then Doc Finn,
beloved local physician and the best friend of Goldy's
godfather, Jack, is killed when his car tumbles into a
ravine. Jack thinks Doc was murdered because of the
research he was doing at the local spa—allegations
that are confirmed when Jack himself is attacked.

So Goldy adds more work to her plate and dons
chef's whites to go undercover at the spa, where
coffee is outlawed in favor of smoothies. But if she
doesn't find the clever killer on the spa grounds
who's watching her every move, catering weddings
and cooking low-fat foods might just be the death of
Goldy Schulz. . . .

CRUNCH TIME

"Terrific."
Richmond Times-Dispatch

Colorado caterer Goldy Schulz cooks up big trouble as she tries to help her longtime friend and fellow chef, Yolanda Garcia. When the rental house shared by Yolanda and her irrepressible aunt Ferdinanda is destroyed by arson, the pair move in with cop-turned-PI Ernest McLeod. But then Ernest is shot dead and his house is set on fire, nearly killing Goldy, Yolanda, Ferdinanda, and nine beagle puppies that Ernest had recently rescued from a puppy mill.

Concerned for her friends, Goldy invites them to stay with her while the sheriff's department looks into the crime. Yet even Goldy's house isn't safe, and after a failed break-in by an unknown intruder, a cop is sent to keep an eye on things. Then a second body is found. Swapping her chef's hat for a sleuthing cap, the intrepid Goldy steps up the investigation. But she's got to move fast, because it's crunch time to close in on a killer, before he can close in on her.

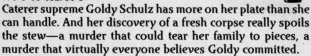

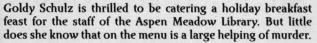